The Ragged Heiress

Dilly Court grew up in North-east London and began her career in television, writing scripts for commercials. She is married with two grown-up children and four grandchildren, and now lives in Dorset on the beautiful Jurassic Coast with her husband. She is the bestselling author of twenty novels. She has also written six novels under the name of Lily Baxter.

Dilly Court

The Ragged Heiress

arrow books

14

Arrow Books
20 Vauxhall Bridge Road
London SW1V 2SA

Arrow Books is part of the Penguin Random House group of companies
whose addresses can be found at global.penguinrandomhouse.com

 Penguin
Random House
UK

First published in Great Britain by Arrow Books in 2010

www.penguin.co.uk

A CIP catalogue record for this book is available from the British Library.

Typeset in Palatino by Palimpsest Book Production Limited,
Falkirk, Stirlingshire

Penguin Random House is committed to a sustainable future for
our business, our readers and our planet. This book is made from
Forest Stewardship Council® certified paper.

MIX
Paper from
responsible sources
FSC® C018179

Printed and bound in Great Britain by Clays Ltd, Elcograf S.p.A.

For my cousins Celia and Barrie

Chapter One

The London Fever Hospital, Islington 1874

The cold passionless light of early morning filtered through the narrow windows of the female ward, and the overpowering smell of carbolic floated in a miasma above the freshly scrubbed floor. The eerie silence was broken by an occasional feverish moan and the rasp of laboured breathing from the regimented rows of iron bedsteads. Following in Sister's brisk footsteps, a young houseman struggled through a haze of sheer exhaustion to complete his ward round. He had already been on duty for seventy-two hours and had at least another twelve to survive before he could even think of sleep.

'Is there any hope for this one, Dr Harcourt?' Sister stopped by the next bed and tidied the tumbled sheets, smoothing them to pristine glassiness with a practised hand.

Dr Harcourt studied the patient's temperature chart and he frowned. 'It's too early to say, Sister, but I'd say her chances are slim.'

Inclining her head slightly, the nurse was unsurprised. She had seen many patients succumb to the dreaded typhoid fever. 'We can but hope and pray for her, the poor soul.'

1

'Have any relatives come forward to claim her?' Dr Harcourt brushed a stray lock of dark hair from his eyes, forcing his tired brain to concentrate. 'Do we know her name?'

'No, doctor. There were few survivors from the sunken vessel and she was only wearing her night-clothes when she was taken to Bart's. They said that there was nothing about her person which would identify her.'

'All alone in the world,' he murmured. 'That is sad indeed.' He lifted the girl's wrist, examining the palm as he took her pulse. 'This is not the hand of a working woman. I'd say this girl has never done a hard day's work in her short life.' Gently he laid the limp hand back on the coverlet, and he suppressed a sigh. It was difficult to remain detached and professional when faced with such a tragedy. He had three sisters of his own, the youngest of whom was probably the same age as this survivor of a collision on the river in which more than fifty souls were known to have perished. The schooner *Caroline*, laden with cargo from the East Indies and just an hour or two from port, had been struck by a steamship in thick fog, and had sunk within minutes in the polluted water near the Beckton sewage outfall. Bodies were still being washed up on the foreshore, most of them totally unrecognisable.

Dr Harcourt noted the patient's temperature on the chart and hooked it over the rail at the foot of the bed. Slowly he dragged his scattered thoughts back to the present, but as he observed the outline of the girl's emaciated body beneath the covers he could not help being affected by how pathetically small and vulnerable she looked. Despite her sickly pallor and sunken cheeks, the heart-shaped face retained traces of her youth and undoubted former beauty. He glanced at the nurse's rigidly controlled expression, noting with some surprise that her lips were moving as if in prayer. They had done everything known to medical science in order to save the girl's life – now it was up to a higher power. Despite his strict Protestant upbringing, Giles Harcourt had seen too much suffering to be able to believe unconditionally in a merciful God. Even so, he too offered up a silent prayer for the girl. It seemed such a criminal waste for a young life to be snuffed out before it had barely begun.

'The next few hours will be critical, Sister,' he murmured in answer to her unspoken question. 'Should anyone come to see her you may allow them in.'

'Yes, doctor.' The nurse made a move towards the next bed, hesitating and glancing over her shoulder with one winged eyebrow raised when the doctor did not immediately follow her. She too was tired and hungry. It had been a long night and her feet ached miserably. She yearned for the relative peace and quiet of the tiny ward kitchen where she could enjoy a refreshing cup of hot, sweet tea and a slice of buttered toast, but she was too well schooled in the rigid discipline of her profession to allow her impatience to show in front of the young houseman. She was, after all, just a nurse and must always defer to the superior intellect of the male physicians, even the junior doctors

3

like this pale-faced young man who looked as though he was going to collapse at any moment. She stood with her hands folded meekly in front of her and her eyes cast down, but in her imagination she could hear the singing of the kettle on the gas ring and smell the heady fragrance of Darjeeling as boiling water was poured onto the tea leaves.

In spite of his desperate need to sleep, and entering an almost dream-like trance, Dr Harcourt found himself wishing that the girl's delicate, translucent eyelids would flutter open to reveal what he was certain would be a pair of blue eyes. But they remained stubbornly closed as if weighed down by the crescents of thick, corn-coloured eyelashes that rested on bruised smudges above sweet cheekbones. Her hair had not been shaved, as had been the custom in past times, but had been confined to a white linen cap, and escaping tendrils of sunlight-gold gave a tantalising clue as to what this fragile creature must have looked like before the shipwreck that had almost cheated her of life.

The sister could stand it no longer and she tut-tutted beneath her breath, hastily covering her lapse of etiquette by tucking the girl's stick-thin arm back beneath the covers. 'I doubt if anyone will come to see her after all this time, doctor. It's been nearly three weeks since the accident.'

Dr Harcourt came back to earth with a jolt. 'Yes, of course,' he said hurriedly. 'Just make certain that she is kept well hydrated, Sister. I'll stop by again before I go off duty this evening.' He forced his weary legs into motion and he moved on to the next bed where another woman, this time much older and almost certainly terminal, lay moaning softly in her delirium. She was, the doctor decided, noting the sickly colour of her skin and the shallowness of each painful breath, much closer to meeting her maker than she had been when he had examined her last evening. 'I think this one will not see the light of another day, Sister. Have her bed moved nearer to the door so that when the inevitable happens the other patients will not be disturbed.'

'Yes, doctor. It will be done immediately.'

In the echoing cathedral-like reception area of Bart's hospital in West Smithfield, an irate man hammered his fist on the polished mahogany desk, glaring at the clerk. 'Come off it, mate. There weren't that many survivors from the *Caroline*; you must have a list of them as was admitted that night.'

The clerk swallowed hard and his fingers twitched nervously as he flipped through the pages of the admission book. 'I wasn't on duty that night, sir.'

'Well someone was. You can't tell me that it ain't wrote down somewhere. I'm looking for me sister and I won't budge until I get some information.'

'Perhaps if you told me your name I might be able to assist further.'

'What's that got to do with anything?'

'Er – there's no need to take that tone with me, sir. Without a name I can't help you.'

'Stranks,' the man growled. 'Me name is Stranks. Now are you going to help me or do I have to choke the information out of you?'

The clerk gazed round the busy atrium of the hospital, raising his hand to attract the attention of a passing porter. 'Er, Mr Simms, could you spare a moment?'

Flexing his muscles, Simms strode over to the desk. 'Having trouble, Mr Blunt?'

The clerk took a step backwards even though the high counter stood between him and the angry man who had marched in off the street making unreasonable demands. 'This gent seems to think we are keeping something from him, Mr Simms. I've told him that I'm not in a position to give out the information he requires.'

'Look, mate . . .' Stranks modified his tone as he stared up at Simms' lantern jaw and beetle brows drawn together in a warning scowl. 'I'm looking for me young sister. We was both passengers on the ship what went down in the river three weeks ago, and I been searching for her ever since. I been round every hospital in London making enquiries and someone told me that you'd taken some of the survivors in here. It ain't much to ask, is it? I just want to know if little Lucy was one of 'em.'

Simms glanced at the desk clerk and his expression softened slightly. 'Seems a reasonable request, Mr Blunt. Have you anyone on your books answering to that description?'

'Like I told the gent, I wasn't on duty that night, Mr Simms. But if the person would give me his sister's full name, I'll see if there's a matching entry.'

'Lucetta Froy, that's her name. She's about so high.'

Stranks raised his hand to the level of his shoulder. 'Pretty little thing she is, with yellow hair and blue eyes. You wouldn't forget her if you'd seen her.'

'No family resemblance then,' muttered the clerk, flicking through the pages of the tome.

'I heard that, cully,' Stranks said, fisting his hand. 'Any more lip from you and I'll . . .'

Simms tapped him on the shoulder. 'No need for that, mister. Let the man do his job.'

Blunt flicked through the pages of the admission book, studying the entries with the tip of his tongue held between his teeth. 'Nothing in that name, sir.' He looked up, his face alight with curiosity. 'You say her name is Froy, and yet yours is Stranks.'

'She's me half-sister,' Stranks muttered through clenched teeth. 'Any more quaint remarks from you, mister, and you'll be sorry.'

Blunt closed the book with a snap. 'No mention of Froy or Stranks,' he said triumphantly, but on seeing the look on Stranks' face he changed his tune. 'But there was a young woman who might fit the description. She developed a fever and was sent to the Fever Hospital in Islington.' Blunt shook his head. 'Typhoid, I believe – you might be too late.'

But he was speaking to thin air. Stranks had raced from the building, barging through the half-glassed doors and almost knocking down a woman and child in his haste.

'Well!' Simms said, shaking his head. 'He's a rum 'un and no mistake.'

'I'd say the young lady would be better off in the

7

next world than living with a brute like him,' Blunt said, adjusting his spectacles with the tip of an ink-stained index finger.

'You wasn't as close to him as I was,' Simms said, grimacing. 'He smelt like a midden and I'll wager he's a stranger to soap and water.' Simms leaned across the desk, speaking in a low voice. 'I heard that there was prisoners being brought back from the East Indies for trial on board the *Caroline*. I wouldn't be at all surprised if he weren't one of them.'

'Well, we'll never know, Mr Simms,' Blunt said, glancing nervously over his shoulder. 'Don't look now, but Matron has just come out of her office, and she's coming this way.'

Stranks erupted into Duke Street and was immediately seized by the scruff of the neck. 'Did you find her?'

'Let go of me, Guthrie.' Stranks jerked free from the hand that held him. 'She ain't there.' He glanced up and down the street. 'There's a copper over the road – best move on afore he spots us.' Shoving his hands in his pockets he put his head down and crossed the busy street with Guthrie hobbling along as fast as his gammy leg would allow.

'For God's sake, man,' Guthrie said breathlessly. 'I can't keep up with you. Anyway, they ain't looking for us. We're dead – drownded in the Thames. We're free men.'

Stranks dodged in between a costermonger's barrow and a brewer's dray where a couple of burly delivery-men were unloading barrels and rolling them down a

8

ramp into a pub cellar. 'Shut up,' Stranks muttered. 'D'you want the whole of London to hear you?'

Guthrie stopped by the open trapdoor and he inhaled the smell of beer with a gasp of pleasure. 'I say let's stop for a jug of ale. It's what I missed the most out there in that heathen land.'

'No time for that,' Stranks said, grabbing him by the arm and dragging him down the street. 'And no money until we've got the heiress safe and sound.'

Guthrie fell into step beside him. 'All right then. Have it your way, but where is the little trull?'

'Looks like they took her to the Fever Hospital in Liverpool Road. Hurry up, mate, there's no time to lose. The silly cow went down with typhoid. We've got to get to her before she croaks or there's no money in it for us.'

'You're so sure of yourself,' Guthrie grumbled. 'How do you know that her family will pay up?'

Stranks stopped for a moment, breathing hard. 'We've been over this a dozen times, you idiot. Her pa was a wealthy merchant with a house in the best part of Islington and she was his only child.'

Guthrie grinned, revealing a row of broken and blackened teeth. 'And we know the parents didn't survive, don't we, cully? You saw to it that they never come up for air.'

'Keep your voice down, you fool,' Stranks hissed. 'I never touched his missis. She went down like a stone, but her old man was made of tougher stuff. I thought he was going to pull me under, so I had no choice. Anyway, there was no witnesses so we're in the clear.'

9

'If you say so, Norm. You're the boss.'

'That's right, you keep that fact in your thick head, Guthrie. Remember that we're officially dead so we're free men, and when we collect from the family we'll be set up for life. There must be a fortune to be had from the Froys for the safe return of their little angel.'

'I've always wanted to be rich,' Guthrie said, sighing. 'They used to call me a clodpole in the workhouse. They said I'd never amount to nothing, but I'll show 'em.'

'Come on then, mate. What are we waiting for? Let's get to the hospital and find out if we've got the right girl.'

Half an hour later, having decided that it was too risky to claim the unidentified girl as Lucetta Froy, Stranks decided that it would be safer to refer to her as Lucy Guthrie, just in case the police became involved, as his name was synonymous with crime and a sure giveaway.

'Are you certain that this is your relation?' the ward sister demanded, unconvinced. She did not like the look of these two men, whom she deemed to be ruffians of the worst order, and her sensitive nostrils twitched as the rank odour of their bodies overpowered the strong smell of disinfectant.

A lady of breeding, Sister Eugenia Demarest had trained at the London Hospital in Whitechapel, and she was used to dealing with people from all walks of life, from the high-born to the lowest of the low. She knew instinctively that these two men fitted into the latter order, but as the young houseman had pointed out, the girl was of a different class altogether.

'She is our little Lucy,' Stranks said, baring his teeth in what he hoped was a pleasant smile. 'We had almost given her up for lost, and now she's found.'

'Thank the Lord,' Guthrie said piously. 'Us will go to church to give thanks for her safe return to the bosom of her loving family.'

Stranks gave him a savage dig in the ribs with his elbow. 'Don't overdo it,' he muttered. He turned back to the nurse, who looked as though her knickers were starched as well as her pristine white cap and apron. He knew that she was suspicious and that she was looking down her long pointed nose at them. He'd like to get that one on her own down a dark alley – he'd soon have her cut down to size and begging for mercy, or maybe for more. Perhaps that was what the sad old virgin needed.

'Have you any proof of identity?' Sister Demarest demanded. These two ruffians might have fooled the almoner, but then Miss Parry was an innocent and thought the best of everyone. Sister Demarest folded her arms across her flat chest. 'Well, have you?'

'All lost when the ship went down, Sister,' Stranks said, meeting her stern gaze with a straight look. He was good at lying. He had learned to lie as soon as he could talk. With a drunken scoundrel of a father and a mother who was no better than she should be, life had been hard in the slums of Hoxton, and Norman Stranks had existed on the streets since he was eight years old. Cheating, lying and stealing had come easily when it meant the difference between survival or the less attractive alternative. A brief spell in the workhouse had further hardened him and a year in Pentonville prison had completed the process. It was there that he had met the simple-minded Guthrie and for good or ill they had been accomplices in crime ever since. Now he could see a way out of the vicious circle of reoffending, capture and imprisonment and he was going to grab it with both hands. The only problem was that the answer to all their problems lay close to death on the bed before them.

Stranks fell on his knees and buried his face in the snow-white coverlet. 'Don't die, little Lucy. Oh, my duck, please don't leave us.' He looked up at Sister Demarest and the tears that trickled down his cheeks were real. 'Get her better, Sister. Us wants to take our little angel home.'

The girl's eyelids fluttered and her lips parted in a long sigh. Her eyes opened and she stared uncomprehendingly at Stranks. For a moment it seemed that the fever had abated and Sister Demarest pushed Stranks aside so that she could take the patient's pulse.

'You must leave now,' she said firmly. 'You are disturbing my patient.'

Stranks scrambled to his feet, wiping his eyes on his sleeve. 'Is she coming round, Sister? Is she going to get well?'

'I can't say, but she must be allowed to rest. If you don't leave I will have to summon a porter to escort you from the ward.'

Guthrie took Stranks by the arm. 'Come on, mate. Do as she says.'

'All right, but we'll be back later,' Stranks said grudgingly. 'But you ain't going to keep us from our sister now we've found her.'

'Keep your voice down, and go,' Sister Demarest said, pulling the curtain around the bed. 'Come back tomorrow and with God's grace you might find that the fever has broken and the patient will be able to recognise you.'

In the dim recesses of her fevered brain, Lucetta could hear the murmur of vaguely familiar male voices and an inexplicable fear seized her. Then there was the unmistakeable clink of brass rings as the curtains were drawn around her bed and she forced her heavy eyelids to open, but a shaft of fear ran through her body. Everywhere was white, except for the flower print on the curtains. She had no idea where she was – or who she was. She closed her eyes and drifted off to another place and another time. A place of safety and calm – somewhere achingly familiar – somewhere else.

Chapter Two

The scent of the Spice Islands was not the sweet, nutty aroma of cinnamon and cloves or the spicy tang of pepper, cardamom and ginger that Lucetta had romantically expected it to be. The cloying odour of rotting vegetation, hanging like a steamy mist in the tropical heat, had come as a shock after months at sea with nothing to breathe but the cool salt-laden air. The first sight of the mountainous, palm-fringed island, bright with exotic blooms of frangipani and hibiscus had hit her senses in a flood of colour. Everything here was so dramatically different from the pale northern watercolour landscape of England or the sepia tints of London that it had left her breathless with wonder.

Now, after three months in this island paradise, she was used to the strange smell of the jungle that permeated the stuccoed walls of the British consul's residence in Denpasar. The odour was all-pervading and even managed to seep into the sandalwood chests that contained her clothes. When she dressed, with the help of Naomi, the flower-like Balinese girl who had been assigned to her as a personal maid, Lucetta had been horrified to find that her new gowns, which had cost a small fortune in London, felt damp to the touch and hung limply from her slender body.

Perhaps this exotic place was not paradise after all, and if the truth were told she had not wanted to come to this strange land, but Papa must be obeyed in all things. He had decided that a sea voyage would be beneficial to her mother's delicate constitution, and there was no question of leaving sixteen-year-old Lucetta alone in London with only the servants to care for her. The only alternative had been to invite Aunt Eliza and Uncle Bradley to stay with her in Islington, and that meant enduring the company of their son, spoiled, spotty-faced Jeremiah. Lucetta had disliked him intensely when they were younger, and although they had seen little of each other while he was away at boarding school, she doubted whether he had changed very much and if he had, then it was probably not for the better.

Lucetta had reluctantly opted to accompany her parents, and she had not regretted her decision. She had fallen in love with what she had seen of the island and its gentle people. If only she had more freedom to explore its mysterious interior she would have been content to stay longer than the intended four months while Papa toured the neighbouring islands in search of merchandise to stock his wholesale warehouse in London. But she soon discovered that the same strict rules applied even though they were so far from home. It seemed to Lucetta that Queen Victoria's influence had spread from the outposts of the British Empire to the Dutch East Indies. The British consulate was dominated not by the consul, Sir John Boothby, but by his wife, Pamela, who observed all the niceties and traditions of English upper class life, even down to afternoon tea with cucumber sandwiches and toasted muffins. Despite the tropical heat, steaming bowls of brown Windsor soup were served at dinner, followed by a fish course and then the inevitable roast meat with at least two boiled vegetables. Lucetta would not have been surprised if suet pudding and custard had appeared on the table as a dessert, but this was either beyond the scope of the Balinese cook, or Lady Boothby had been persuaded that fresh fruit was more palatable after a heavy meal.

Lucetta would have liked to learn more about the Balinese culture and she tried desperately to communicate with her maid Naomi, but as the girl only spoke her native tongue and a few words of Dutch, and Lucetta spoke neither, they had mostly to resort to sign language interspersed with inevitable fits of the giggles. Naomi's given name was Nyoman, but Lucetta had such difficulties with pronunciation that she opted for a more English-sounding alternative. When this seemed to delight rather than to offend Naomi, Lucetta gave her a hug and presented her with a bead necklace by way of setting a seal on their friendship, to which Naomi responded by taking a spray of frangipani from her sleek dark hair and tucking it behind Lucetta's ear.

The days of enforced leisure passed pleasantly enough but Lucetta longed for a little excitement. There were occasional trips into town with Lady Boothby, when the good woman was not otherwise occupied with her charity work, but these were infrequent and

Lucetta was not allowed to explore unless chaperoned by Miss Dodd, Lady Boothby's steely-eyed maid, who complained bitterly of the heat which made her feet swell and played havoc with her varicose veins.

Other than this, Lucetta spent most mornings attempting to entertain her mother, either by reading to her or taking her for short walks in the rose-scented gardens before the heat became too oppressive. Once a month the wives of minor officials and senior clerks were invited to the consulate to take afternoon tea, and there were occasional card parties in the evening, but the guests were mostly middle-aged and Lucetta longed for the company of young people, although she knew better than to complain. She was only too well aware how important this business trip was to her father, and she would not upset Mama's delicate constitution for all the tea in China, or even all the spice in the Spice Islands. She resigned herself to another few weeks of idleness, and resolved to make the best of things.

On a morning that was indistinguishable from any other, breakfast was brought to Lucetta on the vine-shaded veranda outside her ground floor bedroom. She sipped her coffee wondering what she would do today. Papa would almost certainly be off somewhere on the island buying up all the intricately carved teak-wood, seagrass and rattan furniture that he intended to ship back to England and sell for a handsome profit. Lucetta had heard him tell Sir John that he had already purchased enough to fill the entire hold of the *Caroline*, the clipper ship that would take them home when Papa was satisfied that his business was done. She sighed, thinking of London and the pleasant life that she had left behind. She did not often allow herself to yearn for home, nor would she have admitted the truth to her mother, but Lucetta missed the trips to the theatre, the outings to the Zoological Gardens and Madame Tussaud's and meetings with her old school friends from Miss Milton's Academy for Young Ladies, which she had left last spring.

It would be autumn by the time she returned to London and there was much to look forward to. She thought longingly of her blue and white bedroom on the second floor of the elegant townhouse in Thornhill Crescent, one of the best parts of Islington. All the memories of her happy childhood were encapsulated in that bright, sunny room. Her dolls with their beautiful wax faces still sat on the sofa beneath the window, although it was several years since she had played with them, but they were too well loved to be packed away in tissue paper and stored in the far recesses of the attics. Her favourite books were neatly displayed on the white-painted bookshelves and a rosewood escritoire awaited her return in the alcove next to the fireplace. It was there she wrote in her journal every evening before she went to bed. She had brought it with her, but there was little enough to write about. Life in the consulate was comfortable but hardly exciting.

A waft of frangipani from the blossom tucked into Naomi's glossy black hair brought Lucetta back to the present and she turned her head to see her maid tipping the contents of a china jug into the bowl on the washstand.

Lucetta acknowledged her presence with a cheerful smile. 'Thank you, Naomi.'

Naomi moved gracefully to the cedar chest and opened it. She held up a sprigged muslin morning gown. 'Yes, missy?'

'Not that one, thank you,' Lucetta said, shaking her head. 'I think I'll wear the blue silk.'

Naomi's eyes clouded and her lips trembled. '*Saya tidak mengerti, missy.*'

'No, I'm sorry. Of course, you don't understand me and I haven't the slightest idea what you just said.' Lucetta swung her legs off the teak steamer-chair and stood up. Even this early in the morning her flimsy cotton wrap clung to her skin where perspiration had pooled between her shoulder blades. She reached for her leather shoes and found that they had sprouted a white fungal bloom overnight. She sighed, handing them to Naomi. 'I'd be grateful if you would clean them.' She made a polishing motion with her hand and Naomi nodded, smiling as she took the shoes.

'Blue silk dress,' Lucetta repeated slowly. She pointed to the azure sky. 'Blue – like sky.'

'Ah! Blue.' Naomi repeated the word triumphantly and disappeared back into the relative darkness of Lucetta's bedchamber.

Shuffling barefoot across the grass matting, Lucetta followed her into the cool room.

Naomi selected the gown from the cedar chest and held it up for Lucetta to see. 'Blue dress for Missy.'

'Well done,' Lucetta said, clapping her hands. 'Thank you, Naomi.' She reached out to take the dress but it felt damp and the strange jungle odour emanated from its folds. Lucetta would not have been surprised to find mushrooms growing from the seams, but a few minutes in the hot sunshine would put that to rights. It would be too complicated to explain this to Naomi and she went outside to drape the garment over the wooden railing. She returned to the room to find Naomi watching her with a worried frown puckering her smooth brow.

'Missy no dress?'

'No, thank you. I can manage on my own. You go and get your breakfast, Naomi.'

'Breakfast?'

Lucetta raised her hand to her mouth, making a pretence of eating, and she rubbed her tummy. 'Yum, yum – breakfast,' she said, chuckling. 'You go now, Naomi.'

Naomi's lips parted in a wide smile and her almond eyes danced with laughter. 'I go now, missy.'

When she was alone, Lucetta allowed the cotton wrap to fall to the floor. She stretched her arms above her head, revelling in the caress of the cool air that wafted through the open French windows. Padding over the marble tiles to the washstand, she dipped her flannel in the bowl of water scented by rose petals floating on the surface. She shivered with pleasure as the liquid streamed down her neck, trickling sensuously between her firm young breasts.

She repeated the action again and again, taking

delight in the relief of feeling fresh and clean, although she knew that by noon she would be just as hot and sticky and in desperate need of another wash. But first she must go through the motions of dressing and putting up her hair, after which she would seek out Lady Boothby and make polite conversation, enquiring about her hostess's health and her charitable work at the hospital in Denpasar. By that time Mama would have left her room and be comfortably ensconced on the chaise longue in the drawing room while Naomi's seven-year-old sister fanned her with a palm leaf. Lucetta would read to her mother or simply sit and listen while Evelyn Froy reminisced about her idyllic childhood in the Hampshire vicarage where she had been born and raised. After taking luncheon in the dining room the ladies would retire to their rooms for an afternoon nap, to be awoken by their maidservants at four o'clock in time to dress for tea. The day ahead was as predictable as sunrise and sunset and not nearly as exciting.

Quite suddenly, Lucetta had the urge to escape from the confines of the compound and an irresistible need to do something different and even dangerous. With droplets of water still glistening on her skin, she pulled her fine lawn shift over her head and rang the bell for Naomi.

'I've changed my mind,' she said as Naomi came through the French doors with the blue silk gown draped over her arm. 'I'm going riding, Naomi. I'll need my riding habit, please.'

* * *

Outside the cool interior of the consulate the heat was so intense that it hit Lucetta with a force that took her breath away. She hitched up the long skirt of her riding habit and made her way through the gardens safe in the knowledge that the morning parlour, where Sir John and Lady Boothby took breakfast, was on the far side of the building. Mama would not have risen from her bed, and Papa would have left for the north of the island at dawn. There was no one apart from an aged gardener to see her making a bid for freedom.

She crossed the gravelled compound, making her way to the stable block where the little mare she normally rode whinnied in recognition at the sight of her. The head groom hurried to greet her, and although he eyed her doubtfully he was too well trained to question the consul's guest when she asked for her mount to be saddled. Lucetta stroked the horse's soft muzzle and spoke softly to the animal. She had taken a chunk of sugar crystals from her breakfast tray that morning and secreted it in her pocket. She offered it now to the mare on the palm of her flattened hand. She smiled at the gentle touch of the horse's velvet lips on her skin, and her heartbeats quickened in anticipation of doing something as daring as leaving the consulate unchaperoned. She waited while the groom saddled the mare and led the animal to the mounting block. He held the reins while Lucetta climbed onto the side-saddle.

'Thank you,' she said, acknowledging his assistance with a smile. 'You can let her go now.'

But the groom held on to the reins, shaking his head. 'Missy not go alone.'

'It's quite all right,' Lucetta said firmly. 'Sir John said I might take the horse for a short ride. I won't go far.'

'No, missy. Not safe.' The groom signalled to one of his underlings who led a heavy-looking mule of an animal from the stables and prepared to mount.

'No,' Lucetta said, snatching the reins from the startled groom's hand. 'Thank you, but I will go alone. There is no need to trouble your man.'

She could see by the groom's set expression that he had not understood, or if he had then he was feigning ignorance. 'Thank you, but I don't need an escort.' She urged the mare forward using her riding crop to tap the animal gently on its flank. They were off at a smart trot before any of the startled stable hands could stop them. By chance the consulate gates had been opened to admit a despatch rider with a satchel of mail for the consul, and Lucetta rode through them before the gatekeeper had a chance to obey the shouts from the stables.

A triumphant cry escaped her lips as she encouraged the little mare to canter along the road that led away from the town. Soon they were galloping along the edge of a palm-fringed beach. The white sand and the sparkling turquoise sea looked so inviting that Lucetta was tempted to stop and tether her mount in the shade of the palms, but there were people around: local farmers leading donkeys laden with panniers filled with rice for the market; fishermen dragging their nets in the lagoon where the distant sound of thunder was not a threatening storm but the crashing of breakers on the coral reef. Lucetta was not bold enough to go on the beach unattended; at least not until she found a place that was completely deserted.

She rode on, heading inland and pausing for a moment to gaze in wonder as the land dropped suddenly into a deep valley where narrow terraces had been carved out of the hillside to form paddy fields for the cultivation of rice. Shaded by tall palms, the lush green land was misted with heat haze. Lucetta remembered having come this way once before, with Papa and one of Sir John's grooms. If memory served her correctly, there was a fascinating Buddhist temple not far distant from this place. She had spotted it then and had asked to be allowed to explore, but the groom had shaken his head, murmuring something in his native tongue, and Papa had been in too much of a hurry to reach a workshop where he had hoped to make trade.

Lucetta patted the mare's sleek neck and with a gentle pressure of her heels encouraged the animal to walk on. Within minutes she was riding through a village lined with minute dwellings constructed of bamboo, with dirt floors and thatched roofs. Open at the front and sides, they were so different from the brick and stone buildings with which Lucetta was familiar that she could hardly believe that whole families lived in such a way. Chickens roamed freely, pecking at the ground, and mangy-looking curs lay sleeping in the shade, apparently indifferent to Lucetta's presence. Small children stopped their play, plugging their thumbs in their mouths to gaze at her wide-eyed, while their mothers barely glanced up from washing clothes in what was little more than a drainage ditch at the side of the road.

Feeling like an intruder, Lucetta allowed her horse to continue plodding along the dirt road, which seemed to be leading nowhere. Just as she was thinking that she must have come the wrong way the track opened out into a clearing at the foot of steep cliffs. She gasped in wonder at the sight of a temple hewn into the rock and covered in intricate carvings of strange-looking beasts and deities. Without thinking, Lucetta dismounted and, clutching the reins, she approached the gaping mouth of the god figure that framed the entrance to the pitch-dark interior of the temple.

Without warning, she found herself surrounded by monks in blue robes who were shaking their fists and shouting at her in their native tongue. The mare reared in terror and the reins were snatched from Lucetta's hand. Terrified and unable to make them understand that she meant no harm, Lucetta looked round for a means of escape, but found her way blocked by women and children who had appeared seemingly from nowhere. They surrounded her, pointing and staring as if she were an animal in the zoo. A small boy wrenched the riding crop from her hand and ran off shrieking with laughter as he wielded it in the air, and a toothless old woman snatched Lucetta's hat and put it on her own head. The other women began to laugh and taunt her, but the monks turned on them and started pushing them away. In the midst of all this chaos Lucetta did not hear the sound of approaching hoofbeats until a group of men, dressed in the manner of European sailors, burst into the clearing and reined in their horses, throwing up clouds of grey dust.

'Hello there.' A young officer leapt off his horse, pushing his way through the chattering women and children. The Balinese were small by comparison and they scattered before him as he approached Lucetta. He doffed his cap. 'You seem to be in a spot of bother, ma'am,' he said, grinning broadly.

Lucetta couldn't help noticing that his companions were laughing as they dismounted, and instead of rushing to his aid they stood back watching with obvious amusement.

'You save your maiden in distress, young Galahad,' one of them shouted above the din.

Lucetta felt her cheeks burning with humiliation. Fear was replaced by embarrassment. She knew that she must look a sorry sight, hatless and with her hair having escaped from the tight chignon at the nape of her neck. Her cream linen riding habit, made especially for her by Mama's dressmaker in London, was stained with sweat and dust and her plumed riding hat was now perched jauntily on the head of the old woman who had stolen it moments earlier. Lucetta brushed a stray lock of hair from her brow and drew herself up to her full height. 'Thank you, sir. But it was a simple misunderstanding.' Despite her brave words she was uncomfortably aware that her voice shook and she was trembling from head to foot.

'Are you hurt, ma'am?'

She shook her head but her reply was lost as one of

the monks stepped forward uttering a tirade of angry words. The women and children fell silent as he spoke, or perhaps, Lucetta thought, it was due to the fact that the sailors wore side arms and had formed a tight line behind the young officer. He stood his ground, and taking a handful of coins from his pocket he dropped them into the monk's outstretched hand. This brought an immediate reaction from the women, who surged forward clamouring for money, but this time it was the monks who stepped in and with a few words delivered in ominous tones they dispersed the crowd. With a final impassioned few words from their leader, the monks disappeared into the dark interior of the temple and there was silence except for the chattering of monkeys in the trees and the background chorus of the tropical birds.

Shaken and secretly ashamed of herself for causing such a scene, Lucetta forced herself to appear calm although she was inwardly quaking. 'Thank you. I'm very grateful to you, sir, but it was a simple mistake. I was out riding and lost my way.'

He held her hand for a brief moment. 'Which could have proved extremely dangerous for you, Miss Froy.'

'You know my name,' Lucetta said, staring at him in astonishment. 'Have we met before?'

His serious expression melted into a charming smile. 'You would not have noticed me, ma'am. I'm the first mate on the *Caroline*.'

'I'm afraid I don't remember you, Mr . . .'

'Sam Cutler, miss.'

Lucetta felt her blush deepening. This was so

embarrassing. She must have seen this young man every day during their six-week voyage and yet she had absolutely no recollection of him. 'I'm sorry, but then it was a big ship, and . . .' Her voice tailed off as she realised that the men accompanying Sam Cutler were listening with unconcealed interest and obvious amusement.

'And you were strictly chaperoned by that stern missionary lady with no sense of humour,' Sam said helpfully. 'Miss Trim, wasn't it? I believe she even tried to convert some of these heathen fellows with me.' He turned to his shipmates. 'No success there then, mates? They have neither manners nor morals according to that lady. You must forgive my men, Miss Froy; they meant no disrespect to you earlier.'

The man who had spoken out before had the grace to look slightly abashed. 'No offence meant, miss.'

'None taken,' Lucetta said, smiling. 'It was fortunate for me that you all happened along when you did.'

'I would escort you home, Miss Froy, but we have important business to attend to. Have you far to go?'

'Only to the British consulate, but I'd be grateful if you would put me on the right road.'

Sam bowed from the waist, signalling to the man who had teased him for his chivalry. 'Bates, fetch Miss Froy's horse.'

'Aye, aye, sir.' Bates ambled over to the mare. She had found a patch of grass in the shade of a pandanus tree and was munching away placidly. He led the animal back to Lucetta and tossed her effortlessly onto the saddle. 'There you are, ma'am. Best get back home as fast as you can. There are a couple of dangerous men on the loose.'

'Thank you, Bates. That will do,' Sam said, frowning.

Lucetta was quick to hear the warning note in his voice and her curiosity was aroused. 'Who are these men, Mr Cutler?'

'Two criminals who were transported to Australia for life, but somehow managed to escape from the penal colony and made their way here, goodness knows how, but they did. We have the unenviable task of taking them back to London in irons, but they jumped ship last night.'

'But isn't that a task for the army or the Navy? Aren't there any policemen in Bali?'

'Apparently we're the best they've got at the moment,' Sam said with a wry smile. 'You'll be safe enough on the main road, so there's no need to be afraid.' He swung himself up into the saddle with the ease of an accomplished horseman and when the animal attempted to unseat him, he brought the spirited creature under control with a firm hand and a few softly spoken words. 'Follow us, Miss Froy. We'll put you on the road to Denpasar, if you're sure you can make it back from there.'

'Thank you,' Lucetta murmured shyly. 'I hope you catch your criminals, Mr Cutler.'

He smiled and his teeth gleamed white and even in his suntanned face. 'We will, never fear. And may I suggest that you take a groom with you next time?'

Lucetta knew that she had been foolish, but she didn't need a ship's officer to speak to her as if she were a naughty child. The admiration she had felt for him just moments ago was replaced by indignation, quickly followed by humiliation. She was about to put him in his place when he leaned towards her and planted a kiss on her lips. It was over in a flutter of a butterfly's wing and his touch was just as light, but the brief salute brought a cheer from his men and a gasp of shock from Lucetta.

'H-how dare you?' she murmured breathlessly.

'I'm sorry, Miss Froy, but you have the most adorable pout that I've ever seen. You must forgive my bad manners, but I couldn't resist the temptation.'

'Come on, sir.' Bates called from the edge of the clearing. 'We'd best leave the temple before the monks turn nasty.'

'Lead on, Bates. We'll follow.' Sam tightened the reins, wheeling his horse around. 'We will escort you as far as we can, but do take care on the way back to the consulate. Don't stop for anyone or anything.'

Angry, shaken and yet oddly disturbed by the fleeting touch of his lips, Lucetta chose to ignore this last warning and she urged the little mare forward at a brisk trot. She had not realised how far she had strayed from the beaten track, and as she followed the cloud of dust thrown up by the horses' hooves she had to admit that she would have had great difficulty in getting back to the main road on her own. When they parted at the crossroads, Sam reined his horse in so that they were side by side with their knees almost touching. 'We have to leave you now, Miss Froy.'

'Thank you, I know my way now,' Lucetta said, avoiding his intense gaze. 'I hope you catch the criminals.'

'And I hope that you sail with us again on the *Caroline*. Perhaps we might be on nodding acquaintance then.'

This brought her chin up and she met his eyes, suspecting him of teasing, but to her surprise she saw no hint of mockery in them. He was not handsome, she thought, or even particularly good-looking but his eyes crinkled at the corners when he smiled and his mouth curved humorously even when he was being serious.

Lucetta gulped and swallowed. She had lost her riding hat to the old woman at the temple and she was most likely suffering from a touch of the sun. 'I must be on my way,' she murmured. 'I have to get back to the consulate before I'm missed.'

She was about to ride on but he reached out to hold the reins. 'Take care, Miss Froy.'

'Lucetta. My name is Lucetta.'

He took her hand and raised it to his lips. 'Goodbye, Lucetta. We will meet again, I'm certain.'

'I don't want to hurry you, sir,' Bates called from a little further along the road where the men had reined in their horses, 'but we'll never catch them at this rate.'

Sam rode off, leaving Lucetta staring after him. She had lost her riding crop as well as her hat, and she could almost hear the freckles popping out on her nose and cheeks. She would be in for a scolding from Mama when she reached home. The sun was high in the sky and the heat was oppressive, but the ride back to the consulate was uneventful until Lucetta came to a stall by the wayside where two men had stopped to buy fresh coconuts. Her heart sank as she realised that it was her papa and his guide Agung who were sipping the cool sweet coconut milk. There was no chance of getting past them without being seen and she reined in her horse.

'What in heaven's name are you doing riding out alone?' Henry Froy demanded angrily. 'Have you no idea how dangerous it is for a young person such as yourself to be abroad unchaperoned in a foreign country?'

'I'm sorry, Papa. I just wanted to get some fresh air.'

'Fresh air? Are you mad, girl?' Henry peered at her through the heat haze. 'Just look at you, Lucetta. How did you come to be in that dishevelled state? Where is your hat? You'll get a touch of the sun, that's for certain.'

Lucetta could see Agung staring at her with his mouth open and her father's face had flushed to the colour of a boiled beetroot, but before she could think of a suitable reply a sudden tropical downpour spilled from the skies as if someone up above them had turned on a tap. The rain hit the ground hissing and spitting as it evaporated into steam and in seconds they were all soaked to the skin, but at least it put a stop to the interrogation and saved her the necessity of making excuses. She dared not tell Papa about the near catastrophe at the temple. If he knew the extent of her foolhardy escapade he would be justifiably angry and she would be punished. Granted a temporary reprieve by the rainstorm, Lucetta suffered an uncomfortable ride back to the consulate following in the wake of her father and Agung.

The downpour ceased as suddenly as it had begun and their clothes were almost dry by the time they rode through the gates of the consulate compound and into the stables. Henry dismounted and tossed the reins to a groom but he left it to an underling to help his daughter from the saddle as if to underline his displeasure. 'Go to your room, Lucetta. I'll deal with you later.'

'Yes, Papa. I'm very sorry. I didn't stop to think . . .'

'No, that's your trouble, Lucetta. You do things without giving a thought to the consequences.'

'It won't happen again, Papa. I promise you.'

'That won't wash this time, Lucetta.' Henry glared at her, his dark eyebrows drawn together in a frown. 'You have been foolish in the extreme. There are dangerous men on the loose and anything could have befallen you. If I can't trust you to behave like a grown-up then I must treat you like the child that you undoubtedly are. You may be seventeen but you have behaved as irresponsibly as a six-year-old. You will remain in your room until I have decided on the most suitable punishment for you. Do you understand me, miss?'

Chapter Three

It was evening before Lucetta was allowed to leave her room. The tropical night had come down suddenly like a black velvet curtain. Paper lanterns cast a soft glow over the gardens and formed lazily shifting shadows on the veranda. The air was filled with the croaking of frogs and the noisy chorus of cicadas. In the drawing room, Eveline Froy reclined on silk cushions, fanning herself vigorously. Her pale oval face glistened with beads of perspiration and her voice was raised in querulous complaint. 'How could you be so silly, Lucetta? Why did you go riding without a hat? You've got freckles all over your face and you've ruined your complexion.'

'Calamine lotion will help with the sunburn,' Lady Boothby said briskly. 'And lemon juice will make the freckles fade, but it was both foolish and dangerous to ride out unattended, young lady. Heaven knows what might have happened if the men from the *Caroline* had not been out hunting for the escaped convicts.' She glared at Lucetta over the rim of her coffee cup. 'You could have caused a serious political incident by such irresponsible behaviour.'

'I realise that now, ma'am,' Lucetta said humbly. 'It won't happen again.'

'Quite right. It won't happen again.' Lady Boothby slammed her cup and saucer down on the sofa table. 'Sir John has given orders to the grooms that you are not to be allowed out on your own again under any circumstances. You will not leave the consulate without a chaperone. Is that understood?'

Lucetta nodded her head mutely. She knew that she had done wrong, but she was weary with apologising. And was she sorry? If she were to be quite honest, no, she was not. Now that the danger was past, she realised that she had had a great adventure and she had received her first kiss from an impossibly attractive young man. She might have been outraged at the time, but in retrospect she could still feel the soft touch of his lips on hers and the memory sent her heart fluttering wildly in her breast.

'Is that understood, Lucetta?' Lady Boothby repeated forcefully. Her impressive bosom rose and fell as she took deep breaths, causing the strands of pearls that hung round her neck to clatter together as if her rather large, prominent teeth were chattering with cold – a virtual impossibility in this steamy heat.

Lucetta came back to earth with a start. 'Yes, ma'am.'

'I'm so sorry, Pamela,' Eveline murmured, clasping her hand to her forehead. 'You've been so generous in your hospitality, and I'm ashamed that my daughter has seen fit to abuse your trust.'

'Now, now, Eveline, don't upset yourself. You'll only bring on one of your megrims again.'

'Yes, you're right.' Eveline closed her eyes and sighed. 'It's your fault, Lucetta. I thought a trip abroad might tame that rebellious spirit of yours, but it seems I was mistaken. I don't know what I'm going to do with you.'

Lady Boothby raised her lorgnette and stared hard at Lucetta. 'Marry the girl off at the first opportunity.'

'But she's only seventeen, Pamela. Lucetta won't be eighteen until Christmas.'

'I was married at seventeen,' Lady Boothby said stiffly. 'My papa arranged the match and I did as I was told. You may be in trade, my dear, but I'm sure that Mr Froy could set the girl up with a handsome dowry. There are plenty of young men from good families who will overlook the lack of breeding.'

Lucetta held her breath, glancing anxiously at her mother to see if she had taken offence at the slur on their background, but to all outward appearances Mama seemed quite calm.

'I expect that's true,' Eveline said meekly. 'But I'm afraid we don't move in those circles at home in London. We live a quiet life in Islington.'

'Then you must think about changing your way of living. If your husband makes as much money from this voyage as he hopes, then why not arrange a London season for the girl? There are plenty of dowagers who will happily undertake the responsibility for a generous remuneration.'

Lucetta was concerned to see her mother's eyes fill with tears and her lips had begun to tremble. 'Please don't say any more, Lady Boothby. Can't you see that you are upsetting my mama?'

'Lucetta,' Eveline cried faintly. 'Remember your manners.'

Lady Boothby drew back her neck and her eyes glittered like a cobra preparing to strike. 'How dare you speak to me like that?'

'I don't mean to be rude, ma'am, but I won't stand by while you insult my parents. They may not be what you consider to be top drawer, but they are good honest people and worthy of respect.'

'Well!' The word exploded from Lady Boothby's lips and her eyes bulged in their sockets. 'I've never been spoken to in that tone in my life, you insolent creature.'

A groan from Eveline was lost in the sound of approaching footsteps and the murmur of male voices interspersed with bursts of laughter. Lucetta glanced from her mother's tear-stained face to Lady Boothby's outraged expression and she realised that she had gone too far. Papa was still angry with her and he would be even more furious when he discovered that she had spoken out against their hostess. A waft of Havana cigars and brandy preceded Sir John and Henry as the double doors were flung open, but Lucetta did not wait to be tried and sentenced – she made her escape through the French windows and fled down the veranda steps into the all-enveloping darkness of the garden.

She ran, stumbling through flower beds and tripping over tree roots, stopping only to catch her breath. She was shaking uncontrollably and her heart was pounding against the whalebone cage of her tightly laced stays. She glanced over her shoulder to make certain that she had not been followed but all was quiet. The single-storey white stucco consulate appeared to float serenely in a pool of light emanating from the drawing-room windows and the paper lanterns hanging from the roof of the veranda. Lucetta could hear the soft murmur of voices from within, and it was not difficult to imagine the main topic of conversation, but she had no intention of returning to face the inevitable lecture. That could wait until tomorrow when hopefully everyone would have calmed down after a good night's sleep.

Still slightly breathless but intent on reaching the sanctuary of her own room, Lucetta made her way along a path between hedges of tall oleanders, their scented pink and white blossoms standing out palely against the dark night sky. A rustling sound in the undergrowth sent a shiver down her spine. It might be some harmless nocturnal creature or it could be a poisonous snake. She quickened her pace, sighing with relief when the path ended on the carriage sweep at the front of the building. The wide expanse of gravel was illuminated by cressets on either side of the main entrance and Lucetta would have to cross it in order to reach her room. It should have been quite deserted at this time in the evening but a commotion outside the gatehouse made her freeze in her tracks. Holding a lantern above his head, the gatekeeper was arguing fiercely with a person or persons on the road outside.

She paused for a moment, but realising that the gatekeeper was fully occupied she decided to take advantage of the diversion. Bracing her shoulders she forced herself to walk on at a steady pace, as if it were quite normal for her to be out alone after dark. Her feet crunched on the small jagged stones and the hairs stood up on the back of her neck when she realised that someone was following her. Commonsense deserted her and gripped by panic she broke into a run, but the footsteps were coming closer and she realised that someone was calling her name.

'Miss Froy. Stop, please.'

Ignoring the plea, she raced towards the shrubbery, but her pursuer caught up with her before she could disappear into the shadowy undergrowth. She spun round to find herself looking up into the face of Sam Cutler.

'Miss Froy, we seem doomed to meet in unusual circumstances.'

Struggling to regain her composure, Lucetta eyed him coldly. 'Mr Cutler, I live here. You have no right to scare me like that.'

'That wasn't my intention, I can assure you.' He snatched off his peaked cap and tucked it under his arm, bowing from the waist with a rueful smile. 'If I did, then I apologise, but I didn't expect to find you skulking around on your own in the dark. I'm not sure that the consul would approve.'

He was standing with his back to the light and she could not make his features out clearly, but Lucetta heard the laughter in his voice and now she had recovered from her fright the humour of the situation was not entirely lost on her. 'But I'm not on my own now, am I? You are here, although you haven't given me a reason for this unexpected visit. Have you come to see my papa?'

He shook his head. 'No, Miss Froy, I came to beg

your pardon. I didn't want to abandon you this morning and I had to make certain that you got home safely. Unfortunately the fellow at the gate didn't understand my motives for this rather late call.'

Lucetta glanced over his shoulder. The gatekeeper had summoned help from the stables and a group of men were advancing purposefully but warily. She could see that they meant business. 'You're right. I think the gatekeeper is about to have you thrown out.' She slipped her hand through his arm. 'Come with me. They won't dare do anything if I take you into the consulate.'

'I don't want to make things awkward for you.'

'Never mind that. I'm in enough trouble already and a little more won't make a scrap of difference.' Lucetta pulled him purposefully towards the steps which led up to the impressive double doors. They opened as if by magic and a liveried servant stood aside with a respectful bow. Lucetta thanked him with a smile and a nod, hoping that she appeared more nonchalant than she was feeling as they entered the cool white-marble entrance hall with its elegant console tables imported from Europe, gilt-framed wall mirrors and ormolu candle sconces. Three wide corridors led off the reception area; one led to Sir John's official suite of rooms and the other two to the private apartments and servants' quarters. 'Come with me,' Lucetta whispered. 'Hurry.'

'Why are you hiding and who are you hiding from?' Sam demanded as she dragged him towards the consul's private dining room. 'Is it a game of hide and seek?'

'Are you laughing at me?' Lucetta demanded suspiciously. 'I'm not a child, you know.'

His eyes crinkled at the corners and his lips twitched. 'No, I can see that. You are very much a young lady, and a beautiful one too if I might be so bold.'

'Oh, stuff and nonsense. Now I know you're teasing me,' Lucetta said, turning away to hide her blushes. 'Quick, I think someone's coming. We can get out through the dining-room window.'

Without waiting for his response she opened the door to the deserted dining room, where all traces of the recent meal had been cleared away and a clean white damask cloth had been laid ready for breakfast next morning. The floor to ceiling windows had been left open to clear the room of tobacco smoke and Lucetta darted out onto the veranda. She leaned against the balustrade, safe in the knowledge that the velvet darkness on this side of the building would protect them from prying eyes. Her heart was beating a tattoo in her breast, which must, she thought, be due to nervous excitement. But then she realised that she was trembling, and this time it was not fear that was making her pulses race, but the close proximity of a young man who had put himself to a degree of trouble for her sake. She was acutely aware of his presence and overcome by shyness. At a loss for words, she stared down at the ground, unable to look him in the face.

'So tell me what this is all about, Lucetta,' Sam said gently. 'May I call you that?'

She nodded mutely.

'Why were you wandering about in the grounds after dark? Perhaps you had a tryst with a lover?'

This brought her head up with a start. 'Certainly not.'

'I must say I'm glad. You would be wasted on any of these Imperial pen-pushers and mealy-mouthed civil servants who cling to the edge of the Empire.'

Even in the dark she sensed that he was smiling but she had no experience of flirting and she did not know how to respond to his banter. Sam Cutler was unlike any man she had ever met and strange new feelings clouded her mind so that it was impossible to think clearly. 'I don't think you ought to say things like that,' she said, making an attempt to sound grown up and in control of the situation. 'I think I'd better go to my room now, so I'll bid you goodnight, Mr Cutler.'

He took her by the hand. 'After all we've been through today I think we can drop the formalities. My friends and family call me Sam.'

His hand was warm and held hers as tenderly as if it were a baby bird that had fallen from its nest. Lucetta felt herself melting inside and she was alarmed. She knew she ought to pull her hand away, but it felt so comfortable in his grasp. 'And did you catch the escaped convicts, Sam?' Her voice sounded strained even to her own ears, but she knew she must retreat to safer ground.

'No, but we will resume our search at daybreak. They won't get far without food or water and the people in outlying villages have been warned to look out for them.'

'I hope you catch them,' Lucetta murmured. 'Goodnight, Mr – I mean Sam.'

He released her hand only to pull her into his arms.

Lucetta made a vague attempt to struggle free, but without much conviction. Her brain told her to resist, but somehow her body would not respond. Her feet refused to move and in an involuntary movement her arms slid round his neck. She could feel his warm breath on her cheek as she raised her face, half shy, half daring him to make the next move. His lips when they claimed hers were soft and sensual, caressing her mouth with tender kisses until her lips parted with a sigh. She closed her eyes and abandoned herself to the moment. His mouth tasted of fresh pineapple and honey and she could feel the warmth of his body through the thin cotton of his shirt. The male scent of him made her dizzy with desire and her body seemed to fit his so closely that they had become as one being. She returned his embrace with a passion she could never have imagined possible. This might be their first real kiss but she knew in her heart that it would not be the last. Too soon he drew away, holding her at arm's length.

'You are beautiful, Lucetta Froy,' he said softly, tracing the outline of her lips with his forefinger. 'I don't want to leave you but I must go now. I will return tomorrow.'

'No,' Lucetta whispered breathlessly. 'You must not come here. Papa would not permit it.'

'I will speak to him. Everything will be all right, I promise you.' He blew her a kiss and backed away into the darkness.

Lucetta stood motionless, hardly able to believe what had just happened to her. Nothing seemed real.

She was floating above the ground. She was totally and completely happy. Life was wonderful – she was in love.

In spite of everything, Lucetta slept well and awakened next morning with a feeling that something amazing was about to happen. Hundreds of butterflies seemed to be fluttering about in her stomach and she felt that she was invincible. There would, of course, be a long and uncomfortable session with Papa. He would lecture her at length on her inappropriate behaviour, but the worst he could do to her would be to forbid her to leave the consulate, or to stop her allowance. She stretched luxuriously and smiled. What did money matter when she had found the man she would love forever? Sam had promised to return today and her heart leapt at the thought of seeing him again. She must look her best. What gown would she wear? She must get Naomi to dress her hair in the most becoming style so that when he saw her he would fall in love with her all over again.

Lucetta snapped upright in bed. Had he said he loved her? Fingers of fear gripped her heart. Had she dreamed the whole thing? She raised her hands to her temples, closing her eyes, and then she opened them again, smiling. How foolish she was. He might not have told her he loved her in so many words, but his actions spoke for themselves. Surely a man could not kiss a girl with such passion if his heart were not well and truly lost to her?

She reached for the bell pull and tugged at it to

summon Naomi before leaping out of bed. Ignoring the fact that she was clad only in her nightgown, she threw the French windows open and stepped outside onto the veranda. Birdsong filled her ears like a heavenly chorus and a flock of white Balinese starlings took off from a banyan tree, chattering and flapping their black-tipped wings, the iridescent blue feathers on their heads glinting in the sunlight. Why had she never noticed how beautiful everything was before? She lifted her arms, raising her face to the sun as she inhaled the scent of the champak which grew close by. Reaching out she plucked a blossom from the bougainvillea that spilled in a waterfall of purple from the roof of the veranda, and she tucked it behind her ear, native style. The lush foliage and flowers in the neatly tended garden sparkled in the sunshine as the raindrops from last night's tropical downpour evaporated in a steaming mist.

The click of the latch on the bedroom door made Lucetta turn her head to see Naomi enter her room with a jug of hot water and fresh towels.

'Good morning, Naomi,' Lucetta said happily. 'Isn't this the most glorious day?'

'Good morning, missy,' Naomi replied, smiling as she filled the bowl on the washstand and replaced the soiled towels. 'You sleep well?'

Lucetta went back into the room with her feet barely touching the ground. She gave the startled maid a hug. 'I slept so well. Thank you for the clean towels and the hot water. You are wonderful. Everything is wonderful.'

Naomi looked at her doubtfully. 'Missy?'

'And you haven't understood a word I said,' Lucetta said, giggling. 'Never mind. You may go now, but come back after breakfast and help me choose my most becoming gown. I want to look absolutely stunning today.'

Naomi's doe-eyes widened and she shook her head. *'Ma'af, missy. Saya tidak mengerti.'*

'I know you must be confused, my dear,' Lucetta said sympathetically. 'I'll try to make you understand later, but I'm absolutely starving.' She rubbed her tummy and mimed eating and drinking. 'Breakfast, please. I'd like coffee, rolls and lots of fruit.'

'Ah!' Naomi said, smiling. 'Yes, missy.' She clasped her small brown hands together and bowed from the waist. 'I go now.'

Lucetta could barely restrain herself until the door closed and then she did a little dance, but on catching sight of her reflection in the cheval mirror she came to a sudden halt, staring at the young woman who peered back at her with a surprised expression on her pale face. Slowly, staring at the stranger in the looking glass, Lucetta undid the buttons on her nightgown and allowed it to slip to the ground. The blood rushed to her cheeks as she eyed her naked reflection and she struggled with her conscience. Well brought up young ladies were supposed to be modest and pure in thought and deed. That was the mantra which had been drummed into the girls at Miss Milton's Academy. Ladies took no pleasure in the lusts of the flesh; that was the province of the lower classes and fallen women.

The female form had to be imprisoned by whalebone and covered at all times. Décolletage was allowed in the ballroom but a gentleman must never see so much as the turn of an ankle, let alone a shapely calf.

Lucetta allowed her hand to stray over her breasts and flat belly, and her thoughts were anything but pure as the warm, moist air caressed her naked flesh. Mama and Lady Boothby had talked about marrying her off to some wealthy suitor, a prospect that had seemed to be so far in the future that it need not be taken too seriously, and she had barely given a thought to the intimate side of married life – until now. Quite suddenly she was seeing herself in a new light. In an instant her whole life had changed.

Last night a man whom she barely knew had held her in his arms and kissed her. In his tender embrace she knew that she had found a safe haven – she had come home. She could still feel the warmth of Sam's embrace. The taste of him lingered on her tongue and her whole being was consumed by desire for something that she did not fully understand. She had no clear idea of what constituted married love, just the vague rumours that the girls had hinted at in whispers and giggles under cover of darkness when the dormitory was supposed to be sleeping.

Lucetta shuddered with pleasure as she felt her nipples harden. She pulled a face at the girl in the mirror who stood with her feet planted wide apart and her back arched. She shuddered as a warm tingling feeling struck her in the most private of all places and she closed her eyes, wrapping her arms around her body as she tried to imagine that it was Sam Cutler who caressed her. A man's arms would not feel soft and rounded like a girl's. Lucetta had seen navvies at work in the streets with their bare sinewy forearms, their bulging muscles gleaming with sweat and rippling as they moved. She opened her eyes again, staring at herself open-mouthed with horror. She would go to hell for such wicked, lascivious thoughts. She seized the bowl of rapidly cooling water and tipped it over her head.

Trembling with shame and the shock of a sudden drenching, she snatched up her cotton wrap and flung it over the mirror. Water pooled on the tiled floor and she could only hope that Naomi would assume that the spillage was an accident. Having towelled herself dry, Lucetta slipped on her shift and struggled with the laces of her stays, tugging at them until she could hardly breathe. She could hear Miss Milton's voice ringing in her ears. 'Self-control, young ladies. Self-control and self-discipline are the two factors that made this nation great. When you go out into the world you must always remember this.'

By the time Naomi arrived with the breakfast tray, Lucetta was sitting primly on the veranda combing her wet hair. The aroma of the coffee mingled with the flower-scented air and Lucetta drank two cups, one after the other. She devoured a plateful of sliced mango and then peeled the wrinkled purple-brown skin off a mangosteen, sinking her teeth into the crisp white segments. She would miss all these exotic fruits when she returned to London. Apples and pears were nothing compared to sweet, delicately scented star fruit or a succulent, slightly acidic rambutan.

Lucetta sighed. Just thinking of leaving this island paradise made her sad. A few short hours ago she had been dreaming of home and the diversions that she missed most, but meeting Sam had changed all that. She would have been happy to stay here forever, as long as he was with her. She tore a freshly baked bread roll in half, spreading each section with the strawberry jam that Lady Boothby had sent to her in a regular order from Fortnum and Mason's. While she ate, savouring each mouthful, Lucetta decided that she could not exist for a whole day without seeing Sam. The need for him was consuming her like a fever, and if he could not come to her then she must go to Benoa harbour and seek him out.

There was just one flaw in this plan – Papa had forbidden her to leave the consulate. She must catch him before he left on his next buying expedition, and apologise humbly for her bad behaviour. Despite his gruff manner, she knew that she could wrap Pa round her little finger if she tried, and she was genuinely sorry for causing him so much distress. Perhaps she could persuade him that she was in desperate need of a new riding hat and crop as hers had been taken from her at the temple, and these could be purchased in Denpasar. He might have threatened to stop her allowance but no one could accuse Pa of being mean, and a hat was an absolute necessity in this climate. If he agreed to her request she would take Naomi as chaperone and it couldn't be too far from the town to Benoa harbour where she was sure to find the *Caroline*. It was a simple plan and hopefully foolproof.

'Mr Froy left for the other side of the island shortly before daybreak, miss.' Jackson, Sir John's English butler, stared at a point just above Lucetta's shoulder. 'I believe a consignment of teakwood furniture has come to grief at the bottom of a ravine.'

'Do you know when he is expected to return?' Lucetta asked, assuming an innocent air and trying hard not to look pleased by the unexpected reprieve.

'No, miss.'

'Is Sir John at home?'

'No, miss. Sir John has gone to Lombok on official business and Lady Boothby is at the hospital, as is her custom on this day of the week.'

'And my mother?'

'Is in her room. She is not to be disturbed.'

'Thank you, Jackson.' Lucetta could hardly believe her good luck. She watched Jackson as he stalked off towards the servants' quarters with an irritated hunch of his shoulders. She knew that he did not approve of her, or her nouveau riche parents, but she did not care. Today nothing was going to upset her. This was the beginning of the rest of her life and that life included Samuel Cutler.

She hurried back to her room where Naomi was clearing the breakfast things and a maid was mopping the wet floor.

'Leave that, Naomi,' Lucetta said, taking the tray from her hands and thrusting it at the astonished maidservant. 'Please tell the girl to take it back to the kitchen. You and I are going to Denpasar.'

Lucetta shooed the maid out of the room, closing the door behind her. 'Denpasar,' she repeated, pointing to Naomi and then to herself. 'You and me. We go to Denpasar now, this minute. No time to lose.' Without waiting for a response, she went to the heavily carved wardrobe and selected a straw bonnet with blue ribbons that exactly matched the shade of her eyes, and a lace shawl. Her fingers shook with excitement as she put the bonnet on her head and tied the ribbons in a jaunty bow just below her left ear. She draped the shawl around her shoulders and made for the door, but then she realised that Naomi was standing like a statue in the middle of the room. 'What's the matter? Don't look so scared. We're only going to Denpasar, not the moon.'

Naomi shook her head. '*Tan, missy. Tan.*'

Lucetta understood enough Balinese to know that this was a point blank refusal. She could hardly drag the unwilling maid all the way to the docks and there was no one else whom she could trust to accompany her without reporting to Jackson. She would just have to go alone.

In the stables, the head groom met her request with a firm refusal. Sir John and Lady Boothby had taken both carriages and he had strict instructions that Missy should not ride out alone. Lucetta tried everything but no amount of wheedling could make him change his mind, and she was forced to retreat, temporarily beaten. Reluctantly, she returned to her room, pacing the floor and racking her brains for a solution to her problem. She took off her bonnet and tossed it onto a chair where a length of songket, a beautiful fabric used for ceremonial sarongs, had been left to await the dressmaker who was supposed to be coming later that morning in order to take her measurements. The delicate material interwoven with gold thread would make a stunning evening gown, but suddenly Lucetta had another use for it.

She fumbled with the tiny fabric-covered buttons at the back of her morning gown and stepped out of the crinoline cage, allowing it to glide to the floor. Taking a white cotton blouse from her wardrobe she put it on and then, copying the manner of dress of the Balinese women, she wrapped the length of cloth around her body to form a sarong. She studied her reflection in the cheval mirror, but to her chagrin she looked like a young English girl in fancy dress. With her pale complexion and silver-blonde hair she would never pass as a local girl. She rummaged feverishly in the cedar chest and found a long, multi-coloured silk scarf which she wound around her head. The result was far from convincing, but, she reasoned, who would give her a second glance? If she kept her head down and stuck to the shade of the pandanus and palm trees, who would notice yet another village girl hurrying to market in Denpasar?

Slipping out of the consulate grounds was easier than she anticipated. The gatekeeper was busy raking the gravel and the rest of the servants were going about their daily tasks. No one gave her a second glance as she left the compound. She crossed the dusty road and set off in the direction of the town, but she had no idea how far it was. It had only seemed a short carriage ride from the harbour to the consulate, but she soon found that walking in the heat of the day was a very different proposition from being driven in the consul's well-sprung landau. Within minutes she was hot and thirsty and cursing herself for not thinking of equipping herself with a water bottle. She had some coins tucked into her bodice for emergencies and with luck she might come across a wayside vendor selling coconut milk. As the sun rose in the cloudless sky the heat became even more intense; far hotter than she could have imagined when confined to the marble coolness of the consulate or the shady gardens.

A cloud of dust in the distance and the muffled sound of horses' hooves was enough to send her stumbling for cover into the thick undergrowth at the side of the road. The riders went past at a spanking pace, throwing up miniature dust storms. Choking and covering her face with her hands, Lucetta backed further into the tangle of pandanus roots and oleander bushes. She did not hear the snap of a twig or realise that there was someone else hiding in the undergrowth until a rough hand clamped over her mouth, and strong arms lifted her off her feet. She fought and kicked but she was powerless to save herself from being dragged deeper and deeper into the bush.

Chapter Four

'Shut your face, you little whore.'

The harsh cockney accent ripped through Lucetta's consciousness. The smell of unwashed flesh made her feel physically sick, but she was more angry than afraid. Struggling and kicking out with her feet she sank her teeth into the grimy hand that covered her mouth. Her attacker loosened his grip with a grunt of pain and she stumbled, clutching at an overhanging branch to save herself from falling. She backed away from the man, who was sucking his injured hand and glaring as if he would like to finish her off there and then. 'You've made a big mistake. Just wait until the consul hears about this.'

'Bloody hell, Stranks. You've snatched an English-woman.'

Lucetta turned her head to stare at the speaker, who lay on a matted bed of dry leaves, his right leg twisted in a most unnatural position. 'Yes, I'm English, and you'll both end up in jail if you don't let me go this instant.'

'Hoity-toity, begging your pardon, ma'am.' The man called Stranks executed a mocking bow. 'If I'd have known you was a lady, I'd have asked your permission afore I grabbed you.'

'I–I'm not a lady. I'm a lady's maid and you'd better let me go, or my master will have the law on you.'

'Send the trollop on her way, Stranks,' the man on the ground muttered wearily. 'We don't want no more trouble than we got already.'

'Shut up, Guthrie, and let me think.' Stranks wiped his bruised hand on the seat of his pants, staring hard at Lucetta. 'What's an English maidservant doing in them fancy duds, then? Answer me that?'

'I know who you are,' Lucetta said slowly. 'You're the escaped convicts that the men from the British merchant ship were looking for.'

'You know a lot more than is good for you, and I don't believe you're a lady's maid,' Stranks said suspiciously. 'Who are you, girl?'

Guthrie raised himself on his elbow, wincing with pain. 'We're done for, mate. Might as well give ourselves up.'

'Shut up, you fool.' Stranks spat on the ground, just missing Lucetta's feet. 'D'you want to go back to London clapped in irons? It'll mean the gallows for certain.'

'How far d'you think we'll get with my leg busted?' Guthrie collapsed onto the ground with a low moan, covering his face with his arm.

Lucetta watched in horror as a huge centipede appeared from the rotting vegetation and scuttled across his body to disappear into the folds of his shirt. She held her breath, waiting for him to realise that something strange was happening, but he didn't appear to notice. 'Your friend needs a doctor,' she said in a matter-of-fact voice. 'And the thing that just crawled inside his clothes could be poisonous.'

'Shut your face,' Stranks said, fisting his hands. 'One more charge against me won't make no difference, so you button your lip.'

Lucetta was quick to hear the note of panic in his voice. 'If you don't let me go there'll be another search party and this time they'll be looking for me. You can't exactly make a run for it with him in that condition, now can you?'

'Stop going on at me,' Stranks muttered through gritted teeth. 'I ain't never hit a woman, but there's always the first time.'

Lucetta turned her back on him and she knelt on the ground beside Guthrie, running her fingers gently along the contour of his twisted limb. 'It's broken all right and the bone has come through the skin. He must get medical attention or the wound will go septic in this heat.'

Guthrie let his arm fall to his side. 'Oh, God. I'll lose me leg. I'll die of gangrene. I'm burning up already.'

Lucetta laid her hand on his forehead. 'He might have a fever. It's hard to tell.'

'Then you fix him up, girlie,' Stranks said brusquely. 'We got to get away from here afore they finds us.'

'I can't do anything without clean water and bandages. Anyway, I don't know how to set bones. He must see a doctor.'

Stranks seized her by the arm, his strong fingers bruising her soft flesh as he dragged her to her feet. He ripped the scarf from her head. 'There's yer bandages, the water will have to wait. Now get on with it.'

Lucetta's blonde hair swung loose around her shoulders as he shook her until her teeth rattled. 'Let me go, you big brute.' She was terrified, but she was determined not to let it show. 'If you want me to help him I'll do what I can, but I can't promise anything.'

Stranks pushed her away from him, wiping the beads of sweat from his brow with the back of his hand. 'Just see to him then.'

Lucetta frowned as she tried to remember what had happened when the gardener's boy at the Academy fell from an apple tree. The branch that he had been pruning had given way beneath his weight and his screams of pain had been heart-rending. The girls had stood round helplessly, some of them in tears and others pale with shock and unnaturally silent. When the doctor arrived he had taken charge of the scene in the most admirable way. He had instructed the agitated teachers to take the distraught girls back into the building, and he had organised those who wanted to help, which had included Lucetta, to go in search of wooden slats to provide support for the injured limb before the boy was hefted onto a hurdle and carried back to his surgery.

'He'll need a splint,' Lucetta said firmly. 'You must cut some lengths of bamboo.' Ignoring the outpouring of bad language as Stranks stomped off into the bush she went down on her knees beside Guthrie. 'This will hurt a bit.'

'Just do it, miss. Just do it.'

Taking the knife from his leather belt, Lucetta slit the coarse canvas of his trouser leg. The breath hitched in her throat and a feeling of nausea almost overcame her as she saw the bloody mess where the fractured bones had pierced his skin. Flies swarmed over the wound, attracted by the smell of fresh blood. Lucetta swallowed hard. She must keep calm. She must appear to be in control and then, when the opportunity arose, she would make a dash for the road and safety. She leaned back on her haunches, listening to Stranks crashing through the undergrowth as he hacked at the bamboo. It occurred to her that she could make her escape now, but somehow she could not bring herself to leave the injured man. She covered the exposed wound with her headscarf, and she was busy keeping the flies at bay with a palm leaf when Stranks reappeared carrying an armful of bamboo canes.

'Get on with it,' he said, dumping them down beside her. 'Set the bones so that he can walk out of here.'

Lucetta lifted the scarf, pointing to the injury and shaking her head. 'I can't. I haven't got the strength. It must be done properly.'

'Bloody useless female,' Stranks said scornfully. 'I've seen this done a dozen times or more in the penal colony.' He bent down and without a word of warning he yanked the leg so that the bones snapped back into position with a sickening cracking sound.

Guthrie let out an agonised howl and fainted.

'There,' Stranks said, grinning. 'I told you there weren't nothing to it. See to him now while he don't know nothing about it.'

With perspiration dripping into her eyes, Lucetta fashioned a rough splint and bound it in position with her scarf. 'There,' she said, rising unsteadily to her feet. 'I've done what I can. Now let me go.'

'Not on your life, missy.' Stranks seized her before she had a chance to run, and he twisted her arm behind her back. 'You're our ticket to freedom.'

'You won't get away with this,' Lucetta said, wincing with pain as he gave her arm a savage twist. 'You'll never get off the island.'

Stranks chortled with laughter, although there was no humour in the sound. 'You may think I'm stupid, but I know who you are. Guthrie and me was waiting to be taken on board the *Caroline* when you come ashore in your fancy clothes and with that pretty little nose stuck in the air. I don't know who your pa is but I can smell money a mile off. I'm sure he'll be only too happy to pay for the return of his little darling, and the authorities won't touch Guthrie and me while we've got you in tow.'

He released Lucetta with a savage push that sent her staggering. She would have fallen to the ground had she not clutched a liana which hung from a tall banyan tree.

'How far do you think you'll get with him in that condition?' she demanded. 'Your friend can't stand, let alone walk, and do you know where you're headed? If you go back to Benoa harbour you'll be caught for certain.'

'And you've got a lot of lip for someone in your position,' Stranks said, scowling. 'But if you must know, we're making for Gilimanuk. Guthrie and me can get a boat to Java from there. We got money and we can buy a passage to somewhere the law won't catch up with us.'

'Gilimanuk is miles away to the north. You'll never make it.'

'I'll make it all right, and the first thing I'll do when we get there is wring your neck and feed you to the sharks.'

'But why burden yourself with a woman and an injured man?' Lucetta said softly. 'You could make Gilimanuk in a couple of days if you went alone.'

'And leave you to set the law on me? D'you think I'm a complete fool?' Stranks raised his hand as if to strike her but a low moan from Guthrie diverted his attention.

'Water. For God's sake give me water.'

'There ain't none,' Stranks said gruffly. 'Hang on there, mate. I'm parched too, but I've got to sort this trull out afore I go looking for water.'

He took a step towards Lucetta, pulling a knife from his belt, and for a terrifying moment she thought he intended to kill her, but he hacked a length off the liana and seizing her by the shoulders, he pinned her arms behind her back. He lashed her wrists together and cutting a longer length of the vine, he bound her to the trunk of the banyan tree. 'There, that'll hold you until I get back.'

Lucetta was about to scream for help, but Stranks slapped his hand over her mouth, holding his knife to her throat. 'One peep from you, missy, and I really will slit your gullet.'

She did not doubt that he meant every word he said, and she was barely surprised when he ripped a length from the hem of her sarong and gagged her so that she could not utter a sound. He grinned, revealing an uneven row of blackened teeth. 'That'll keep you quiet for a bit, Miss High and Mighty.'

He was gone for what seemed like hours and Lucetta had to suffer the torment of flies buzzing around her face while ants crawled over her feet and made exploratory trips up her bare legs. Guthrie lapsed in and out of consciousness, begging for water in his lucid moments, his eyes beseeching Lucetta for help that she was unable to give. His groans of pain became unintelligible gibberish as fever racked his body. Lucetta could only watch helplessly and wait for Stranks to return.

A green snake slithered from the undergrowth and she held her breath as it moved towards Guthrie's inert body. She hoped that he would remain unconscious as the reptile stopped, its forked tongue flicking in and out as it absorbed the scent of the man lying on the forest floor. Don't let it come near me, Lucetta prayed silently, as sweat trickled down her face and neck. The snake raised its flat head and stared at her with basilisk eyes, then just as suddenly as it had come it disappeared into the undergrowth. Shuddering violently, Lucetta felt tears of relief pouring from her eyes.

Guthrie moaned and began thrashing about and a bubble of hysteria rose in Lucetta's throat; if he'd come to moments sooner the snake would almost certainly have struck one of them. She was shaking from head to foot with sheer relief and she didn't know whether to laugh or cry.

The sound of cracking twigs and muffled footsteps brought her abruptly back to her senses. Had she been missed? Could this be a rescue party? Her hopes were dashed when it was Stranks who stumbled through the bamboo and pandanus fronds followed by two sturdy Balinese men carrying long bamboo poles and a rolled up seagrass mat. While the men constructed a rough stretcher, Stranks produced a rush basket filled with coconuts. Piercing one with the tip of his knife he held it to Guthrie's parched lips. Some of the cool milk trickled into his mouth although most of it seemed to run down his chin, but it had the desired effect and Guthrie's eyelids fluttered and opened.

'That's the ticket, mate,' Stranks said. 'Drink some more.'

Guthrie coughed and spluttered as he slipped back into unconsciousness and Stranks rose to his feet, tossing the coconut into the bushes. Brandishing his knife he moved towards Lucetta and cut her bonds. 'Don't try and speak to them,' he said, jerking his head towards the men. 'They don't understand English.' He took the gag from her mouth and pressed a coconut in her hands. 'Drink this and we'll be on our way. Try to escape and I'll kill you.'

Their progress through the dense rainforest was slow. Stranks tied Lucetta's hands in front of her and she found herself tied to him with an umbilical cord of liana fastened to his waist. He charged on ahead of the stretcher bearers, slashing at the undergrowth with his knife. Lucetta stumbled in his wake and soon her legs were scratched and bleeding, making every faltering step even more painful. Guthrie's moans and feverish cries echoed through the forest, startling the macaques and black monkeys as they swung from branch to branch in the leafy canopy overhead. Lizards darted across their feet and to her horror, Stranks almost bumped into a python that hung like a trapeze artist from an overhanging limb of a flame tree. Seemingly more startled than they were, the snake coiled itself up and disappeared into the foliage.

Lucetta almost fell when she twisted her ankle in a hole where some animal had made its burrow. She managed to regain her balance but Stranks stopped and swore at her. 'You nearly had me over, you silly bitch.'

'Have a heart,' Lucetta murmured, clutching her side as a painful stitch almost doubled her up. 'We can't go much further. It will be dark soon and we won't be able to see a thing.'

'Tell me something I don't know,' Stranks hissed.

The stretcher bearers had laid Guthrie gently on the ground and the elder of the two men came scurrying towards Stranks, talking volubly and waving his hands.

'Can't understand a word, mate,' Stranks said, shrugging his shoulders.

Pointing to a tiny patch of sky above them, the man chattered on, shaking his head.

'I think he's trying to tell you that it will soon be

nightfall,' Lucetta said, folding her arms across her chest as a shiver ran down her spine. The thought of spending a night in the forest was too terrifying to contemplate. The local men seemed to agree with her as they eyed Stranks warily, shaking their heads. Lucetta found herself wishing that she had learned some of their language instead of expecting Naomi and the other servants to master the English tongue. If only she could make them understand that her father would give them a rich reward for her safe return.

'Move on,' Stranks ordered.

The men shook their heads, speaking in unison. '*Tan*.'

It was the one word that Lucetta understood. It was a very definite no.

'Not tan, you bloody native,' Stranks roared. He drew a leather pouch from his pocket and tipped some coins into his hand, holding it out to them. 'Me pay more, savvy?'

'Don't speak to them like that,' Lucetta protested. 'Do you want them to abandon us in the middle of the jungle?' Infuriated by his stupidity, she tugged on the liana which joined them together, catching him off balance so that he fell to his knees. His shouts and curses were drowned by the men's laughter; they seemed to think it was the funniest thing they had ever seen. The older man picked up the coins that Stranks had dropped and threw them at him. Still laughing, they turned on their heels and vanished into the bush.

Stranks rose to his feet, slashing at the liana and freeing Lucetta. 'This is all your fault. I should slit your throat here and now.' He raised the knife as if he meant to kill her but a sudden downpour drenched them to the skin in seconds. The shock of the warm rainwater cascading over him stopped Stranks as if he had been turned to stone. He raised his face to the sky and opened his mouth, swallowing the water in noisy gulps. Lucetta followed suit. Never had fresh water tasted so sweet. Momentarily forgetting about her captors, even though her wrists were still bound, she raised her arms above her head and allowed the tropical rain to wash the dust and sweat from her body. Even Guthrie seemed a little quieter as the water cooled his fever and moistened his dry lips.

It was over as suddenly as it had begun. Stranks seized Lucetta by the hair and just when she thought she had breathed her last, he brought the knife down and slit the liana fibres that bound her wrists. He pushed her away from him. 'You won't get far, so don't try to escape.'

She rubbed her chafed flesh, eyeing him warily. 'What are you going to do?'

'Not that it's any business of yours, but I'm going to find a safe place to get some rest. You stay here and look after Guthrie.' He trudged off, his booted feet squelching in the newly formed mud.

Lucetta's knees gave way beneath her and she sank down on a dead log. Stranks was right; she wouldn't get far on her own. She was completely lost and in a very short time the tropical night would wrap itself around them like black velvet. Already she could hear the 'geck-oh' night call of the geckos and the contin-uous croaking of frogs. The undergrowth surrounding them was alive with sound and the foliage above her head rustled with the movement of bats and other nocturnal creatures. Guthrie had quietened considerably and was muttering feverishly as he lay on the now sodden matting.

Her stomach rumbled and she realised that she was extremely hungry. She picked up the sack that Stranks had bought from the Balinese villagers and emptied it onto the ground. Two coconuts rolled onto the forest floor followed by a bunch of finger-sized bananas and a couple of star fruit. Without stopping to think how Stranks might react when he discovered that some of the fruit was missing, she peeled a banana and sank her teeth into the sweet flesh, barely chewing it before swallowing. She ate another and was about to gobble a third when she realised that Guthrie had opened his eyes and was staring at her. She knelt down beside him, breaking off a small piece of banana and holding it to his lips. 'Try to eat. You need to keep your strength up.' As obedient as a small child, he opened his mouth and chewed the soft fruit, gulping it down with an effort.

'Water,' he croaked. 'Give me water.'

Lucetta picked up a coconut and tried smashing it against a stone, but the hard shell withstood the shock and it bounced out of her hand. Stranks was the only one who possessed a knife and the milk would have to remain inside the nut until his return. She tore a strip from his shirt, which was still damp enough to moisten his cracked lips. She could not be certain, but she thought he smiled at her as he lapsed into merciful unconsciousness. There was nothing more she could do and she returned to the log, sitting down and wrapping her arms around her knees as the darkness enveloped them.

She thought about her parents. Father would be frantic by now and Mama would be prostrate on her bed with a cold compress on her brow and a vial of hartshorn clutched in her hand. Sir John would be furious and Lady Boothby would say it was only to be expected of a wilful young girl who spent her time idling round the house instead of helping the sick and disadvantaged at the charity hospital. Lucetta made a silent vow to atone for her disobedience, but imagining her parents' distress was too painful and even worse, she might die here in the Balinese jungle and never have the chance to say that she was sorry.

She buried her face in her hands, attempting to conjure up the face of Sam Cutler, the man who had stolen her heart and for whom she had risked her reputation, and it would seem, her life. She could not exactly describe his features one by one, although she remembered the way his hazel eyes crinkled at the corners when he smiled, and the way her heart fluttered at the sound of his voice. He had awakened something within her that threatened to consume her and had made her reckless with the need to see him again. Would he still be searching for the escaped convicts? Or would he and his men have given up and returned to the *Caroline*? Did he know that she was missing, and if he did, would he come to her rescue?

It was pitch dark now and she could not see Guthrie

even though he lay just a few feet from her. The rustling sounds in the undergrowth seemed to be even louder and growing closer minute by minute, and she felt as though they were being watched by unseen predators. The foolhardiness of her escapade sat on her shoulders like a heavy mantle. Her pampered, protected life had not equipped her for survival outside the walls of her comfortable home. She had never had to do anything for herself; there had always been servants at her beck and call, ready to carry out the simplest of tasks. She had never felt so lost or so alone in the world. She even found herself wishing that Stranks would return. He was a villain and a ruffian but at least he was human. Who knew what horrors lurked behind every bush and tree?

Lucetta opened her eyes. She could see a faint glimmer of light filtering through the ghostly grey trunks of the trees and she could hear the sound of men's voices, the heavy tramp of booted feet, the splitting of cane and the crack of broken twig. It was, of course, just another dream: she had been dozing fitfully all night and then waking with a start as the pain in her cramped limbs became unbearable. Each time she opened her eyes it had been to suffocating darkness, like being stone blind. The noises that she had heard had been the night sounds of the rainforest, punctuated by feverish moans from Guthrie, but this time it was different; the men were speaking English. She pinched herself and it really hurt; she was not dreaming. She was wide awake and help was close at hand.

She opened her mouth and tried to call out, but no sound came from her dry throat. For a dreadful moment she thought the rescue party were going to miss them and she reached out with her hands, feeling for a branch or a stone, anything that she could throw to attract their attention. Then her fingers curled around the hard, hairy shell of a coconut and she scrambled to her feet, flinging it with all her might. She heard a soft thud followed by a loud curse and raised voices.

'Where did that bleeder come from? It hit me square on me head.'

'It came from over there. Bring the torches, men.'

Dazzled by the sudden bright light of a flaming torch, Lucetta shielded her eyes. She could just make out the dark silhouettes of men breaking through the tangle of banana palms and tree ferns. Someone called her name and her heart leapt against her ribs as she recognised Sam's voice, but relief quickly turned to humiliation as she realised what a sight she must look. The once beautiful songket clung damply to the natural contours of her body and her hair must be in a terrible mess. She was filthy, exhausted, and she knew that she must smell absolutely terrible.

'Lucetta! Thank God.'

Recognising her father's voice, Lucetta leapt up and flung herself into his arms. 'Oh, Papa, I'm so glad to see you.'

'Are you all right, Miss Froy?' Sam asked anxiously.

Tears of relief flooded down Lucetta's cheeks and she buried her face against her father's shoulder.

'My little girl will be all right now, thank you, Cutler.' Henry wrapped his arms protectively around his daughter's trembling body. 'I'll take her back to the consulate. You'd best set about catching the villains who abducted her.'

It was dawn when they reached the consulate and the stucco was tinged rose pearl by the rising sun. Lucetta was still dazed and disorientated and she was stunned to see her mother and Lady Boothby waiting for them on the veranda. Mama never left her bed this early; it was unheard of. She was even more astonished when her mother ran towards her.

'Oh, my poor child. What have they done to you?' Eveline threw her arms around Lucetta but then stepped away, wrinkling her nose. 'You must have a bath immediately.'

'She is quite obviously in a state of shock, Eveline,' Lady Boothby said, eyeing Lucetta critically. 'I've sent for the doctor and I think he should examine her first, if you know what I mean.'

'Oh, no. You don't think . . .' Eveline paled alarmingly and dropped her hands to her sides.

Lady Boothby nodded emphatically. 'Virgo intacta, my dear. We must ascertain the truth.'

Lucetta had not paid much attention in Latin classes and she had no idea what virgo intacta meant, but she could tell by the expression on Mama's face that it must be something quite serious. 'I'm not hurt, Mama. I'm just tired and dirty and I would love a bath.'

Eveline sank down on the nearest rattan chair,

fanning herself vigorously. 'You must do as you're told, Lucetta. Henry, please tell her that we know best.'

'Pa?' Lucetta turned to her father and was shocked by the fury in his normally gentle brown eyes, and the white lines around his tight lips.

'Best if you wait, poppet,' he murmured, giving her a hug. 'Do as your mama says, there's a good girl. I have some unfinished business with Sir John.'

Lady Boothby took Lucetta firmly by the shoulders. 'I'll look after her. You will find Sir John in his office, Henry.'

With a curt nod of his head, Henry strode purposefully into the house.

'What did those brutes do to you, my darling?' Eveline asked faintly. 'Did they – did they molest you in any way?'

Lady Boothby pressed Lucetta down on a cushioned chair. 'You must tell us the truth, my dear. We know that they must have been lurking in the grounds just waiting for the chance to abduct you. No one is blaming you, Lucetta, and you mustn't be afraid to tell us everything, so that those criminals can be brought to justice for their appalling crime.'

Lucetta closed her eyes as the bougainvillea-drenched roof of the veranda began to swim dizzily towards the balustrade. She was faint with hunger, fatigue and emotional exhaustion. 'Please, I don't want to talk about it,' she murmured.

'I think I'm going to swoon,' Eveline said, clasping her hand to her forehead. 'I can't bear to think what you must have suffered.'

Lady Boothby snatched up a bottle of sal volatile from the table and waved it beneath Eveline's nose. 'Get a hold on yourself, woman. Having a fit of the vapours won't help the situation.'

Eveline coughed and spluttered as the potent fumes had their effect. 'I've suffered terribly but then you wouldn't understand, Pamela. Only a mother could know what I've been going through.'

'Poppycock! You're just being hysterical and that's the last thing the girl needs.' Lady Boothby turned to a male servant who had been standing mutely by the door. 'Kadek, go and see if the doctor has arrived, and tell Nyoman to have a warm bath prepared for Miss Lucetta. We will also need salve and lint. Those cuts and scratches will have to be attended to soon or they will suppurate. And fetch Miss Froy's wrap from her room,' she added, staring with obvious distaste at the flimsy sarong which left little to the imagination. 'We can't have you running about the consulate in that state of undress.'

Kadek bowed and slipped silently into the dark interior of the house.

Lucetta stared down at the tattered songket which had been destined for better things, and she was even more acutely aware of her unsightly appearance. 'I would like to go to my room, if you please, ma'am.' She attempted to rise from her chair but was overcome by a bout of dizziness.

'Stay where you are,' Lady Boothby ordered in the commanding tones of a general addressing his troops. 'You're as white as a sheet. Are you in pain?'

Lucetta shook her head. 'Do you think I could have something to eat and drink, please?'

Lady Boothby stared at her as if she were asking for something outrageous. 'Not until you've been seen by the doctor.'

'I can't bear it,' Eveline cried, shuddering. 'My poor baby girl. I feel quite faint at the thought.'

'Hush, Eveline. Don't frighten the child.' Lady Boothby angled her head, holding up her hand for quiet. 'Hush, I hear carriage wheels. It must be the doctor. Lucetta, I'll help you to your room. Eveline, if you can't control your emotions, you had best remain here.'

'I don't understand,' Lucetta said, rising unsteadily to her feet. 'What is going to happen to me, Lady Boothby?'

Chapter Five

If her experiences in the rainforest had been terrifying they vanished into the realm of a bad dream when compared to the shock and embarrassment of the examination by an elderly English doctor, who smelled disturbingly of brandy and stale tobacco. He performed the most intimate of medical procedures without telling her what he was going to do or explaining the reasons why it was considered necessary, leaving Lucetta stunned and on the verge of tears. He washed his hands and pronounced that she was indeed virgo intacta, which seemed to come as a disappointment to Lady Boothby who had stood at the bedside throughout, grim-faced and seemingly ready to pounce on Lucetta and hold her down if she dared to resist the doctor's probing fingers.

Naomi fluttered into the room after they left and she made sympathetic noises as she helped Lucetta into the hip bath filled with warm, scented water. She bathed her mistress as gently as if she had been a small child, washing her hair and drying it with a towel. Even though they could not communicate verbally, it was quite obvious to Lucetta that the servants were well aware of her ordeal, and Naomi's gentle doe-eyes were brimming with concern.

Despite her recent trials, Lucetta had not lost her appetite. She ate a hearty breakfast of buttered eggs, toast and fresh fruit, washed down by several cups of strong black coffee. Although she had intended to get dressed and behave as though nothing had happened, she was overcome by a feeling of lassitude and she decided to lie down and rest for a few minutes before getting dressed.

She slept dreamlessly and awakened at noon feeling refreshed and surprisingly free of any ill effects from her time in captivity. The scratches on her arms and legs were sore, but the salve applied by the doctor had eased the pain, and even at this early stage they showed signs of healing; unlike her conscience. What had happened yesterday had been almost entirely her fault. If she had not ventured out alone in that feeble attempt to disguise herself as a Balinese woman, she would not have stumbled into the path of the escaped convicts.

She lay in bed weighing up the pros and cons of confessing everything to Papa, or of taking the easy way out and going along with the fiction that Stranks and Guthrie had abducted her from the consulate grounds. After all, it would be her word against theirs, and they were already in such deep trouble that no one would believe them. She tugged at the bell pull to summon Naomi and she sat up, swinging her legs over the side of the bed. Her plan to see Sam might have gone disastrously wrong, but in the end it was he who had come to her rescue. She was certain that she had not imagined the relief in his voice when he had found her in the rainforest. The knowledge that he really cared for her was balm to her soul, and an irrepressible bubble of excitement rose to her throat, making her want to sing for joy. It was a pity that she had been in such a sorry state, but perhaps he had not noticed; after all it had been quite dark and no one could survive a night in the bush without looking a complete fright.

She rose to her feet and ran lightly across the room to fling the French windows wide open. The steamy heat of midday enveloped her in a warm embrace as she stepped outside onto the veranda. Above the chatter of the starlings she was suddenly aware of gamelan music and the babble of voices emanating from the servants' quarters. She could feel the excitement in the air and it matched her own, for today she knew that she would see Sam again. Now he had a valid excuse for visiting the consulate, as Sir John would want to be certain that the prisoners were safely under lock and key.

She held her arms out to the sun and felt its soft caress on her cheeks. If the truth came out she was prepared to take the consequences, but she was certain that Sam loved her as she loved him. Whatever the outcome, she felt it was a truly wonderful day, although she might still have some explaining to do. Mama and Lady Boothby might be content to know that she had suffered no long-lasting physical harm, but Papa would not be so easily satisfied. She pushed the niggling worry to the back of her mind. She would cross that particular bridge when she came to it. She rang the bell for Naomi again. The most pressing problem now was to decide what to wear.

In the end and after much deliberation, she chose an afternoon gown made from white muslin sprigged with forget-me-nots. It had a quite daring décolletage and the wide crinoline made her waist look even tinier than the eighteen inches Naomi had achieved by lacing Lucetta's stays so tightly that she could hardly breathe. Satisfied that she looked a completely different person from the frightened and dishevelled girl the search party had discovered in the rainforest, Lucetta went in search of her parents.

The reception rooms were deserted and echoing with silence, although there seemed to be much activity in the servants' quarters and outside the compound it sounded as though there was a huge party in progress. Mystified, Lucetta sought out Jackson. She came across him in the entrance hall, and if he knew about her ordeal he gave no sign of it. When questioned he informed her that Mr Froy had gone inland to organise the retrieval of the consignment of furniture from the bottom of the gorge. Sir John was out somewhere on official business and Lady Boothby had left earlier for the charity hospital. Mrs Froy had taken to her bed with a migraine and was not to be disturbed. He turned to walk away but Lucetta called him back.

'Yes, miss?'

'What is all that noise? It's normally so quiet here.'

Jackson sniffed and his mouth creased into the shape of a small prune. 'A native festival, I believe, miss. Some outlandish name – Nyepi, or something similar.'

'Nyepi? What does that mean?'

'I wouldn't know, miss. But apparently at the end

77

of the rainy season the locals celebrate their pagan festivals with processions, feasting and the din that they call music. It's some heathen notion of casting out devils, I believe, which goes on day and night until sunrise tomorrow, when thank the Lord everything goes back to normal.'

'How fascinating, Jackson. Do tell me more.'

'There's nothing more to tell, except that tomorrow the natives won't do a stroke of work. They believe that if they keep quiet the evil spirits will think the island is deserted and simply go away. It's unchristian, that's what it is.'

'But it's their religion, and rather beautiful, I think. Perhaps we should be more tolerant of other people's beliefs.'

'Undoubtedly, miss.' Jackson inclined his head and stalked off, visibly offended.

Lucetta sighed. She had not meant to hurt his feelings, but the man was such a bigot. The sound of the gamelan orchestra floated through the open windows and she could hear bursts of laughter. She would have loved to go outside and join in with the celebrations but she did not dare flout Papa's instructions to stay within the compound. She wandered into the drawing room and picked up a morocco-bound copy of Mrs Gaskell's *Wives and Daughters*, which she had been attempting to read on and off for a month or more. She took the book out onto the veranda and sat down, opening the page at the bookmark, but try as she might the black print danced before her eyes and she could not concentrate on poor Molly's problems.

The gamelan orchestra was playing a tune that was strange to her ears. The noisy, jingly percussion of the gangsa sounded something like a xylophone, and the repetitive rhythmic beat of the kendang drums was both hypnotic and thrilling. The music and the sound of people having a good time made her feel restless and she closed the book with a snap. Abandoning Molly to her fate, Lucetta jumped to her feet and ran down the steps into the searing heat of the garden. Within seconds, her thin shift was sticking to her back and she could feel the freckles popping out on her nose, but she did not care.

She closed her eyes, holding her arms outstretched as she walked along the gravel path in an attempt to see how far she could go without bumping into something. It was a game that she had played as a child when she used to hide from her governess in the shrubbery of their London garden. It had ended then, as it did now, when she missed her footing and stumbled into a tree or shrub. In Islington it had been the sooty branches of laurel or the prickly leaves of a holly bush that stopped her fall, but here in Bali it was the lush stems and opulent blossoms of the oleander that enveloped her. She opened her eyes and giggled. It was a silly, childish thing to do and without realising it she had come as far as the carriage sweep.

Over the top of the wall surrounding the compound she could see prayer flags flapping gently in the breeze, and above the general hubbub outside she heard the sound of a horse's hooves pounding on the dirt road. Her heart was drumming to the same rhythm and for a moment she felt quite faint. She knew who the caller was even before he drew his mount to a halt outside the gates, and she clapped her hand across her mouth to prevent herself from calling out his name. She took a step forward and then stopped. She had known that he would come, but now she felt suddenly shy. She had been in a dreadful state when he last saw her. She glanced down at her gown which was now smeared with green sap from the oleander, and the hem was covered in mud from the flowerbed where the gardener had recently watered the plants. She was hatless and her hair had come loose from the elaborate style created by Naomi's nimble fingers. She did not want him to see her like this.

She picked up her skirts and was about to make a dash for her room, but too late. The gates creaked on their hinges and Sam rode into the compound. She froze on the spot and was transfixed by the sight of him in his white, open-neck shirt with sleeves rolled up to reveal muscular forearms. He had abandoned his peaked cap and his hair was ruffled by the breeze giving him the tousled look of a romantic poet. The sun had bleached golden glints into the dark auburn and he ran his hand carelessly through his thick locks, brushing an irritating strand from his forehead. He leapt from the saddle, handing the reins to a groom who had appeared as if by magic at his side.

Curbing a sudden impulse to rush from cover and fling her arms around his neck, Lucetta backed into the shade. She wanted to greet him like a lady, not a hoyden as Miss Milton had once called her when she had been caught running through the school grounds barefoot and hatless. She held her breath, hoping he would head for the main entrance and walk past, giving her time to get to her room and make herself presentable. She moved back a little further but the snapping of a twig gave her presence away.

'Miss Froy, is that you?' Sam strode towards her hiding place and parted the fronds of green leaves. 'Lucetta, thank God. I've been out of my mind with worry. Are you all right?'

'I-I'm well, thanks to you.' She met his anxious gaze and felt her heart melt like warm chocolate. 'If you had not found me I dread to think what might have happened.'

'I would have searched for you all night if necessary.' He took her hand and raised it to his lips. 'I got my men together as soon as the alarm was raised. We would have scoured the whole island until we found you.'

'I'm very grateful to you all.' Lucetta felt herself blushing as she snatched her hand free. Her heart was thudding against her ribcage and she wished that vanity had not led her to demand such tight lacing of her stays. She was finding it almost impossible to remain calm when he was standing so close to her that she could feel his breath on her cheek. She turned away and began to stroll along the shady path, clasping her hands tightly in front of her.

His booted feet crunched on the gravel behind her. 'Did those brutes harm you in any way? I swear to God if they did . . .'

She stopped, glancing over her shoulder and shaking her head. 'No, I was not physically harmed. Stranks was going to demand a ransom from my father. He wouldn't have been stupid enough to injure me in any way.'

Sam lifted his hand to tweak an oleander petal from her hair, and he smiled. 'You are wonderful, Lucetta. I don't know many young ladies who would have been so brave under similar circumstances.'

'I wasn't brave but I was more afraid of the snakes and wild animals than I was of Stranks and Guthrie. What will happen to them?'

'They're in irons on the *Caroline* and that's where they'll stay until we get back to London, where they'll go straight to jail to await sentencing. They could face the hangman's noose.'

A shiver ran down Lucetta's spine despite the heat. 'Did they say anything about the way they'd found me?'

Sam took both her hands in his, looking deeply into her eyes. 'Don't think about it, sweetheart. Put the whole sorry affair out of your mind.' Drawing her to him, he kissed her gently but with mounting desire.

She leaned into him, sighing and closing her eyes as her lips parted. The lectures on propriety from Mama and Miss Milton flew from her head and she returned his kisses, holding nothing back. This was what she had been longing for, and for which she had risked her reputation and possibly, if things had gone differently, her life. When at last they drew apart, Lucetta glanced nervously through the fronds of oleander to see if anyone might have seen them from the house, but the windows were shaded by blinds and there was no one in sight. She slipped her hand into the crook of his arm. 'Walk with me, Sam. There is so much I want to know about you.'

'There's nothing I would like more, my love, but I came on official business and I'm afraid I can't stay long. I have a report to hand to the consul and a message for your father from Captain Sharpe.'

So he had not come expressly to see her. Disappointment threatened to choke her. 'I see,' she said coldly, withdrawing her hand. 'Well they are out on business, so I'm afraid you have had a wasted journey.'

He took her by the shoulders, gazing deeply into her eyes. 'I didn't mean it that way, Lucetta. I had to have an excuse to come ashore or Captain Sharpe would not have allowed me to leave the ship, but I couldn't live another hour without seeing you.'

There was no doubting the sincerity in his eyes and Lucetta smiled mistily. 'Nor I you, Sam.'

'You don't know how happy that makes me, my darling,' he whispered, taking her once again into his arms and holding her as if he would never let her go. 'But knowing that you feel as I do is going to make our parting even harder.'

'You're leaving?'

'Not from choice, sweetheart. The *Caroline* is due to sail for England the day after tomorrow.'

'But surely Captain Sharpe won't leave without a full cargo, and part of it is stuck at the bottom of a gorge in the north of the island. That's where Papa went today.'

'I don't know about that, Lucetta. I just obey orders.'

'But Papa has shares in the *Caroline*. Captain Sharpe must do what he wants, surely?'

Sam shook his head. 'That's a matter for them to discuss. All I know is that I must speak to Mr Froy and take his response back to Captain Sharpe.'

Lucetta swallowed a lump in her throat that threatened to engulf her in a flood of tears. 'But we can't be parted so soon. We've only just found each other.'

'I will return with the *Caroline* in September by which time I hope I will have my master's ticket. I will then be in a position to ask your father's permission to marry you.'

'Marry me?' Lucetta could hardly believe her ears. She felt the blood drain from her face and for a moment she thought she was going to faint. She took a deep breath. 'Did you just propose to me, Sam?'

He smiled gently. 'Isn't that what a man does when he meets the love of his life?'

'But we hardly know each other.'

'I knew from the first moment I saw you that you were the girl for me,' Sam whispered, raising his hand to stroke her cheek. 'I couldn't believe my luck, and I thought you felt the same.'

'I do. You know I do, but my parents would never agree to it.' Lucetta hesitated, biting her lip. She could not bring herself to tell him that her mother, and probably Papa also, had plans for her to marry a much wealthier man than a young seafarer.

Sam gripped her hands in his. 'I know that you are very young, my love. But I'm prepared to wait, and during that time I'll work hard. When I am captain of my own ship I will be in a position to keep a wife in comfort, although maybe not as much style as this.'

The pressure of his strong fingers was reassuring and his voice was so full of confidence that Lucetta almost believed him. 'But that will take years,' she murmured. 'I want to be with you now and forever.'

Sweeping her in a close embrace, his passionate kisses robbed her of breath and also of reason. In his arms she felt that the world was theirs. Anything was possible. He released her slowly, laying a gentle finger on her trembling lips. 'You have my heart and my life in your hands. I will always be true to you, Lucetta, and I will win your father round somehow. We will spend the rest of our lives together, you and I, you have my solemn promise on that.'

Tear spilled unchecked from her eyes, but they were tears of happiness. 'I will be true to you too, Sam. I'll never look at another man as long as I live. I'll wait for you, even if it's a hundred years or more.'

He chuckled deep in his throat although his eyes were moist. 'I hope we don't have to wait that long, my love.' He leaned over to kiss her on the tip of her nose. 'Now I must find Sir John and your father, or I will be in trouble with Captain Sharpe.'

Lucetta clasped his hand and raised it to her cheek. 'I understand, but I can't bear to part with you like this. If the *Caroline* sails without waiting for Papa's last consignment we may not get a chance to see each other for months.'

'That won't happen if I have anything to do with it, but I will come back this evening when the whole island will be feasting and dancing. Will you come with me to watch the procession and the bonfires?'

'Papa would forbid it,' Lucetta said, staring down at their entwined fingers. Sam's were so slim, tanned and strong and her hand was pale and tiny by comparison, but together they made an entrancing whole. She looked him in the eyes and smiled. 'But what he doesn't know won't hurt him. Come to my window after dark. I'll leave a lantern on the table outside my room, and I'll be waiting for you.'

That evening at dinner Lucetta's lack of appetite was commented upon and became the main topic of conversation. Eveline urged her husband to send immediately for the doctor, who must be persuaded to prescribe a tonic for their daughter, but Lady Boothby declared this to be quite unnecessary. A spoonful of castor oil would be more efficacious, she said firmly, or perhaps a dose of the new medicine from America, *Cascara sagrada*, which was used in the hospital to great effect. The girl was in need of a purgative, which would soon restore her to good health. Treating her in a namby-pamby fashion would do her no good at all.

Lucetta said nothing to all this. She kept her eyes meekly cast down and when the meal was over she followed her mother and Lady Boothby into the drawing room. They subsided onto the damask-covered sofas, stuffed to bursting point with prickly horsehair, and their wide crinolines spread out around them in pools of delicately coloured silk. A maid served coffee which the ladies sipped decorously while they waited for the gentlemen to join them. Lucetta glanced anxiously at her mother, who was visibly wilting in the oppressive heat and humidity, but Lady Boothby seemed oblivious to physical discomfort. Beads of perspiration stood out on her brow and damp patches stained the purple silk of her tight bodice, but she sat bolt upright like the image of Britannia on a coin of the realm. Lucetta would not have been surprised if the silver teaspoon clasped between Lady Boothby's thumb and forefinger had suddenly turned into a trident, and her lace fan into a shield. She bit her lip to suppress a giggle but her vision of Britannia dissolved into a disapproving Lady Boothby, who was glaring through narrowed eyes. She seemed about to demand an explanation for Lucetta's apparent amusement when the door opened and Sir John strolled into the drawing room.

'It makes sense, Henry,' he said, making for a side table laden with crystal glasses and decanters. 'Should you miss this sailing, the *Caroline* is not due to return here until September, and your business here, I believe, is completed.'

'It is,' Henry said, frowning. 'But taking only half a consignment back to London will slice into my profits and barely make the trip worthwhile.'

Sir John poured two measures of brandy, handing one to Henry. 'That is true, but surely it would be better for you to be in London to manage your affairs and have the damaged furniture restored by our local craftsmen and sent on at a later date.'

'I had my heart set on going home, Henry,' Eveline said plaintively. 'This climate is far too hot for my liking and now the monsoon season is over it is going to become unbearable.'

Henry went to sit by her side on the sofa. 'Come, come, my dear. It's not so very bad. I've been trading in these parts for more than twenty years with no ill effects. I'm sure you could hold out for a few more months if necessary.'

'I haven't got your iron constitution,' Eveline said plaintively. 'I've never been strong.'

Lucetta nodded vigorously. She was genuinely concerned for her mother's wellbeing, and she was also desperate to sail on the *Caroline*. The thought of seeing Sam every day for the next five or six weeks made her bold. 'That's right, Papa. You know that Mama is delicate. I think the voyage home would do much to restore her good health.'

'I'm well aware of that, poppet,' Henry said fondly. 'But business is business. There is a lot of money tied up in that cargo.'

'I'm sure I don't care about money, Papa,' she retorted, tossing her head. 'I'd rather be happy than rich.'

Sir John threw back his head and laughed. 'Oh, the innocence of youth, Froy.'

'My dear child,' Lady Boothby said with a patronising smile. 'You don't know what you're saying.

Money may not be able to buy happiness but you would be shocked if you saw the deprivation suffered by the poor in this country and at home in London.'

'I'm sure that Lucetta didn't mean to sound uncaring,' Eveline murmured faintly. 'She may be a little naïve in the ways of the world, but in some part I think she is right. What use is money if one hasn't one's health?'

Henry eyed her anxiously. 'It's not possible, my love. The teakwood furniture is still stuck at the bottom of a gorge, several inches deep in mud. Tomorrow everything comes to a standstill and no one can be persuaded to work. The *Caroline* will sail next day regardless and there's nothing I can do about it.'

Eveline's bottom lip trembled ominously and her blue eyes swam with unshed tears. 'I really want to go home.'

Lady Boothby rose majestically to her feet. 'Perhaps you ought to reconsider your decision, Mr Froy?' She beckoned to the manservant who was standing to attention in the doorway. 'Take Mrs Froy to her room and send for her maid.'

Lucetta saw her chance to escape. 'It's all right, Lady Boothby,' she cried, jumping up and rushing to her mother's side. 'I'll take Mama to her room.'

Having left her mother in the capable hands of Gertie, the ageing maidservant who had faithfully served her mistress for more than twenty years, Lucetta hurried to her own room. She opened the French doors and went out onto the veranda. Her hands shook with excitement as she struck a vesta and lit a lantern, placing it on the rattan table. She leaned on the balustrade taking deep breaths of the heavily perfumed night air. White-winged moths appeared as if from nowhere to flutter around the light, and fronds of bougainvillea swayed like ballet dancers in a gentle whisper of a breeze.

The tropical darkness outside the compound was pierced with light from flaming torches and Lucetta could hear an excited chatter of voices as the procession made its way along the road outside the compound, moving to the rhythmic sounds of the gamelan orchestra. Above the wall she could just make out the heads of the ogoh-ogoh, huge brightly painted monster dolls that would eventually be tossed onto the many bonfires that turned night into day. She could sense the excitement of the unseen crowds and their strange magic added to her own heightened emotions as she paced the veranda, waiting for Sam and praying that he would come soon.

Time seemed to have stopped, or to be going backwards, as her nervous anticipation increased. Perhaps he had been unavoidably delayed or worse still he might have had his shore leave cancelled. Just as she was beginning to despair of seeing him, she heard a soft rustling in the bushes. She held her breath, hardly daring to hope, and then he appeared, emerging from the darkness to take the steps two at a time. He swept her into his arms and his mouth claimed hers in a kiss that made her senses reel. He smelt of the sea, fresh and clean, so different from the cloying smell of the rainforest. She closed her eyes and abandoned herself to the strange and wonderful new sensations that made her blood fizz through her veins like champagne. When he released her to draw breath she still clung to him, wanting more.

'We must go now,' he whispered softly. 'Are you sure you want to do this, Lucetta?'

'Of course I do. I'd go anywhere with you, Sam.'

His eyes were luminous in the lamplight. 'You are quite amazing, but I don't want you to get into trouble with your parents. Perhaps I ought to go and see your father and ask his permission to take you to the festival.'

Lucetta shook her head vehemently. 'No, it's all right. I didn't want Papa to think badly of you so I asked him if we might go outside the consulate compound just to see the procession and the bonfire, and he said yes.'

Sam grinned broadly. 'That's splendid. I wouldn't want to upset Mr Froy, since I mean to ask for his daughter's hand in marriage.'

Lucetta slipped her hand through the crook of his arm. Papa would be absolutely furious if he discovered her deception, and she would undoubtedly go to hell for telling such dreadful lies, but she was determined to snatch this piece of heaven for herself. She smiled up at him. 'I'm ready, Sam. Let's go.'

There was no one to prevent them from leaving the compound. Either the gatekeeper was asleep or else he had joined in the procession. As they left the consulate grounds it seemed to Lucetta that they had entered another world where people from miles around were heading for a huge celebration party. Holding hands, they tagged onto the end of a long procession, becoming part of a human chain babbling with excitement and anticipation as they headed for the place where a great bonfire shot tongues of orange flame into the night sky. Women carried baskets on their heads piled high with offerings of fruit and food, and young girls wearing bright robes had garlands of fragrant frangipani and hibiscus around their necks and blossoms tucked into their dark hair. The ogoh-ogoh were being transported on bamboo poles and the gamelan orchestra played on and on.

Keeping well to the back of the crowd, Lucetta watched the dancing and the strange rituals with delight, but all the while she was acutely aware of Sam holding her hand and standing so close to her that she could feel the warmth of his body. She felt that they were in fairyland: an enchanted place where time did not exist. She wanted this night to go on forever, but all too soon it came to an end as the monster figures were sacrificed to the flames.

'We'd best leave now,' Sam whispered, squeezing her fingers.

'Oh no, please let's stay a bit longer.'

He shook his head. 'They might have locked the gates and I don't think you could climb the walls in that gown.'

With the utmost reluctance, Lucetta turned her back on the revellers, knowing that she would remember this night for the rest of her life. She looked up into

Sam's smiling face and was reassured. There was no trace of deceit or dishonesty in his candid gaze and no evidence of ill temper or meanness of spirit in the generous curve of his lips. His firm jaw and strong features breathed trust and dependability, and his hazel eyes shone with intelligence and good humour. She knew instinctively that she could trust this man with her life, and that her heart was his now and forever. There was no need for words, and arms entwined they walked back to the consulate.

As luck would have it, the gatekeeper had not returned and the house servants appeared to be too busy celebrating the festival to bother about small details such as locking the gates. They slipped into the compound unnoticed and Sam drew Lucetta into the shadows beneath the champak trees. She slid her arms around his neck and her lips parted with a sigh. In the heat of the night, with the distant sounds of revelry, feasting and music in her ears, and the intoxicating scent of the champak, jasmine and roses making her head swim, Lucetta felt desire flare between them like a bushfire. Sam's lips travelled down the slender column of her neck to the swell of her breasts above the low neckline of her evening gown. She felt her whole body respond to his caress.

Gently, so gently, he slid his fingers beneath the silk of her bodice, exposing one breast. He kissed her nipple, teasing it with his tongue until it became hard and erect. He closed his lips around it, taking it in his mouth, nuzzling and sucking until Lucetta moaned softly with pleasure. Her legs gave way beneath her and they sank to the soft mossy ground beneath the trees. She moved instinctively against him, spreading her legs and arching her body as he lifted her silken skirts and his hand stroked the inside of her thighs, fondling and caressing her flesh until he found the forbidden place. Sensations that she could never have imagined were setting her whole being aflame with desire. Although she did not know what would follow next, she knew dimly in the deep recesses of her mind that she wanted him to complete the act of love, and when he withdrew a little from her she opened her eyes, staring blindly into his shadowy face. 'Don't stop. Please.'

'I can't take advantage of your youth and innocence. I love you too much for that, Lucetta.' He bent his head and kissed her tenderly on the lips. 'Not yet, my darling. Not yet.'

'I love you too . . .'

'My God. You young bastard. I'll have you flogged for this.'

Blinded temporarily by the light of a lantern, Lucetta screamed as Sam was dragged to his feet, leaving her semi-naked body exposed for all to see.

Chapter Six

'Sir, I can explain.'

'Explain!' Henry's tone deepened from a shout to a roar. 'You deflower my innocent daughter and you tell me that you can explain.' He reached for Lucetta's arm and hauled her unceremoniously to her feet. Raising his hand, he slapped her hard across the face. 'Cover your shame, you little trollop. I expected more of you, Lucetta. I'm disgusted by such wanton behaviour. D'you hear me? Disgusted.'

Lucetta's hand flew to her bruised cheek and she stared at her father in disbelief. He had never in all her seventeen years raised a hand to her and now he was staring at her as though he hated her. She tugged at her bodice with her free hand, turning away to cover her naked breasts.

'Don't vent your anger on Lucetta. If you want to strike someone, hit me.' Sam made a move towards Henry but Sir John stepped in between them.

'I think you've done enough harm this night, young man,' he said sternly. 'I suggest you leave now before you make matters worse.'

'I love Lucetta, Mr Froy,' Sam said, pushing past Sir John. 'I want to marry your daughter, sir.'

'I'll see you clapped in irons for what you've done

to my innocent child,' Henry raged. 'As to marrying her, you won't be in a position to support a cat let alone a wife when I've done with you.'

'It was my fault as much as Sam's,' Lucetta cried passionately. 'I love him.'

'Go to your room, Lucetta. Stay there and don't you dare leave it until I say so. I'll deal with this young libertine.'

Lucetta ran to Sam's side, flinging her arms around him. 'I won't let you harm him, Pa. Can't you understand that we love each other? I will marry him whether you like it or not.'

'Marry a penniless seafarer? You've gone off your head, girl. I've heard that that happens sometimes in the tropics and now I believe it's true. You will marry the man of my choosing, that's if anyone will have you now. You're damaged goods, Lucetta, and all because of him.' Henry's face was suffused with purple as he pointed a shaking finger at Sam.

'You can't do that,' Sam said through gritted teeth. 'I won't allow it. Nothing untoward occurred between us. I would rather cut off my right hand than harm your daughter.'

'You're a liar, sir. I know what I saw.' Henry lunged towards him, but Sir John caught him by the arm.

'This is a bad business, Froy, but perhaps we should all calm down. We can sort this matter out tomorrow.'

'Calm down, Sir John? I'll kill the young devil.' Fisting his hands, Henry took a swipe at Sam, missing him by inches as the younger man dodged the blow.

'Stop,' Lucetta cried, wringing her hands. 'Please

stop all this. I am as I was when I left the consulate, Papa. I am still virgo intacta or whatever that doctor called it.'

Henry froze to the spot and he let out a strangled cry. His eyes started from his head and his florid complexion paled to ashen as he crumpled to the ground.

Lucetta screamed and fell to her knees beside him. 'Speak to me, Pa. I didn't mean to upset you.'

Sir John leaned over to feel for a pulse in Henry's neck. 'He's alive, but I think he's had some kind of seizure.'

'I'm sorry, Pa,' Lucetta sobbed. 'I'm so sorry.'

Sam lifted her gently to her feet. 'Don't be afraid, my love. I'll ride to town and fetch the doctor.'

'Mr Froy needs complete rest and quiet,' the doctor said, taking off his spectacles and polishing the lenses with a clean white handkerchief. 'I've seen this condition afflict many gentlemen of a certain age and constitution. The outcome, I'm afraid, is not always what one would hope for.'

'Is he going to die?' Lucetta asked, glancing anxiously at her mother who lay on the chaise longue pale-faced, tears coursing down her thin cheeks.

The doctor shook his head. 'I'm afraid the prognosis in these cases is very hard to predict.'

Lady Boothby rose from her seat by the open window. 'You may rest assured that Mr Froy will have everything he needs while he is under our roof, doctor.'

'Absolutely,' Sir John agreed. 'Although perhaps he should be removed to the hospital?'

'With all due respect, Sir John,' the doctor said, closing his medical bag with a decisive snap of the brass locks, 'I think you are forgetting that the natives are still celebrating Nyepi. Nothing will move on the island until tomorrow, and then in my experience things will only gradually get back to normal.'

'This is all my fault,' Lucetta said, choking back a sob. 'I did this to him and I am so sorry.'

Eveline covered her face with her hands and wept.

'Come now, Eveline,' Lady Boothby said briskly. 'Giving way like this won't help anyone. But I'm glad to see that someone has learned a lesson from this.' She cast a contemptuous glance at Lucetta and then turned her attention to the physician. 'What do you suggest we do for the patient?'

'My advice would be to take Mr Froy back to England as soon as possible. If Mrs Froy can book a passage for the family on the *Caroline*, which I believe is due to sail tomorrow evening that, in my opinion, would be the best course. A long sea voyage would be most beneficial. I believe that in his home surroundings, with the best medical attention that London has to offer, the patient has an excellent chance of making a full recovery.'

Lady Boothby nodded her head sagely, as if this pronouncement coincided with her own experience of medical matters gained in the charity hospital. 'Exactly so. I think that makes excellent sense.'

Eveline dropped her hands to her sides. 'Are we really going home?'

'It would seem to be the most sensible course to take, ma'am. I'm sure that your daughter will help you to take care of Mr Froy,' the doctor said, eyeing Lucetta sternly.

'I'll do anything I can,' Lucetta murmured, staring down at her tightly clasped hands as she struggled with her conscience. The prospect of seeing Sam every day during the long sea voyage made her heart sing, but guilt weighed heavily on her soul.

The doctor picked up his medical bag, nodding to Sir John and Lady Boothby. 'I'll call again in the morning, but if Mr Froy's condition should deteriorate, please send for me.'

'I'll sit up all night with him,' Lucetta said hastily. 'It's the least I can do.'

The doctor patted her on the arm and for the first time that evening his lined face cracked into a half-smile. 'The apoplectic fit could have occurred at any time, my dear. But another seizure could prove fatal. I strongly advise you to sail for London on the *Caroline*.'

Captain Sharpe rose from behind his desk as Eveline and Lucetta were ushered into his day cabin. 'Good morning, ladies. This is a pleasant surprise.' He pulled up two chairs. 'Please be seated.'

'Thank you, Captain,' Eveline said, perching on the edge of the chair with her hands folded primly in her lap. 'I came to inform you that in the light of my poor dear husband's present condition, I will be taking over his business affairs.'

Lucetta took a seat beside her mother feeling slightly in awe of the stranger who seemed to inhabit Mama's frail body. She barely recognised this determined woman whose whole demeanour had changed overnight. This was not the fragile invalid who took to her bed at the slightest upset or the first hint of a headache. This was a woman hell bent on snatching her husband back from the jaws of death and woe betide anyone who attempted to gainsay her.

Captain Sharpe seemed similarly nonplussed. He cleared his throat, shifting awkwardly from one foot to the other. 'I was sorry to learn of Mr Froy's indisposition, ma'am. I trust he is on the road to recovery?'

Eveline eyed him coldly. 'I won't beat about the bush, Captain. I understand that the *Caroline* is sailing for England this evening.'

'That is so, ma'am.'

'The doctor says that my husband should return home at the first possible opportunity.'

Lucetta held her breath, crossing her fingers. She wanted this for Papa but even more for herself and Sam. She knew it was selfish of her, but the desire for his company filled her soul with an urgent need that was frightening in its intensity.

'And you require berths on the *Caroline*?' Captain Sharpe said, visibly relaxing.

Eveline inclined her head. 'Yes, Captain. Is that possible?'

'It can be arranged, ma'am. We have a full complement of passengers but I will be pleased to allocate my own cabin to you and Mr Froy. We can accommodate

Miss Froy and your maid, but I am afraid they will have to share.'

'I don't mind in the least,' Lucetta said earnestly.

Eveline shot her a withering look. 'Thank you, Lucetta. I think we might take that for granted.'

Captain Sharpe mopped beads of perspiration from his brow with a pristine white handkerchief. 'Is there anything else, ma'am?'

'Yes, indeed there is, Captain. As I'm sure you are aware, at least half my husband's consignment of cargo is stuck at the bottom of a gorge in the north of the island. It must be retrieved and loaded before we sail.'

Captain Sharpe's mouth opened and closed several times, reminding Lucetta forcibly of a goldfish that she had once owned. It had swum round and round in its glass bowl until one day the cat decided it was hungry enough to go fishing and had gobbled it up, leaving a sad little fishtail in evidence of the evil deed. She clenched her fists in her lap as a bubble of near hysteria rose in her throat. She willed her mother to accept the fact that fate had intervened and the wretched furniture was as good as lost.

'I'm afraid I cannot delay the ship's departure, ma'am.'

'I might remind you that my husband has shares in your company,' Eveline said coldly.

'I am well aware of that, Mrs Froy, but I'm afraid what you ask is impossible. The natives have only just commenced work again after Nyepi, and I'm afraid it would take more than a day to retrieve the goods.'

'Then I insist that you defer sailing until such time as the cargo is complete.'

Lucetta glanced anxiously at Captain Sharpe and her heart sank. She could tell by his expression that his reply was going to be in the negative.

He shook his head. 'That is impossible, I'm afraid, Mrs Froy. We sail on the tide this evening and I have orders to pick up another cargo in Java.'

Lucetta jumped to her feet. 'Mama, surely it is better to take half the merchandise and get Father safely home?'

'Leave this to me, Lucetta,' Eveline said, rising from the chair. She faced up to Captain Sharpe, even though he was the taller by a good head and shoulders. 'My husband will report your intransigent attitude to the board of governors when we get home, Captain.'

'That is his prerogative, ma'am. But, if you so wish, I can arrange for the remainder of the cargo to be shipped by the *Caroline*'s sister ship. The *Louisa* should be in Sydney by now and is due to arrive here in about a month's time.'

Eveline met his gaze with a look of pure steel. 'That really isn't good enough. Do I have to remind you that you were supposed to take the whole shipment back to London?'

'With respect, ma'am, I cannot challenge the orders I receive from the company's agent in Bali. If Mr Froy was well enough he would acknowledge that profit comes before everything, and he would appreciate that fact.' Captain Sharpe's voice deepened and his bushy grey eyebrows snapped together over the bridge of his bulbous nose, which was suspiciously red at the tip.

Lucetta glanced anxiously at her mother, expecting her to collapse beneath a look that might have quelled a mutiny at sea, but to her astonishment Mama did not seem in the least perturbed. In fact she seemed almost to be enjoying this battle of wills.

'Don't think you can browbeat me, Captain. My husband's profits depend on shipping the whole consignment back to England.'

'Then what do you suggest, Mrs Froy?'

'I'll agree to your terms providing I can be certain that the rest of the cargo will be retrieved, restored and made ready to be taken on board the *Louisa*. And I want someone trustworthy and resourceful left in charge of the entire operation.'

'I'm sure the company's agent will be only too happy to oversee matters, ma'am.'

'No, Captain. I want Mr Cutler to stay behind and take full responsibility for a valuable cargo.'

'Mama, please,' Lucetta cried, clutching her mother's arm. 'Don't do this.'

'Be silent, Lucetta. This doesn't concern you,' Eveline said, focusing her full attention on Captain Sharpe. 'Do you agree to my terms, sir?'

'You drive a hard bargain, ma'am, but you leave me little choice. Mr Cutler will remain in Bali as you request and I will make him responsible for the retrieval, storage and shipping of your goods.'

'Thank you, Captain Sharpe,' Eveline said graciously. 'I knew we could come to a civilised arrangement.

Lucetta, we must return to the consulate immediately. There is much to do.'

Lucetta stared at her mother in disbelief. The heat in the cabin was intense and she was finding it difficult to breathe. Her mother's pale oval face swam before her eyes and she felt herself falling into nothingness.

'She's coming to. Fetch Sister Demarest.'

Lucetta opened her eyes and saw a fresh young face hovering above her. For a moment she thought she was dead and that she was looking up at an angel, but then she realised that the halo was merely a white cap with sunlight reflecting off its starched surface, and there was an almost overpowering smell of disinfectant in the air. She was dimly aware of the sound of scurrying footsteps and the soft murmur of female voices. She licked her dry lips and tried to speak but she was weak, so very weak that the words would not come. Where was she, and – even more frightening – who was she?

'Don't try to talk,' the disembodied face said, smiling. 'You've been very poorly but you're on the mend now.'

'That will be enough, Nurse Hastings.'

The smile faded and the young nurse drew back respectfully as Sister Demarest arrived at the bedside. She thrust a thermometer under Lucetta's tongue and took her pulse, all done efficiently but in stony silence. 'You are lucky, young lady,' she said at last, in a cool clipped voice. 'Nurse Hastings, give the patient a bed bath and then she may be able to take a little gruel.'

'Yes, Sister.'

Nurse Hastings scuttled away to do her bidding and Sister Demarest stood over Lucetta, staring down at her with an impassive expression on her sculpted features. 'Are you able to tell me your name?'

Lucetta tried to focus her eyes on the face above her, but there seemed to be an impenetrable fog in her brain. She felt panic rising in her chest as she tried to remember who she was. She must have a name. Everyone had a name, so why couldn't she remember hers? She closed her eyes and opened them again, hoping that perhaps this was a bad dream, but nothing had changed. She shook her head as hot tears spilled from her eyes and ran down her neck to dampen the pillow beneath her head.

'Never mind,' Sister Demarest said in a softer tone. 'It will come back to you. Rest now.' She glided away, moving gracefully as if she were skating on ice.

After a futile attempt to raise herself onto her elbow, Lucetta realised just how weak she was. She could barely lift her hand to brush the tears from her cheeks, but with an effort she managed to turn her head very slightly from side to side. She could see uniform rows of beds with pale-faced women lying as stiff as corpses beneath crisp white coverlets. It dawned on her then that she was in a hospital but how she came to be here and why, were two of the unanswered questions that both terrified and confused her.

Nurse Hastings bustled up to the bedside carrying an enamel bowl, a sponge and a towel. 'Here we are again, miss. I'm sorry I don't know your name, but we call you Daisy between ourselves.' She set the bowl down on the bedside cabinet. 'I'll just pull the curtains, Daisy, and then I'll give you a nice wash. You'll feel heaps better then, and maybe you could manage to eat some gruel.'

Nurse Hastings chattered away cheerfully as she performed the bed bath routine efficiently but gently and with respect for her patient's modesty. Lucetta was suddenly aware of her wasted limbs and emaciated body. Had she always been so stick-thin? She really could not remember.

'There we are, Daisy,' Nurse Hastings said, slipping a clean cotton nightgown over Lucetta's head. 'You'll feel better in no time. I'll just get rid of the slops and then I'll bring you your breakfast. Hold your arms up so I can get them into the sleeves, there's a good girl.'

As obedient as a small child, Lucetta did as she was told and then fell back on the pillows completely exhausted by the effort. 'Wh-where am I?' she whispered.

'You're in the London Fever Hospital. You've been here for almost three weeks and your brothers have been very worried about you. They'll be so pleased to know that you're on the mend. Now you rest, while I go and get that nice hot bowl of gruel.'

Lucetta absorbed this information in silence as she watched Nurse Hastings draw the curtains with swift bird-like movements. She hurried off taking the bowl and towel with her and her small feet made pitter-pattering sounds on the bare linoleum.

Brothers! The idea of having brothers seemed so alien to Lucetta as to be impossible. She closed her eyes and drifted off to sleep.

It was pitch dark and all around her people were shouting and screaming. The deck was wet and slippery and tilted at an alarming angle.

'Abandon ship.'

'Oh, my God. We're sinking.'

'Get out of me way, girl.'

She was being pushed and jostled by frantic people wearing nothing but their night clothes. Children were crying and clinging to their mother's skirts. Dazed and disorientated, Lucetta tried to push her way back towards the captain's cabin where she had left her parents before retiring to the small cabin she shared with Gertie, but it was impossible to go against the surge of panic-stricken passengers. The deck lurched beneath her feet and then tilted crazily. She was slipping and sliding towards the ship's railings as people jumped overboard in order to avoid being crushed by the weight of those being thrown against them. There was nothing she could do to save herself. She tripped and would have fallen but someone grabbed her by the arms and she found herself lifted off her feet and tossed into the air. For a few brief seconds she was flying upwards but then she plummeted down into the inky black waters. She was going down, down, down. She couldn't breathe. She was drowning.

'Wake up, Daisy.'

Someone was shaking her gently by the shoulders. Struggling for breath, Lucetta felt the waters release her body and she opened her eyes.

'You were having a bad dream,' Nurse Hastings said, raising her to a sitting position and piling pillows behind her back. 'You'll feel better when you've had something to eat. Can you feed yourself, or would you like me to help you?'

Lucetta clasped her hand to her chest. The dream had seemed so real. The cries of the desperate people rang in her ears and the taste of the filthy polluted water lingered on her lips. 'What happened to me?' she whispered. 'Why am I here?'

Nurse Hastings held a spoonful of gruel to Lucetta's lips. 'You were shipwrecked, Daisy. The *Caroline* collided with a paddle steamer in thick fog. It was in all the newspapers. You were one of the lucky ones, but then you took sick with the typhoid and that's why you were transferred here.'

Lucetta swallowed a mouthful of warm sweet gruel. 'In my dream there was darkness and the water was cold.'

'Do you remember your name?'

'No. I wish I could, but I can't.' Shaking her head, Lucetta blinked back tears of weakness. 'I don't know who I am.'

Nurse Hastings fed her another spoonful of gruel. 'You will, Daisy. It will all come back to you as you regain your strength. And there are two people very eager to see you.'

*   *   *

'I don't know you,' Lucetta said, staring at the two rough-looking men who claimed to be her brothers. 'I think you have the wrong girl.'

Stranks curled his lips in an ingratiating smile. 'Come now, Lucy my duck, you must remember me. I'm Norman, your big brother what used to dandle you on his knee when you was a baby.' He nudged Guthrie who was standing at the foot of the bed, clutching his cap in his hands. 'As did you, Lennie. Ain't that right?'

'That's it,' Guthrie muttered. 'We're your brothers, Lucy.'

Lucetta stared at them trying in vain to place their faces. They looked vaguely familiar but surely she would have instantly recognised blood relations. She shook her head. 'I'm sorry, but I don't remember you at all.'

Stranks laid a badly wrapped paper parcel on the end of the bed. 'We brought you something to wear, ducks. You can't come home in your nightgown.'

'Come home?' Lucetta said faintly. 'I am not well enough to leave hospital, am I?'

She cast a pleading look at Nurse Hastings who was standing by her side with the protective attitude of a small but determined guard dog.

Nurse Hastings eyed Stranks and Guthrie with obvious distaste. 'It's not up to me, Daisy. I mean, Lucy. It's for the doctor to say if you're fit enough to leave our care.'

'The young doc who's been looking after you says you can home if there's someone to look after you,'

Stranks said, shooting a look of pure malice at Nurse Hastings. 'It ain't up to you, nurse.'

'I really don't know you,' Lucetta protested weakly. 'I think there's been some mistake.'

Nurse Hastings laid her hand on Lucetta's arm. 'Don't upset yourself, my dear. I'll go and speak to Dr Harcourt. He'll sort this out.' She marched off towards the office at the end of the ward.

'Get dressed, girl,' Stranks said gruffly. 'We're taking you home and that's that.'

'Hold hard there, Norm,' Guthrie said in a low voice. 'Don't scare her. She's been very sick.'

Lucetta warmed to Guthrie. He had the look of a shaggy old mongrel, but she was quick to hear a note of genuine concern in his voice. 'I have been ill,' she agreed. 'And I'm still very weak. Perhaps I should stay here for a while longer.'

'They need the bed for someone who's really sick,' Stranks said impatiently. 'We'll leave you to get dressed and then we're taking you out of here, like it or not.'

'C'mon, Norm,' Guthrie muttered. 'We'll wait outside the ward until she's ready.'

'All right,' Stranks said reluctantly. 'But we're not going without you, Lucy. If the doctor says you're well enough then you're coming with us.'

Lucetta lay back against the pillows and watched them leave with a sinking heart. Dr Harcourt had already told her that she was well enough to go home, providing he was satisfied that she would be well cared for. He was a nice young man, earnest and pleasant-looking if not exactly handsome. She had grown to like him during the past week when she had been recuperating on the ward. She had discovered that not only had he several younger sisters but that he and Nurse Hastings were first cousins. It was obvious that they were fond of each other, but Lucetta suspected that Mary Hastings' feelings went a little deeper than mere cousinly affection. Her cheeks would flush prettily if Dr Harcourt teased her, something he would only dare to do if Sister Demarest was otherwise occupied.

With her world shrunk to the size of the hospital ward, Lucetta wove fantasies around the young couple during the long nights when sleep evaded her. She imagined Mary dressed in her wedding finery, smiling happily on the arm of her new husband Dr Giles Harcourt. Closing her ears to the sighs and moans of the other women on the ward, Lucetta saw herself as a guest at the wedding, welcomed into the two families. She knew that it was only a dream, but escaping to her imaginary world was a comfort during the lonely hours of darkness. After almost a month, Lucetta had begun to feel quite at home on the ward. Her own identity continued to evade her and she was quite frankly terrified of leaving the security of the hospital, particularly if that meant accompanying the two uncouth strangers who claimed to be her next of kin. She lay rigid and frightened with the sheets pulled up to her chin as she kept her gaze fixed on the office door, waiting with bated breath for it to open.

She did not have to wait long, and the expression on Mary Hastings' face confirmed her worst fear.

'I'm sorry, Daisy, but Dr Harcourt thinks you are

quite well enough to go home with those two who claim to be your brothers.'

Lucetta snapped to a sitting position. 'You don't think they are related to me, do you?'

Mary turned away to draw the curtains around the bed. 'It's not for me to put ideas in your head, but I will say that I don't see any family resemblance between you and them. They're not your sort, if you know what I mean.'

'I think I do, or rather I don't feel as though they're my blood relations.' Lucetta clutched her forehead with both hands, squeezing her skull as if by doing so she could force her memory to return. 'I can't remember anything. I just can't.'

'There, there, Daisy. Don't upset yourself. I'm sure it will come back in time.'

Lucetta shook her head, allowing her hands to fall to her sides. 'I just don't know, but it seems I have no choice but to go with them. Will you help me dress, please, Mary?'

Nurse Hastings turned away abruptly, clearing her throat. She snatched up the package and made an attempt to untie the string, but when the knots proved stubborn she tore at the greasy brown wrapping. 'Well,' she said, wrinkling her nose as she pulled out some grubby-looking undergarments and a blouse that might once have been white but was now yellowed with age and frayed at the cuffs, followed by a linsey-woolsey skirt that had also seen better days. 'Looks like they bought this stuff from a stall in Petticoat Lane or a dolly shop in Hoxton.'

Lucetta fingered the coarse calico chemise and the odour of stale sweat emanating from the material made her feel sick. 'This can't be mine, Mary. I'm certain I've never worn such a garment in all my life. It doesn't smell like me.'

'Perhaps you'll find something more suitable to wear when you get home,' Mary said hopefully. 'I expect they tried their best, but they're only men, poor things.'

Despite an overwhelming feeling of foreboding, Lucetta allowed Mary to help her dress, but the stays appeared to have been made to fit a much larger person and had to be discarded. The chemise hung off her like a shroud, as did the blouse, and the skirt trailed on the floor, threatening to trip her each time she took a step. Mary begged some pins from Sister Demarest and spent a good ten minutes on her knees taking up the hem. 'I'll grant that you've lost weight since your illness,' she said, clambering to her feet, 'but you can't have shrunk four inches in height. I think your brothers have got some explaining to do, Daisy.'

'It's simple,' Stranks said, eyeing Nurse Hastings as if he could cheerfully throttle her. 'Our sister's clothes were all lost when the ship went down. We had a bit of a rush to find her something to wear, but our little Lucy will have nothing but the best when we get her settled at home.' He hooked his arm around Lucetta's waist. 'Come along, ducks. Lennie's gone to find a cab. We'll have you home safe in no time at all.'

Fighting back tears, Lucetta turned to Mary who was standing side by side with Dr Harcourt. 'Thank you both for looking after me. I might have died but for your care.'

Giles Harcourt smiled, shaking his head. 'You are made of stronger stuff than that, Daisy.'

'She ain't Daisy,' Stranks said belligerently. 'It's Miss Guthrie to you. Miss Lucy Guthrie.'

Giles acknowledged this intervention with a stiff nod of his head. 'I beg your pardon.' He turned to Lucetta with a shy smile. 'Goodbye, Lucy, and good luck.'

'Here, what d'you mean by that, mate?' Stranks demanded, pushing Lucetta aside and squaring up to the doctor. 'Ain't we good enough for your little Daisy?'

'I meant no disrespect, sir.'

'It's just a manner of speaking, Mr Guthrie,' Mary said hastily. 'We always wish our patients the best of everything when they leave our care.'

Lucetta gave her an impetuous hug. Parting from Mary was physically painful. She had come to think of her as a friend. 'Goodbye, Mary. I will miss you.'

'Come and see me when you are settled,' Mary said tearfully. 'I stay in the nurses' home when I'm on night duty, so I'm quite easy to find.'

Stranks caught Lucetta by the arm. 'Come on, Lucy. I'm taking you home, girl.'

Chapter Seven

The cab ride seemed to last forever. Squashed in between Stranks and Guthrie, Lucetta could scarcely breathe. Their body odour mixed sickeningly with the foetid smell of the second-hand clothes that she had been forced to wear. Worse still, her skin had begun to itch and she suspected that the garments harboured fleas. 'Where are you taking me?' she demanded.

'Shut your trap,' Stranks muttered, staring straight ahead.

Lucetta turned to Guthrie, sensing a more sympathetic soul. 'Who are you really? I'm sure I would remember you if you were my brother.'

'I said shut up,' Stranks roared before Guthrie had a chance to answer. 'One more word from you and you'll feel the back of my hand across your chops.'

Lucetta sank back against the leather squabs, her worst fears realised. Whoever these men were they could not be related to her. How they knew her, or what they wanted from her, was a mystery. She was trapped, helpless and terrified. Whatever they planned for her, she was certain that they were up to no good. She considered throwing herself from the moving vehicle, but she was wedged firmly between them and there was nothing she could do other than bide her time. At least she had someone on her side. She knew that she had one friend in London, and when the opportunity arose she would escape and make her way back to the Fever Hospital and find Mary. She closed her eyes, blotting out the view of the busy streets as they flashed past the cab.

Lucetta awakened with a start as the cab came to an abrupt halt, and her hand flew to her mouth as the smell of the river almost choked her, conjuring up terrifying visions of darkness and panic. She could feel the cold waters of the Thames closing over her head. She couldn't breathe. She was drowning. The memories of that dreadful night began to surface through the haze that had dulled her mind during her fever. 'The ship,' she cried. 'It sank. People were drowning—'

Stranks clamped his hand over her mouth and he held her to his side, squeezing her until she could hardly breathe. 'Stop that noise or I'll break your neck.'

'He means it, girl,' Guthrie whispered. 'Best do as he says.'

Stranks thrust some coins into Guthrie's hand. 'Pay the cabby.'

Lucetta struggled, but Stranks only tightened his hold. 'One word from you and it'll be your last.' He waited until Guthrie had clambered down from the cab before lifting Lucetta bodily from the vehicle. 'She's been ill,' he remarked conversationally to the cabby. 'Poor girl had typhoid. Nasty disease, but she's on the mend now. Let's get you inside, ducks.'

Lucetta opened her mouth to cry for help but Stranks tossed her over his shoulder and suddenly her world was upside down. The cobblestones swam before her eyes and she almost bumped her head on the top step as Stranks descended into the gloom of the foul-smelling area that led into the basement. Guthrie had gone on ahead and Lucetta heard the grating of a key in a lock followed by the groan of a door opening on rusty hinges. Her view of slime-encrusted stone steps and cracked flagstones gave way to dusty wooden floorboards speckled with mouse droppings and empty carapaces of dead cockroaches. 'Put me down,' she demanded, beating her fists against the back of Stranks' legs.

He dropped her unceremoniously onto a pile of filthy sacks. 'Lock the door, Lennie, and give me the key. We don't want our little investment to wander off and get lost in the wicked city.'

Guthrie did as he was told, handing the key to Stranks with a deprecating grin. 'We done it, Norm. We got our pot of gold.'

'Not quite,' Stranks said, slipping the key into his pocket. 'We got to convince her family that she's alive and well and worth the ransom money.'

Lucetta made a vain attempt to get to her feet but the room spun dizzily around her and she sank back onto the sacks. She clutched her hands to her forehead as the cries of drowning people filled her ears. 'The ship was in a collision – I remember it now. The smell of the river brought it all back to me. I must find Mama and Papa. Were they rescued too? You must take me to them. They will pay you for your trouble.'

'Mama and Papa.' Stranks mimicked her girlish

voice. 'They're dead and gone, ducks. You're an orphan, but you're a rich one. We should get a lot of money for you.'

'No!' Lucetta cried. 'No, I don't believe you. You're lying.'

Stranks made a move towards her, fisting his hands. 'No one calls Norman Stranks a liar.'

'Leave her be,' Guthrie said, grabbing him by the arm. 'She's just a slip of a girl.'

Stranks shook off his restraining hand and he leaned towards Lucetta, thrusting his face close to hers. 'You'd better believe me, Miss Lucetta Froy, because you are coming into a fortune and your loving aunt and uncle are going to pay handsomely for your return.'

'I know you now,' Lucetta said slowly. 'You're the escaped convicts.'

Stranks grabbed her by the throat. 'And there's no search party looking for you now, girlie. As far as the world is concerned you're dead along with your mum and dad and the rest of the passengers and crew.'

Lucetta huddled against the damp brick wall, turning her head away from the disgusting stench of his foetid breath. She did not want to believe him, but in her heart she knew that what he said was true. The horror of the shipwreck was slowly coming back to her, and she knew that Stranks was speaking the truth. Neither of her parents would have been able to survive for long in the water. Her past life flashed before her as if she too were drowning, not physically, but in sorrow. She had been desperate to regain her memory while she was in hospital, but now she wished wholeheartedly that it had not returned. She longed for the oblivion of fever to wipe away the pain of losing both parents in such a tragic way. She hung her head, not wanting her captors to see the tears that coursed down her cheeks.

'That's shut her up,' Stranks said triumphantly. 'Let's get out of here, Lennie. I could do with a drink after all this.'

Guthrie eyed Lucetta warily. 'Should we leave her like this, Norm? I mean she's just come out of hospital. We don't want her to get sick again.'

'Stop acting like an old woman,' Stranks said impatiently. 'She'll be all right for an hour or two. Maybe a spell on her own with the rats and mice for company will quieten her down a bit.' He made for the door and unlocked it. 'You'd best behave yourself, girl. There's no way out, so save your strength. C'mon, Norm. Don't stand there like a fool.'

'I'm coming,' Guthrie said, taking off his jacket and wrapping it around Lucetta's shoulders. 'We'll bring you back something to eat and drink.' He lowered his voice. 'I ain't forgotten how you looked after me in that bloody jungle. I might have lost me leg if it weren't for you.'

Stranks wrenched the door open. 'If you don't come now I'll lock you in with your little friend.'

'Leave it out, Norm,' Guthrie said, limping across the floor to retrieve his walking stick. 'She's just a kid.'

Stranks' reply was lost as the door closed on them. Lucetta threw Guthrie's jacket off in disgust at the mixed odours of stale tobacco, beer and sweat, but it was cold in the basement and she was still very weak. Reluctantly she picked up the garment, which still retained some of Guthrie's body heat, and she draped it around her shoulders. The coarse material scratched her skin but as warmth began to seep into her chilled bones she felt strong enough to stand. Getting to her feet she walked slowly round the dingy room, peering into dark corners where fungi sprouted from the damp walls, and moss grew in cracks on the flagstone floor. On the far wall there were two wooden beds with straw-filled palliasses and coarse woollen blankets left in untidy heaps. A rickety deal table in the centre of the room was streaked with snail trails of dried gravy where the resident rodent population had carried off the remnants of a meal, and the dirty plates were thick with flies.

Wrinkling her nose, Lucetta picked up a chipped enamel jug, hoping that it might contain water, but a cloud of blowflies rose angrily from the sticky puddle of sour ale at the bottom and she dropped it with a cry of disgust. She was hungry and thirsty and she was still very weak. She walked slowly to the window but it was barred against intrusion from outside. The panes were thick with grime both inside and out and festoons of spiders' webs hung like curtains from the beams above her head. She could see daylight through the railings on top of the area wall, but little else. She tried the door in the vain hope that Stranks had forgotten to lock it, but it held firm. She was a prisoner, and there was nothing she could do about it. Beyond tears, and overcome by sheer exhaustion, she stumbled over to one of the wooden cots and lay down, covering herself with a tattered blanket which smelt suspiciously of horses. Her mouth was dry and her head ached miserably, but she drifted off into a fitful sleep.

It was pitch dark when she opened her eyes, awakened by the sound of loud voices and drunken laughter as Stranks and Guthrie barged into the room. She stiffened, hardly daring to breathe.

'Light a candle for God's sake, Lennie,' Stranks muttered in a voice thickened by drink.

'Hold on a minute, Norm. I can't find the vestas.'

A tin plate fell from the table hitting the flagstones with a resounding clatter and Guthrie swore beneath his breath. Lucetta huddled beneath the blankets, waiting for inevitable discovery when Guthrie eventually managed to strike a match. After several attempts he succeeded and Stranks swore loudly. 'Hold the damn candle up, Lennie. Where's the little bitch gone?'

Guthrie raised the candle above his head and he chuckled. 'She's made herself comfortable, mate. Over there.'

Stranks tottered over to stand beside the bed, glaring down at Lucetta with his square jaw out-thrust. 'Get up. You ain't a little princess now.'

'Leave her be,' Guthrie said mildly. 'She ain't doing no harm.'

'It's your bed she's taken, mate,' Stranks muttered. 'You can sort her out.'

Lucetta pulled the covers up to her chin. 'I'm not

sleeping on the floor, and if I die in this dreadful place you won't get a penny from my family.'

Stranks raised his hand, scowling. 'Shut up. You've got too much to say for yourself.'

'Never mind her,' Guthrie said, wiping one of the plates on his sleeve. 'Come and get your grub.'

'All right, but she can go without. She won't be so cocky when her belly is empty.' Stranks turned away from Lucetta and scuttled crabwise over to the table. He slumped down heavily on a stool, and snatching a meat pie from its wrapping of newspaper he sank his teeth into it, munching noisily and smacking his lips as he gobbled the food.

'She's right though, Norm,' Guthrie said, chewing thoughtfully. 'We need to keep her in good health if we're to get the ransom money. Starving her ain't the answer.' Ignoring Stranks' muttered protests he put a slice of pie and a generous helping of pease pudding on a plate, and heaving his bulk from the stool he limped over to Lucetta. 'Get this down you, girl, and no turning your nose up at good vittles, because it's all you're getting.'

Lucetta struggled to a sitting position and took the plate from him, trying to forget that not so long ago it had been a skating rink for flies. 'Thank you. Could I have something to drink, please?'

'Would your ladyship like champagne or claret?' Stranks muttered through a mouthful of pie.

Guthrie went back to the table and filled a mug with ale. 'You'll have to make do with small beer, Lucy. The water in these parts will kill you.'

'If I don't do it first,' Stranks said darkly. 'You're turning into a real old woman, Lennie. Sit down and eat, for God's sake.'

Guthrie resumed his place at the table. 'It weren't her fault we was caught, and she was good to me in the jungle. I don't forget a favour.'

'That's it. I knew you was turning soft.' Stranks thumped his hand down on the table top. 'We're off to Islington to start negotiations with the family first thing in the morning. The sooner we get rid of her, the better.'

'Yeah,' Guthrie agreed enthusiastically. 'We'll be rich, Norm. We'll live like lords for the rest of our naturals.'

After the bland hospital diet the meat pie lay heavily in Lucetta's stomach and her captors' combined snoring made the rafters shake, but despite this she managed to sleep reasonably well on Guthrie's palliasse. He had retired to the pile of sacks and Stranks was so drunk that he collapsed insensible on his bed without any further arguments. She was awakened by what she thought at first was the sound of torrential rainfall, but when she opened her eyes she was horrified to see Stranks relieving himself in a bucket placed in the far corner of the room. The stench of strong urine laced with alcohol made her feel physically sick and she pulled the blanket over her head. She covered her ears with her hands, but moments later the covers were dragged from her head and she looked up to see Stranks bending over her with a knife clutched in his hand.

'Scream and I really will slit your pretty throat,' he

hissed, cutting a lock of her hair with one swipe of the blade. He held it up to the daylight that filtered hazily through the windowpanes. 'This should be enough to convince your family that you're alive and kicking.'

Lucetta raised herself on one elbow. She was trembling with fear but she was desperate to escape from this hellish place. 'Why should they believe you? Take me with you so that they can see I am alive.'

'Do you take me for a fool? They'd set the coppers on us straight away. While we got you prisoner they won't take no chances. Ain't that right, Lennie?'

Guthrie rose from the sacking, stretching and groaning. 'Another night on that bloody floor and I'll be crippled. Let's get on to it right away, Norm. The sooner she's back with her folks the better for all of us.'

Lucetta watched them leave with a feeling of relief tinged with a certain amount of trepidation. She did not relish the idea of being left on her own in the bleak basement room for any length of time. She crawled out of bed and, as there was no alternative, she was forced to make use of the bucket in the corner. She could hardly believe she had sunk so low, but the will to survive was stronger than her fear of what the future might hold. She comforted herself with the knowledge that Uncle Bradley and Aunt Eliza would be certain to pay the ransom demanded by her kidnappers. Uncle Bradley would complain, as he always did when he had to part with money, and Aunt Eliza might be a bit put out to have her niece foisted on her, but they were family and Papa had always said that families must stick together. Hopefully Stranks and Guthrie would return with good news. She would just have to put up with this awful place for a while longer.

Focusing her thoughts on a positive outcome of their dealings with her aunt and uncle, Lucetta decided that she must be ready to leave as soon as they returned. What she needed desperately was a wash and some clean linen, but that was out of the question in this sordid bolt-hole where the rats only ventured out to steal leftover food before scurrying back to their nests behind the rotten skirting boards. She shuddered as a flea crawled out from beneath her sleeve and latched onto the skin of her wrist. She brushed it off with a cry of horror and began stripping off her clothes, shaking them and draping them over the stools until she stood naked and shivering in the middle of the floor. She crossed her arms over her breasts, shuddering at the sight of angry red lumps where the parasites had feasted on her blood during the night. She thought longingly of the days when Naomi had been at her beck and call, bringing scented water for washing and assisting her to dress in freshly laundered, sweet-smelling undergarments made out of the finest cambric and trimmed with lace. She had taken so much for granted then, but it had all changed in that split second when the two vessels collided on the river.

If only she could turn back time and return to the life that had been stolen from her, she would tell her parents how much she loved them and how bitterly she regretted having been the cause of Papa's apoplectic fit. The return of her memory had brought with it a crushing feeling of guilt. None of this would have happened had she not been so wilful and headstrong, and yet she did not regret a moment that she had spent in Sam's company. At least he was safe in Bali, and she had Mama to thank for that, even though she had railed against her mother's decision at the time. Had Sam been on board the *Caroline* he might have drowned, but when the news of the disaster reached across the oceans he might believe that she was dead and find someone else to love. They had only known each other for such a brief time, and yet she knew for certain that he was the one man in the world to whom she could give her heart and soul.

Lucetta gulped back tears as she pulled the coarse calico shift over her head. Sam would scarcely recognise her now. If he returned to London and discovered that she had survived, would he love a girl whose bones stuck out like white marble beneath her skin? Would he be attracted to someone who undoubtedly smelled as bad as her captors and her stinking surroundings? She was not at all certain of the answer. Sam Cutler had fallen in love with a spoilt young girl who had been petted and cosseted and told that she was beautiful from the cradle onwards, and, until now, she had had no reason to doubt it.

Lucetta slipped her arms into the yellowed-cotton blouse but her fingers were shaking so badly that she found it almost impossible to do up the buttons. With a great deal of effort she managed to finish dressing and her hand flew automatically to her hair. It hung around her shoulders in a mass of knots and tangles and she had neither a brush nor a comb. It was, she thought with a touch of her old humour, a good thing that Stranks and Guthrie did not possess a mirror. She dragged her hair back from her face and tied it with a strip of material torn from the hem of her shift and then she began a methodical search of the room, looking for something which might help her to escape.

Perhaps there was a spare key hidden somewhere under a loose brick, or beneath the palliasses on the wooden cots? There was plenty of dust and dirt piled in the corners of the room which might have been used to conceal something as small as a key. She took a spoon from the table and began digging as if prospecting for gold, but she found nothing other than nests of woodlice and crawly things with dozens of legs. In desperation she tried to open the window, even though the bars on the outside were too closely set together to allow anything bigger than a cat to slide through them, but the window was nailed shut and the door remained firmly locked. There was no way out and she was both hungry and thirsty. She went back to the table, but if there had been anything left after last night's meal, the rats and mice had devoured the last crumb. The jug was empty except for the flies forming a moving crust in the bottom as they feasted off the dregs of small beer. The stale smell made her retch and she pitched the jug at the wall. The violent action did nothing to assuage the pangs of hunger or thirst that tormented her, but it went some way to relieve her feelings.

She perched on one of the stools, leaning her elbows on the table and cupping her chin in her hands. She closed her eyes and imagined herself back on the veranda outside her room in the consulate. She could smell the scent of the champak blossoms and the fragrance of hot coffee and freshly baked bread. She could taste the sweet flesh of the finger-size bananas, mangosteens and rambutans. She could hear Sam telling her that he loved her and repeating his promise to ask her father for her hand in marriage. But it was all a dream, so far distant from the reality of this dreadful place that it seemed like another life.

Lucetta jerked upright as something warm and furry ran across her feet. Opening her eyes she saw a black shape disappearing into a hole in the wall. With one sweep of her hand she cleared the table, sending greasy newspaper, spoons and mugs flying onto the floor. She climbed onto the table and sat with her knees drawn up to her chin and her arms wrapped tightly around her legs. She must keep her thoughts positive and not give way to fear. She began to recite poems that she had been forced to learn at Miss Milton's Academy for Young Ladies. She had never been fond of poetry, but bringing some of them to mind prevented her from agonising about what might happen when her captors returned. She managed to recall a few lines of Keats' *La Belle Dame sans Merci*, but having exhausted that particular work, she went on to Wordsworth and his daffodils. Finally, just as she was almost halfway through Coleridge's *Rime of the Ancient Mariner*, which she rather liked, she heard the sound of booted feet tramping down the stone steps, and the rattle of the key in the lock. She slid off the table to perch on the stool. She would not let them see that she had been close to despair. She eyed them coolly as they clattered into the room.

'Well?' she said, hoping that they did not notice the tremor in her voice. 'Are you going to take me home now?'

Stranks dragged off his cloth cap and hurled it at the wall. 'We might as well toss you back in the river. Your stuck-up relations won't have nothing to do with us. They don't want you back.'

Lucetta stared at him in disbelief. 'That can't be true.'

'It ain't exactly the case, Lucy,' Guthrie said, scowling at Stranks. 'They didn't believe us, that's more like it. They was convinced you'd drowned and we was telling lies.'

'It don't matter which,' Stranks countered. 'The result is the same. They ain't paying up and now we're stuck with her.'

'Lennie's right,' Lucetta said, using his given name to emphasise the fact that he was on her side. 'That lock of hair could have been anybody's and they would have no reason to believe you. You must take me to them right away. It's the only way they will know for certain that I am alive.'

Stranks scratched his head. 'I dunno. It's too much of a risk.'

Lucetta was quick to see a hint of uncertainty in his eyes. 'But wouldn't it be worth it, if you get what you want?'

'We ain't got much money left, Norm,' Guthrie said earnestly. 'I say we take her there now and show them we mean business.'

Stranks cocked his head on one side, staring hard at Lucetta as if calculating her value, pound for pound. 'All right, we'll do it,' he said, pulling a clasp-knife from his pocket. 'But if she tries to escape I'll stick her with me chive, and put an end to her moaning for good.'

Guthrie took Lucetta by the elbow. 'She won't do nothing stupid, will you, Lucy?'

'No, you have my word I won't try to escape. My aunt and uncle will reward you handsomely. I know they will.'

The butler faced them with a stony stare. 'As I told you before, my good man, Mr and Mrs Froy are not at home to the likes of you.'

With his jaw out-thrust, Stranks took a step towards him. 'You tell your master that I've brought proof and she's standing here beside me on the pavement. This here is Miss Lucetta Froy; you must know who she is unless you're blind as well as stupid.'

The butler flinched visibly, but held his ground. 'Don't take that tone with me, my man. As it happens I'm new here and I wouldn't know what the young lady looked like.'

'Please, you must tell my aunt and uncle that I am here,' Lucetta cried, struggling to free herself from Guthrie's firm hold. 'If Uncle Bradley will just come to the door he will see for himself.'

'You heard her,' Stranks roared. 'Fetch your master and be quick about it.'

'Wait here.'

The door closed in their faces and Stranks beat on it with his fists. 'Open up, or I'll break the door down.'

'Hold on, mate,' Guthrie said urgently. 'They'll have the cops on us if you keep that racket up.'

'My uncle will come,' Lucetta said confidently. 'Just give him a moment. It's a big house and the drawing room is upstairs.'

'Oh, the drawing room,' Stranks mocked. 'Pardon me, your highness. I forgot I was dealing with the toffs.'

Lucetta bit her lip. Her nerves were jangling like the pots and pans on a tinker's cart, and her heart was beating so fast that she felt quite faint. She glanced upward at the drawing-room windows, and she thought she saw Aunt Eliza's pale face peering from behind one of the velvet curtains, but whoever it was withdrew instantly.

Stranks hammered on the doorknocker. 'What's keeping you? We ain't got all day.'

The door opened and Lucetta gasped with relief as Bradley Froy stepped past his butler and stood, stiff and unsmiling, on the top step. 'If you don't go away this instant I will send for the police.'

Stranks seized Lucetta by the arm, dragging her from Guthrie's less savage grasp and he thrust her forwards. 'Here's the proof you wanted. This here is your niece, Miss Lucetta Froy. Now let's talk business.'

'Uncle Bradley, please give them what they ask,'

Lucetta pleaded, her voice breaking on a sob. 'Give them the money. I want to come home.'

Bradley stared at her coldly, his face a mask of indifference. 'This is not my niece. Lucetta lost her life when the *Caroline* sank on that terrible night. This is a cruel hoax. If you value your freedom, leave now.'

'Uncle, it is me,' Lucetta cried in desperation. 'I know I look awful but I can't have changed that much in less than a year.'

'I've never seen this young person before,' Bradley said, backing into the vestibule. 'Go away or I'll send for the police.'

'No,' Lucetta screamed. 'It really is me, Uncle. I escaped drowning but I caught typhoid and was in the fever hospital. You can check with Sister Demarest, she will confirm my story.'

'Give us the money, guv,' Stranks said, changing his tone to a wheedling whine. 'Half of what I asked for earlier, if you must. But take the little trull. She's no use to us.'

'This farce has gone far enough,' Bradley said angrily. 'Close the door, Jenkins, and send the boot boy for the police.'

'No.' Lucetta heard herself screaming the word as she tumbled headlong into a pit of darkness.

She came to her senses in the increasingly familiar upside down world over Guthrie's shoulder. 'Put me down,' she cried, pummelling his back with her fists. 'Put me down.'

Guthrie stopped and dumped her unceremoniously

on the pavement outside the Angel public house. The smell of malt and hops and tobacco smoke drifted out through the open doorway. Stranks sniffed the air. 'I need a drink.'

'We can't take her in there,' Guthrie protested.

'Let me go then. I'm no further use to you,' Lucetta said hopefully.

Stranks stared at her, frowning. 'Shut your trap, girl. I need to think.'

'Well getting drunk ain't going to help,' Guthrie said, jerking his head in the direction of the open pub door. 'And we only got a few coppers left. We need it for vittles.'

Stranks' hand shot out to grab Guthrie by the throat. 'Me mind's clearer when I've got a few pints in me belly. You take the bitch back to our place and I'll see you later, when I've worked out what to do with the little doxy.'

'Perhaps if I went to see Uncle Bradley on my own,' Lucetta suggested tentatively. 'It's no wonder he didn't recognise me looking like this.'

'You stupid little cow,' Stranks snarled. 'He knew you all right. The truth is that he don't want you back because he'd rather have the money. I never saw that coming, but I should have known better.'

Lucetta stared at him in disbelief. 'No, he wouldn't – I mean – he just wouldn't do something like that. He's my father's brother.'

'And he's inherited the house, the business and the money. Why would he want a spoilt brat like you? Tell me that?'

Lucetta's bottom lip trembled and she bit it hard to prevent herself from crying.

Guthrie patted her awkwardly on the shoulder. 'Maybe he really didn't recognise you,' he said gruffly. 'Perhaps if we got you cleaned up a bit . . .'

'You're as daft as she is,' Stranks said savagely. 'Get rid of her. Take her to Seven Dials and see what you can get for her in one of the knocking-shops. Don't take less than a tenner for her neither. It ain't what I was hoping for but it's better than nothing.'

'Give over, Norm,' Guthrie protested. 'Lucy was brung up to be a lady. She's worth more than that.'

'Put her up for auction then,' Stranks snapped. 'Sell her to the highest bidder. I don't care what you do with her but get as much for her as you can. If you don't, I'll wring her bleeding neck and throw her off London Bridge, so help me.' Shoving his hands in his pockets, he strolled into the pub, leaving Guthrie and Lucetta standing on the pavement, staring after him.

Chapter Eight

Thinking fast, Lucetta turned to Guthrie. 'Let me try to see my uncle again, please, Lennie. I'm sure he didn't recognise me, but if I could just speak to him . . .'

'It's no use, girl. Norm's right about that one. Your uncle don't want to be bothered with you, all he wants is the money. He's a black-hearted villain if ever there was one.'

'He's my uncle. I don't understand how he can do this to me.'

Guthrie raised his hand as if he were about to stroke her hair, but he let his arm fall to his side with a sympathetic grunt. 'I dunno what to say.'

His face crumpled as if he was going to cry and Lucetta found herself comforting him. She patted him on the shoulder, making an effort to sound unafraid although inwardly she was quaking. 'So what are you going to do with me, Lennie?'

'I – I dunno,' Guthrie said, staring down at his misshapen leg. 'I don't want to sell you to one of them places, but Norm will have me guts for garters if I don't bring back some reddy and I ain't got nothing to trade but you, ducks. Ain't you got no other relatives what would cough up money for you?'

'Not in London. I have a maiden aunt living

somewhere in Surrey, but my mother's family disowned her when she married Pa. I never met any of them and I wouldn't know where to find them.'

'Ain't there no one in London you could turn to?'

'There's Mary, the nurse who was kind to me when I was in the fever hospital, but I doubt if she has any money. Papa had plenty of business acquaintances. We could try some of them.'

Guthrie seized her by the hand. 'We will. That's what we'll do. If you could get one of them to speak up for you it would put the old bugger to shame. He'd have to take you in.'

'And I would see that you get a reward,' Lucetta said earnestly. 'You need not share it with Stranks and you could start a new life somewhere a long way from London.'

Guthrie grabbed her by the hand. 'I don't want to see you end up on the streets. It just wouldn't be right. Who shall us try first?'

Lucetta racked her brains as she tried to recall her parents' friends and business acquaintances. She had been a weekly boarder at Miss Milton's Academy before they sailed for Indonesia, and she had not been considered old enough to attend the lavish dinner parties hosted by her parents. Occasionally, if the guests had been very well known to her father, she had been allowed to join them for dessert, but she had rarely been invited to accompany her parents when they received reciprocal invitations to dine at the wealthy merchants' houses.

'Think hard, ducks,' Guthrie urged, staring nervously

over her shoulder at the pub door. 'We'd best start walking in case he's watching out of the window.'

Lucetta fell into step beside him as he limped along, leaning heavily on his cane. 'You shouldn't be walking so far on that bad leg, Lennie.'

'Don't worry about me, ducks. You're the one who's in desperate need.'

She came to a sudden halt, very nearly unbalancing Guthrie. 'There is one person who might remember me.'

'Speak up then. We'll go and see this cove.'

'Mr Wilkinson owns a saw mill and timber yard not far from here. I haven't seen him since I was twelve or thirteen, but he might recognise me. He used to bring me chocolates when he and his wife came to dine at our house. I remember him because he was round, like a robin, and he had kind eyes. He laughed a lot and his chins used to wobble like blancmange above his starched collar. I know my papa liked him because they used to laugh and joke together, but Mrs Wilkinson looked as though she lived on lemon juice and vinegar. I don't think my mama liked her at all.'

'Where do we find this bloke? We ain't got much time, girl.'

The City Road Basin was crammed with vessels tied up alongside the many wharves. The air was thick with dust as the glistening nuggets of coal were unloaded from the holds of barges. Men with blackened hands and faces struggled to tote heavy sacks of fuel to the manufactories where gutta-percha and lead were being produced by the ton. Steam from the laundry billowed into a sky that was already filled with clouds of noxious gases and a steady drizzle of dust and soot rained down on their heads. Lucetta felt certain that this teeming industrial landscape must be the equivalent of hell on earth and she clutched Guthrie's hand as they made their way over grimy cobblestones towards Wilkinson's timber yard and mill. She covered her ears as the screaming saw sliced through baulks of timber throwing up showers of sawdust. Guthrie marched her to the office door and thrust it open with the toe of his boot. 'It's up to you now, Lucy. I'll wait outside.'

'Won't you come in with me?'

'I ain't taking the chance that someone might recognise me. I did time in Pentonville and I seen some familiar faces working here.' He pulled his cap down over his eyes and leaned against the brick wall, crossing his arms over his chest. 'Get on with it, double quick.'

Lucetta patted him on the shoulder. 'You're not a bad man, Lennie. If ever I get a chance to do something for you in return, I promise you that I will.'

'Never mind that. Go inside and do what you must.' He gave her a gentle shove through the open doorway.

'We don't employ women.'

Lucetta blinked and stared at the bald-headed clerk standing behind the high counter. 'I wasn't after employment. I came to see Mr Wilkinson.'

'And what would the likes of you want with the likes of him?'

'That's my business, sir,' Lucetta said icily. 'Please tell Mr Wilkinson that Miss Lucetta Froy would like to see him.'

The clerk stared at her with narrowed eyes. 'It was in the newspaper,' he said slowly. 'Miss Froy was drowned along with her parents when the two ships collided in the fog. Mr Wilkinson went to their funeral.'

'Well, as you can see, that isn't true. I was saved and I want to see him now, please.'

'He's busy, miss. Put your request in writing and I'll see that he gets it.' The clerk went back to writing in a ledger, dismissing her with a wave of his hand.

Lucetta glanced over his shoulder and a shaft of pale sunlight filtered through the window, illuminating the gold lettering on the door behind the desk. *Edwin Wilkinson, Esq., Proprietor*. She went up to the counter and tapped on it to attract the clerk's attention. 'If I might have the use of a pen and paper?' She met his startled gaze with a straight look. 'I can read and write.'

Reluctantly, he pushed an inkstand towards her. He tore a sheet of paper from a notebook and handed it to her silently, although his disapproving expression spoke louder than words.

Lucetta wrote a note in her best copperplate hand and she folded it in half, sliding the paper across the polished mahogany counter. 'Please give this to Mr Wilkinson, and you can tell him that I will wait even if I have to stay here all day.'

With a deep-throated sound halfway between a grunt and a growl, the clerk snatched up the note. He knocked on the office door before entering, and he closed it before Lucetta had a chance to peer inside. She paced the floor, wringing her hands nervously. Her whole future depended on Mr Wilkinson recognising her. She spun round at the sound of the door opening. 'Well?' she breathed. 'Will he see me?'

With his lips pencilled into a thin line of disapproval, the clerk lifted a hatch in the counter and stood aside to allow her to pass. 'Mr Wilkinson will see you, but if I hear a commotion I'll send for the police.'

Lucetta sailed past him with her head held high. She might look like a skivvy, but she knew how to act like a lady. She was still Miss Lucetta Froy of Thornhill Crescent who had until recently resided with the British consul and his wife in Bali. She entered the office and found herself facing Mr Wilkinson, whose huge bulk was partially concealed behind a large pedestal desk with a green tooled-leather top. He leaned forward, steepling his fingers. 'So, young woman, you claim to be Lucetta Froy.'

'I am she,' Lucetta said firmly. 'I was not drowned when the *Caroline* sank. Somehow I was saved, although I don't remember anything about it.'

'A convenient loss of memory, although I have to tell you that I was present at the funeral of Miss Froy and her parents and a very sad occasion it was to be sure.'

Lucetta felt her confidence ebbing away as she met his cold glance. This was not how she recalled her father's old friend. 'That wasn't me. I don't know who they buried in my stead but I am Lucetta.'

'That is quite enough of this charade, my girl. The body was identified by Miss Froy's uncle.'

'Then he was mistaken. I am very much alive, as you see.' Lucetta took a step nearer the desk. 'You must remember me, Mr Wilkinson. You used to bring me chocolates when you came to our house in Thornhill Crescent.'

Edwin Wilkinson lowered his hands, placing them palms down on the desk top and smoothing the leather as if he were stroking a cat. 'Answer me this. If you are who you say you are, why are you not at home with your surviving family?'

'That is easy to explain. I caught typhoid and was confined to the fever hospital for several weeks. I lost my memory—' She broke off, clasping her hands tightly in front of her. If she told him about Stranks and Guthrie she would endanger Lennie, who was trying to help her.

'Answer my question, girl, or else leave my office.'

Lucetta met his stern gaze and she knew she must tell the truth, even though it went against her. 'I went to Thornhill Crescent this morning and my uncle treated me like a stranger. He must have recognised me but he made it clear that he wants nothing to do with me.'

'You had better be careful what you're saying, miss. Bradley Froy is a respected businessman. You won't get very far making wild accusations against him.'

'I am just telling you what happened, sir. I know I am roughly dressed, but you can see that I am not a common girl. I was educated at Miss Milton's Academy for Young Ladies, and my father was Henry Froy. We had just returned from Indonesia when the *Caroline* was in collision with another vessel on the river. I beg you to believe me.'

Edwin leaned back in his chair and the wood creaked beneath his considerable weight. 'It is not I you must convince. If your uncle fails to recognise you then the world will assume that you are an imposter.'

'But I am not . . .' Lucetta cried, her voice rising on a sob. 'I am who I say I am. My uncle wishes to disown me so that he can keep what is rightfully mine.'

'Stop there!' Edwin raised his hand and his piercing blue eyes flashed angrily. 'That is slander and you could go to prison for defaming a respectable man's character.'

Lucetta bowed her head, overwhelmed by the knowledge that she was losing ground. 'I am telling the truth,' she whispered. 'Why won't you believe me?' She turned to leave the room, stumbling blindly as tears blurred her vision.

'Wait a minute.'

She stopped, turning her head to look at him and hardly daring to breathe. Had he changed his mind? Was it possible that he believed her? 'Yes, sir?'

'I must admit that there is something very familiar about you, although the Lucetta Froy I remember was a rosy-cheeked young girl with tumbling golden curls and a charming smile. You on the other hand are thin and gaunt and your hair is so dirty that I cannot tell whether you are dark or fair. There might be a fleeting resemblance to my old friend's daughter, but I could not stand up in court and swear on the Bible that you are who you say you are, even though there is a shadow of doubt in my mind.'

'I realise that I am much changed,' Lucetta said slowly. 'But as I was attempting to explain, I have been ill with typhoid fever. My clothes and everything that might identify me were lost in the shipwreck, and my parents are both dead. I cannot be the carefree girl you recall.'

Edwin stared at her thoughtfully. 'You might be an imposter, but it's obvious to me that you are not a common, uneducated girl. Who are you really?'

Lucetta shrugged her shoulders with a heartfelt sigh. 'There is no use repeating my name if you refuse to believe me.'

'I believe that you are desperate enough to perpetrate this deception, claiming to be a young woman who would have inherited a considerable fortune had she lived. Who put you up to this, my girl? You look too young and innocent to have conceived such a plan.'

'No one,' Lucetta said, grasping the doorknob with trembling fingers. 'I've taken up enough of your time.'

'No, wait.' Edwin heaved his bulk from the chair with an effort that pearled his forehead with beads of sweat. He waddled round the desk to face her. 'I can see that you are in desperate straits. Have you anywhere to go?' He thrust his hand into his inside pocket and took out a bulging wallet. 'Do you need money for food and lodging?'

'I don't want your money, sir,' Lucetta said, shaking her head. 'I didn't come here to beg.'

'But have you anywhere to stay? Are you in employment?'

'No, sir.'

'Are you willing to work?'

Lucetta looked into his eyes and she saw genuine compassion in their clear blue depths. 'Yes, sir.'

'I am not offering you a life of ease and luxury, but

if you are prepared to work hard and do as you are told, I may be able to help you.'

'I will do anything that is legal, sir.'

A shadow of a smile lit Edwin's eyes. 'I'm pleased to hear it, but I cannot help you if you continue with your claim to be Lucetta Froy. I'll ask you just once and I want an honest answer – what is your name?'

The words stuck in her throat like a fishbone, but Lucetta knew that she would get nowhere with the truth. If she lost this opportunity to return to the world she knew, she could end up in a brothel or even worse. 'Lucy,' she whispered. 'My name is Lucy Cutler.' She looked away to hide the tears that sprang to her eyes as she took Sam's name. He was lost to her and she would never see him again, but by using his name she felt she could keep a small part of him for herself.

Edwin plucked his top hat from a stand in the corner of the room, and set it on his head. 'Then come with me, Lucy Cutler. I return home for luncheon at this time of day, and you shall come with me. I believe our cook is looking for a girl to help in the kitchen. It might not be the sort of work that you are looking for, but it pays ten pounds a year all found. How does that sound to you?'

Disappointment and desperation threatened to over-come her, but a small voice in her head was telling her to accept his offer. Going into service was preferable to being sold to a brothel-keeper, and at least she would have a roof over her head. Almost anything would be better than returning to the rat-infested dungeon that Stranks and Guthrie called home. 'I'm grateful, sir.' She stood back, waiting for him to open the door for her, but at the sight of his raised eyebrows she quickly realised her mistake. She bobbed a curtsey and allowed him to precede her into the office.

'Is everything all right, sir?' the clerk demanded, shooting a suspicious glance at Lucetta as he lifted the hatch in the counter.

'Quite all right, thank you, Potter.' Edwin paused, eyeing Lucetta thoughtfully. 'Wait outside for me, Miss Cutler. I won't be long.'

Lucetta had been wondering how she was going to explain Guthrie's presence, but now she had a golden opportunity to send him safely on his way. She hurried from the building and found him waiting where she had left him. He straightened up, taking his hands out of his pockets. 'You've been long enough,' he grumbled. 'What went on in there?'

'You must go quickly, Lennie. I don't want Mr Wilkinson to see you or he might start asking awkward questions.'

Guthrie stared at her, frowning. 'So is this cove going to help you?'

'He thinks his wife might find me a place as a servant and I can't afford to be fussy. You can go back to Stranks and tell him what you will; I don't care, just so long as he thinks I'm safely out of the way. I don't want to be looking over my shoulder every time I walk out and about.'

'But did he recognise you?'

'No. He thinks I'm an imposter, trying to get money under false pretences, but one day I'll prove my identity and when I come into my rightful inheritance I'll do what I can to help you. Now please go, before he comes out.'

Guthrie gave a start as the office door creaked on its hinges. 'Good luck, nipper.' He backed away from her, dodging behind a pile of timber as Edwin emerged from the building.

Lucetta fell in behind her prospective employer. Guthrie and his evil partner were part of her past and she was heading towards the future, whatever that might hold. She held her head high in an attempt to give herself courage, but her stomach felt as though it was tying itself into knots and she felt sick with nerves.

Edwin walked at a surprisingly brisk pace for such a large man and his huge frame swayed from side to side with each step. He could have been regarded by some as a caricature of a man or pointed out as a figure of fun, but Lucetta was quick to notice that working men tipped their caps to him and their bosses stopped to pass the time of day with jovial remarks and much shaking of hands. It became apparent to her that Mr Wilkinson was a much-liked and well-respected man in this area of Islington. She could only hope that in time he would come to believe her story and then he might actually remember her. If such an important man were to take her side Uncle Bradley would be forced to admit that she was his niece and her father's rightful heir. With her fortunes restored she would search the globe until she found Sam Cutler. She had taken his name and in her heart she would always be his. She comforted herself with the thought of their blissful reunion.

'Come along, Lucy. Don't dawdle.'

Edwin's voice shattered her reverie and she quickened her pace in order to keep up with him as they left the filth and bustle of the wharves. Memories came flooding back to Lucetta as they reached Duncan Terrace. There were gardens now where the New River had flowed freely between the rows of elegant Georgian houses before it was culverted. It now ran its course underground, but in her mind's eye Lucetta could see herself as a lively six-year-old, walking sedately along the riverbank with her nanny while Mama and Papa were being entertained by the Wilkinsons. She couldn't recall exactly what had attracted her curiosity on that hot June day, but something in the water had caught her eye and she had broken free from Nanny's restraining hand and run to the river's edge. Leaning over a little too far she would have fallen head first into the fast-flowing water if a fisherman had not abandoned his rod and hauled her to safety. She grimaced as she remembered the spanking she had received for that piece of bad behaviour. Her backside had been sore for days afterwards and she had never again been invited to accompany her parents to the Wilkinsons' home.

Puffing and panting, Edwin walked up the path to the front door. He rapped twice on the brass knocker. 'No nonsense now, miss,' he wheezed. 'Mrs Wilkinson is a very fair woman but she won't be trifled with and she was very fond of the late Mrs Froy. I don't want you to say anything that will upset her. Do you understand me?'

The door opened and Lucetta acknowledged his warning with a nod of her head.

Edwin stepped over the threshold, handing his hat and gloves to the uniformed maidservant, who shot Lucetta a deprecating glance beneath sandy eyelashes.

'Is my wife in the parlour or the dining room, Ruby?'

'In the parlour, sir.'

'That will be all for now, Ruby.' Edwin beckoned to Lucetta. 'Follow me, Miss Cutler.'

Lucetta hesitated for a moment. She could sense the maidservant's animosity towards her, which Ruby underlined with a scornful curl of her lip and a twitch of her thin shoulders as she placed her master's hat and gloves on the hallstand. Lucetta knew that she was being watched closely as she followed her new protector along the narrow hallway with its highly polished oak floorboards and white walls lined with mezzotints, etchings and watercolours of rural scenes.

Edwin entered a room at the end of the passage but Lucetta hesitated on the threshold. She was suddenly nervous, wondering if Mrs Wilkinson might recognise her where her husband had failed. Her whole fate seemed to hang in the balance and she held her breath.

'You're late, Edwin.'

The sharp tone of Fanny Wilkinson's voice was not encouraging, but Edwin seemed unperturbed as he crossed the floor to kiss his wife on her leathery cheek. 'I'm sorry, my dear, but I was delayed at the office.'

'Who is that ragged creature hovering in the doorway?' Fanny raised a lorgnette to her eyes and peered myopically at Lucetta. 'You haven't brought one of your charity cases home again, I hope, Edwin.'

'This young woman has fallen on hard times, Fanny,' Edwin said mildly. 'Come in, Miss Cutler. I want you to meet my lady wife, who I am sure will be well disposed towards someone who is genuinely down on their luck.'

Hardly daring to hope that Mrs Wilkinson would see some resemblance to the schoolgirl she had been when they last met, Lucetta stepped into the room and was almost overpowered by the heat. Despite the sweltering June weather, a fire burned in the grate and the curtains were half drawn, excluding most of the natural light. As her eyes grew accustomed to the dimness, Lucetta could see that the room was crammed with furniture that might have come straight from a shop window. She would not have been surprised to see price tags dangling from the arms of the chairs. A black marble clock ticked sonorously from the mantelshelf where porcelain figurines of shepherds and shepherdesses seemed to elbow each other, jostling for position with grinning pot dogs, spill jars and candlesticks complete with dangling lustres. The air was heavy with the scent of lavender beeswax and pot pourri and Lucetta was finding it increasingly hard to breathe.

Resplendent in royal purple, Mrs Wilkinson sat bolt upright on a chair which resembled a throne, while her husband stood dutifully at her side like an obedient consort.

Lucetta approached her with a sinking feeling in

her heart. She saw no hint of recognition in those melt-water eyes and no evidence of kindness in the thin lips that were drawn together in a pencil line.

'What has this young person's ill-fortune to do with us, Edwin?' Fanny demanded.

'Miss Cutler came to me seeking employment, and I know that Cook needs more help in the kitchen.'

'Our domestic arrangements are my domain, Edwin. I wish you would not interfere,' Fanny retorted in a low voice.

'Miss Cutler assures me that she is a good worker, and you are known for your charitable deeds, my love. Perhaps a week's trial might be appropriate?'

Lucetta clasped her hands demurely in front of her, keeping her eyes cast downwards to hide the bitter disappointment raging in her breast. All her hopes of finding an ally in the mistress of the house were fading fast.

'How old are you, girl?'

Fanny's sharp voice made Lucetta jump and she looked up. 'Seventeen, ma'am.'

'Too old to train,' Fanny snapped. 'Show me your hands.'

Lucetta held her hands out for inspection, but she knew that they would give her away. She had seen the calloused fingers and palms of the kitchen maids and tweenies in her parents' house, although she had taken little notice of them at the time. It had never occurred to her that their reddened and rough skin was due to hard work; it had simply been a fact of life amongst the lower classes.

'This girl has never done a hard day's work,' Fanny announced triumphantly. She leaned towards Lucetta, eyes narrowed. 'You have never worked in a kitchen, have you, Miss Cutler?'

'No, ma'am.' Lucetta cast a despairing glance at Edwin, but he answered with a slight shrug of his shoulders.

'I thought as much,' Fanny said with obvious satisfaction. 'Leave the room, if you please. I want a word in private with my husband.'

Lucetta was only too glad to get away from the stifling atmosphere of the parlour, but she left the door ajar, eavesdropping unashamedly.

'The girl is obviously up to no good,' Fanny said angrily. 'It's obvious that she has never done manual work. What cock and bull tale did she tell you, Edwin?'

'She is unemployed through no fault of her own, Fanny. She is destitute and needs our help.'

'She was probably dismissed for pilfering her mistress's jewellery or having an illicit liaison with one of the male servants,' Fanny hissed. 'I won't have a girl like that in my household, Edwin. She will corrupt our maids and most probably do a moonlight flit with the best silver plate.'

'I think you are being a little harsh in your assessment of Miss Cutler's character, my love.'

'Harsh? I am the most public spirited of women, as you well know, Edwin. I work tirelessly for charity, but there are limits. Send her on her way and don't encourage her by giving her money.'

Lucetta backed away from the door as she heard Edwin's heavy tread on the floorboards. He emerged from the room with an apologetic smile. 'I expect you heard most of that, Miss Cutler.'

'I did, sir. I'm sorry I put you in such an awkward position.'

He regarded her with a thoughtful frown. 'I don't know what your true story is, but I can see that you have come down in the world.'

For a moment she thought he might have seen just a little similarity to her former self and she met his gaze without blinking. 'What I told you was the truth, Mr Wilkinson.'

'I'm sorry, but I see no resemblance between you and the person you claim to be. I think my wife may have been closer to the truth when she said you were a lady's maid. Perhaps you were on the *Caroline* and your mistress was drowned, leaving you without a character or the means by which to live. Perhaps you saw this as an opportunity to better yourself, and who could blame you. I have eyes in my head and I know what a harsh world it can be, especially for young females such as yourself.' He put his hand in his pocket and produced two silver crowns, pressing them into her hand. 'I'm sorry I can't help you more, but this will pay for a few nights' lodgings, and enable you to seek employment elsewhere. Good luck, Miss Cutler.'

The sun blazed down from a clear sky and sparrows skittered about on the grass, pecking and squabbling over minute scraps of food. Lucetta stared up at the house where once she had been a welcome guest, but the door was firmly closed to her and she was alone, friendless and homeless. She shivered despite the heat, and her belly growled with hunger. She had not eaten since last evening and then it had only been a doorstep of bread smeared with what was left of the dripping after Stranks and Guthrie had had their fill. She had not completely recovered from her illness and the living conditions in the basement room had not been conducive to a speedy convalescence. Her knees trembled and she feared that she might faint.

Taking a deep breath she forced her weary legs to move, although she had no idea where she was going. For some unknown reason she found herself heading back towards the City Road Basin. Perhaps she hoped to find Guthrie, who seemed to be her one friend in the whole of London. She was tired, hungry and confused and one way seemed as good as another. Most important of all, she knew that she must find food quickly before her strength ebbed away. Within minutes, she found herself walking alongside the Regent's Canal in Frog Lane. The smell of beer and tobacco smoke belched out of open pub doorways, mingling with the enticing aroma of hot savoury pies and roasting meat, but the raucous sound of male voices and laughter made her think twice before entering such alien territory. The coins were hot in the palm of her hand, and she clutched them tightly as she tried to choose between the Fox and Cub, the Flower Pot or the inn facing her with an intriguing sign of two frogs pulling a plough. Suddenly their bowed green legs began to move and their pop-eyes bulged as they attempted to pull the heavy farm implement. Lucetta blinked and looked again. She must be delirious. The fever had returned. She must get food . . .

Chapter Nine

Something wet was trickling down her face. She was drowning. She struggled for breath and opened her eyes with a strangled cry for help, but it was not the dark waters of the Thames that met her terrified gaze, but a swarthy face masked with a beard, moustache and sideboards that merged into a head of curly black hair.

'The frogs,' Lucetta murmured dazedly. 'They were moving.'

'She's either mad or out of her head with fever, Bob.'

Another face, this time a woman's, peered down at her. Lucetta made a feeble attempt to sit up but a further bout of dizziness made her collapse back onto the hard wooden settle. 'I must have fainted. I'm all right now.'

The man called Bob jerked upright, staring down at her as if she had just spoken in a foreign tongue. 'This ain't no guttersnipe, Peg. What have we here, I wonder?'

Peg pushed him aside. 'Get back to the bar, and serve the customers afore they goes next door for their ale.' Wiping her hands on a none-too-clean apron, she helped Lucetta to a sitting position. 'You collapsed in the road outside the pub, ducks. One of our regulars brought you in, although there's plenty as would have left you there thinking you was dead drunk. I hope you ain't got nothing catching.'

Lucetta managed a wobbly smile. 'No, I'm not sick, just hungry.' The rich aroma of roasting meat and hot pastry made her stomach rumble as if to confirm her words. 'Might I have something to eat, ma'am? I can pay.' She unclenched her fingers but to her horror her palm was empty. 'I – I had money. I must have dropped it outside.' She struggled to her feet. 'I must find it.'

Peg pushed her back down on the seat. 'Even if that's true, it won't be there now, love.'

'I'm not mad and I'm not lying,' Lucetta protested. 'I had two silver crowns in my hand. I felt dizzy and the frogs on your signboard were moving, I'd swear to it.'

Bob stuck his head round the kitchen door. 'Two steak and kidney pies and mash with plenty of gravy, Peg.'

'Coming up.' Peg moved away to the range where a tray of hot pies was being kept warm beneath a piece of grubby cloth.

Lucetta's mouth watered as she watched creamy mashed potato being heaped onto plates to accompany the pies, and she licked her lips as Peg ladled rich brown gravy to form a pool around the steaming food.

'Don't move from there,' Peg said sternly. 'I know exactly how much grub there is so don't go picking bits off the crusts of me pies. I'll see to you when I get back.' She opened the door with the toe of her boot and backed into the taproom with a plate grasped in each hand.

Lucetta fumbled in the pocket of her skirt, hoping

that by some chance she had put the coins in a safe place before the dizzy spell had overtaken her, but her searching fingers found nothing. She sat staring numbly into space. Without money she was well and truly lost and she doubted if she had the strength to cross the flagstone floor, let alone walk out of the pub in search of work. She turned her head as the door opened and Peg staggered into the kitchen carrying a pile of dirty crockery.

'I could wash those for you, in return for something to eat.' Lucetta said hopefully. 'A slice of bread and butter will do, and a cup of tea – anything.'

Peg cleared a space on the table with her elbow, setting the plates down with a clatter. 'You ain't no skivvy. I can tell by the way you speak. You look like a common drab, but you talk like a lady. Who are you, girl?'

The appetising smells were a torment and when she attempted to move her head swam. Lucetta knew there was no point in telling her story to this kindly but suspicious woman. 'My name is Lucy Cutler,' she said, eyeing a piece of crust that someone had left on their plate. She licked her lips and swallowed hard. 'I was a lady's maid and my mistress was drowned when the *Caroline* went down in the Thames a few weeks ago. I was saved but I lost all my possessions and now I have no money and no one left alive to give me a character.'

Peg's eyes widened and she made sympathetic clucking noises. 'Well now, there's a pickle and no mistake.' She spooned mashed potato onto a clean plate, covering it with a steady stream of gravy. 'Eat this, ducks. We'll talk about payment later.' She thrust the plate into Lucetta's hands.

Lucetta murmured her thanks, spooning a little of the sticky mash and gravy into her mouth. It was not the type of meal that would have been served at home or at the British consulate in Bali, but it was undeniably tasty and much better than anything she had been given by her former captors. She abandoned table manners and began shovelling heaped spoonfuls into her mouth.

'Slow down, you'll choke yourself,' Peg said, chuckling. 'I'll make us a nice cup of tea and then you can tell me what it's like living with the toffs. We don't get no carriage trade here in Frog Lane.' She bustled about making the tea but was interrupted by Bob who poked his head round the door to demand five more pies with plenty of gravy and two servings of sausages and mash.

'Rushed off me feet, I am,' Peg grumbled as the door closed on him. 'It's like this every day of the week and that stupid workhouse girl has been took off to hospital with a quinsy. I haven't had time to go for a replacement, but they're a sickly bunch, always getting poorly with something or other.' She rolled up her sleeves and began plating the food. 'If you've finished, you could give us a hand, ducks. Then we'll have that cup of split pea.'

Lucetta scraped her plate in order to spoon up the last of the gravy. She resisted the temptation to lick it clean, and she rose a little unsteadily to add it to the pile of dirty crockery. She felt better already, and she was able to look round the kitchen without feeling dizzy, but what she saw filled her with dismay. The ceiling was blackened with soot and grease and the roughly plastered walls were scabbed yellow where the whitewash had peeled off in huge flakes. Strings of onions and dried herbs hung from the beams and a couple of hams dangled in the ingle nook above the range, their skins glistening with salt as the smoke from the fire cured the blackened flesh. What should have been a sight that would gladden the heart of any cook was spoilt by the clouds of bluebottles buzzing around the meat, and the spiders' webs which festooned the herbs and onions, some of which looked shrivelled like prunes and gave off a distinctly unpleasant odour.

It was stiflingly hot in the room and the one small window which overlooked the back yard remained firmly closed. A door on the far side led into what looked like a scullery. Lucetta could just make out a clay sink and a wooden draining board cluttered with pots and pans. Dirty crockery was piled on the floor and small grey mice were busily feasting off the congealed grease.

It was obvious that Peg needed all the help she could get, and Lucetta rolled up her sleeves. She had never washed a dish in her life, but it couldn't be that difficult. Without disturbing Peg, who was busy with the food orders, she picked her way carefully over the greasy flagstones and mice scattered in all directions as she entered the scullery. If the kitchen was grubby and untidy, the scullery was a filthy mess. Cobwebs hung from the ceiling like fishermen's nets put out to dry, and the cracked windowpanes were opaque with dirt. Flies buzzed around her head and the sink was green with slime. The smell rising from the drain was evil enough to fell an ox, and Lucetta thought for a moment that she was going to be sick. She opened the door that led into the yard and gulped in a lungful of the city air. It was not country fresh but anything was better than the rank odour in the scullery.

She looked around for a bucket and found one outside the back door. Taking it into the kitchen, she filled it with hot water from one of the boilers on either side of the range. Peg was too occupied to pay her any attention and Lucetta staggered back to the scullery to fill the sink. The green slime waved at her like water-weed in the river that had once flowed outside the Wilkinsons' home in Duncan Terrace, but there did not appear to be anything to help cleanse the dishes other than soda crystals and a crock filled with sand on one of the shelves. As a small child, Lucetta had sometimes ventured into the kitchens of Thornhill Crescent where Cook had been a kindly soul and had allowed her to sample jam tarts or a slice of seed cake still warm from the oven. She had watched the scullery maid pouring Hudson's extract of dry soap into hot water when she washed the dishes from breakfast or luncheon, but on finding no similar product to this, she threw a handful of soda crystals into the water and hoped for the best.

Within minutes her hands were red and wrinkled but she was determined to repay Peg's generosity, and she continued to wash the crockery, piling it on the draining board and leaving it to dry in the humid air.

'Well now, you've done a better job than Poppy and that's for sure.'

Lucetta had not heard Peg come into the scullery and she almost dropped a plate as she turned with a start. 'I wanted to repay your kindness, Mrs er . . .'

'It's Potts,' Peg said, grinning. 'But everyone calls me Peg. Anyway, you done enough for now, ducks. It's gone quiet in the bar and I've sold out of pies and sausages. We'll have that cup of tea I promised you a good half-hour since.'

The water in the sink was tepid and thick with grease, and Lucetta's back was aching. She was only too glad to follow Peg into the kitchen.

'Take the weight off your feet, ducks,' Peg said, pouring tea into two china cups. 'You've paid for your dinner, so what are you going to do now? Have you got lodgings nearby?'

Lucetta accepted the cup of tea and sank down gratefully on the wooden settle. 'No. I've nowhere to go and no money now.'

Peg lowered herself onto a chair at the table. 'Ain't you got no family?'

'I'm an orphan,' Lucetta said truthfully, and her eyes filled with tears. Until this moment she had been too intent on survival to dwell on her loss, but now the realisation that she would never see her parents again hit her forcibly. She bowed her head, to hide the tears that flowed freely down her cheeks. 'And I have no relations living in London,' she whispered. 'I must find work.'

Peg cleared her throat noisily. 'Well, love, I don't want to hurt your feelings, but you won't get a job anywhere looking like something the cat's dragged in. I seen better dressed scarecrows than you.'

Lucetta wiped her eyes on her sleeve, sniffing. 'I know, but I've nothing else to wear. I've lost everything.'

'But the family you worked for,' Peg said, frowning thoughtfully. 'Where was they from? Did they have a house in London? If they was rich enough to employ a lady's maid, they must have had other servants who would vouch for you.'

Lucetta choked on a mouthful of tea. 'I went to the house, but the master's brother and his wife live there now. They sent me away and told me not to bother them again.' She shot a sideways glance at Peg, wondering if she would swallow such an unlikely story.

'That's the way of the world,' Peg said, nodding sagely. 'There's one rule for the toffs and another for the likes of us. Tell you what, love. You can stay on here and help in the kitchen until Poppy gets out of hospital. I'll pay you in food and you can have her cot in the attic for nuppence a week. How does that sound to you?'

Lucetta glanced down at the grime-encrusted flagstones and the small mounds of vegetable peelings left to moulder away under the deal table. It would take a Herculean effort to create a semblance of cleanliness and order in this chaotic kitchen, but Peg was kindly and she was a good cook. A cot in the attic was preferable to sleeping in a shop doorway, and Stranks would never find her here. She looked up and met Peg's enquiring gaze with a smile. 'It's a fair offer, and I'll do my best.'

'That's settled then.' Peg refilled her cup with tea. 'You can make a start by peeling them spuds.' She pointed to a bulging sack under the window.

'All of them?' Lucetta said faintly.

Peg chuckled. 'Not unless you're expecting an army to come for their supper. You start peeling and I'll tell you when to stop.' She put her feet up on a stool. 'When you've done that you can chop up the beefsteak for the pies. Anyone can do that but it takes a proper cook to make pastry as light as mine.'

By the end of the day Lucetta was so exhausted that she could hardly put one foot in front of the other as she climbed the narrow staircase to the attic. The flickering pool of light from Peg's candle bobbed unsteadily ahead of her and the flame was almost extinguished by the draught from the open door.

'There's your bed,' Peg said, pointing to a narrow wooden cot set against the wall. 'You'll sleep without rocking tonight, girl, but I expect you up at six to clean the grate in the bar and get the fire going in the range. If you was a kitchen maid in one of them big houses you'd be up at five, so think yourself lucky. Sleep well.' She left the room, closing the door behind her.

Lucetta blinked as her eyes grew accustomed to the dim light filtering in through a small roof window. There was head height in the middle of the room only and she had to duck under the rafters in order to reach the bed. The bare boards creaked beneath her feet and she had no idea what lurked in the dark corners, but she was too tired to care and she fell, fully dressed, onto the lumpy mattress. Every bone in her body ached and her hands were chapped and raw. She felt the blisters bursting on her fingers as she pulled off her boots, but at least her stomach was full. Peg might be a hard taskmaster but she was generous with food, insisting that a person could not be expected to work on an empty belly. It was past midnight but the sounds of carousing from the bar filtered up two storeys to the attic, and there seemed to be a brawl going on in the street outside. Hysterical screams and shouts were accompanied by the scrape of hobnails striking the cobblestones, and the grunts of opponents as fists came into contact with soft flesh. Lucetta closed her eyes. At least she was safe up here beneath the eaves. She hoped that the illness which had laid poor Poppy so low was not catching, but she was really too tired to care very much. Despite everything, she drifted off to sleep.

She was lying with Sam beneath a champak tree in the consulate compound. The scent of the blossoms crushed beneath their warm bodies would linger in her memory forever. The soft touch of his hands on her bare flesh sent the blood racing through her veins and the taste of his mouth was achingly familiar. She could hear his voice whispering words of love in her ear, and she was in heaven.

'Get up, you lazy little trollop.'

Wrenched cruelly from her sweet dream, Lucetta opened her eyes to see Bob Potts towering over her. He tore the coverlet from the bed, staring down at her with an angry curl of his lips. 'You was hired to work not to laze about all day.' His dark eyes raked her bare legs where her skirt had ridden up past her knees.

The expression on his face both startled and alarmed her and she sat up in bed, cracking her head on a rafter.

'Bob!' Peg's voice cracked like a whip from the doorway.

He backed away from the bed, dropping the coverlet on the bare floorboards. 'I was just telling her to get her idle body out of bed, ducks.'

'I'll deal with her,' Peg said coldly. 'Your breakfast's on the table in the taproom. Cold beef and beer. I'll deal with our little princess.'

Bob shrugged his wide shoulders and shuffled past his wife without looking at her. His footsteps echoed on the wooden treads as he descended the steep stairs.

'I'm sorry,' Lucetta said, swinging her legs over the side of the low bed and reaching for her boots. 'I didn't mean to oversleep.'

'I'll let you off this once, being as how it's your first day, but you'd best be up and about afore my husband. He's got a mean temper when it's roused.'

Lucetta pushed her feet into the ill-fitting boots that Guthrie had bought for her in a dolly shop. 'I'm ready.'

Peg eyed her dispassionately. 'You look a mess, girl.' She jerked her head in the direction of a boxwood chest, the only other piece of furniture in the room. 'There's some of Poppy's duds in there. She's about your size.'

'Are you sure she won't mind?'

'Lor-a-mussy, girl. She ain't in no position to care one way or the other. I ain't telling you a second time. Change into something half decent and put your hair in a mobcap. We'll see about cleaning you up later, but it'll be the pump outside in the yard for you and a bar of carbolic soap when the morning rush is over.' Having made this pronouncement and leaving no doubt in Lucetta's mind that she meant business, Peg swept out of the room to follow her husband downstairs.

Lucetta eyed the chest doubtfully. It didn't seem right to take poor Poppy's clothes when her life hung in the balance, but it would be wonderful to feel clean linen next to her skin. She had to bend almost double to open the lid of the chest and she knelt on the floor to examine the contents, which were pitifully few. The smell of camphor was almost overpowering, but at least it seemed to have kept the moths at bay. She pulled out a coarse woollen skirt which was obviously Poppy's winter wear, together with a calico blouse in an indeterminate shade of grey. There was a clean although much-darned shift and, at the very bottom of the chest, a faded cotton-print dress and a white mobcap.

'Don't take all day about it,' Peg shouted from the bottom of the stairs. 'There's work to be done.'

Making as much haste as she could when hampered by sore fingers that fumbled painfully with buttons and laces, Lucetta donned Poppy's clothes. The garments fitted well enough although the faded print gown barely reached her ankles, but it would have to do. She made her way down to the kitchen.

'That's better,' Peg said, thrusting a besom into her hands. 'Now you look like a workhouse girl and we won't have no trouble from the customers taking liberties with you. You have to watch out for men when they've had too much to drink. When you take food into the bar, keep your eyes down and your trap shut.'

Lucetta stared at her in horror. What if by some unhappy chance Stranks or Guthrie should choose to drink at the Frog Inn? 'But I thought I was just working in the kitchen. You didn't say anything about going into the bar.'

'You'll do what you're told, Lucy Cutler. You ain't no lady's maid now. I can put you out on the street as soon as look at you and don't you forget it. Now sweep the floor like a good girl, and then you shall have some breakfast.'

All morning, Lucetta worked harder than she could have imagined possible. She swept and mopped the floors in the taproom as well as the kitchen and scullery. She prepared vegetables, washed dishes and hefted hods filled with fuel from the coal shed to the fire in the bar and the kitchen range, which seemed to need feeding every half-hour like an insatiable ravening monster. She scuttled in and out of the taproom, doing as Peg said and keeping her head down, but whether it was by accident or simply due to the confined space behind the bar she was uncomfortably aware that Bob brushed against her every time she attempted to get past him. Sometimes his hand strayed to touch her behind, although he withdrew it so quickly that she couldn't be certain whether or not it was deliberate. By the end of the midday rush, she was beginning to think that she had more to fear from the landlord of the Frog Inn than from the punters.

Having served the last customer with a meat pie and mash, Lucetta was allowed to sit down at the kitchen table with Peg and they finished up what was left of the food they had prepared that morning. Bob had taken his meal in the empty taproom and had gone out on business of his own, leaving Peg and the ancient potman, Charlie, to deal with any customer who might wander in on a quiet summer's afternoon.

'We don't get much passing trade,' Peg explained through a mouthful of bread and cold sausage. 'We get busy again when the workers knock off at six or seven, though there's not much call for food until later on and then it's mainly hot pies for the men to take home as a peace offering for spending their hard-earned wages on booze.'

'You work hard,' Lucetta said, mopping up the last of the gravy on her plate with a hunk of bread. 'Don't you ever get a day off?'

'Everyone works hard round here, ducks. If you don't work, you don't eat. It's as simple as that. You'll learn.'

'I have already,' Lucetta murmured, licking her fingers one by one. 'I'm very grateful to you for taking me in, Peg, but I must start looking for a more permanent position.'

'You won't find no better employers than us,' Peg said, frowning. 'I'd forget about being a lady's maid if I was you, Lucy. You're still young, but if you ain't careful you could end up on the streets. Life is hard in these parts, and that's a lesson you need to learn quick if you want to survive.'

Lucetta realised too late that she had said the wrong thing. She had no intention of staying any longer than was absolutely necessary, but it would have to do until she could find someone who remembered her as Lucetta Froy, or she had found a more suitable position.

'That's enough chat,' Peg said, pushing her plate away. 'Get these dishes washed and sweep the floor. I'm going to have a nap upstairs on me bed while Bob's out. Charlie will see to the bar and you, miss, can give yourself a good wash down in the yard while it's quiet. You smell worse than the drayman's horse, and that's saying something.'

Lucetta rose to her feet, hiding her blushes by stacking the dirty crockery. For a brief second she was glad that her mother had not lived to see her daughter's humiliation. To be upbraided for her lack of personal hygiene by a slattern such as Peg would have been less painful if it were untrue. Lucetta had not seen herself in a mirror since the night of the shipwreck, but her hair felt like tow and she knew she must look a sight. As she washed the last of the dishes in the stone sink, she gazed down at the greasy grey water thinking longingly of her bedroom at home. Every morning the maid had brought hot water to fill the violet-patterned china basin which stood on the wash-stand. Lined up against the tiled splashback were glass jars filled with sweet-smelling soft soap, made to the housekeeper's own special recipe, hand cream scented with rose petals and cut-glass bottles filled with cologne and attar of roses. She had taken it all for granted then, never thinking that this way of life might end. She sniffed, wiping her nose on her sleeve, and her eyes filled with tears. What had she come to? She did not even possess a handkerchief.

Suddenly she was angry. A cold white fury gripped her belly and she brushed away her tears. Uncle Bradley had robbed her of everything that was rightfully hers. Poor Papa would be turning in his grave if he knew what his wicked brother had done. She hiccuped on a sob as she realised that she did not even know where her parents were buried. Perhaps it would have been better if her memory had deserted her permanently. Her time spent in the fever hospital seemed like halcyon days compared to life since Stranks and Guthrie had claimed to be her brothers. She could see Mary's fresh face and sympathetic smile, and Dr Harcourt had been kind and considerate. For a moment Lucetta could not recall his name, but she seemed to remember that he and Mary had been related in some way. Cousins – that was what Mary had said. 'Come back and see us when you are fully recovered, Daisy,' Mary had cried as she waved goodbye.

Lucetta had almost forgotten Mary while she was imprisoned in the damp, disgusting basement room, but she remembered her now and she felt as if someone had just given her the most precious present of all. She had a friend. She jerked the plug from the sink and watched the filthy water as it gurgled away down the drain. She stacked the clean dishes on the kitchen dresser, and picking up the rough piece of towelling that Peg had given her, she went out into the yard with renewed hope in her heart. She would seek out Mary and enlist her help in proving her identity. But first she must wash away the dirt that seemed to have become ingrained in her skin, or Mary might not recognise her.

Taking a quick glance around her, Lucetta was reassured that no one could see her as she stripped off her clothing. The inn yard was shielded from public view by its own outbuildings and high brick walls. Double wooden gates were securely padlocked against intruders and those who might attempt to pilfer a barrel or two, and shards of broken glass were cemented into the top of the walls. The autumn sunshine filtered through a haze from smoking chimneys, and having stripped off her clothes Lucetta closed her eyes as she worked the pump handle. The chilly air made her bare flesh tingle and when she finally worked up the courage to duck beneath the gushing jet of cold water, the shock took her breath away. Peg had given her a sliver of green soap which smelt strongly of carbolic. It was a far cry from attar of roses, but it formed a lather of sorts when she rubbed it over her body and into her hair. She watched the grime leach off her body and trickle down her slender legs to form pools at her feet. She was chilled to the bone but she felt cleansed. Her spirit had been crushed but it had not been broken. She was still Miss Lucetta Froy of Thornhill Crescent. She was the legal heir to her father's estate, whatever that might be, and she was going to prove it if only for his sake. Once she had claimed her fortune she would be in a position to search for Sam, even if it took her to the other side of the world. She would find him and then . . .

The sun had gone behind a cloud and she sensed that someone was watching her. She spun round, folding her arms across her naked breasts.

Chapter Ten

Bob was standing in the shadows by the scullery door. His beard and moustache masked his expression, but to Lucetta he looked like a panther preparing to pounce on its unfortunate prey.

She reached for the towel and wrapped it around her slender body. She wanted to run but there seemed to be no way of escape: the gates were padlocked and Bob was blocking her only exit from the yard. They stood like statues, staring at each other for what seemed to her like an eternity. She willed him to go away or to break the dreadful silence that hung between them with an apology, but he might as well have turned to stone. She made a feeble movement with her hand and this seemed to bring him to his senses. Without a word, he turned his back on her and disappeared into the scullery.

As if on cue, the sun reappeared from behind the clouds and the yard was once again bathed in warmth and light. She leaned against the pump, controlling her erratic breathing with a supreme effort. Drying herself as best she could on the scrap of towelling, Lucetta pulled her shift over her head, followed by Poppy's faded print frock. She was shaking uncontrollably, even though there had been no spoken threat to her person, but her instincts screamed out a warning. Her doubts had been confirmed and she was certain that it was not safe to be alone with Bob Potts. Perhaps that was why Poppy had departed so suddenly. Maybe she was not in hospital after all, but had run away from her employer's lewd looks and grasping hands?

Lucetta slipped her wet feet into her boots and towelled her hair until it was almost dry. Her lips trembled as she realised that she did not possess something as basic and necessary as a comb. Once, not so long ago, her dressing table had boasted silver-backed hairbrushes and tortoiseshell combs. She had had maidservants to wait on her and parents who loved and cherished her, but that life was gone forever and she might never find the man to whom she had given her heart and soul. It was all gone like a puff of smoke. She clenched her fists. 'I will survive,' she whispered. 'I won't be bullied and browbeaten and I won't stay here a moment longer than I have to.' Holding her head high, she walked slowly across the cobbled yard. She paused outside the scullery. She was afraid, but she was not going to let Bob Potts see her fear. She took a deep breath and stepped inside.

There was no one in the scullery and the only person in the kitchen was old Charlie the potman who was sitting at the table drinking a cup of tea. He looked up as she entered the room and gave her a gummy grin. 'You're new here, ain't you?'

Lucetta could have rushed over and hugged him simply for not being Bob. 'I'm just here until Poppy gets better.'

Charlie pulled a face. 'She won't come back. She's gone to a better place.'

'Oh, the poor child. Is she dead?'

'Dead?' Charlie said, cackling with mirth. 'No, she run off, didn't she? She'll be working in one of them knocking-shops or gone back to the workhouse. Either way it'll be better than what she had here, but don't tell the guvner that I said so.'

This statement confirmed Lucetta's worst fears, but she managed a smile. 'Well, I won't be here long, Charlie. As soon as I find another position I'll be off too.'

'Good luck, girlie. I'm afraid you're going to need it.' Charlie rose hastily to his feet as Bob put his head round the door.

'Where's that barrel of ale you was supposed to be fetching? Hop to it, Charlie, or I'll find a younger bloke to take your place. This ain't a charity institution.' Bob glared at Lucetta. 'And you tidy yourself up. Where's Peg? She should be down here seeing that you don't laze about like that last little trollop. Get to work, the pair of you.'

That night, Lucetta heaved the pine chest into place across the door to the attic room. She knew that it would not stop a strong and determined man if he set his mind on entering, but it might make him think twice, and the noise would waken her from the deepest sleep. It was past midnight and she was bone weary. Peg had not allowed her to have a candle in her room in case she burned the place down, although Lucetta thought she was just being mean. Peg might appear to be open-handed but she was a thrifty housekeeper, and when Lucetta had asked if she might have an hour or two off one afternoon, the answer had been a firm negative.

Lucetta made her way to her bed, ducking her head so that she did not collide with the rafters. A storm was rumbling around outside and clouds had obscured the moon. It was hot and stuffy in the attic and the darkness was filled with the sound of tiny feet scrabbling about beneath the eaves. A sudden flash of lightning turned night into day and Lucetta collapsed onto the hard little cot. She pulled off her boots and slipped the frock over her head, laying it across the foot of the bed. She would make certain to be up early and fully dressed so that Bob had no excuse to come to her room.

She lay down, listening to the thunder as it rumbled around the city. She knew now that she was almost as much a prisoner here as she had been when held captive by Stranks and Guthrie, and she was a virtual slave. Peg had no intention of paying her other than with food and lodging, and she had denied her right to time off. Lucetta had begun to appreciate the fact that her parents had been good employers. All their servants from the stable boy to the housekeeper were entitled to one afternoon off a month, and paid the going rate for their work. No wonder Poppy had run away, she thought sleepily. She would not stay here a moment longer than was necessary. She closed her eyes and curled up in a ball. Mary woud help her. She must think of a way to contact Mary.

But it was not that easy. Lucetta was guarded more closely than the crown jewels. She was kept busy from early morning until late at night and she was never allowed out of the building even on the simplest errand. It seemed that the Potts had lost too many girls that way, Poppy being the last one to defect and take her chances in the outside world. Lucetta grew adept at avoiding Bob's clumsy advances, and Peg was constantly alert, watching her husband's every move.

As the days turned into weeks and autumn was overtaken by winter, Lucetta became more and more frustrated. She had written to Mary, and to her surprise Peg had agreed to post the letter, but when she received no reply Lucetta suspected that it had never reached the post office, let alone its destination at the fever hospital. The days became progressively colder and Lucetta's attic room was filled with icy draughts that kept her awake at night, shivering beneath the thin coverlet.

The cotton frock that had once belonged to Poppy was so worn that the pattern was no longer distinguishable and it had begun to fall apart at the seams. Lucetta had found a coarse linsey-woolsey skirt in the chest but it was theadbare, and would not last the winter. She had learned to sew a straight seam at Miss Milton's Academy, although most of their lessons had been devoted to the art of embroidery, but she was able to alter the garments that Stranks had brought to her at the hospital so that they now fitted reasonably well. Peg had given her a shawl but this was little protection against the bitter cold of early morning when Lucetta had to fetch water and coal from the yard. Chilblains were a constant torment and her calloused hands were cracked and bleeding by the end of each long day. She had not given up hope but she had learned to live with her situation, and she had formed a working relationship with Peg, who was easy-going unless provoked. It was Bob who gave her the most cause for concern. Outwardly jovial and an excellent mine host in the taproom, he continued to be a brooding sexual menace. Lucetta took care never to be alone in his company and for the sake of peace she said nothing to Peg about his groping hands or the way his eyes raked her body as if he were mentally undressing her. She hated every minute that she was forced to slave away in Frog Hall, as the locals called it, but even though beneath the surface she rebelled she tried to maintain an outward appearance of meek acceptance.

She watched and waited for the opportunity to slip unnoticed from the pub and it came unexpectedly one afternoon in early December, when Charlie was laid low with a chill and she was called upon to fill the coal scuttle in the taproom. The yard was slippery with a thin coating of ice and the first flakes of snow were tumbling from a grey featherbed of clouds. She tied her shawl around her shoulders and she hefted the heavy bucket, slipping and sliding as she staggered over the cobblestones. Snowflakes settled on the frilled edge of her mobcap, melting as she entered the kitchen and trickling down her face. The wet cotton flopped over her eyes, obscuring her field of vision so that she accidentally barged into a man standing by the bar.

'Look where you're going, you stupid trull.'

The voice was instantly recognisable and Lucetta dropped the bucket, spilling nuggets of coal all over the flagstones. Bob cursed her as he lifted the hatch and erupted into the taproom, apologising to the irate customer. He seized Lucetta by the arm, shaking her so violently that her mobcap fell to the floor and her long blonde hair tumbled about her shoulders.

'Bloody hell, it's you.'

The irate punter grabbed her by her free arm and she found herself in the middle of a tug of war between Bob and Norman Stranks.

'Let her go, mister,' Bob roared. 'This girl works for me.'

'Don't push me, mate,' Stranks growled, pulling even harder on Lucetta's arm.

'This is my pub.' Bob released Lucetta as he squared up to Stranks. 'No one tells me what to do in here.'

Stranks shoved Lucetta aside as he swung a vicious punch, aiming at Bob's jaw. She would have fallen but a strong arm caught her round the waist. 'I dunno what you're doing here, Lucy,' Guthrie muttered in her ear. 'I'd run for it if I was you.' He gave her a push towards the door which had just opened to admit a couple of burly draymen.

She needed no second bidding. She barged past the newcomers and escaped outside into the swirling snowstorm. She picked up her skirts and ran. There was only one place where she might find sanctuary and she headed in the direction of Liverpool Road. It was mid-afternoon but it was almost dark. The lamplighters had not yet reached this part of Islington, but Lucetta was more afraid of being pursued and caught than of what might linger in gloomy alleyways and narrow side streets. She slipped and fell several times, grazing her hands and knees, but she felt no pain. She ran and kept on running until she reached the imposing neo-classical buildings that constituted the London Fever Hospital. She had often passed this way in Papa's carriage, but she had never before come on foot. She made her way along the low brick walls topped by railings to the impressive wrought iron gate where gas lamps shone dully through a veil of snowflakes.

She tried to open the heavy gates, but she had used every last scrap of strength in her flight from Frog Hall and her legs gave way beneath her. She fell to her knees, clutching the ice-cold metal until it burned her chilled fingers. 'Let me in,' she sobbed. 'Oh, please let me in.'

'May I help you?'

With her hands still locked around the bars, she looked up. The voice was vaguely familiar but the man's face was in shadow. 'I c-can't open the g-gate. W-will you help me, sir?'

He bent down and attempted to help her to her feet. 'You will have to let go first, miss. I'm not strong enough to lift you and half a ton of metal.'

The humour in his voice was not lost on her, and she relaxed her grip. He held out his gloved hand and she grasped it like a drowning woman. He raised her gently and, supporting her weight with his free arm, he opened the hospital gate.

'Thank you, sir,' Lucetta whispered. 'I can manage now, I think.' She took a step forward and stumbled on the icy cobblestones. He was at her side in an instant and slipped his arm around her waist.

'Allow me to help you into the hospital. They will take care of you.'

'No, I'm not sick, sir. I am looking for a friend.'

'Well, whatever your business, we must get you inside before you catch your death of cold.'

Lucetta accepted his help and allowed him to lead her across the forecourt. As they entered the vestibule, which would have done justice to a Palladian mansion, Lucetta could not quite repress a shudder. The smell of disinfectant mixed with the slight odour of coal gas brought back hazy memories of the day when Stranks and Guthrie had claimed her as their sister.

'Here we are,' her companion said, taking off his top hat to reveal a head of thick, dark hair that seemed to have a life of its own, springing up in rebellious spikes where the application of Macassar oil had obviously failed to do its job. He stared at her, frowning. 'Are you sure you are not in need of medical attention?'

Lucetta recognised him instantly. 'Dr Harcourt. I thought I knew your voice.'

'Do I know you?'

'I was a patient here, doctor. I was admitted suffering from typhoid and you looked after me until I was well again. I came here looking for Miss Hastings; she was so kind to me.'

'That sounds like Mary,' he said, smiling. 'But she is not on duty today. I'm afraid you have had a wasted journey, Miss er . . . I'm afraid I can't recall your name.'

'I'd lost my memory and Nurse Hastings nicknamed me Daisy, but now I'm known as Lucy Cutler, although that isn't my real name. It's a long story.

'I can see that,' he said, staring curiously at her shabby attire. 'You speak like a lady, but if you'll forgive my saying so, you look as though you have fallen on hard times.'

'I have, sir, and that's why I came looking for Mary. I thought she might be able to help me.'

'I think you'd better sit down for a moment.' Giles Harcourt took her by the arm and guided her to a row of wooden chairs lined up against the wall. 'I only came to collect some books. Perhaps you'll allow me to see you home.'

Lucetta shook her head. 'I have nowhere to go, sir. I was hoping perhaps I could stay here for tonight.'

'Apart from the fact that it is strictly against hospital rules, you would risk infection from a number of deadly diseases.'

'Then I must look elsewhere.' Lucetta attempted to rise but her legs stubbornly refused to bear her weight and she sank back onto the hard seat.

'Have you any money?'

'No, sir.'

'That settles it. I cannot allow a young girl like you to tramp the streets in a blizzard. You'd be found frozen to death in a doorway or worse.'

'I'm seventeen, sir,' Lucetta said, realising that he thought her little more than a child. Her eyes filled with tears. 'Actually, I'm eighteen. I'd quite forgotten but today is my birthday.'

'Come now, there's no need to cry about it. I've had ten more birthdays than that and I'm still a cheerful fellow.' Giles thrust his hand into his coat pocket and pulled out a spotless white handkerchief. 'Dry your eyes, Miss Cutler. If you would care to wait here for a few minutes while I collect my books, I'll take you to Lonsdale Square where Mary lives. She'll look after you.'

Lucetta accepted the handkerchief with a grateful smile. She wiped her eyes and blew her nose, watching his tall figure as he crossed the encaustic-tiled floor to the wide stone staircase where he took the shallow steps two at a time. She buried her face in the hanky, inhaling the delightful scent of freshly laundered cotton dried outside in the frosty winter air. It was such a simple thing and yet it reminded her painfully of the home she had been denied by her devious uncle. As she waited for Giles to reappear, she decided that she would tell Mary everything. She had nothing to lose and everything to gain.

'Well!' Mary exclaimed, round-eyed with amazement. 'What a tale you have to tell, Daisy. Or should I call you Lucetta?'

Lucetta stretched her bare feet towards the fire blazing away in the grate. Steam rose from her damp skirts and her boots were visibly cracking as they dried out on the hearth. 'Lucetta is my real name and everything I've told you is true,' she said earnestly. 'You must believe me.'

'Oh, I do,' Mary cried, nodding vigorously. 'We both believe every word, don't we, Giles?' She turned her head to give her cousin a pleading glance as he sat beside her on the sofa.

'Of course I believe her,' Giles said thoughtfully. 'But

I cannot think that a man would deny his own brother's child in such a way. Maybe he didn't get a proper look at you, Lucetta. Perhaps he was scared off by those two villains who abducted you.'

'Yes, dear,' Mary added hastily as Lucetta opened her mouth to argue. 'You had been very poorly and your appearance might have changed considerably since he last saw you. Maybe you ought to give him another chance.'

Lucetta looked from one earnest face to the other. There was a striking likeness between them; they might have been brother and sister instead of cousins and they seemed to share an unshakeable faith in the innate goodness of their fellow human beings. She realised with a sense of shock that not so long ago she would have thought as they did now. The harsh experiences of the past few months had been a stark revelation after her protected and pampered upbringing. She had witnessed the worst of human nature and it had not been a pretty sight, but she had not the heart to tell them they were wrong. She twisted her lips into a smile. 'I hope what you say is true.'

Mary slid off the sofa to kneel at Lucetta's side. 'I'm sure it is, my dear. You've had a terrible time but that's all over now. You must stay here tonight and tomorrow we will all go to Thornhill Crescent and confront your uncle, won't we, Giles?'

He was silent for a moment. Twin furrows creased his brow and he shook his head. 'I think it might be better if I went to see Mr Froy on my own,' he said at length. 'It might save embarrassment all round if I presented him with the facts, and gave him time to get over the shock of having his niece restored to the family.'

'And I'm on duty all day,' Mary said, shaking her head. 'I'd almost forgotten. But I think Giles has a point. He might do better speaking to your uncle man to man.'

'You are very kind,' Lucetta murmured, brought close to tears by their unquestioning belief in her. 'But are you sure that your parents won't mind me staying here?'

'My father is visiting his constituency in Dorset and he will be away for another day or two,' Mary said, resuming her seat on the sofa. 'My mother died when I was three, so you see I am mistress of the house and I am inviting you to be our guest, but I can assure you that Papa would do the same if he were here.'

'I don't know how to thank you,' Lucetta murmured.

'I'm sure we'll think of something,' Giles said with a roguish twinkle in his eyes. 'When you are restored to your fortune you might like to make a generous contribution to the hospital funds, or donate a bursary for poor medical students.'

'Or a slap-up dinner for hungry nurses,' Mary said, giggling. 'But seriously, my dear Lucetta, you must have something to eat and then we'll go upstairs to my room where I'll sort out some fresh linen for you. I think perhaps those clothes have seen better days, and are not really suited to Miss Lucetta Froy of Thornhill Crescent.' She leaned over to tug at the bell pull. 'We'll have supper on a tray before the fire. Giles is always hungry so I know he won't refuse.'

'My cousin maligns me,' Giles countered with a good-natured grin. 'If you listen to Mary you will think

I have the appetite of a donkey and the manners of an ape, all of which is quite untrue.'

'Lucetta can be the judge of that,' Mary said, ruffling his already tousled hair. 'But you have the untidiest head in London, Dr Harcourt. You should see him before ward rounds, Lucy. He drenches his hair with Macassar oil and it still won't lie down. Sister Demarest has threatened him with the scissors many a time.'

Giles picked up a velvet cushion with long silk tassels and took a half-hearted swipe at her, but Mary was already on her feet and dodged his aim just as a prim-faced maid entered the room.

'Oh, Phyllis,' Mary said breathlessly. 'We'd like supper brought up on a tray. Please ask Cook to make it something special as we have a guest.'

Phyllis flicked a sideways glance at Lucetta but if she was surprised to see a bedraggled street girl sitting in her mistress's parlour, she was too well disciplined to allow it to show. She bobbed a curtsey. 'Yes, Miss Mary. Will there be anything else.'

'A bed for the night,' Giles suggested helpfully.

'For you, sir?' Phyllis's features relaxed into a genuine smile.

Mary shook her head. 'It's not for Mr Giles. My friend, Miss Froy, will be staying for a night or two. Please make up the bed in the room next to mine and tell the tweeny to light a fire in there, and make certain that the sheets are properly aired.'

'And bring a bottle of my uncle's best claret, Phyllis,' Giles added. 'It's Miss Froy's birthday and it shouldn't go unmarked.'

'Yes, sir. Will that be all?'

'And some glasses wouldn't go amiss.'

'Oh, sir,' Phyllis exclaimed, blushing. 'You are a one, sir.' She left the room in a flurry of starched white petticoats.

'Giles, you are such a tease,' Mary exclaimed, picking up the cushion he had just dropped and throwing it at him. 'Poor Phyllis, she never knows quite how to take your jokes.'

He caught the flying object deftly with one hand. 'Caught and bowled,' he said, laughing. 'I may not be the best doctor in the world, Lucetta, but I am an expert when it comes to the game of cricket.'

'And he is so modest too, Lucetta. He thinks he is perfect and I keep telling him that he is not. Someone has to keep his massive ego in check.'

Lucetta smiled at their playful badinage, but beneath it she still sensed that perhaps Mary's fondness for her cousin went a little deeper than familial affection. Whether or not Giles reciprocated her feelings was another matter, but he was an undeniably attractive man with an easy charm and an engaging sense of humour. Lucetta jumped as he reached out to touch her on the arm.

'Are we tiring you, Lucetta? I think we're forgetting that you've been through a terrifying ordeal.' There was no hint of mockery in his eyes, which were the colour of rich dark chocolate with a hint of honey.

She felt a lump rise in her throat and she swallowed hard before answering. 'I am a little tired, but I can't tell you how good it is to be here with both of you. I can hardly believe my good fortune. Any moment I think I might wake up and find myself back in that dreadful basement, or in the attic with snow blowing through gaps in the roof.'

'I can't bear to think of it,' Mary said with feeling. She held her hand out to Lucetta. 'I think we'd best get you a change of clothes before supper or you might end up with pneumonia.'

'Best hurry then,' Giles said, leaning back in his seat and closing his eyes. 'I might be tempted to eat your suppers if you spend too long upstairs.'

'Take no notice of him,' Mary said, pulling a face at her cousin. 'Giles is all talk, and if he doesn't behave I'll set Brutus on him.'

'A threat indeed,' Giles responded without opening his eyes. 'I'm terrified.'

'And so you should be.' Mary held the door open for Lucetta, closing it firmly behind them.

'Who is Brutus?' Lucetta asked, glancing anxiously up and down the hallway, half expecting a savage hound to come bounding up to them or at the very least a stern-looking family retainer.

Mary giggled. 'It's a joke. I was never allowed to have a dog as a pet. Papa thinks they are dirty unhygienic beasts and will not have one in the house. So I pretended that I had an Irish wolfhound puppy and I named him Brutus. I was an only child and he was very real to me. I used to threaten Giles with him when he teased me, but of course it was only a joke.' She led the way up the wide staircase that led to a galleried landing, and up another slightly less grand flight of stairs to the second floor. Gas lights flickered inside opalescent glass shades, casting a warm glow on the richly patterned wallpaper and reflecting in the gilt-framed mirrors and oil paintings that lined the wide corridor. A door was open at the far end, spilling light into the shadows at the end of the passage, and Lucetta caught the flash of a white pinafore as the tweeny and Phyllis made up the bed.

'That will be your room,' Mary said as she opened the door of the neighbouring bedchamber. 'This is mine. Come in and we'll see if I have anything which might fit you.'

Lucetta followed her into the large room, warmed by a coal fire and the glow of gaslight. The maids had obviously been busy in here also, as the bed sheets were turned down and a white lawn nightgown lay in readiness on the satin coverlet. Rose-pink velvet curtains were drawn across two tall windows and button-back chairs upholstered in similar material were placed strategically on either side of the white marble mantelpiece. Lucetta gazed round appreciatively at the simple yet elegant style of the armoire, dressing table and washstand made from glowing burr walnut. The scent of roses filled the room even though it was midwinter, and watercolours of birds and flowers adorned the walls. It was a lady's room and yet there were signs that Mary had not quite abandoned her childhood. A huge doll's house occupied the space between the two windows and two shelves were crammed with beautifully dressed dolls of all sizes. Their painted smiles never wavered and their glassy eyes seemed to stare at Lucetta as she hovered in the doorway, taking in the scene with a nostalgic and slightly envious pleasure.

'Come in,' Mary said, hurrying over to the armoire and opening the double doors. She began pulling out gowns, skirts and blouses and flinging them haphazardly onto the bed. 'Take your pick, Daisy. See if you can find something that will fit you, although you are so slender I fear they might all be too large.' She glanced at her own slim figure in the cheval mirror and frowned. 'I can get my waist down to twenty inches on a good day, with Phyllis tugging at the laces of my stays, but I'd say yours is closer to eighteen. I am quite jealous.'

Lucetta stared down at the fine fabrics in a rainbow of colours. She touched the material and the coarse skin on her work-worn fingers snagged the delicate silk. She shook her head. 'I can't take any one of these, Mary. They must have cost a small fortune and I have no way of repaying you.'

'Don't be a goose,' Mary scolded. 'I wouldn't think of accepting anything in return.' She delved amongst the garments and pulled one from the bottom of the pile, holding it up to the light. 'Now this is an old one. I haven't worn it for at least three years. In fact I don't know why it is still in my wardrobe.' She thrust the cornflower-blue silk gown into Lucetta's hands. 'I was about your age when I last wore this, and a little thinner, too. Try it on and see how it feels.' She turned away and began rummaging in one of the drawers. 'You will need a shift and some unmentionables, as well.' She selected the necessary undergarments and thrust them into Lucetta's hands. 'There, put these on. I won't look.'

She sat down on one of the chairs by the fire and picked up a fashion journal, flicking through the pages while Lucetta struggled out of her damp clothes.

The sheer luxury of having fine lawn next to her skin made Lucetta's spine tingle. She sniffed appreciatively at the scent of dried rose petals and lavender that permeated the soft fabric, and when she slipped the silk gown over her head she felt that she had died and gone to heaven. But she came back to earth with a bump as her sore fingers could not fasten the tiny pearl buttons and she let out a sigh of sheer frustration.

Mary dropped the magazine and leapt to her feet. 'What's the matter?'

'I can't do up the buttons,' Lucetta said, stifling a sob and holding out her hands for Mary to see.

'You poor thing,' Mary said with her own eyes brimming with tears. 'Let me help you and then we can go downstairs for supper. I don't know about you, but I'm starving.'

Giles rose to his feet as Mary entered the parlour first. 'Good God, what kept you? I was about to start without you . . .' His voice tailed off as Lucetta followed Mary into the room. His eyes widened and for once he seemed at a loss for words.

'What do you think, Giles,' Mary demanded, laughing. 'Doesn't Daisy look absolutely splendid?'

'Stunning! Absolutely stunning and her name is Lucetta.'

Lucetta felt the blood rush to her cheeks. 'It's a lovely gown. I can't thank you enough, Mary, and I really don't mind if you call me Daisy.'

'The name seems to suit you, my dear. And it's not the gown, Giles, it's the young woman who is wearing it,' Mary said, smiling happily. 'I knew it would suit you, Daisy. It brings out the colour of your eyes and complements your lovely golden hair, although if we had had more time I would have put it up for you. What do you think, Giles?'

'I think that all women with hair like Lucetta's should wear it just like that: hanging loose around their shoulders.' He drew up a chair. 'Won't you take a seat, Miss Froy?'

Lucetta was only too glad to sit down. Exhaustion both emotional and physical was almost overwhelming and she was faint with hunger. The food had been laid out on a dainty hexagonal tea table set in front of the fire. Lucetta gazed hungrily at the assortment of cold roast meats and a pie with a glistening golden-brown crust and her mouth watered.

Mary began serving the food while Giles poured wine into three glasses. He raised one in a toast. 'Happy birthday, Lucetta Froy. Tomorrow morning first thing I'm going to Thornhill Crescent to see your uncle. I'm certain that when he sees you looking like that he will have no difficulty in recognising you.'

Mary looked up from cutting into the pie. 'She must wear gloves though. No one would believe she was a young lady of fortune with those work-worn hands.'

'I doubt if a small detail like that would bother a man of intelligence,' Giles said confidently. 'Once I've explained everything I'm certain that Lucetta's uncle will welcome her with open arms.'

Chapter Eleven

'I'm so sorry, Lucetta,' Giles said, taking both her hands in his. 'I did my best but your uncle is a hard man. He simply wouldn't listen and kept insisting that he had identified the body and that his niece was buried alongside her parents.'

Lucetta stared down at their entwined fingers; his were the unblemished hands of a gentleman and hers, although tiny by comparison, were the hands of a scullery maid. She bit her lip to prevent herself from crying out in despair. She had dared to hope, but in her heart she had known that Uncle Bradley was an ambitious man who had always been jealous of her father's success in business and had resented being the junior partner. She realised now that he was dishonest as well as greedy and that there had been no mistake. He had deliberately chosen not to recognise her and he had no intention of allowing her to claim her inheritance.

She raised her eyes slowly to Giles' face and was touched to see a look of genuine concern in his eyes. 'I had no real hope, but thank you for trying.' Her voice broke on a sob and he released her hands to wrap his arms around her in a brotherly embrace.

'I really thought that I could convince him that you

had survived the shipwreck,' he murmured into her hair. 'Perhaps I was wrong in going there alone. If you were to accompany me next time . . .'

Lucetta drew away, turning her head so that he would not see the tears coursing down her cheeks. 'No, Giles. Thank you, but no. Mama always said that Uncle Bradley was a devious man, and I knew that she did not like Aunt Eliza, although she never said as much, but when you are a child you sense these things . . .'

Giles pressed a clean handkerchief into her hand. 'I don't know what to say, Lucetta. I believe your story absolutely, but it will be almost impossible to prove who you are unless you can find reputable witnesses who would swear to your identity.'

Lucetta sank down on the chair where she had sat the previous evening while they drank a birthday toast. Her hopes had been high then, but now as the cold grey light of a snowy morning filtered through the windowpanes in the Hastings' parlour, she knew she must face reality. She blew her nose and wiped her eyes. 'We were away for almost a year and before that I was a boarder at Miss Milton's Academy in Highbury, just a schoolgirl. The servants would know me, but I expect Uncle Bradley has thought of that and has sent them packing. I certainly didn't recognise his footman, and I can only assume that Mama's maid perished when the *Caroline* sank.'

Giles took a seat opposite her. 'Perhaps a visit to the shipping company would help. If the captain or any of the ship's officers were among the survivors they would be able to testify in your favour.'

Lucetta felt herself blushing as she thought of Sam, but their brief time together in Bali had taken on a dream-like quality. That whirlwind romance might have happened to another girl, living in a different world. The reality was here and now, but the one thing she did know was that the loss of her home and fortune would pale into insignificance if she were to be reunited with the man she loved. She nodded in agreement. 'Yes, Captain Sharpe and the ship's officers would know me.'

'Then we must find out if the captain was amongst the survivors.' Giles glanced at the ormolu clock on the mantelshelf. 'Unfortunately I have to return to the hospital at midday and will be on duty for thirty-six hours or even longer, but I believe Mary has some time off tomorrow. She would be more than willing to accompany you to the shipping office.'

'I'm not afraid to go out alone, Giles.'

'I wouldn't advise it. Anyway, the roads are treacherous. You would do far better to stay indoors today and rest.'

His expression was so serious that Lucetta could not resist teasing him. 'Is that your professional opinion, doctor?'

This brought the twinkle back to his eyes. 'Both professional and personal. Try not to worry, Lucetta. Mary and I will do everything in our power to help you establish your identity.'

'But what about Mary's father? What will he say when he finds a penniless orphan foisted upon him?'

'Uncle Hector is a good man, despite being a politician. He will understand and may even be persuaded to take up your cause, so you have no need to worry on that score.' With a reassuring smile, Giles patted her hand. 'Now, I really must go or Sister Demarest will report me to my superiors and I will be in trouble.'

'Thank you, Giles,' Lucetta said softly. 'I am truly grateful for everything you and Mary have done for me.'

He hesitated for a brief moment, meeting her earnest gaze with an unreadable expression in his dark eyes, and then he turned away abruptly and left the room.

Lucetta ran to the window and watched him as he walked down the front path and opened the gate leading into the square. He hailed a passing cab and was gone, but she could still see his footsteps in the freshly fallen snow. She shivered as a cold draught forced its way between the sash-window frames and she wrapped Mary's cashmere shawl more closely around her shoulders. Turning away from the monochrome wintry scene, she went to warm herself by the fire. She stared into the leaping orange and yellow tongues of flame as they licked around the shiny lumps of coal and caressed the fireback, setting alight the tiny flecks of soot which clung there. The intense heat reminded her of Bali and in her mind she crossed the thousands of miles of ocean.

She closed her eyes as she conjured up the precious images of Sam from the moment they had met at the temple until their tearful parting on the quay. But at least a merciful providence had spared him from drowning in the polluted waters of the Thames. Giles' words rang in her head and now the answer seemed blindingly obvious. She must go to the shipping office and make enquiries as to Sam's whereabouts now. He had been due to return on the *Louisa*, the *Caroline's* sister ship, and he might even be on leave in London at this very moment. She clutched her hand to her bosom, hardly able to breathe. If that was so, Sam would have been told of her demise. He would think she had been buried in the cold earth and was lost to him forever.

She turned away from the fire and moved swiftly to the chair where she had left the reticule that Mary had given her before leaving for the hospital that morning. She opened the embroidered silk purse and tipped its contents into the palm of her hand. Mary had insisted that Lucetta might need some money for essentials, and she had been more than generous. Having counted the coins, Lucetta was satisfied that she had enough for a cab fare to Wapping Wall where the offices of the Far Eastern Shipping Line were situated. She would need to borrow some outdoor garments from Mary's wardrobe, but she did not want the servants to think that she had taken them without permission. She decided to brave the redoubtable Phyllis and she reached out to tug the bell pull. She paced the floor while she waited, reminding herself that she was Miss Lucetta Froy of Thornhill Crescent and she was used to giving orders to servants. 'Come in,' she said firmly in answer to a knock on the door.

Phyllis entered the room, standing stiffly to attention. 'You rang, miss?'

'I have to go out and Miss Mary said I might borrow a cloak and bonnet.'

'Very well, miss.'

Lucetta breathed a sigh of relief as the door closed behind Phyllis. So far so good. She had not expected it to be that easy.

The cab drew up outside the shipping office in Wapping Wall. 'Wait for me please, cabby,' Lucetta said as she alighted from the vehicle. Without waiting for his reply she made her way carefully through the ankle-deep slush. A bell jangled as she entered the office, closing the door carefully behind her. She paused as her eyes grew accustomed to the gloom of the oak-panelled room with its high counter and walls lined with hard wooden seats. A coal fire smouldered in a grate but its feeble glow gave off little heat, and the candles in the wall sconces guttered, almost extinguished by the draught of ice-cold air that had followed her in from the street.

The clerk perched on a high stool behind the counter was wearing a muffler and mittens and the tip of his nose was cherry-red. 'May I help you, miss?' His nasal voice had a rasp to it which suggested that he was suffering from a head cold, and he peered at her with watery red-rimmed eyes. 'If it's your allotment you're after we don't pay out until midday Saturday.'

Lucetta shook her head. 'No, I came for information only.'

'If it's sailing times you want, then they're posted up on the board,' he said, jerking his head in the direction of the wall behind his head.

'No, that's not it either,' Lucetta said, forcing herself to be patient. After all, the poor fellow looked as though he ought to be at home tucked up in bed with a stone hot water bottle at his feet. 'What I wanted to know was if you have a list of survivors from the wreck of the *Caroline*?'

'I'm not at liberty to give out such information.'

'I just want to know whether Captain Sharpe was amongst the survivors.'

'I can say that he was, miss.'

'And do you know where I might find him?' Lucetta held her breath, waiting for his answer.

'In the mad house, miss. Sadly the captain lost his mind completely and had to be locked away for his own safety.'

Lucetta stared at him in disbelief and horror. The man she remembered had seemed like a tower of strength; she could not imagine him collapsing either mentally or physically. 'But the other officers, did they survive?'

'No, miss. Sadly not. Although I believe the first mate was not on board at the time of the tragedy.'

'That would be Mr Cutler.'

The clerk took a ledger from beneath the counter and leafed through its pages. 'Yes, miss. He arrived back in London on board the *Louisa* at the end of June.'

'And his whereabouts now?' Lucetta gripped her

gloved hands together so tightly that she felt her knuckles crack. She hardly dared to breathe as she waited for him to search for the information.

'Mr Cutler was paid off. He is no longer in the employ of the Far Eastern Shipping Line. I can't help you any further. Good day, miss.'

'You must have his home address on your books.'

'Like I said before, miss, I'm not at liberty to give out such information. Now I must ask you to leave as I need to speak to the shipping manager.'

Tucking the ledger beneath his arm, he slid off the stool and was about to open the door directly behind him when Lucetta called him back. 'Wait, please. I am desperate to find Mr Cutler. Can you not stretch a point just this once? I would not ask if it were not so desperately important to me.'

'Like that is it?' The clerk pulled a red and white spotted handkerchief from his pocket and sneezed into it. Wiping his nose, he eyed Lucetta's waistline. 'You don't look very far gone, but then we all know what these boys are like when they come ashore.'

Lucetta's cheeks burned but she made no attempt to hide her blushes. She met the clerk's gaze with a beseeching look. 'Please, sir, have pity on a poor girl.'

He stuffed the handkerchief back in his pocket and replaced the ledger on the counter top. 'Well, if I am called away on business and you are overcome by curiosity, I daresay I can't be blamed.' He opened the inner door and left the office without a backward glance.

Lucetta seized the leather-bound volume and flipped

through the pages, peering at the lines of neat copper-plate writing. She ran her finger down the entries beginning at *A* for Adams, until she came to *C* for Carson, Carter, Clarke and finally *Cutler, Samuel, first mate. Cutler's Boatyard, Union Street, Salcombe, Devonshire.* Lucetta did not need to write the address down. It would be engraved on her heart forever. She closed the ledger and hurried out to the waiting and extremely irritable cabby, who complained that he would have to charge her double for keeping his horse standing about in such inclement weather. She could not have cared less. If it took all the money in her purse it would have been worth it to discover Sam's address, even if he lived at the far end of the country. She had no idea how she would get to Devonshire but if there was no alternative, she was prepared to walk all the way.

'No, absolutely not,' Mary said firmly. 'That is utter folly.'

'But I love him, Mary. Sam would have been told that I had drowned with the rest of the unfortunates on board the *Caroline*. The clerk said that he had been paid off and I can only assume he would have gone home to Salcombe.'

Mary stopped brushing her long dark hair and she turned her head to give Lucetta a direct look. 'You have no proof of that. He might have signed up for a voyage with another shipping company. He could be anywhere in the world by now. After all, it is almost six months since he learned of your unhappy fate.'

Lucetta swung her legs as she perched on the edge of Mary's bed. 'His family must live at that address, and they'll know where he is. I will find him, Mary.'

'Then write him a letter. Send it to his home. You could have a wasted journey if you travel all that way on the off chance, and you may even learn something that will break your heart.'

Lucetta leapt to her feet. 'What do you mean by that?'

'He might have had a sweetheart waiting for him in Devonshire. You knew him for such a short time, and if he believed that you were lost to him, he might even have married.'

Lucetta covered her ears with her hands. 'No. No, I won't believe that. Sam loved me as desperately as I loved him. He would never have betrayed me in such a way.'

'He is a man, Daisy. And you were supposed to have been dead and buried. Write that letter, I beg of you. Stay here with us until you hear one way or the other.'

'I know what you say makes sense, but I can't bear to sit around doing nothing.'

'Papa will be home tomorrow. Maybe he can help you trace Sam, and in any event he will be able to give you much better advice than I. Please reconsider. Wait just another day before you make any rash decisions.'

'I don't know,' Lucetta said, pacing the floor. 'I just don't know what to do for the best.'

'Write to him,' Mary said firmly. 'Phyllis will take the letter to the post office first thing in the morning, and in the meantime, perhaps we ought to pay a visit to your old school. The teachers there are certain to remember you, and with their testimony as proof of your identity I'm sure Papa will take up your case. Your uncle would be forced to recognise you and you would be restored to your home and your rightful inheritance. Think what your papa would have wanted for you, Lucetta.'

'You're right, I suppose.' Lucetta sank down on the window seat, staring out onto the gaslit square. Moonlight reflected off the fallen snow, turning the railed gardens into a fairyland of sparkling whiteness.

Mary rose from the dressing stool and came to sit by Lucetta's side, taking her cold hand in a warm grasp. 'The snow makes everything look clean and beautiful, doesn't it?'

Lucetta nodded wordlessly. Her head ached almost as much as her heart and she drew her hand away, staring down at her calloused palms. 'Perhaps I could wait until after Christmas.'

'Your hands will heal and I doubt if Sam would care anyway,' Mary said, smiling gently. 'Go downstairs and write that letter or you won't get a wink of sleep tonight.'

Lucetta threw her arms around Mary and hugged her. 'You are so good to me. I can't think what I have done to deserve friends like you and Giles.'

'I can't speak for my cousin, but I've always wanted a sister and there was something appealing about you, Daisy, even when you were so very ill in hospital. I knew then that you were a special person.'

'Don't, Mary. You'll have me in tears if you go on like that.'

'I'm not working tomorrow so we'll take a cab to Highbury and pay a call on Miss Milton. Then we can present my father with the facts of the matter.'

Next morning, Phyllis was sent off to the post office with the letter that had taken Lucetta half the night to compose. She had thought it would be easy to put her thoughts and emotions onto paper, but when she was faced with a blank sheet the words would not flow. The Sam Cutler she had known in Bali seemed to be worlds away from the son of a boat builder in Devon, and for the first time she was assailed by doubts. Would he remember her as fondly as she remembered him? And if they did meet again, would he love a homeless and penniless girl who could bring nothing to their marriage other than herself?

'Stop worrying,' Mary scolded as they settled themselves inside the hansom cab, having given the driver instructions to take them to Miss Milton's Academy in Highbury. 'Nothing will have changed if Sam really loves you.'

Lucetta nodded, staring down at her gloved hands. 'It's been a long time since we were in Bali. Perhaps it was just a flirtation on his part. The clerk in the shipping office seemed to think that girls like me are abandoned all the time. He thought that I was . . .' She hesitated. 'You know what I mean, Mary.'

'Then shame on him,' Mary said, chuckling. 'Anyone with half a brain can see that you are an innocent.

Giles said as much the other day and he has plenty of experience with young ladies.'

Lucetta stared at her in surprise. 'Is Giles a flirt then?'

'No. Well, not more than any other good-looking man of his age, but he has three younger sisters, so he is used to tears and tantrums and broken hearts. You will meet the Misses Harcourt on Christmas Day when we go to their house for dinner.'

'No, really, I can't. I mean, they don't know me.'

'Nonsense, Daisy. Giles will have told them all about you and they will be longing to hear your romantic story. They are nice girls really and they won't bite.'

Lucetta was not convinced. She lapsed into silence, staring out of the window at the snow-covered streets and pedestrians muffled to the eyes against the cold as they went about their daily business. Steam rose from horses' sweating hides and their breath curled up around their heads in clouds. Crossing sweepers worked extra hard to keep the roads free from the slush mingled with horse dung and straw, and ragged urchins hung about on street corners, begging for money. Lucetta shuddered at the sight of their pathetic bare limbs turning blue with cold and their haunted eyes that seemed too large for their pinched faces. She recalled her flight from Frog Hall when she had stumbled through the snowstorm with nothing more than a thin shawl to keep her warm and dry, and she wished that she could do something to help the poor and needy. But for the grace of God and the kindness of Giles and Mary, she would be living on the streets now.

She closed her eyes, shutting out the sight of a carter beating his ancient nag that had fallen to its knee between the wooden shafts of a wagon that was too heavy for it to pull. She closed her ears to the cries of a woman being beaten by a ruffian who no doubt claimed to be her legal spouse. No one went to her aid. Passers-by crossed the street so that they did not get involved.

It was a relief when the cabby finally drew his horse to a halt outside the imposing building in Highbury Crescent where Lucetta had spent most of her childhood. As she stepped down from the cab she felt an almost overwhelming wave of sadness. The first time she had arrived here it had been in the family carriage with her father, who had accompanied her into the building to make sure that Miss Milton received his daughter cordially. He had not left until he was satisfied that the strait-laced headmistress had grasped the fact that his only child was to be treated with kindness and respect. Papa had not believed in the use of corporal punishment for young ladies, but he had been a strict disciplinarian as well as a loving parent. Lucetta's heart was heavy with guilt as she remembered the terrible night when he had suffered a stroke after finding her in the consulate garden with Sam. Papa might be alive now if they had not made that fateful voyage on the *Caroline*. She jumped as Mary laid a hand on her arm.

'It must be hard on you, Daisy, but I'm afraid we will perish from cold if we stand here much longer simply staring up at the building.'

'Of course,' Lucetta murmured, hurrying towards the school gate. 'They will know me here. Of course they will.'

'Are you sure this is your old school?' Mary asked, pointing to the signboard which nestled amongst the laurels in the garden. 'It says *Principal, Miss Martha Shannon*. Didn't you say that the headmistress was Miss Milton?'

Lucetta frowned. 'This is the right place. I should know; after all, I spent eight years of my life here.'

'Best knock on the door, Daisy. There must be someone who will remember you.'

Lucetta rapped on the knocker and waited, holding her breath in anticipation of seeing a familiar face. Would it be Maisie or Ada who opened the door? They had been maids at the school when she first started and had been little more than children themselves, having been selected by the redoubtable Miss Milton from the Foundling Hospital. Lucetta recalled how Maisie, who could not have been much more than twelve or thirteen at the time, had comforted her when she had cried for her mother, and had wiped her tears away on the corner of her apron. She hoped it would be Maisie who opened the door, but it was a stranger who faced them with an incurious expression on her plain face.

'School's closed for the holidays.'

Lucetta placed her foot over the threshold as the girl seemed about to shut the door in their face. 'I've come to see Miss Milton.'

'She's left.'

'Then I'd like to see Miss Shannon.'

'Have you got an appointment?'

'No, but I used to be a pupil here.'

Reluctantly, the girl allowed them into the vestibule. 'What name shall I say?'

'Miss Lucetta Froy.'

'Wait here then, and don't touch nothing.' The girl scuttled off into the dim recesses of the entrance hall and her footsteps echoed eerily off the high ceilings.

'It's very quiet,' Mary whispered. 'Do all the girls go home for the holidays?'

'Some of them used to stay, particularly if their fathers were in diplomatic service or the army and lived abroad.'

'That must have been hard for them.'

'It was, particularly for the younger girls. My best friend's father was a senior government official in Delhi. Serena hardly saw her parents during her school years, but she had a grandmother living in a castle in Scotland.' Lucetta turned at the sound of approaching footsteps, but it was not the maid who came towards them, but an older woman wearing a black bombazine dress with a starched white collar and cuffs.

'Miss Froy?'

'Yes, ma'am.'

'I am Miss Shannon, the principal. How may I help you?'

Lucetta exchanged wary glances with Mary. Miss Shannon did not look like the sort of person for whom help was a byword. She cleared her throat. 'I was a pupil here and I wanted to see Miss Milton, but I understand that she has left.'

'Quite so. Miss Milton took early retirement due to ill health.'

'I'm sorry to hear it. Her illness must have been quite sudden. She always seemed to be the picture of health.'

'Who can tell? Now if that is all, Miss Froy, I am rather busy.'

'Miss Jones, then. Is she here?'

Miss Shannon shook her head. 'I do not know that person. She is not in my employ.'

'But Miss Jones was the English teacher.'

'She may have been then, but she is not here now. I'm afraid you have had a wasted journey.'

Miss Shannon turned on her heel and began to walk away but Lucetta ran after her.

'No, wait, please. It's less than two years since I was here. There must be someone here who would remember me.'

'Perhaps, although I doubt it. My teachers are all hand-picked by me, and most of Miss Milton's staff decided they would prefer to find work elsewhere,' Miss Shannon said, eyeing her coldly.

'Can you tell me where I might find them? Miss Parkin, for instance. She took us for art and needlework. Then there was Miss Brown who taught music . . .'

'As I said, they are no longer in my employ. Now I really must ask you to leave.'

Lucetta was desperate. 'Serena Daubenay was my

particular friend. She was a pupil here. Could you give me her address?'

Miss Shannon stiffened. 'It is not my policy to give information to anyone other than close relations. Good day, Miss Froy.' She swept off with a rustle of starched petticoats, leaving a strong scent of eau de Cologne in her wake.

Lucetta turned to Mary who had been standing quietly by the door. 'I don't believe her, Mary. There is something very wrong here.'

'Is it possible that your uncle could have a hand in this?' Mary asked in a low voice. 'Do you think he would go that far?'

'I don't know. I simply don't know.'

The sound of brisk footsteps made them turn their heads, but it was just the young maidservant who approached them. She opened the door with a flourish. 'Mistress says good day to you, ladies.'

With a last long look at the school which had been such a large part of her life, but where all knowledge of her existence seemed to have been eradicated, Lucetta stepped outside into the biting cold. She shivered as the door closed on them. 'No one knows me, Mary. It's as if I never existed.'

'There must be a logical explanation,' Mary said through chattering teeth. 'The most important thing at the moment is to find a cab to take us home. Judging by those clouds, it's going to snow again any moment now.'

'Look, there's one dropping off a fare,' Lucetta cried, running down the stone steps and out through the gate. She waved frantically to attract the cabby's attention. 'He's seen me. Come along, Mary.'

The cab drew to a halt at the kerb. 'Wapping High Street, please, cabby.' Lucetta picked up her skirts and climbed inside, leaving Mary no alternative but to follow her.

'I thought we were going home,' Mary protested. 'What is there at Wapping?'

'My father's warehouse,' Lucetta said, closing the folding wooden doors as the cab moved forward. 'Most of the employees have known me since I was a child. I wonder I didn't think of it before.'

'But your uncle owns the business now. If he has seen fit to put pressure on Miss Shannon, don't you think he will have done the same thing to those who work for him?'

'Perhaps, but it's my last chance to prove my identity. Pa's clerk, Tommy Hall, has known me all my life. He wouldn't be afraid of Uncle Bradley. And there's Jim Jenkins, one of the warehousemen, who was my father's first employee. I don't doubt his loyalty to Pa. Either or both of them will speak up for me, I'm sure of it.'

Chapter Twelve

'Tommy Hall retired a month ago, miss.'

Lucetta stared at the unfamiliar face behind the desk in the office of Henry Froy, Importers and Shippers, only now the name in gold above the door had been changed to Bradley Froy and Son. 'Are you certain about that? I mean, Tommy didn't seem that old to me.'

'He was forgetting things, miss. Mislaying bills of lading and other important documents. Mr Froy had to let him go.'

'Can you give me his home address then,' Lucetta said urgently. 'It's very important.'

The clerk shook his head. 'I believe Tommy went to live with his sister in the country, but I don't know where. I'm sorry, miss. I can't help you.'

Lucetta leaned over the counter. 'Let me speak to someone else who might know where I can contact him. Pip, the office boy, knew Tommy well.'

'Pip proved unsatisfactory, miss. He left about the same time as Tommy.'

'Jim Jenkins then,' Lucetta said urgently. 'Jim has worked in the warehouse for years.'

'I don't know anyone of that name, miss.'

Lucetta stared at him in disbelief. 'What is your name, sir?'

'Perks, miss. I've only been here a short time. I believe everything changed after the tragedy, but you must know all about that if you're a friend of the family.'

'Yes, I do, which is why I'm here. Is there anyone who was here in the old days when Mr Henry Froy ran the business?'

Perks' face lit up in a genuine smile. 'Yes, miss. Mr Jeremiah manages the warehouse. Perhaps he could help you?'

Lucetta opened her mouth to disagree, but Mary plucked at her sleeve. 'I don't think this is helping, Daisy. We'd best leave.'

Lucetta glanced over her shoulder as a tall, broad-shouldered man entered from the warehouse.

'Having trouble, Perks?' He rolled his sleeves up, glaring at Lucetta and Mary beneath lowered brows.

'I'm sure the young persons are about to vacate the premises, Ned,' Perks said nervously. 'There'll be no need for brute force, will there, ladies?'

Lucetta realised that she had little choice. This was not the time for heroics. 'We're going,' she said, taking Mary by the arm.

'Sorry I can't be of help, miss,' Perks called after them.

The door slammed behind them and once again they were outside in the bitter cold. Large flakes of snow were tumbling around them like feathers from a burst mattress.

'That proves it,' Lucetta cried angrily. 'Now I know that my uncle is at the back of all this. He must have sacked everyone who was loyal to my papa. I wouldn't be surprised if he engineered the collision that dreadful night. He is a nasty, evil man and quite ruthless.'

'That big fellow is watching us through the window,' Mary said nervously. 'We'd best start walking, Daisy. I don't fancy meeting him in a dark alley.'

Lucetta suppressed a shudder. 'Me neither. If we walk towards the Thames Tunnel we might find a cab in the High Street. I hope we do because my boots are leaking and I can't feel my feet.'

It was quite dark by the time they reached home. Snowflakes swirled around the street lamps, appearing to dance upwards in the yellow beams before floating softly to the ground. The rumble of the cab wheels and the clip-clop of the horse's hooves were muffled by the thick icy carpet covering the cobblestones, and Lucetta's booted feet crunched on the frozen surface as she and Mary made their way up the path to the front door. It opened as if by magical command.

'I saw the cab stop outside, miss,' Phyllis said by way of explanation. 'I thought it might have been the master.'

'I hope he won't be delayed by this awful weather,' Mary said, stepping into the light and warmth of the entrance hall. She took off her bonnet and cloak, handing them to Phyllis. 'Is there a fire in the morning parlour?'

'Yes, Miss Mary, and one in the drawing room too.' Phyllis held her hand out to take Lucetta's damp outer garments. 'I posted your letter, miss. Although I doubt if it will get there until the snow clears. The roads outside of London are blocked, so the post office clerk said.'

'Yes, thank you, Phyllis.' Mary glanced over her shoulder as she opened the parlour door. 'We'll take tea now if you please, and some of Cook's seed cake would be nice.'

'Yes, Miss Mary.' Phyllis shot a look of silent disapproval at Lucetta as she went off to do Mary's bidding.

'She doesn't approve of me,' Lucetta said, making a face as her feet squelched inside her sodden boots. 'And who could blame her? I turn up on your doorstep a penniless girl whom no one remembers. I'm beginning to doubt my own identity.'

'Don't let them upset you, Daisy.' Mary perched on the edge of a chair close to the hearth and held her hands out to the blaze. 'Come and sit down. It really doesn't matter what Phyllis thinks.'

'You see,' Lucetta said, taking the seat opposite her, 'even you call me by the name you gave me in hospital when I had lost my memory. It's as if Lucetta Froy never existed.'

Mary's eyes clouded with concern. 'Don't talk like that, Dais— I mean, Lucetta. I'm so sorry. I won't call you Daisy if it upsets you.'

'No, it's I who should apologise.' Lucetta tugged off her sodden boots, stretching her chilled feet out towards the fire. 'You have been kindness itself. I don't know what I would have done if you had not taken me in.'

Mary reached across to pat her hand. 'You'll feel better when you're warm and dry and have had something to eat. I had quite forgotten about food but we missed luncheon and I for one am extremely hungry.'

'I was so convinced that Miss Milton would be there,' Lucetta murmured. 'I can't believe that she retired of her own free will and the same goes for Tommy Hall and Jim Jenkins; in fact all the men who were in my father's employ. None of them would have left willingly.'

Mary opened her mouth as if to reply, but she closed it again, angling her head to listen. She leapt to her feet and ran to the window. 'I thought I heard the sound of horses' hooves. It's Papa. Thank goodness, he's home safely.' She crossed the room to open the door, almost bumping into Phyllis who was balancing a tray on her knee whilst attempting to let herself into the room.

Mary took the tray from her. 'The master has arrived, Phyllis. I'll take this; you go and let him in and bring another cup and saucer.' She set the tray down on a side table. 'Now you'll meet my pa, Lucetta. He'll know what to do for the best.' With a happy smile wreathing her face, Mary hurried out to meet her father.

Lucetta visualised the scene with a lump in her throat, for hadn't she greeted her own father with just as much enthusiasm on so many occasions in the past when he had returned from one of his trips abroad? His clothes had borne the inevitable travel stains and had smelt of steam engines, leather squabs and stale tobacco, but in his pockets he had concealed small packages containing little gifts for her: necklaces made from exotic seashells, fans painted with foreign flowers and ladies in brightly coloured kimonos, or tiny wooden or ivory carvings of animals and fishes. She had kept them all in a box beneath her bed. She wondered who slept in her old room now and if they had found her treasures.

The door opened and she stood up, attempting to conceal her bare feet beneath the damp hem of her dress as Mary entered the room followed by a tall, distinguished-looking gentleman who came towards her holding out his hand. 'How do you do, Miss Froy. As you must have guessed, I am Hector Hastings, Mary's father.'

'Sir Hector,' Lucetta said, bobbing a curtsey. 'I hope you don't mind . . .'

He silenced her with a wave of his hand. 'My dear, I don't in the least. Mary has given me a brief outline of your story, and I look forward to hearing the rest from you, but only after I have had time to enjoy a cup of tea and a slice of Cook's seed cake.' He sat down in the wingback chair close to the fire, accepting a cup of tea from Mary with a grateful smile. 'Thank you, my dear. I can't tell you how relieved I am to be home. The journey from Dorset seemed interminable and several times I thought we would be stuck in a snow-drift or that the carriage would slide off the road and I would have to spend an uncomfortable night in a hedge.' He took a sip of tea. 'Excellent. Now, Miss Froy, please tell me your story from the beginning.'

Lucetta swallowed a mouthful of seed cake. Mary had been right; it was delicious and the tea had refreshed her flagging spirits. Sir Hector might be an important politician but he was not the unapproachable martinet that she had imagined him to be, quite the contrary. He was a man in his middle years, not handsome, but good-looking in an intellectual way with a high forehead and piercing blue eyes that sparkled with a youthful zest for life. She found it quite easy to tell him everything, from the events leading up to the tragic sinking of the *Caroline* to the humiliation of being evicted from her papa's former office in Wapping High Street.

Mary refilled her father's cup. 'It would appear that Mr Bradley Froy is at the bottom of all this, Father.'

'That is a grave charge, Mary. The apparent disappearance of the people who would know Lucetta could be purely coincidental.'

'And very convenient, Papa,' Mary said, resuming her seat. 'What do you say, Daisy?'

'If only my uncle would see me, I'm sure we could come to some arrangement. I really don't care about the business or the money, but I want to be me again.' Lucetta stared down at her hands clasped tightly together in her lap. She heard her voice break with emotion and she could not bring herself to meet Sir Hector's gaze. He might think she was an imposter too, and all her hopes would be dashed.

He cleared his throat. 'You said that my nephew had paid a call on your uncle, is that correct?'

Lucetta nodded her head. 'Yes, sir.'

'Giles has been very good, Papa,' Mary said hastily.

216

'He would have done more but you know what dreadfully long hours he keeps at the hospital.'

'As do you, my dear girl. I am still not happy about you working there, or working outside the home at all if it comes to that. But we won't speak of such matters now. What is more important is to help Lucetta regain her rightful place in society.'

'What will you do, Papa?' Mary asked anxiously.

'I think the obvious course is for me to visit Mr Bradley Froy. He might be able to browbeat a young fellow like Giles, but I don't think he will try that with me.'

'Thank you, sir,' Lucetta said wholeheartedly. 'I don't think my uncle would lie to a man like you.'

'That is most flattering, but we will see.' Sir Hector placed his empty cup and saucer on the sofa table and he rose to his feet. 'Now, I must go to my room and change for dinner. I hope that Cook has excelled herself tonight. My housekeeper in Dorset employs what one would call a good plain cook, but I've really missed Mrs Bullen's cooking.'

'Well,' Mary said, turning to Lucetta with a smile as the door closed on her father. 'I told you that Papa would take your side. Aren't you pleased?'

'I'm delighted and very relieved. Your father is a real gentleman, Mary. My uncle will crumble when faced with such a man.'

The snow had ceased by morning, leaving a winter-white world glistening in the sunshine. Lucetta gazed out of her bedroom window with a feeling of renewed optimism. Sir Hector's arrival had given her fresh hope. She had been so excited at the prospect of his challenge to Uncle Bradley that she had hardly slept, but she did not feel the least bit tired. She had been wide awake when the chambermaid came to clear the ashes from the grate and light the fire, and a tweeny had brought a jug of hot water and fresh towels. Lucetta had risen as soon as the maids had left the room and she had washed and dressed herself, struggling with the laces on her stays and the tiny buttons on the back of her gown; managing as best she could without help.

She sat at the dressing table, brushing her hair and thinking longingly of Naomi's nimble fingers working swiftly and expertly to create the most flattering coiffures. If she closed her eyes she could shut out the cold white northern light and imagine herself back in sun-drenched Bali, and that made her feel closer to Sam. He was never far from her thoughts and just knowing that his family lived in Devon made their separation a little easier to bear. She could only hope and pray that her letter would reach its destination, and that his feelings for her had not changed.

She captured a strand of silver-blonde hair that had escaped from the chignon she was attempting to create and secured it with a hairpin, although she could do nothing to confine the small tendrils that insisted on curling around her forehead in the most unfashionable manner. She sighed. She would never achieve the sleek style adopted by Mary, whose thick dark hair was worn parted in the centre and drawn back like two glossy raven's wings to lie in a heavy knot at the nape of her neck. Lucetta stood up, smoothing the crumpled skirts of Mary's old gown and hoping that no one would notice the dried mud and water stains on the hemline. She wondered what had become of the winter clothes that had been left hanging in her wardrobe at home. The frocks would be sadly outdated now and maybe a little too short, since she was certain she had grown an inch or two since they had left the cold shores of England, but at least they belonged to her. The thought that her things might have been given away or thrown out for collection by the dustman was too painful to contemplate. She must be positive and think only of the future. With that thought in mind, Lucetta made her way downstairs to the dining room.

Sir Hector was just finishing his meal, and he half rose from his seat as she entered. 'Good morning, my dear. I hope you slept well.'

'Yes, thank you, sir.' A polite lie was better than admitting the truth. Lucetta went to the sideboard to help herself to a plate of buttered eggs and sautéed kidneys. She took her place at the table. 'Mary is not up yet?'

Sir Hector dabbed his lips with a starched white-linen table napkin. 'She left for the hospital an hour ago. I wish I could persuade her to give up working like a slave for so little money, but my daughter has a mind of her own.'

'She is a very good nurse, sir,' Lucetta said with feeling. 'I can vouch for that.'

'I know, and it does my heart good to hear you say so, but I think that young women are being exploited by their employers, and that goes for all trades and professions.'

'You are very liberal-minded, sir.'

'And you are a very intelligent young woman, Miss Froy.' Sir Hector flashed a charming smile in her direction. 'I can see that we are going to get on very well.' He drew a gold half-hunter watch from his waistcoat pocket and he frowned. 'I am due in my office in less than ten minutes for a most important meeting.'

Lucetta dropped her fork with a clatter. 'But, sir, I thought you were going to see my uncle today.'

Sir Hector rose to his feet. 'And I will, my dear. I always keep my promises, but constituency business comes first, and I have urgent matters to attend to. I will pay a call on your uncle after luncheon. I'm afraid you must be patient for a little while longer.' He paused as he was about to leave the table, and taking a wallet from his inside breast pocket he selected a ten-pound note and laid it on Lucetta's side plate.

She stared up at him, wide-eyed with embarrassment. 'What is that for, sir?'

'I am not blind, Lucetta. I can see that you are in desperate need of some new clothes, and if we are to convince your uncle and the world in general of your true identity, then at least you should look the part. I suggest you take a cab to Oxford Street and visit some of the fashionable department stores where they sell ready-to-wear garments. It will pass the day pleasantly for you and take your mind off your problems.'

'It's too much, sir. I really can't accept . . .'

He raised an eyebrow and his eyes twinkled.

'Charity? Think of it as an advance on your rightful inheritance, Lucetta. Now I really must go. We will meet again at dinner this evening.'

Despite feelings of embarrassment and guilt at accepting money from a relative stranger, Lucetta spent a blissful day shopping. She had visited some of the department stores in Oxford Street shortly after they opened, but then she had been accompanied by her mother and Mama's maid had tagged dutifully along behind them ready to carry any purchases they chose to make. When her parents were alive Lucetta had never been allowed to venture out alone and the experience was as daunting as it was delightful. She received some strange glances from shop walkers and shop assistants alike, but their attitudes changed subtly when they discovered that she had the means to pay for her purchases. By mid-afternoon she was the proud possessor of two new gowns, one for evening in gauzy pink Barèges, and one for afternoon wear in dove-grey tussore trimmed with dashing purple braid. For morning wear she purchased a more practical navy-blue serge skirt and two white cotton blouses, three pairs of lisle stockings, two plain lawn shifts, a pair of stays, three pairs of unmentionables and, lastly, a pair of black boots with high heels that she simply could not resist. She had not thought as far as protective outer garments, but she was sure that Mary would allow her to borrow the warm woollen cloak and the grey-silk bonnet for just a little longer.

Laden with bandboxes, she hailed a cab outside

Peter Robinson's store in Oxford Circus. She had forfeited luncheon in order to save the cab fare back to Islington, although she had been tempted by the delicious aromas coming from the restaurants inside the larger stores and she was now extremely hungry, but a young woman eating out alone was unheard of. She had taken one look through the half-glassed doors at the head waiter in his black tailcoat and she had known instinctively that she would not be welcome in his domain. She had hurried off in the opposite direction and ignoring hunger pangs she had found fresh delight in the millinery department. Now it was almost dark and the lights from the store windows shone out across the snowy pavements. The shop dummies in their elegant costumes seemed to beckon to her like Lorelei but she was not to be seduced any further. A cab drew to a halt by the kerb and she tossed her purchases onto the seat, climbing in after them. The cabby peered at her through the roof window. 'Been spending your boyfriend's hard-earned cash, have you, miss?'

She chose not to respond to his cheeky grin. 'Lonsdale Square, please, cabby.'

She closed the folding doors and huddled beneath her cloak as she came back to earth with a bump. The cabby had seen her for what she was, just as Phyllis had done. Without a proper identity or the means to support herself she was less than the servants. She was a nobody and they saw through her as though she were as transparent as a pane of window glass.

She arrived back at the house to find Mary and Giles

together in the parlour, their faces flushed with effort as they decorated a Christmas tree that in Lucetta's estimation must be at least nine foot tall. Giles was balancing precariously on top of a wooden pair of stepladders, while Mary was putting the finishing touches to the lower branches.

'Oh, there you are,' Mary exclaimed, turning to Lucetta with a beaming smile. You're missing all the fun. Isn't this a splendid tree? Giles brought it from the market as a surprise just for us. Lord knows what his sisters will say when they see it. They'll be green with envy.'

Giles leaned at a dangerous angle as he pinned a gold star to the topmost branch. 'I bought one for my sisters too. They will be fighting over the glass baubles and candle holders as we speak, but I prefer the quiet sanity of my uncle's house to the bedlam wrought by three young women all vying for attention.'

Mary pulled a face. 'Don't listen to him. He loves women really, he just likes to pretend that he is superior to us in every way.' She squealed as Giles shook the tree, sending a shower of pine needles to rain down on her head. 'Giles, you brute. If you do that again I'll pull the ladder out from under you.'

Lucetta found herself laughing at their playful badinage, although their obvious closeness struck a painful chord of loneliness deep within her. 'It's a beautiful tree,' she said, giggling. 'But it will be quite bare of needles if you treat it so badly, Giles.'

Mary fastened the last glass ball on the tree. 'There, that's done. Now you must tell me what you bought today. Phyllis said that you had gone shopping. Did you get what you wanted?'

'Yes, and more. I'm afraid I've been too extravagant. Your father was very generous, Mary, but I will repay him every penny as soon as I come into my inheritance.'

'I shouldn't worry on that score,' Giles said, grinning down at them. 'My uncle can afford grand gestures. He was a barrister before he went into Parliament, and I think he misses the theatre of the law courts. He is a great one for posturing, like all politicians.'

'And some doctors,' Mary said wryly. 'Get down before you fall down, Giles. You won't enjoy Christmas if you end up with your leg in splints or worse.'

'I'd quite forgotten that tomorrow will be Christmas Eve,' Lucetta said dazedly. 'I had lost count of time.'

Mary's smile vanished and twin lines appeared between her delicate winged eyebrows. 'Of course you have, Lucetta. After all you've been through, who could blame you? Why don't you sit down and I'll ring for tea.'

Giles climbed down the ladder. 'That is a capital idea. We were so busy at the hospital that I missed luncheon.'

'And so did I,' Lucetta said with a wry smile. 'But only because I was too shy to go into a restaurant on my own.'

Giles lifted her chin with the tip of his finger and he smiled, but there was sympathy in the depths of his dark eyes. 'You were quite right, Lucetta. Ladies should go nowhere unattended. I am a modern man but I am

224

deeply conservative at heart.' He dropped his hand to his side and turned away. 'Where is Phyllis? Did you ring the bell, Mary? I'm absolutely ravenous.'

'Of course I did,' Mary said, pulling a face at him. 'If you are so impatient go down to the kitchen and hurry them up.'

'Do you know, I will.' Giles clambered over the empty cardboard boxes which had contained the decorations. 'And don't talk about me when I've gone.'

'Don't flatter yourself.' Mary dismissed him with an airy wave of her hand. 'I thought he would never go. Now you can tell me in detail what you bought. Men only hate one thing more than shopping, and that is listening to females talking about it. So what did you buy?'

Lucetta sank down on the sofa. 'I can hardly remember, but we can go upstairs after tea and I will show you everything.'

Mary paused as she tidied the boxes, stacking them in the corner by the door. 'I'd like that, and when I next go shopping you must come with me. It will be fun, and we will have luncheon in a restaurant. It will be quite proper if there are two of us.'

'I'll look forward to that,' Lucetta said sincerely. 'And if Sir Hector has had any success with Uncle Bradley, I will be a young woman of means.'

'Papa will be home in time for dinner. We will know then. I'm keeping my fingers crossed for you. Now tell me what you bought. I can't wait a moment longer.'

By the time Lucetta had run through her string of

purchases, Giles returned with a smug smile on his face. 'It always pays to be nice to the resident cook,' he announced as he took his seat by the fire. 'Just you wait and see.'

Minutes later, when Phyllis and the tweeny brought tea to the parlour it was a much grander affair than normal, or so Giles insisted. He munched his way through half a plateful of salmon and cucumber sandwiches, followed by hot muffins dripping with melted butter, and several slices of dark chocolate cake oozing with cream. Mary nibbled at the food, declaring that she had eaten well at luncheon, but Lucetta ran Giles a fair second, earning his enthusiastic approval, which made her blush and gave her a warm feeling of belonging. She was sorry to see him leave, but he departed for home shortly after tea, saying that he had to go and separate his sisters, who would undoubtedly be at the hair-pulling, name-calling stage at this time of day, sending their mother into a fit of the vapours. He kissed Mary on the cheek and Lucetta secretly hoped that she might receive a similar salute, but he raised her hand briefly to his lips and then he was gone.

'He can be most charming when he puts his mind to it,' Mary said, folding her napkin neatly and placing it back on the tea tray. 'But don't read anything into it, Lucetta. Giles is an accomplished flirt.'

Lucetta turned her head to stare at Mary in surprise at the sudden sharp note that had crept into her normally gentle voice. For a moment so fleeting that Lucetta wondered afterwards if she had imagined it, she thought she had seen a hint of jealousy in Mary's eyes, but it was gone in an instant and Mary rose to her feet with her usual sunny smile.

'I'm dying to see your new clothes. You will be able to change for dinner tonight and show Papa how well you have chosen.'

Sir Hector rose to his feet as Mary and Lucetta entered the drawing room. 'My dear Miss Froy,' he said, bowing from the waist. 'I must compliment you on your choice of gowns. You look every inch the lady.'

Lucetta was not quite sure whether he was sincere or if he was teasing her, and she looked to Mary for reassurance.

'I couldn't have chosen better for her,' Mary said, taking a seat on an elegant, if slightly uncomfortable-looking, chaise longue.

Slightly overawed by the splendour of the room, Lucetta perched on the edge of an upright chair uphol-stered in slippery damask, which threatened to slide her onto the floor if she lost concentration for a single moment. She clasped her hands nervously in her lap as she watched her host pouring sherry from a cut crystal decanter into three glasses. 'Sir Hector, I wonder if . . .'

He handed one to her. 'You want to know if I had any success with your esteemed uncle, Mr Bradley Froy. I'm sorry to tell you this, Lucetta, but he is prob-ably one of the most objectionable characters whom I have had the misfortune to meet. If he weren't standing between you and your rightful inheritance, I would say that you are well rid of any connection with him and his sour-faced wife.'

'Oh, Papa, no.' Mary accepted a glass of sherry, casting a pitying glance at Lucetta. 'I am so sorry, Daisy.'

Lucetta swallowed hard. 'What did he say?'

'Nothing more than he had told Giles. He said that he had identified the bodies of his niece and her parents and that he had attended their funerals. He insisted that you are an adventuress and he threatened to have you arrested if you attempted to further your claim. I am convinced that he was lying, but unless we can find someone who would swear to your true identity the case would be impossible to prove in a court of law. I am so sorry, Lucetta. So very sorry, my dear.'

The glass slipped from Lucetta's nerveless fingers and fell to the floor. She stared in horror at the dark stain on the Persian carpet. It seemed as though her last hope had been dashed and her life blood was seeping from her, pooling at her feet like the sherry wine. Uncle Bradley had robbed her of everything, even her name. She was less than no one now. She was vaguely aware of Mary's voice.

'Don't be upset, dear Daisy. You mustn't give up hope.'

Sir Hector cleared his throat noisily. 'Hmmph. You'll feel better when you've eaten, my dear. We'll talk this over after dinner.'

Lucetta rose unsteadily to her feet. Her throat felt as though it was closing up and the mere thought of food was making her feel sick. 'Th-thank you, but I'm not hungry. If you don't mind, I'll go to my room.' She fled from the drawing room, almost knocking Phyllis down as they collided in the doorway. Picking up her skirts, Lucetta raced along the landing and up the next flight of stairs to her bedchamber. She closed the door, leaning against it and gasping for breath. She felt the solid oak vibrate behind her as someone rapped on the door.

'Lucetta, may I speak to you?' Sir Hector's voice was filled with concern.

'Please go away, sir. I need time to think.'

'A few minutes, that's all I ask.'

It was his house after all, and she was a guest in his home. Reluctantly, Lucetta moved away from the door. 'Come in.'

She snatched a towel from the rail on the washstand and mopped her streaming eyes, but she could not bring herself to meet his gaze as Sir Hector entered the room. He went to the fireplace and leaned over to shovel coal onto the fire. It was such a commonplace and homely action, more fitting for a servant than the master of the house, that Lucetta breathed a sigh of relief. She had expected to receive a stern lecture, but Sir Hector seemed more intent on riddling the dying embers of the fire than on scolding her for her lack of manners. 'It's a cold night,' he said as if continuing a discussion about the weather. 'I daresay we will have more snow by morning.'

'I'm sorry about the carpet,' Lucetta murmured. 'I hope the stain will come out.'

Sir Hector straightened up, standing with his back to the fire. 'Don't worry about that, my dear. I am the one who should apologise. I should have broken the news more gently, instead of stating the facts as though I were in court.'

Lucetta sank down on the edge of the bed. 'It's all the same in the end. I cannot impose on your hospitality any longer. My case is a hopeless one; my uncle has seen to that.'

'I admit that things look bad, but as Mary said, you must not give up hope.'

'I was not trained to do anything useful, Sir Hector. My expensive education has been wasted, since without a character I cannot even apply for the position of governess or a lady's companion.'

'That is exactly why I wanted to talk to you, Lucetta. Perhaps I should have begun our conversation with the idea that occurred to me on my way home this evening.'

Clutching the damp towel to her bosom, Lucetta raised her eyes to his face. 'What idea would that be, sir?'

Chapter Thirteen

Sir Hector regarded her seriously. 'I need an amanuensis, Lucetta. Of course I have an official secretary when the House is sitting, but my correspondence does not cease simply because Parliament is in recess. Your expensive education as you call it would be put to good use in helping me.' He paused, eyeing her as if gauging her reaction.

'You're very kind, Sir Hector, but I would still feel that I was imposing on your good nature.' With the towel still clutched firmly in her arms, Lucetta rose slowly to her feet. 'I must learn to be independent and not rely on your generosity, even though it is very much appreciated.'

'And with this new-found independence you intend to make the journey to Devonshire to find your young seafarer,' Sir Hector said, smiling. 'Mary told me.'

'As soon as the weather improves I must try to find him, even if I have to walk all the way to Salcombe.'

'I won't try to stop you, my dear.' Sir Hector took a step towards her, taking the towel gently from her grasp. 'And I suggest that you purchase some handkerchiefs with your first week's pay, Lucetta.'

'You still want to employ me, even on those terms?'

'I am a hard taskmaster, Miss Froy. Tomorrow is Christmas Eve but I will expect you to be in my study ready to begin work as soon as you have finished breakfast. I trust that you write with a fair hand.'

Responding to his smile, Lucetta felt the tension ebbing away from her taut muscles. 'I was top of the class in handwriting, sir.'

He proffered his arm. 'Then we have a bargain, Lucetta. Now perhaps you will allow me to escort you downstairs to join Mary for dinner. She was most anxious about you, and if we tarry much longer I'm afraid that Cook might hand in her resignation. Mrs Bullen would be almost irreplaceable.' He paused, smiling down at Lucetta with a quirk of his eyebrow. 'Unless, that is, you have hidden culinary talents?'

Lucetta slipped her hand through his arm. 'Unfortunately not, sir. But I did learn how to peel vegetables in the kitchen of Frog Hall.'

'And you say that you have no useful accomplishments. If you prove to be a poor secretary, we might find you a place in the scullery. I believe talented vegetable peelers are at a premium, especially so close to Christmas.'

Light-headed with relief and bubbling with optimism, Lucetta allowed her new employer to escort her downstairs to the drawing room.

Mary rose from her seat with an expectant smile. 'Papa?'

'It's all settled, my dear,' Sir Hector said cheerfully. 'Lucetta has agreed to my proposition. Now we can do justice to Mrs Bullen's excellent meal.' He held his free arm out to his daughter. 'I've worked up quite an appetite.'

All next day, Lucetta worked away in Sir Hector's study at the back of the house, taking down his dictation in note form and then transcribing it back in her best copperplate hand. She worked conscientiously, stopping briefly to eat her midday meal alone in the morning parlour as Sir Hector had gone to his club and Mary was on duty at the hospital. Neither of them returned until late that evening and, daunted by the prospect of eating alone in the wainscoted dining room, Lucetta had once again requested a tray be brought to her in the parlour. Replete, and satisfied that she had at least earned her living that day, she sat by the fire watching its light play on the glass baubles and tinsel on the tree. She recalled the previous evening when Giles and Mary had laughed and teased each other as they dressed the green boughs. The scent of the pine needles filled the room and the fizzing and popping of the gas mantles accompanied the crackling and spitting of the burning coals in the grate. Lucetta drifted off to sleep but suddenly the room around her seemed to change. She did not recognise her surroundings. It was a much larger room with oak-panelled walls and mullioned windows. She could see Mary seated on a chair with her face buried in her hands and she appeared to be sobbing uncontrollably. Giles and Sir Hector were pacing the floor. She could not hear what they were saying. Their lips moved but it was like watching a mime. She could feel their distress but she had no idea what could be the cause. And yet she knew it had something to do with her. She wanted to put her arms around Mary and comfort her, but it was as if her limbs were turned to stone. She tried to speak but no words came from her lips and she realised with a feeling of utter panic that they could not see her. She did not exist. She opened her mouth to scream . . .

Someone was shaking her, calling her name. She opened her eyes and focused blearily on Mary's smiling face.

'You were dreaming, Daisy. It must have been a nightmare judging by the way you were struggling. You are quite safe, dear. It was just a dream.'

Lucetta sat up straight, rubbing her eyes. 'What time is it?'

'Very late, close to midnight. We were so busy that I had to stay on in the ward, but I'm home now, and I have tomorrow off. We will have a wonderful time across the way with the Harcourts.'

'The Harcourts?'

'We always have Christmas dinner with my aunt and the Harcourt cousins. You will meet Giles' sisters. I'm sure they are dying with curiosity.'

The sun had forced its way through ominous-looking clouds to reveal a tantalising patch of blue sky that seemed to promise a hint of spring even though the air was bitingly cold. Lucetta, Mary and Sir Hector crossed the square, their breath spiralling into columns above their heads as they picked their way through the ankle-deep snow. Lucetta had been reluctant to accept the invitation, preferring to spend Christmas day on her own rather than feeling like an outsider in the family party, but Mary and Sir Hector flatly refused to leave her at home. She had tried to put her emotions into words but they had simply not understood that this was her first Christmas since she had lost her parents, and that accompanying them to a family gathering would only emphasise her orphaned status. With obvious good intentions they seemed to think that being alone was the same as being lonely. Lucetta could have put them right on that score but in the face of their genuine concern for her wellbeing, she gave in. Mary had been kind but firm and Sir Hector had insisted that the company of young people was just the thing to cheer Lucetta's flagging spirits.

To make matters even worse, that morning at breakfast Mary had presented her with a beautiful shawl which was so delicate that it might have been fashioned from a cobweb, and Sir Hector had given her a box of Swiss lawn handkerchiefs, embroidered with flowers and trimmed with lace. She had no gifts for them, and she had felt even guiltier for spending so much money on herself. Her shame had been compounded by Mary and Sir Hector's refusal to accept that she had done anything wrong, or that she had behaved thoughtlessly. Their generosity was over-whelming and Lucetta felt even more unworthy of their kindness as she followed them into the Harcourts' residence on the far side of the square.

A silver-haired butler, who seemed more like a respected family member than a servant, welcomed them at the door with obvious pleasure. Their outer garments were spirited away by a maidservant who in contrast to the dour Phyllis was all smiles and cheerful nods. The butler led them up the sweeping curve of the staircase to the drawing room. Lucetta could hear the aged retainer's joints creaking with every step, but if his rheumaticky knees were painful, he gave no evidence of his discomfort.

Mrs Harcourt and her three daughters were seated on spindly antique chairs with their crinolines spread about them like the petals of exotic flowers. Sunlight poured through the tall windows and a fire blazed up the chimney. The pastel furnishings and floral-patterned wallpaper gave the room a delicate feminine look, and the scent of hothouse flowers mingled with the expensive perfumes favoured by the girls and their mother. The scene might have been the subject of a water-colour painting of genteel family life, but the serenity was broken the moment the visitors entered the room. The three sisters rose like a flock of brightly coloured parakeets, laughing and chattering as they descended on Mary and her father.

'Merry Christmas,' they carolled in a chorus.

Lucetta hung back in the ensuing flurry of kisses and fond greetings, but Mrs Harcourt rose majestically from her seat by the fire and sailed over to her, embracing her on both cheeks. 'You must be Miss Froy. Welcome to our home, my dear.'

Lucetta felt her throat constrict as she inhaled the achingly familiar aroma of a perfume that had been her mother's favourite. 'Thank you, ma'am.'

Mrs Harcourt clapped her hands for silence. 'Girls, do be quiet for a moment.' She turned to Lucetta with a charming smile. 'Miss Froy, may I introduce my daughters. Jemima, the eldest, Chloris and Caroline, my baby.'

'I'm fifteen, Mama,' Caroline protested, pouting.

'And a spoilt brat,' Chloris said, tweaking her sister's dark curls.

Caroline retaliated with a shove that sent Chloris staggering against Jemima who slapped Caroline on the wrist with her fan.

Mary thrust herself between them. 'Girls, what will Lucetta think of you?'

'She started it,' Chloris said, glaring at her younger sister. 'She is a brat.'

Sir Hector raised his eyes to the ornately plastered ceiling rose above his head. 'It's Christmas Day. Can't you girls call a truce for one day at least?'

Mrs Harcourt clapped her hands. 'You're absolutely right, Hector. Girls, look after your uncle and cousin. I want to speak to Miss Froy.' She took Lucetta by the hand. 'Come and sit by the fire, my dear. Leave my girls to get over their excitement, and tell me about yourself. It must be very difficult for you, particularly at this time of the year.'

Lucetta opened her mouth to answer, but was forestalled by Caroline who came bounding over to them like an eager puppy. 'So you are Lucetta. Giles has told us a little of your story, but you know what men are like: they leave out all the interesting bits. Come and sit by me and tell me everything.'

'Caroline,' Mrs Harcourt protested mildly. 'Leave the poor girl alone.'

'Yes, don't monopolise our guest,' Chloris said, pulling a face at her sister.

Caroline scowled and her rosebud lips pursed in a sulky pout. 'Go away, Chloris. Lucetta is going to be my friend, not yours.'

'Don't squabble, girls,' Mrs Harcourt said faintly. 'You'll upset our guest.'

Sir Hector crossed the floor to embrace his hostess. 'My dear sister-in-law, you look younger every time I see you. If I did not know better I would think you were these girls' sister and not their mama.'

Ellen Harcourt blushed rosily. 'Still the same old Hector.'

'I should hope so, my dear.'

Mrs Harcourt held her arms out to Mary. 'Come and give your auntie a kiss. We hardly see you since you started working at the hospital.'

Mary extricated herself from her cousin Jemima's embrace and she crossed the room to kiss her aunt on her cheek. 'I know, Aunt Ellen. But the hours are long and—'

'The pay is so low that it is almost an insult,' Sir Hector said, standing with his back to the fire. 'I've done my best to persuade her to give up nursing, but my girl is as stubborn as—'

'Her father?' Ellen interrupted, smiling. 'Come now, Hector. Would you have taken advice when you were Mary's age? I'm sure that my dear Hubert would not have done, and you two might as well have been twins you were so alike.' She paused, dabbing her eyes with a scrap of lace handkerchief. 'It's just three years since he passed away, but it seems like a lifetime.'

Chloris gave an exaggerated sigh. 'Heavens, Mama. Don't get in a state. This is supposed to be a happy day.'

'Yes,' Caroline agreed, tugging at Mary's sleeve. 'Isn't it time we exchanged presents?'

'You hateful children.' Jemima pushed her sisters aside so that she was between them and their mother. She bristled like an angry cat. 'Greedy Caro and unfeeling Chloris. What will Miss Froy think of us?'

There was a moment's silence as all eyes turned to Lucetta. She felt herself blushing furiously. The sisters were glaring at her as if it was all her fault and yet she had said nothing. She was at a loss for words but Mary turned on her cousin with an angry frown.

'You are all as bad as each other. If you are going to behave like witches, then I'm sure I would rather spend the day at home. What would Giles say if he could hear you now?'

'What indeed?'

Giles' voice from the doorway made everyone turn their heads to look at him. He shook his head, wagging a reproving finger at his sisters. 'Can't you furies keep the peace for one day of the year? Look at Mary and Lucetta; they behave like ladies, not like fishwives from Billingsgate. Shame on you.'

Jemima tossed her head. 'You've only just arrived, Giles. So don't put on that holier than thou face. You didn't hear what was said.'

'I heard you screeching at each other from the bottom of the stairs,' Giles countered. 'And if you can't behave yourselves, then I would be more than happy to leave you to your squabbles and take Mama over to our uncle's house, where we would spend a much more congenial time without you.'

'Come now, Giles,' Ellen said mildly. 'It's just youthful high spirits.'

'Yes,' Sir Hector agreed, patting her hand. 'But you must not upset your mother, girls. And I would remind you that we have a guest in our midst.'

Chloris flicked a sideways glance at Lucetta, her green eyes veiled by thick, dark lashes. 'We won't be allowed to forget it,' she hissed in a barely audible whisper.

'What was that?' Giles demanded. 'I hope you weren't being nasty to Lucetta.'

'Heaven forbid that anyone should offend your favourite, Giles.' Pouting, Chloris slumped down on the sofa, arranging her skirts so that there was no room for anyone to sit by her side. 'We've hardly seen you since Miss Froy arrived on your doorstep.'

'Yes,' Jemima said, addressing her remark to Mary. 'Some of us have had our noses put out of joint by your obvious preference for the unfortunate Miss Froy.'

Lucetta bit her lip as a sharp rejoinder rose to her lips. She was not concerned for herself but she could see that the cousins' spiteful comments had left Mary close to tears. She cast an appealing glance at Giles, whose normally cheerful countenance had darkened to that of a thundercloud.

'Come, come, girls,' Sir Hector said jovially. 'Peace and goodwill to all men, and I believe that includes young ladies too.'

'Yes,' Ellen agreed, rising to her feet. 'There are presents under the tree. I think it's time we exchanged gifts.'

'And a glass of sherry might be in order, Ellen,' Sir Hector said, winking. 'Maybe a little negus for the younger girls might sweeten their tempers.'

'I think chloroform might be more beneficial,' Giles replied with a wry smile. He put his arm around Mary's shoulders. 'Or maybe a few drops of laudanum in their wine might be just as effective. What d'you think, my dear?'

Mary smiled valiantly. 'I think that opening the presents is the best idea.' She turned to Lucetta, holding out her hand. 'Come and sit by me, and we'll open them together.'

Lucetta sensed how much it must have cost her friend to behave with such generosity of spirit. She could have quite cheerfully banged all three sisters' heads together, but she must suppose that their spite had roots in simple jealousy rather than ill nature. She hoped so anyway. She went to sit beside Mary and was rewarded by a smile of approval from Giles.

Ellen resumed her seat with a sigh that could have been one of relief or resignation. She waved a vague hand at Caroline. 'You are the youngest so you may hand out the presents, darling.'

Caroline pushed Chloris out of the way as she made for the Christmas tree in the corner of the room.

Beneath it was a pile of interesting-looking boxes and packages wrapped in gaily coloured tissue paper tied with satin ribbons. 'I'm to do it,' Caroline said crossly. 'Go and sit down, Chloris.'

'Brat,' Chloris muttered as she flounced over to the sofa and sat down, crushing the silk of Jemima's outspread skirt.

'You beast, Chloris,' Jemima cried, pushing her away. 'You've creased my best *faille française* and it cost four and six a yard.'

Chloris sniffed, looking down her sharp little nose. 'There's no need to be vulgar. You're talking like a tradesman's daughter.'

Sir Hector cleared his throat in a way that Lucetta had come to realise signified his embarrassment. He waved to attract Caroline's attention. 'Where are those gifts, my dear? Ours should be on top, since I sent Phyllis over with them last evening.'

'I can't read the labels, Uncle,' she said in a sulky voice. 'Somebody writes like a rheumaticky spider that's fallen in the inkpot and crawled across the paper.'

Mary rose to her feet. 'I'm afraid that was me. I was rather tired when I finished my shift at the hospital.'

Giles pressed her back onto her seat. 'Allow me, Mary. If I can read other doctors' dreadful scrawl, then I will have no trouble deciphering your delicate hand, even if you were exhausted, which I don't doubt for a minute.' Flashing a comforting smile in her direction, he crossed the floor to take the package from Caroline. 'There, that's clear enough, Caro. It says to Aunt Ellen, with love from Mary.'

'Oh, all right,' Caroline snapped. 'Just because you're a doctor you think you're so very clever.'

'I would have studied medicine if I had been allowed to do so,' Jemima said primly. 'But instead I am forced to sit at home and wait for an eligible husband. It's not fair.'

'With a face like that you'll be waiting a long time.' Chloris wriggled to the end of the sofa, out of reach of her sister's flailing hand.

Giles thrust a box tied with scarlet ribbons into Caroline's eager hands. 'This one is for you, Trouble. And this one is for Chloris. Perhaps that will keep her tongue still and give us all a rest.'

'I hope it's a scold's bridle,' Jemima said in a low voice. 'Hurry up, Chloris. Can't you wait until we've all had our gifts before you tear into yours?'

Sir Hector tugged at the bell pull. 'How many of you would like a glass of negus?'

'Imagine them tipsy,' Mary whispered in Lucetta's ear. 'A half-glass of wine and they will love everyone.'

Lucetta smiled a reply, but she thought privately that there was not enough warm port and lemonade in the world to sweeten Chloris into a nice person, and Caroline might have benefited from a stern governess who did not spare the rod. She looked up as Giles came over to them, handing a large bandbox to Mary and to Lucetta's surprise he pressed a small, beautifully wrapped package into her hands.

'Merry Christmas, Lucetta,' he said with a smile that melted her heart. 'The misadventure that brought you our way was our good fortune.'

Lucetta fingered the satin ribbon tied in a bow, and as she raised her eyes to his she felt her heart skip a beat at the warmth of feeling she saw in his gaze. 'Thank you, Giles, but I have nothing to give you.'

'You have given us all something that money cannot buy, Lucetta. You make the dullest winter day seem like summer.' He paused, glancing over his shoulder as he appeared to realise that the room was suddenly silent. He struck a pose, hand on heart. 'If I were a younger fellow or indeed if you were an older woman, I would be on my knees before you, but as it is I am your devoted friend.'

The ensuing silence was broken by Caroline. 'You're only twenty-seven, Giles. I don't call that old.'

He turned to her with a smile. 'And you can be a sweet little sister when you keep your kitten-claws in. Stay like that, Caro, and we will all love you too.'

'Open it,' Mary urged, nudging Lucetta gently. 'Let's see what Giles has given you.'

Reluctantly, Lucetta tore away the tissue paper to reveal a shagreen box, the type that only came from the most expensive jeweller's. Her fingers trembled as she opened it and she gasped at the sight of a gold bracelet fashioned in a delicate filigree pattern. She shot a sideways glance at Mary and to her relief she saw nothing but admiration and approval in her eyes.

'Do you like it, Lucetta?' Giles asked anxiously. 'We can always change it for something else if you don't.'

'I'm sure he wouldn't be so generous to me,' Chloris muttered. 'And I'm part of the family.'

Giles turned on his sister. 'Chloris, if you can't behave

yourself in company I suggest you go to the nursery where it seems you still belong.'

'Mama,' Chloris wailed. 'Are you going to let him speak to me like that?'

Ellen exchanged meaningful looks with Sir Hector and she nodded her head. 'Giles is right. I'm ashamed of all you girls. I thought I had taught you better but it seems that I was wrong. You will all apologise for your rudeness to Lucetta, and then I hope we will see the end of this bad behaviour.'

'I agree,' Sir Hector said sternly. 'Listen to your mother, girls, and do as she says.'

The sisters obeyed grudgingly, mumbling apologies, and then, seeming to forget their disgrace in the flicker of an eyelid, they began tearing the paper off their presents.

Lucetta met Giles' eyes and she smiled. 'Thank you. It is the most beautiful gift I have ever received, but it makes me feel all the worse for having nothing to give you in return.'

'I'll bear that in mind,' Giles replied, laughing. 'And when you inherit your fortune I will remind you that you owe me a present, and I will insist that it is very costly and must be delivered by you into my hand.'

'I promise.'

'Put it on,' Mary urged. 'It is very pretty, Giles. I didn't know you had such good taste.'

He took the bracelet from Lucetta and fastened it around her wrist. 'I am a man of many talents, my dear Mary. I don't think my family truly appreciates me.'

'I do,' Mary said simply.

Lucetta was quick to hear the wistful note in Mary's voice and she hid her hand and wrist beneath the folds of her skirt. She looked up at Giles but he did not appear to have noticed anything amiss. He had moved away to serve the negus that the maid had just deposited on a side table. He handed the silver cups round to his mother and sisters.

Lucetta accepted one and sipped the heady brew which worked quickly to sweeten the sisters' tempers, and soon they were laughing and giggling and had apparently overcome their initial antipathy towards her. She might not have been included in their conversation, but at least they left her alone and refrained from making barbed comments. Mrs Harcourt relaxed visibly and Sir Hector became expansive after several large glasses of sherry, and by the time luncheon was announced the atmosphere in the room had become much more congenial.

'We only dine at midday on Christmas Day,' Ellen explained as she accepted Sir Hector's offer to escort her to the dining room. 'Normally we eat at a more fashionable hour, Lucetta. But on this special day I like to give the servants time to enjoy the festivities.'

'Quite right, Ellen,' Sir Hector said with a nod of approval. 'Excellent sentiments.'

'Are you going to take me in to dinner, Giles?' Jemima asked with an arch smile. 'I am the eldest.'

'And so you are, Jemima, but Lucetta is our guest, and Mary is your senior by a year, so I think she takes precedence.' He proffered an arm to each of them.

'Well, she is not much older than me,' Chloris muttered, eyeing Lucetta with an ominous pout. 'And you don't know who she is, Giles. She could be a dolly mop for all you know.'

Giles turned his head to give his youngest sister a searing glance. 'Chloris, if you can't mind your manners you can go downstairs and eat with the servants.'

Lucetta had begun to enjoy herself, but now the bright bubble of the day had burst. She knew that Chloris had only put into words what most people seemed to think. She was a fraud and an adventuress. She glanced down at her hand as it nestled in the crook of Giles' arm, and the gold bracelet winked at her in the sunlight. She should not have accepted such an expensive gift. First thing in the morning, she would return it to Giles. She hoped that he would understand.

'No, damn it, I don't understand,' Giles said, staring at her in bewilderment. 'I gave you that present because I wanted to, Lucetta, and for no other reason than that. I wanted to make up in some small part for the terrible experiences that have been forced upon you. Why should you not accept it in the spirit in which it was given?'

Lucetta stared down at her unembellished wrist. It had cost her much heart-seeking during the night, but she had come to the same conclusion in the morning. She was upsetting the whole family by her presence and Mary in particular, even though her friend had said nothing to make her feel uncomfortable. 'I can't

247

keep it, Giles,' she said in a small voice. 'It's too costly a gift and it puts me in an awkward position. If anyone should have had such a present, it should have been Mary.'

'Why so? I gave Mary and my sisters what I thought they would like. Why should I not give you something similar?'

'But that's just it. My present must have cost double or more the amount you spent on them. They all saw that and were upset by your generosity to someone who they think is an imposter.'

'My sisters are ninnies and Mary is too good and generous to be jealous about such a trifle. The only problem is in your head, Lucetta. I will be most offended if you refuse to accept my present.' Giles took her hand and placed the box in her palm, closing her fingers over it with a teasing smile. 'Now you wouldn't wish to offend me, would you?'

She shook her head. 'No, Giles.'

'Then we will hear no more of such talk, and I have something to tell you.'

'What is it?'

'My uncle and I had a talk last night after you ladies had retired to bed. We decided that the only people who could identify you and were not going to be intimidated by your uncle were the consul in Bali and his wife.'

'That's true,' Lucetta said slowly. 'But I have not the means to travel all the way to Bali, and a letter would not suffice.'

'It might, if it were to contain a likeness of you. Sir

Hector is going to arrange for a daguerreotype to be taken of you and he will send it to the consulate with a covering letter. It will take several months for the reply to arrive, but in the meantime you will have plenty to do writing letters for my uncle, and keeping Mary company when she is not at the hospital. I think it is a capital solution. What do you say?'

Lucetta raised her eyes to his face and her worst fears were confirmed. She had seen that look in Sam's eyes. Any hope that she had been mistaken as to Giles' feeling for her was dispelled at that moment.

'Giles,' she said slowly, choosing her words with difficulty. 'There's something that I haven't told you.'

He stared at her, eyebrows raised. 'What on earth could it be that makes you look so serious?'

'Please sit down, and I'll explain.'

He took a seat opposite her. 'Go on. I'm listening.'

'I met a young man in Bali, a seafarer who should have sailed with us on the *Caroline*. It's a long story and complicated but I've discovered that his family live in Devon. As soon as the weather improves I must go there. I love him, and he loves me. I don't care about my inheritance. I must find him. You do understand, don't you, Giles?'

Chapter Fourteen

Giles had understood perfectly. Lucetta had no doubts about that, but she realised instinctively that admitting her feelings for Sam had both shaken and hurt the man to whom she owed so much.

During the weeks that followed Giles said nothing to make her feel uncomfortable, but sometimes Lucetta caught him looking at her with a serious, almost wistful expression in his dark eyes. It was gone in an instant, replaced by his normal insouciant smile, convincing her that she had imagined the whole thing. After all, he had never spoken to her of love or romance and he was a good ten years her senior. What would a man of the world like Giles see in a penniless orphan? Despite the generous Christmas present and his obvious pleasure in her company, she decided that he was just being kind. His real interest must lie with Mary, whose feelings were painfully obvious, at least to Lucetta who had grown to love her like a sister.

The days passed pleasantly enough, although the weather continued to be dreadful with continuous snowstorms and reports of drifts several feet deep making travel outside London virtually impossible. Lucetta hoped that this was the reason for the lack of a response to the letter she had sent Sam, but she was still determined to go to Devonshire the moment that winter released its icy grip. She worked diligently for Sir Hector, and even when Parliament returned after the Christmas recess she continued to write much of his private correspondence, for which he paid her a modest salary. She saved every penny of her wages, placing the coins in an old stocking that was too laddered to darn, and stowing it away in a drawer with her clean undergarments.

Soon after Christmas, Sir Hector had taken Lucetta and Mary to the studio of a photographer who was renowned for his daguerreotype portraits. Sir Hector and Mary had their likenesses taken together and separately, posing rather self-consciously amongst potted palms set against a lavish curtained backdrop. Then it was Lucetta's turn to sit on the horsehair sofa for what seemed like hours while her image was captured for posterity and an extra print ordered so that it could be sent to Bali for validation by the consul.

'It seems as though this is the only way we can prove your true identity,' Sir Hector had said. 'Even if you find your young seafarer, I doubt whether his word alone would be enough to convince a magistrate that your uncle is lying.'

When the daguerreotypes were delivered to Lonsdale Square, Lucetta could hardly recognise the elegant young lady who stared dreamily into the distance. The sepia tint gave her an ethereal look. Her eyes looked huge in her pale heart-shaped face and the photographer's flash had illuminated her blonde hair so that it framed her head like a halo. She found it hard to believe that anyone would recognise this person as being Lucetta Froy, even though both Mary and Giles insisted that it was an exact likeness and not even very flattering. The print was duly posted to Sir John Boothby at the British consulate in Denpasar, and once again there was nothing Lucetta could do other than wait for a reply.

Each morning she collected the post from a silver salver on the hall table hoping to receive a letter from Sam, and although she knew it was ridiculous to expect anything from Bali so soon she found herself hoping for a miracle. When there was nothing bearing her name, Lucetta resigned herself to yet another day's delay. She took the correspondence to Sir Hector's study, where he read the letters and dictated replies to those he considered most urgent, leaving Lucetta to answer the more mundane enquiries from his constituents. This took up most of the morning and occasionally an hour or two after luncheon, which Lucetta took alone in the morning parlour. Mary continued to work long hours at the hospital, as did Giles, although when he was doing a night shift he had time off in the afternoon. Rather than return home to the chaotic household where his sisters continued to spend most of their time bickering, he took Lucetta on outings to art galleries and museums, followed by tea at Brown's Hotel. Lucetta had never been up West before, and if she had thought the houses in Lonsdale Square and Thornhill Crescent were the height of luxury, she realised that she had seen nothing to compare with the grand mansions in Mayfair.

'One day, I might have a practice in Harley Street,' Giles had said with a teasing smile. 'What do you think of that, Lucetta? Could you imagine living in such a place?'

His tone had been bantering but there had been an intense look in his eyes which had suggested that his question was serious and required an honest answer.

'No, Giles. Nor can I imagine you taking money from rich people with imagined illnesses. I've seen first hand how dedicated you are to your chosen profession.'

'Yes,' he murmured, turning away to hail a cab. 'Such a life is obviously not for me.'

The weeks turned into months but the snowfalls continued until April, when there was a sudden thaw followed by the welcome first signs of spring. Lucetta had saved enough money for the train fare to Devon, but before she could make the necessary arrangements Mary had gone down with a chill which developed with frightening rapidity into pneumonia. There was no question of Lucetta leaving while her friend was so ill, and she devoted herself to looking after Mary, hardly leaving the sickroom other than to snatch a few hours' sleep while a night nurse took over. But on finding the woman dead drunk one morning and Mary lying in a nightgown soaked with sweat, Lucetta sacked the woman on the spot. She sent for Phyllis and between them they managed to get Mary onto a chair while they stripped and remade the bed with fresh linen. Having sponged Mary's fevered limbs with cool water they dressed her in a clean nightgown and laid her back against the pillows.

'I think she's a bit better, miss,' Phyllis whispered. 'She don't seem quite so hot.'

Lucetta laid her hand on Mary's brow. 'You may be right. We can only hope that the crisis is past, no thanks to that dreadful woman. Mary could have died and that old hag wouldn't have been in a condition to notice.'

'I'll fetch you a nice hot cup of tea, miss. And I'll ask Cook to make up a breakfast tray. You need to keep your strength up too.'

Phyllis whisked out of the room and Lucetta sat down in the chair by the bedside. She smiled, thinking how Phyllis had changed in the past few months. Her initial antagonism and suspicion which she had done little to conceal had vanished, and it comforted Lucetta to know that the servants, all of whom were devoted to Sir Hector and Mary, now accepted her as part of the family. She had had to earn their respect but she knew that those below stairs were often more adept at recognising an imposter than their masters. Satisfied that Mary's breathing was much easier and that she was sleeping peacefully, Lucetta set about tidying the room while she waited for Phyllis to bring the tea.

When the family physician made a house call later that day he confirmed that the crisis was past. With complete rest and constant care, Miss Hastings would undoubtedly regain her full strength, but there was no question of her returning to work in the hospital for some time to come. Mary greeted this pronouncement with a resigned smile, and Lucetta had to face the fact that she must put off her trip to Devon for a while longer. She hid her disappointment, putting on a cheerful face and spending every afternoon in the sick room with Mary who was allowed to sit out of bed for increasingly long periods each day. Lucetta read to her or they pored over copies of *The Young Ladies' Journal*, discussing at length the latest Paris fashions. They marvelled at the elegance of the gowns, the size of the bustles and the length of the trains worn by fashionable ladies. They exclaimed over the tiny hats trimmed with feathers, flowers and ribbons that had taken the place of the more homely bonnet, and as the days began to lengthen they made plans to go shopping together as soon as Mary had regained her strength.

Giles visited almost daily, or as often as his hospital duties would allow. He never came empty-handed and would arrive with bouquets of daffodils or nosegays of snowdrops, boxes of chocolates to tempt the invalid's appetite and baskets of hothouse fruit. As soon as the doctor considered that Mary was well enough to take a little air, Giles arrived early one afternoon, and, despite her protests, he insisted on carrying her downstairs to the entrance hall where Phyllis was waiting anxiously with her mistress's cape, bonnet and kid gloves.

Mary shook her head, laughing. 'Phyllis dear, the sun is shining. It's a lovely warm day. I think a shawl will suffice.'

'No, miss. The doctor says you must be well wrapped up against the chill wind. It might be May, but you can't trust the weather and we don't want you to suffer a relapse.'

Lucetta saw Mary's lips tremble and she took off her own shawl, wrapping it around Mary's thin shoulders. 'Wear this, and I will carry your cape. Then if a wicked wind should rage round the square we will be prepared.'

Phyllis pursed her lips with an ominous frown, but Giles took the bonnet and gloves from her hands. 'Don't worry, Phyllis. I promise to look after Miss Mary. After all, I am a doctor, and I do know best.'

'Very well, sir. But Miss Mary must wear her bonnet.'

Mary reached out to take the straw bonnet trimmed with white lace. 'I will put it on to please you, Phyllis dear.' She placed it on her head, but her hands shook a little as she attempted to tie the ribbons beneath her chin.

Giles took them from her and he tied them in a perfect bow. 'What would you do without me, cousin?'

Mary's cheeks reddened and she gave a shaky laugh. 'What indeed, Giles?'

Phyllis opened the front door. 'Best not keep her out too long, Mr Giles.'

As the door closed on them, Mary uttered a heavy sigh. 'I am quite well now. I do wish everyone would stop fussing and treating me as if I were ten years old.'

Giles tucked her hand into the crook of his arm. 'If you're going to be a crosspatch, I won't tell you what your father and I have planned to speed your convalescence.' Smiling, he proffered his free arm to Lucetta. 'This includes you too, Lucetta.'

She fell into step beside him as they crossed the road to enter the gardens through a gate in the iron railings. 'That sounds interesting, Giles.'

Mary came to a halt, leaning heavily on his arm. 'This is too much excitement for me on my first outing. If you don't tell me at once, I'll have to go back indoors and lie down in a darkened room.'

Her tone was serious but Lucetta noted a twinkle in Mary's dark eyes. 'And I too, Giles,' she said, smiling.

He raised his hands in a gesture of defeat. 'I can't win if the pair of you gang up on me.'

'Then tell us,' Mary insisted. 'Please, Giles.'

He led them to a seat beneath a huge plane tree in the centre of the lawns. Above them the sky was a soft baby-blue dotted with fluffy white clouds and the sun filtered through the fresh summer foliage, making dappled patterns on the grass. Mary sat down but Lucetta remained standing. This was a family matter and she felt quite suddenly that she was intruding.

'Everything is arranged,' Giles said, taking a seat beside Mary. 'We travel to Dorset tomorrow where we will stay for a month while Uncle Hector deals with constituency affairs.'

Mary stared at him wide-eyed with surprise. 'But Giles, I have to go back to the hospital. I can't just take a month off as I please, and neither can you.'

'And I would love to accompany you,' Lucetta said, thinking that this might be the chance she had been waiting for. 'But I must go to Devonshire. I've put it off for too long already.'

'Don't you think you would have heard something before now if your friend wanted to contact you?'

Lucetta met his steady gaze with an angry toss of her head. 'Sam is more than a friend, Giles. You know very well that we are unofficially engaged to be married. He loves me.'

'Then why hasn't he replied to your letter?'

Lucetta gasped as a shaft of genuine pain shot through her breast. The same question had been running through her mind, but hearing it voiced by Giles was more than hurtful and worst of all, it was a just comment. Before she could think of a reply, Mary had risen to her feet.

'Giles, I'm surprised at you. That was uncalled for and unkind. There could be all manner of reasons why Sam hasn't written to Lucetta and the most obvious of all is that he is away at sea and her letter has not yet reached him.'

Giles stood up, shaking his head. 'I'm sorry, but his family must know his whereabouts and one would think they might have either forwarded the letter, or opened it in an attempt to discover the name and address of the sender.'

'It was private,' Lucetta murmured. 'I would not want anyone but Sam to read it.'

'Then you must face the fact that he is either sailing the high seas or has had second thoughts.' Giles moderated his tone with an obvious effort. 'You knew him only for a short time, Lucetta. His feelings might have changed.'

'Giles, that is cruel,' Mary said in a voice that

throbbed with emotion. 'How can you say such things to poor Lucetta? Hasn't she suffered enough?'

'I am being realistic, Mary. I don't want to see Lucetta's heart broken or for her to waste her youth dreaming impossible dreams.'

'You don't know what you're talking about,' Lucetta cried passionately. 'Sam loves me. He loves me, Giles.'

'You're so young,' Giles said gently. 'You have little experience of life. Don't throw yourself away on the first man who says that he loves you. This fellow is a seafarer, one foot in sea and one on shore as the great Bard wrote. You deserve better, my dear.'

Mary laid her hand on his shoulder with a warning glance. 'Giles, stop. You've said enough.'

Lucetta bit back tears of anger and frustration. 'I'm not a child. I will be nineteen at Christmas and I know my own mind and heart. You can take Mary to Dorset, but I am going to Devonshire to find Sam.'

Taking her by the shoulders, Giles looked deeply into her eyes. 'If the man loved you as you say he did, don't you think he would have moved heaven and earth to find you, even if it was just to lay flowers on your grave?'

'He might have done just that. You don't know him, Giles. You are being very unfair. I hate you for saying such things.' Lucetta broke free from his grasp and she raced across the grass heading for the gate. She could not bring herself to return to the house and she left the square, walking briskly with her head down so that she did not have to meet the curious gaze of passers-by who might wonder why a well-dressed young lady was allowed to roam the streets unaccompanied.

She passed the fever hospital in Liverpool Road without giving its impressive façade a second glance. She had no purpose to her walk; she just wanted to put distance between herself and Giles Harcourt, who had the unhappy knack of speaking his mind and hitting on the truth. It was over a year since she had left Sam in Bali. He had thought her dead for almost all that time, and even if he had tried to find her he would have been met by a wall of silence from Uncle Bradley. If he had visited the churchyard he would have seen a grave where some other unfortunate young woman had been laid to rest. Sam might have been sincere in his love for her, but he was young and attractive and one day he would inevitably take a wife. She gulped back a sob, narrowly avoiding bumping into a burly workman carrying a stepladder over his shoulder. He muttered something unintelligible beneath his breath and carried on in the opposite direction. She paused at a road junction, finding herself in the City Road, outside a public house called the Angel. She knew then that she had come too far and she started back the way she had come, but she had lost her bearings, and jostled by the crowds of pedestrians, costermongers and urchins begging at the kerbside she took the wrong route and only realised her mistake when she came to the open space of Islington Green. She was hot and tired but it was quieter here amongst the trees in a place that had retained a little of its rural past. She sat down on the grass beneath an oak tree and blew her nose on one of the handkerchiefs that Sir Hector had given her at Christmas. The gold bracelet on her right wrist glinted in the sunshine, and she was immediately assailed by feelings of guilt. She had shouted at Giles when she knew that he had been thinking only of her welfare, and worse still she had upset Mary, who was convalescing from a near-fatal illness.

Lucetta dabbed her eyes and sniffed. The whole family, with perhaps the exception of the Harcourt sisters, had shown her nothing but kindness. Giles and Mary had taken her in when she had nowhere else to go. They had fed and clothed her and treated her like a sister. They must think that her behaviour rivalled that of young Caroline at Christmas. She rose a little unsteadily to her feet and shielded her eyes against the sunlight, looking around in an attempt to get her bearings. The spire of St Mary's church dominated the skyline; it was a familiar landmark and she could use it to guide her way back to Lonsdale Square. She straightened her bonnet, droped the cape around her shoulders and headed in the direction of home, intent on apologising and begging her friends' pardon.

The journey to Stockton Lacey took a whole day. It could have been accomplished much faster had the family taken the train, but Sir Hector liked to travel in the comfort of his own carriage, stopping frequently at coaching inns to change horses and to allow the family time to stretch their legs and to take sustenance. The mail coach, he said proudly, could travel from

Dorchester to London in twelve hours, but that entailed travelling at breakneck speed and he preferred to progress at a more leisurely pace. The family rode in the landau with the servants and luggage preceding them in the wagonette.

It was almost dark when the party arrived at the Grange, but Lucetta could just make out the house set amongst tall beeches, horse chestnuts and oak trees. The carriage crossed a narrow stone bridge over a fast-running but shallow stream, which Mary said flowed around the property like a moat. And, she added, as the carriage passed through wrought iron gates opened by a boy who had come running from the coach house, there had been an even earlier building on the site, erected by the Norman lord of the manor who had owned the farmland for miles around. The farmhouse had been added to by successive generations and largely rebuilt in the time of Queen Anne when the stone façade had been added.

Giles patted Mary's gloved hand as it lay in her lap. 'There, Lucetta, you have a potted history of the Grange. You can see how Mary loves her old home.'

'I grew up here,' Mary said, smiling. 'I have many happy childhood memories of living in the country.'

Sir Hector had been dozing for the last half an hour but he opened his eyes as the carriage slowed down. 'I hope that Cook has improved on her culinary efforts since I was last here,' he said, as they came to a halt outside the main entrance. 'I've worked up quite an appetite since luncheon.'

Lucetta stared out of the window at the square,

three-storey house surrounded by a flagstone terrace and low balustrades. The warm glow of candlelight flickered in the downstairs windows and bats zoomed about overhead. Starlings swooped and dived in noisy formations as they came home to roost in the tops of the trees and beneath the eaves.

As she alighted from the carriage Lucetta stood for a moment, breathing in the sweet country air, so different from the putrid odours that had descended upon London with the early summer heat. She could smell roses and honeysuckle, mingling with the aroma of new mown hay from the surrounding fields. The Portland stone exterior of the house was mellowed by encroaching ivy and a Palladian pediment framed the main entrance. The door had been flung open to reveal a square entrance hall that was more homely than grand. As she entered the house Lucetta had the feeling that she had stepped back in time. The wainscoted walls were hung with family portraits and generations of the Hastings family seemed to stare at her, their glassy eyes following her every move. She almost felt the need to curtsey to a high-nosed lady who peered at her over a ruff as big as a dinner plate, but she was brought back to the present by the sound of footsteps echoing off the flagstones. Phyllis appeared from the back of the house, adjusting her white mobcap as she ran towards them. She bobbed a curtsey to Sir Hector. 'I'm all of a dither, sir. We've only just arrived ourselves and the men are still unloading the wagonette.'

'That's quite all right, Phyllis,' Sir Hector said,

handing her his top hat and gloves. 'There's no hurry.' He glanced over his shoulder as a tall, gaunt-looking woman appeared from a corridor which Lucetta later discovered led to the servants' quarters.

'Good evening, Sir Hector. I hope you had a good journey.'

'We did indeed, Mrs Comben,' Sir Hector replied affably. 'You are keeping in good health, I trust?'

'Thank you, sir. Tolerably good considering the winter we've had, and the damp that rises from the river and gets into my bones. But here I am going on about my rheumatics and you'll be wanting your dinner, I'm sure.'

'Quite so, ma'am. We're looking forward to sampling your excellent cooking. I hope it will be ready soon.'

'And I too,' Giles said, stepping forward to clasp Mrs Comben's hand. 'It's good to see you again, Mrs Comben. You look a picture of health, quite blooming in fact.'

Mrs Comben's thin cheeks flooded with colour and a smile transformed her taut features. 'Oh, sir, you are a one.'

'Undoubtedly,' Sir Hector said drily. 'But we can't stand about in the hall all evening. I'm sure that the ladies would like to refresh themselves after a long and dusty journey.'

'Your rooms are ready, sir.' Mrs Comben eyed Lucetta with a curious twitch of one eyebrow, but her expression softened as she turned to Mary. 'I was sorry to hear you had been unwell, Miss Mary.'

'I am quite recovered now, thank you, Mrs Comben.'

Mary held her hand out to Lucetta. 'As you know, we have a house guest. This is my good friend, Miss Lucetta Froy.'

Mrs Comben bobbed a curtsey. 'Welcome to Stockton Lacey, miss. I've put you in the room next to Miss Mary. I hope it will suit.'

'I'm sure it will, thank you,' Lucetta murmured, but Mrs Comben had turned away and was heading towards the wide oak staircase.

'Don't worry,' Giles whispered, grinning. 'She's always like this with strangers, but she has a heart of pure brass beneath that steel exterior.'

Mary raised her finger to her lips with a warning frown. 'Hush, Giles, she'll hear you. Come along, Lucetta. Let's hope that Phyllis has had time to unpack our clothes. I want to change before dinner.' Linking her arm through Lucetta's, Mary led her up the shallow flight of stairs which curved round to a galleried landing. The oak floorboards glowed like warm honey in the candlelight and the air was redolent with the scent of beeswax and lavender.

The door to the room at the top of the stairs had been left open and Lucetta could see Phyllis feverishly unpacking garments from Mary's leather valise.

'That is my room,' Mary said happily. 'You will be next door.'

Mrs Comben threw the door open and stood aside. 'I had a fire lit in both rooms. It's not cold but there's always that chill rising from the river.' She shivered. 'It gets into my bones.'

'Yes, Mrs Comben,' Mary said sympathetically. 'I'll

ask my cousin to prescribe some medicine to ease your rheumatics. Giles is an excellent physician.'

Mrs Comben sniffed, but her thin lips curved into a reluctant smile. 'I'm sure he is, miss. Perhaps he could take a look at Cook's bunions while he is here. She never stops complaining about them, but I suffer in silence.'

'Of course you do.' Mary patted her on the shoulder. 'Please tell Cook that we'll be ready to dine in half an hour.' She waited until the light from the housekeeper's candle had vanished into the darkness before turning to Lucetta with an apologetic smile. 'Don't take any notice of Mrs Comben. She's all bark and no bite, but like many country folk she's suspicious of strangers. It doesn't mean anything.'

Lucetta couldn't help wondering if news of her sudden appearance in Lonsdale Square had filtered down to Dorset, and if it had she could hardly blame the housekeeper for being a little suspicious and over-protective of her young mistress.

'It's only natural,' she murmured. 'I expect the servants have told her all about me.'

'It's none of their business, Lucetta. I will have sharp words to say to them if I hear any unkind tittle-tattle and so will Papa.'

Lucetta shook her head. 'I'm sure it won't come to that, and I love my room.' She glanced around at the collection of country-style furnishings, none of which matched, but the eclectic mix had the effect of making the ambience homely and welcoming. A log fire burned brightly in the grate and the flickering light from candles placed on the dressing table and tallboy reflected off the highly polished surfaces of beech wood and burr walnut. The floral pattern of the wallpaper had faded but retained its original charm. The chintz curtains and soft cover on the chair by the fireplace did not match, but somehow it did not matter. Impulsively, Lucetta kissed Mary's soft cheek. 'I love it,' she repeated. 'I feel at home already.'

Mary's eyes lit with a warm smile. 'I knew you would adore it here. This is my real home, although I do like the town house, but my heart will always be in the country.' She moved swiftly to the door. 'We'd best hurry and get changed for dinner. Papa doesn't like to be kept waiting, as I'm sure you have realised.' She left the room, closing the door behind.

Lucetta eyed her dinner gown neatly laid out on the white coverlet. She knew she must change for dinner but curiosity overcame her and she went to the window to draw back the curtains. Despite the summer dusk, there was just enough light in the sky to reveal a sweep of lawn beyond the terrace, and the pale glimmer of a lake beneath weeping willows. She threw up the sash and she could smell the damp earth and hear the tinkling of water as the stream rippled over a bed of stones. She was so used to the constant noise of the city that the sounds of the countryside were strange to her ears and slightly eerie. The hoot of a barn owl hunting, the distant bark of a dog fox and the rustling of the leaves as a breeze caressed the trees were a far cry from the drum of horses' hooves and the incessant rumble of cart wheels.

Reluctantly Lucetta closed the window and went to change her clothes. The Dorset countryside was quite different from the exotic shores of Bali, but on a night like this she found it easy to recall her last clandestine tryst with Sam. Where was he now? Was he thinking of her, or had he buried their love beneath the cold English soil with her supposed corpse? She sighed as she undid the buttons on her blouse and skirt, allowing the soiled garments to fall to the floor. There was only one way to find out. She must persuade Sir Hector to allow her to continue her journey to Devonshire. She made her mind up to broach the subject first thing in the morning when they were alone in his study.

But her plans were doomed to go astray as next morning at breakfast Sir Hector announced that he would be out for the entire day and Lucetta was to enjoy a well-earned rest after their long journey. Mary was openly delighted and began planning a list of local sights to show her. Giles offered to drive them in the dog cart as Sir Hector intended to do the rounds of his constituency in the landau, and Phyllis was despatched to the kitchen to ask Cook to prepare a picnic lunch. Lucetta told herself that another day's delay would make little difference and she hid her disappointment, not wanting to spoil Mary's enthusiasm for their outing.

They set off in the dog cart shortly after breakfast. Giles, looking the part of a country squire in tweeds and riding boots, handled the reins with relaxed expertise and Mary insisted that Lucetta took the seat beside him while she sat in the back with the picnic hamper. It was a bright sunny day with just a hint of crispness in the air and the promise of heat when the sun was high in the sky. The hedgerows sparkled with dew as they tooled along the country lane, past thatched cottages and open fields where cattle and sheep grazed contentedly on the fresh green grass.

'It looks so perfect,' Lucetta said dreamily. 'Like the watercolour paintings of rural life.'

'It may look picturesque,' Giles said, shaking his head, 'but there is as much poverty in the country as there is in the cities. It just looks prettier here.'

'Yes,' Mary added, leaning over the back of the seat. 'Farm workers' wages are disgustingly low and the farmers themselves have been struggling since the land enclosures. Papa will hear many tales of bankruptcy and hardship today, but I daresay he will tell you all about it when you do his correspondence tomorrow.'

Lucetta opened her mouth to tell them that she intended to ask for time off so that she could make the journey to Devonshire, but Giles had drawn the pony to a halt outside a small thatched cottage a few hundred yards upriver from the mill house which they had just passed.

'You must have a wish, Lucetta,' he said, pulling on the brake and securing the reins as he leapt off the driver's seat.

'A wish?' Lucetta turned her head to give Mary a puzzled glance.

'It's the wishing well,' Mary explained. 'The old lady who lives in the cottage serves tea and cakes which she bakes herself and there is a wishing well down by the river's edge. You must throw in a coin and make a wish.'

Giles had come round to Lucetta's side of the trap, and he held out his hand. 'It's quite famous. You must wish but you mustn't tell or it won't come true.' He helped her down from the cart, holding on to her hand just a little longer than necessary and smiling into her eyes with a look that she knew would have warmed the hardest heart. Hers was at this moment as soft as whipped cream.

The moment passed in an instant as Giles released her hand and went round to help Mary alight from the back of the trap. Lucetta watched them together, thinking what a handsome pair they made and what beautiful dark-haired, dark-eyed children they might produce if they were to marry. She wondered why Giles, who was such an intelligent, caring man, could not see that Mary absolutely adored him, and she would make him the most devoted and loving of wives. But he seemed totally oblivious to the silent messages she was sending him. Lucetta wanted to give him a good shake and force him to see Mary with different eyes.

'Come along,' he said affably. 'Don't stand there day-dreaming, Lucetta. You won't get your wish by doing nothing.'

'No, indeed,' Mary said, tucking her hand in the crook of his arm. 'I think I know what Lucetta might wish for, but it's our secret.'

'I know what my heart's desire is, and I shan't tell either of you. That is my secret.'

They walked arm in arm through a wicket gate and down a pathway lined with pink and white hollyhocks to the thatched porch where an old lady sat with a tin cup at her side containing just a few pennies.

'Welcome to the wishing well,' she said with a gummy grin. 'Shall you take tea and some of my scones, sir? I've just took a fresh batch out of the oven, and there's strawberry jam made with berries from my own garden.'

'That sounds wonderful, mother,' Giles said, throwing a silver sixpence into her can. 'Maybe you have some fresh cream too?'

With surprising agility the old woman rose to her feet. 'I'll see what I can do for you and the maidies, sir.'

As Giles led them round to the back of the cottage into a well-stocked garden, Mary pulled a face at Lucetta. 'His charm works every time,' she whispered, giggling. 'Giles has a way with women from the age of seven to seventy.'

'Naturally,' Giles said airily. 'I am particularly successful with martinets like Sister Demarest.' He stopped walking as they reached the river's edge where a crudely made stone well had been erected.

Lucetta leaned over the side, looking down into the clear, shallow water. Nestling on the smooth round pebbles some coppers glinted in the sunlight.

'Be careful,' Giles warned. 'The stones are slippery. You might fall in.'

Just as Lucetta was about to tell him that she was perfectly safe, her leather-soled shoes lost their grip on the wet moss and she would have toppled in had Giles not caught her round the waist. His arms tightened around her and she could feel the warmth of his body as he held her close to his chest. He released her with a sudden movement that caused her stumble and clutch the side of the well for support. The brief moment of physical contact had made her pulses race, and she could feel her cheeks reddening. She glanced anxiously at Mary but she didn't seem to have noticed anything untoward.

'That was a near thing,' Mary said, smiling. 'You wouldn't have drowned had you fallen in the water, but you might have caught a chill. There is always a cool breeze blowing down by the river.'

Giles thrust his hand in his pocket and took out a handful of change, which he pressed into Mary's outstretched hand. 'Here, make your wishes and I'll go and see what has happened to the tea,' he said abruptly.

Lucetta watched him striding up the garden path and her heart was heavy inside her breast. She knew that she must go to Devon as soon as possible. To delay any longer would bring disaster on them all.

Chapter Fifteen

'But I need you here, Lucetta,' Sir Hector said, frowning as he wiped his lips on his table napkin. 'We have much work to do.'

'And I will do it when I return from Salcombe, sir.'

Sir Hector did not look convinced. 'And when will that be? How long do you propose to be away?'

Lucetta shot a glance beneath her lashes at Giles, who had stopped eating his dinner and was staring down at his plate. She turned to Mary who gave her an encouraging smile.

'I don't know, sir. A day or two, I should think. I can catch the train at the nearest railway station, or get the mail coach.'

'Both of which will take the best part of a day by the time you have changed trains or the mail coach has stopped for fresh horses,' Giles said, looking up with a set expression on his face. 'It's not a good idea for a young woman to travel unaccompanied.'

'Indeed not,' Sir Hector said firmly. 'I wouldn't allow Mary to traipse around the country on her own.'

'I could go with her, Papa,' Mary volunteered eagerly.

'Out of the question,' Sir Hector replied, pushing his dinner plate away. 'Really, you modern young women have no sense of decorum, or danger if it comes to that.'

'Please, Sir Hector,' Lucetta said, rising from the table. 'Please reconsider. You knew that it was my intention to seek out my fiancé. I told you that at the outset.'

'Yes, but I had not thought you would leave until I had finished my business in Dorset. It was always my intention that I should accompany you, but that is impossible at the moment.' Sir Hector stared at her with a perplexed frown. 'Please sit down and finish your meal. There are people not so fortunate as ourselves who are starving; I cannot bear to see good food go to waste.'

Reluctantly, Lucetta sat down and picked up her knife and fork, but she only pushed the roast meat around her plate. She knew she could not swallow another morsel.

'I will take Lucetta to Devonshire,' Giles said, breaking the silence. 'She will be safe with me.'

Lucetta raised her eyes to meet his and she was about to refuse his offer but Mary spoke first.

'That's a splendid idea, Giles. And I will come too if Papa will let me. We will be a merry party if we go together.' She turned to her father with a persuasive smile. 'May I, Papa? May I go with Giles and Lucetta? We won't be away for long, I promise you.'

Sir Hector looked from one to the other and Lucetta held her breath. The last thing she wanted was for Giles to accompany her on this particular journey, but if there was no other way she could hardly refuse.

'Go on, Papa,' Mary urged. 'Do say yes. I've never been to Devon and I'm sure that the sea air will be good for me.'

'Very well, I suppose I must honour my promise to Lucetta, but you must not be gone for more than a week. I insist on that.'

Lucetta breathed a sigh of relief. 'Thank you, sir,' she murmured. 'If it's all the same to you, I would like to go tomorrow.'

Despite his initial reluctance, Sir Hector relented so far as to insist that they travelled in the landau. He could not, he said, allow Mary to undertake the journey in any way that might jeopardise her continued recovery, and he could manage very well with the dog cart or make the rounds of his constituency on horseback.

They set off early next morning and the steady rainfall did nothing to dampen their high spirits. Giles and Mary seemed to be in a holiday mood, and despite her state of nervous apprehension Lucetta found herself affected by their ebullient mood.

'No one will know us,' Mary said excitedly as the carriage sped through open countryside. 'We might be brother and sisters, Giles, or even husband and wife.' She paused, glancing at him beneath her lashes and blushing to the roots of her hair. 'Well, you know what I mean.'

He leaned back against the squabs, smiling lazily. 'And which one of you is going to be Mrs Harcourt? Or am I allowed to choose?'

Giles was seated opposite her, but Lucetta could not look him in the eye and she stared out of the window, deliberately ignoring his question.

'I was joking, Giles,' Mary said hastily. 'I just meant

that – well, you know that I was suggesting that we would be free from the constraints put on us by society. Don't tease me.'

'Perhaps I have two wives,' Giles said, chuckling. 'Maybe I am a real life Bluebeard.'

Mary tossed her glove at him. 'Stop it, or I will go and sit on the box next to Crabtree.'

'Oh, look,' Lucetta said in an attempt to change the subject. 'I can see a small town nestling at the foot of the cliffs. Where are we, Giles?'

He leaned forward, following her gaze. 'It must be Lyme Regis.'

'And it has stopped raining at last,' Mary said, flashing a grateful smile at Lucetta. 'Perhaps we can stop at an inn? I would love a cup of coffee.'

Giles leaned out of the window. 'Stop at the most likely-looking inn, if you please, Crabtree. We are in desperate need of sustenance.' He resumed his seat. 'Now which of you lovely ladies is going to be my wife at this stop?'

Lucetta gave him a direct look and dissolved into giggles as she saw the laughter in his eyes. 'If we are going to play let's pretend, then I choose to go first.' She changed seats so that they were sitting side by side. 'I will be the first Mrs Harcourt and you will find me a complete shrew, Giles. I will take every opportunity to complain. I will contradict everything you say and I will nag you until you wish that you had grounds for divorce.'

'This I want to see,' Mary said, clapping her hands. 'You will be sorry you ever thought up this game, Giles.'

He took Lucetta's hand and held it. 'I look forward to every painful moment of being a hen-pecked husband.'

They broke the journey at a coaching inn on the outskirts of the town, and Lucetta took on the role of a peevish termagant so well that she caused some raised eyebrows. Mary seemed amused at first, but as they warmed to their roles she began to look uncomfortable and she begged them to stop, but Giles was obviously enjoying himself. He declared that his favourite play at school had been *The Taming of the Shrew*, and if Lucetta insisted on acting out the part, he might be forced to take sterner measures. Lucetta had also studied Shakespeare under the strict eye of Miss Jones and she would have taken on the challenge but for Crabtree, who appeared at the parlour door, respectfully suggesting that they continue the journey if they wanted to reach Exeter in time to book rooms for the night.

'I think it's just as well we stop the charade now,' Mary said, as they left the inn. 'You and Lucetta were much too convincing as an old married couple, Giles.'

Her tone was light, but Lucetta sensed the pain behind Mary's words. 'It was just play-acting,' she murmured. 'A silly old game, that's all.'

'Mary is right,' Giles said, taking her by the arm. 'We had better not carry on so at the next stop, or we might find ourselves asked to leave. Young Lucetta is too good an actress by far, don't you think, my dear?'

Mary glanced at him over her shoulder as he assisted

her into the carriage. 'And are you a good actor, Giles? I think you must be, since it was a most convincing performance.'

The sun might have come out, but the party was much more subdued as they travelled onwards into Devonshire. Giles closed his eyes and appeared to sleep for the rest of the journey and Mary lapsed into silence, staring out of the window at the gently rolling hills and wooded vales. Lucetta was left to her own thoughts and these inevitably turned to Sam. She tried to imagine their reunion, but she was even more nervous now and unsure of the outcome. When they reached the inn where they were to spend the night, she had to conquer the desire to beg Crabtree to turn the carriage around and head back to Stockton Lacey. She had come this far, she reasoned, and she would never forgive herself if she lost this opportunity to find her lost love.

They enjoyed a good meal in a private parlour and harmony was restored to their little group, with no mention of what had passed earlier that day. Giles was in good spirits, keeping them entertained with accounts of his exploits as a medical student, and Mary listened avidly, hanging on every word, although Lucetta was certain she must have heard it all before.

To her surprise, Lucetta had a good night's sleep. She had expected to lie in the lumpy four-poster bed, tossing and turning into the small hours, but in reality she drifted off the moment her head touched the pillow. Next morning, they breakfasted on hot bread rolls fresh from the oven, smothered with butter, homemade preserve and crowned with dollops of thick yellow clotted cream, washed down by excellent coffee. Giles declared himself to be a devotee of Devonshire food and he tipped the landlord handsomely as they left the inn.

Mary squeezed Lucetta's hand as they settled down in the carriage on the last lap of their journey. 'Not long now, Daisy dear. I'm sorry, I do try to call you Lucetta but today you have something of that lost look which I found so touching when you were in hospital.'

Lucetta managed a weak smile. 'I'm nervous, that's all. And I don't mind being called Daisy. I think it's a sweet name.'

'Sweet, indeed,' Giles said, grinning. 'We will call our first daughter Daisy.' He paused and his smile faded as he met Mary's stern gaze. 'I'm sorry. I had lapsed into play-acting again.'

Mary turned her back on him and she took Lucetta's hand, giving it a gentle squeeze. 'When you meet your Sam again he will be able to confirm your true identity. It may not satisfy your Uncle Bradley, but it might encourage others who knew you to admit the truth.'

Lucetta nodded wordlessly; so much depended on this reunion. Her whole life seemed to be hanging in the balance. She sat in silence for most of the way, lost in her own thoughts, oblivious to Mary's cheerful chatter and leaving the responses to Giles.

The county lanes grew narrower and the banks steeper as they drew closer to Salcombe. The striking beauty of the area took Lucetta's breath away as they crested the brow of the hill and descended into a wide, wooded inlet. As the landau threaded its way through the narrow village streets, she was in a fever of anticipation. Her heart thumped at an alarming rate against the whalebone prison of her stays and she was finding it increasingly difficult to breathe. Her palms were sticky with perspiration and her mouth was dry as Crabtree drew the carriage to a halt and went to make enquiries at an inn. He returned minutes later, smelling suspiciously of ale which suggested that he had downed a pint in a great hurry. He said the inn had no letting rooms, but he had been given particulars of a hostelry on the outskirts of the village which could offer adequate stabling for the horses and superior accommodation suitable for the young ladies.

Lucetta fumed inwardly at the delay and had to resist the temptation to leap out of the carriage and make her way to Cutler's Boatyard on foot, but a sympathetic pat on the arm from Mary persuaded her to be patient for just a while longer. She suffered the rest of the journey in a fever of nervous excitement, and when Mary exclaimed at the beauty of the sandy cove that stretched out before them, Lucetta merely nodded in agreement. At any other time she would have been enthusiastic about the view, but at this particular moment she was too preoccupied with her own thoughts to care.

The landlord came out to greet them and Giles ordered a light luncheon to be brought to the parlour while their rooms were made ready. Food was the last thing on Lucetta's mind, and she was tempted to raise an objection, but Mary was so enthusiastic about the quaint charm of their surroundings that Lucetta had once again to contain her impatience. She made a brave attempt to eat, but she had little appetite. When the meal was over, Giles suggested that they hired a fishing boat. In discussion with the landlord he had discovered that fishermen often ferried visitors to the village, obviating the necessity to travel the steep and tortuous lanes.

The sea was the colour of blue-green glass tipped with foamy white spume as a brisk breeze filled the sails and sent the small boat scudding across the water. Lucetta could taste the salt on her lips and the wind whipped tendrils of hair into wild disarray around her forehead, but she had more important concerns than her appearance as the old fisherman skilfully brought his craft alongside the stone steps leading up to the quay. Her feet barely seemed to touch the ground as they walked the short distance to the end of the street where a sign advertised the site of Cutler's Boatyard. She felt as though the breath had been sucked out of her lungs as they descended the stone steps to the foreshore.

There was no one in sight, and if it had not been for the sound of hammering emanating from the half-completed hull of a fishing vessel, Lucetta would have thought that the yard was deserted. The smell of fresh sawdust took her back to Wilkinson's timber yard and the days following her escape from Stranks and Guthrie. It was not a happy reminder, and she was seized by a sudden and inexplicable sense of foreboding.

Mary touched her gently on the arm. 'There's a shack of some sort over there, behind that great pile of wooden planks. I think I saw someone moving inside.'

Lucetta glanced at Giles, but he was taking a closer look at the vessel under construction and he appeared to have lost interest in their mission. She braced her shoulders. 'Well, I won't find anything out by standing here.' She picked up her skirts, and treading carefully around crates of nails, kedges and coils of rope she made her way towards the wooden shed. She was about to climb the steps to knock on the door when it was wrenched open by a man with his shirtsleeves rolled up to expose sinewy, tattooed forearms. He stared at her with a less than friendly expression on his rugged features. 'Well? What's your business here, maidy? This is a boatyard, not a tea shop.'

Lucetta took an involuntary step backwards. 'I was looking for Mr Cutler. Can you tell me where to find him, sir?'

He leapt from the top step to stand beside her, and his sandy brows drew together in an ominous frown. 'Who wants him?'

'My business is with Mr Sam Cutler or his father, if he is about.'

'You'll have to go to the churchyard to find Bill Cutler. He's been dead these past twenty years.'

His hazel eyes glinted with something like humour, or it could have been malice; Lucetta was not sure which and this unnerved her even more, but she eyed him steadily, refusing to be cowed by his aggressive attitude. 'It's Samuel Cutler I wanted to see. Is he here?' She heard her voice waver and she clasped her hands tightly behind her back so that the unfriendly man would not see how they trembled.

'It wouldn't have anything to do with a letter, would it?' he demanded, angling his head.

The sun had gone in but for a brief moment it forced its way between gathering rainclouds. Lucetta caught her breath to see the man's sweat-darkened hair glint with russet tones so similar to Sam's that she was certain they must be related. 'Are you his brother by any chance?'

He threw back his head and his laughter echoed off the granite quay wall. 'You'm a persistent young maid, to be sure. Well, you've had a wasted journey. Sam isn't here and he can rot in hell for all I care.'

'Hold on, mister.' Giles came striding over the mud to stand by Lucetta's side. 'What's this fellow been saying to you? I don't like his tone.'

Mary hurried towards them, her face pale and pinched with anxiety. 'Is everything all right, Lucetta?'

'Quite all right, don't worry,' Lucetta said firmly. 'This gentleman was just telling me that Sam is not welcome here, although he hasn't had the good manners to introduce himself or to give me a reasonable explanation.'

'What have you to say for yourself?' Giles demanded angrily. 'This is no way to treat a young lady who has travelled many miles to see her fiancé.'

'Fiancé! Bah! Let me tell you this, mate. Samuel Cutler is like all seafarers. Haven't you heard they have a woman in every port? He may be my cousin but I won't have anything to do with him, and I don't know where he is. Now go away the lot of you and leave us be.'

'It's not true,' Lucetta cried, grabbing him by the sleeve. 'You can't just say things like that and walk away. What is your name, sir? Or haven't you got one?'

He turned on her with a scornful curl of his lips. 'I'm Seth Cutler, and my father took Sam in when his ma and pa were drowned. Brought him up like one of his own, he did, and little or no thanks he got for it. Sam is bad news, maidy. You'm better off without him.'

Lucetta was not going to give in so easily. 'You mentioned my letter. Did he receive it?'

'It went on the fire,' Seth hissed. 'Dora read it and threw it into the flames. She watched it burn to ashes like the promises Sam made her before he went off to sea.'

Mary clasped Lucetta's arm. 'Come away. You don't have to listen to this madman.'

'Yes,' Giles added, hooking his arm around Lucetta's shoulders. 'We should leave now.'

Lucetta shook free from them, facing Seth squarely with her chin raised. 'What are you saying? Who is Dora? I must know.'

'She is my wife now. I done the honourable thing and married the wench when Sam deserted her. That's the sort of man he is.'

'I don't believe you,' Lucetta gasped. 'I won't believe it unless I hear it from your wife's lips.'

Seth took a step towards her, fisting his hands at his side. 'Leave my Dora out of this. Go back to London-town or wherever it is you come from. There's nothing but trouble for you in these parts.' He turned away and stomped off towards the vessel where he climbed a ladder and disappeared inside the hull.

Giles took Lucetta by the hand. 'I'm so sorry.'

'And I too,' Mary said, choking back a sob. 'I wish we'd never come here.'

'He must be lying,' Lucetta whispered. 'I don't believe a word of it.'

'We'll go back to the inn,' Giles said gently. 'It's too late to start out for home, but we'll leave first thing in the morning.'

Lucetta shook her head. 'No, I can't go without speaking to Dora. I must find out the truth, no matter how painful it is.'

Giles opened his mouth as if to protest, but Mary laid her hand on his arm. 'She's right, Giles. If I were in the same position I would want to know the worst.'

Lucetta was not going to argue. She made her way back towards the stone steps leaving Giles and Mary little alternative but to follow her. When she reached street level she paused, realising that she had no idea where Seth Cutler lived. Small children were playing on the pavement and Lucetta picked out the eldest, a handsome little fellow with auburn hair and large hazel eyes. She approached him with what she hoped was a friendly smile. 'Hello there, young man.'

The boy, who could not have been much older than three or four, stared at her open-mouthed.

She tried again. 'I'm looking for Mrs Cutler. Do you know where I might find her?'

The child opened his mouth and began to howl.

'No, please don't cry,' Lucetta said, laying her hand on his thin shoulder in an attempt to comfort him. 'I won't hurt you.'

'Hey, there. Leave my boy alone.'

The sound of running footsteps made Lucetta spin round to see a young woman racing across the cobblestones with her fair hair flying out behind her like a flag, and a sobbing baby in her arms.

'Mama!' The boy hurled himself at the woman, clutching her round the legs and stopping her in her tracks.

'I'm sorry,' Lucetta said hastily. 'I didn't mean to frighten him. I only asked where I could find Mrs Cutler.'

Giles and Mary were now standing behind her, and with an angry mother looking as though she was ready to attack her, Lucetta was glad of their support.

'We meant no harm,' Giles said smoothly. 'We can pay for the information we require.'

The woman moved to the edge of the quay wall. 'Seth,' she screamed. 'Come here.'

'You must be Dora.' Lucetta moved slowly towards her, holding out her hand. 'We've just spoken to your husband.'

'What d'you want?' Dora demanded, glancing anxiously over her shoulder as if willing her husband to come to her aid. 'Who be you?'

'I came looking for Sam,' Lucetta said, hoping and

praying that Seth had not heard his wife's cry for help. 'I'm Lucetta Froy. I wrote him a letter.'

Dora curled her lip. 'I read it and then I burnt it for the nonsense it was. Sam's took you for a fool and you ain't the first neither.'

'Maybe, but I need to find him. Can you tell me where he might be?'

'In the family way, are you?' Dora tossed her head. 'Like I said, you wouldn't be the first.'

'Come away, Lucetta,' Giles said, taking her by the arm. 'You won't do any good here.'

Dora turned on him like a fury. 'What's the matter, master? Ain't we good enough to speak to the likes of you and her?'

'We've come a long way, Mrs Cutler,' Mary said in a soothing tone. 'Perhaps we could talk this over in private?' She glanced over her shoulder at the crowd of women who had come out of their homes perhaps to enjoy the spectacle, or to see off the strangers who had disturbed their peace.

'Go back where you come from then,' Dora said, spitting on the ground at Lucetta's feet. 'Sam wooed me with his soft words and winning ways and then he left me on the eve of our wedding. Jilted me, he did, and made me look a fool in the eyes of the whole village. It looks like he done the same to you.' She wiped her son's eyes on the corner of her grubby apron, and taking him by the hand she strode off down the street.

'We'd best go quickly,' Mary whispered, staring nervously at the women who showed no sign of dispersing.

Giles stepped forward, addressing the crowd. 'The show is over, ladies. We're leaving.'

The women melted away, disappearing into their homes and closing their doors behind them. Lucetta walked down the street with her head held high. She was not going to allow the people who had known Sam to see that her heart was breaking and that her life was in ruins, all her bright hopes of love and marriage gone. She could hear Giles and Mary following close behind her and she was grateful to them for their support, but what she wanted most was to be left alone to deal with the emotions that assailed her as she attempted to absorb the Cutlers' savage words. She was hurt and angry, but a small voice in her head kept insisting that it was all a pack of lies. Whatever Sam had done in the past, she could not bring herself to believe ill of him. She might have been a green girl then, but deep down she was certain that Sam Cutler had been sincere when he told her that he loved her and wanted her to be his wife.

Giles caught up with her as she reached the quay where they had left the boatman. 'Are you all right, Lucetta?'

She could not look him in the face and the words stuck in her throat. She nodded her head.

'I told the fisherman to wait for us,' Giles continued conversationally. 'I'll just see if he's ready to take us back to the cove.'

He exchanged meaningful looks with Mary, the significance of which was not lost on Lucetta. She knew they were concerned for her but their kindness was overwhelming. She had tears in her eyes as she watched Giles striding over to the quay wall where the fisherman was sitting on an upturned lobster pot, smoking a clay pipe.

Mary laid her arm around Lucetta's shoulder. 'I don't know what to say, other than I am so sorry things worked out this way.'

Lucetta forced a smile. 'I am all right, really I am. I won't throw myself in the sea if that's what you're afraid of, Mary.'

'No, of course it isn't,' Mary said hastily. 'It was just so horrid for you having to listen to all that hateful nonsense. I'm sure none of it was true.'

'Thank you for being so understanding, Mary, but I know you don't believe that. You and Giles have warned me often enough and I chose not to listen.'

'But what does your heart tell you?'

'I don't know,' Lucetta said sadly. 'I'm so confused, and I really don't want to talk about it. Look, Giles is waving at us. I think the boatman is ready to take us back to the cove.'

'Yes, of course. We'd best hurry, for it looks like rain.'

Mary's fears were proved right and they were all soaked to the skin well before they landed in the cove. Giles stepped over the side knee deep in water and carried Lucetta ashore, returning to the boat for Mary. Lucetta tramped across the wet sand and clumps of slippery seaweed to the inn. She was met by an anxious-looking chambermaid who threw up her hands in horror.

'Best change out of them clothes afore you catch your death of cold, miss. I'll light a fire in your room and you can dry your things.'

Lucetta murmured her thanks, but going down with a chill was the least of her worries. She went straight to her room and as she closed the door she sighed with relief. For once she was grateful for solitude. Keeping up a light conversation with Mary and Giles during the boat ride had been agonising, but she knew that they were only trying to keep up her spirits and she had done her best to respond. She stripped off her wet garments and had just wrapped herself in a silk robe when the maid returned with kindling and a tinderbox.

'Did you find the Cutlers' yard, miss?'

Lucetta stared at her in surprise. 'How did you know where we were going?'

The girl busied herself laying the fire. 'Mr Harcourt asked my pa for directions, miss.' She sat back on her haunches watching the flames lick round the dry sticks.

'Do you know the Cutler family?'

'Oh, yes, miss. Dora Cutler is my cousin, although we don't have nothing to do with her and that man she married. Silly besom got herself in the family way by young Sam Cutler and he left her at the altar, so she married his cousin Seth.'

'Sam jilted her when she was carrying his child?' Lucetta could hardly frame the words, as the awful truth filtered into her brain. 'That's just not possible.'

'The boy is the spitting image of Sam. Young Tommy must be coming on four now and never knew his real pa. Still, that's the way it goes. Can I get you a nice hot cup of tea, miss? You look awful pale.'

Later that evening after dinner in the inn parlour, Lucetta excused herself on the pretext of having a headache, but instead of going to bed she slipped out through the crowded taproom. The cool night air was fresh and clean after the fuggy, smoky atmosphere indoors and a gentle breeze caressed her hot cheeks. A large silver moon hung suspended in a dark sky studded with pinpoints of twinkling stars and a pathway of moonlight slivered across the water to the far side of the estuary. The gentle swish of the waves on the shore had a soothing effect on her shredded nerves. She had tried to appear cheerful throughout the meal, but there had been awkward silences during which Giles and Mary exchanged agonised glances until one of them thought of something else to say.

Lucetta took deep breaths of the salt-laden air. A faint waft of tobacco smoke drifted through the open windows of the taproom and she could hear the muted sound of deep male voices and the occasional burst of laughter. She turned with a start as she heard the crunch of booted feet on the pebbles. Giles smiled as he slipped her mantle, now completely dry, around her shoulders. 'It's chilly,' he said simply. 'Mary was worried that you might take a chill.'

'Thank you, Giles. I'm sorry I was not better company at dinner.'

'We understand, Lucetta. You have nothing to apologise for.'

'You are both so kind to me. I don't know what I have done to deserve such good friends.' She turned away, unable to meet his gaze. 'I'm sorry I dragged you and Mary down here. I should have listened to your advice.'

Giles took her gently by the shoulders, turning her to face him. 'Does anyone ever pay attention to the advice of others? Good or bad.'

The tender smile and sympathetic look in his eyes made her lips tremble. 'Oh, Giles.'

He drew her close. 'Forget him, Lucetta. I was not going to say anything yet, but I can't hold back any longer. You must know how I feel about you, my love.'

Her heart missed a beat. Of course she knew, and had known for a long time, but she had hoped that it might be just a passing fancy. 'Please don't say any more, Giles.' She tried to pull away from him, but his hands tightened on her shoulders and he looked deeply into her eyes.

'I love you.'

He was the last person on earth she wanted to hurt, but panic raged in her breast and she shook her head. 'No, please . . .'

He laid his finger on her lips. 'You are suffering, I know, but please hear me out. I know I am a few years older than you and not your first choice, but I can offer you the protection of my name and a position in society as well as my whole heart. In short, and I know I'm making a complete mess of this, but – will you marry me, my dearest Lucetta?'

Chapter Sixteen

Rejecting Giles' proposal was the most painful and difficult thing she had ever done, but Lucetta had left him in no doubt as to her feelings. She had taken off the gold bracelet and thrust it into his hands before fleeing to the safety of her room, where she gave full vent to her emotions in an explosion of grief. She truly felt that she had lost everything dear to her, including the man whom she had cherished as a dear friend. She was convinced that her heart was broken and would never mend.

Breakfast next morning was a stilted affair and the journey back to Stockton Lacey was completed for the most part in silence. Mary's unspoken sympathy was hard to bear and it was obvious that she had no knowledge of Giles' proposal, which made it even more painful. He had chosen to hire a horse and ride on ahead, making the excuse that he needed the exercise. Lucetta pleaded a sick headache, which was no lie, and she closed her eyes feigning sleep. They stopped to change horses and take some refreshment but Giles decided that they would travel on instead of putting up for the night. It was late in the evening when they finally arrived at the Grange.

If Sir Hector was surprised by their unexpectedly

early return from Devonshire he gave no sign of it. Lucetta could only guess that Giles had given him some sort of explanation when he arrived ahead of the carriage. She was too exhausted to utter anything other than a brief greeting before climbing the stairs to her room. It was sheer bliss to find that it had been made ready for her; the bed sheets turned down, a clean nightgown laid out on the coverlet, a fire lit in the grate and a jug of hot water ready and waiting on the washstand. She undressed, washed and collapsed with a sigh into the soft embrace of the feather bed. She had slept very little the previous night and now, overcome by both physical and mental exhaustion, she sank into a deep and dreamless sleep.

When she awakened next morning, she knew that it would be impossible to keep Giles' proposal of marriage secret while they were staying in the same house. Their relationship at best must appear stilted to those who loved them, and Mary would soon realise that something was wrong. Heavy-hearted and dispirited, Lucetta climbed out of bed. The water in the ewer was cooling rapidly and after a quick wash, she put on a plain grey morning gown. Taking a seat in front of the dressing table she picked up a silver-backed hairbrush and began brushing her hair in long, slow strokes. The sun slanted through the window-panes and outside she could hear the joyous notes of birdsong. Life would go on, although she felt that hers was already at an end. By omitting to tell her of his sordid past, whether it had been intentional, or unintentional, Sam had misled her. How could she have any faith in his protestations of love and devotion when she knew how badly he had treated Dora and his unborn child? And how could she face Mary with Giles' proposal of marriage still fresh in her memory?

Lucetta glared at her reflection in the mirror as she brushed the tangles from her hair. 'Who are you?' she demanded out loud. 'You are nobody. You bring misfortune wherever you go. Mama and Papa might still be alive if you hadn't wilfully disobeyed them by consorting with Sam Cutler. You fell for his sweet words and his lies, and now you are about to bring misery on the person who has done the most for you.' She shook the hairbrush at her reflection. 'Shame on you, Lucetta.'

A soft tap on the door made her jump. 'Yes, who's there?'

'It's Phyllis. Miss Mary sent me to see if you want breakfast brought to your room on a tray, or if you would like to join them in the dining room.'

Lucetta scowled at the pale-faced girl in the mirror. 'Stop being a coward. You've got to face them sometime,' she whispered. Rising to her feet she raised her voice. 'I'm coming right away, Phyllis.'

Sir Hector was seated in his usual place at the head of the dining table with Mary on his left. Lucetta was quick to notice the empty place setting where Giles would normally be taking his meal. She was torn between relief that he was absent and anxiety in case he had merely overslept and might appear at any moment. With a determined effort to act normally, she took her seat opposite Mary and was greeted by a warm smile.

'I trust you slept well?' Sir Hector said, wiping his lips on a starched white linen napkin. 'I must say I would have broken the journey somewhere en route. I wouldn't have fancied sitting all those hours in the carriage.'

'It was Giles who was eager to hurry home, Papa.' Mary rose to her feet, taking her plate to the sideboard where she helped herself to devilled kidneys and a slice of bacon. 'He left for London first thing this morning.' She returned to the table, glancing at her father with a mischievous smile. 'I made him tell me, Papa. I knew there was something going on.'

Sir Hector pinched her cheek. 'Minx! You should have waited until he was ready to share his news.'

Lucetta's hand trembled as she lifted the lid of a silver dish and selected a toasted muffin. 'His news?'

'Yes, the secret is out now,' Mary said gleefully. 'Giles has been offered the medical practice in the village and he's gone to London to sort out his affairs. Papa made it possible, I'm certain, but he won't admit it.'

Sir Hector smiled, shaking his head. 'I wouldn't dream of encouraging nepotism, my love, but I might have put a good word in for the boy, and I might have offered a little financial help.'

'You know you did, Papa. And I think it was a wonderful thing to do. Giles was never cut out to be a fashionable doctor in Harley Street. He cares too much for the poor and needy to make a fortune from rich people who would have him at their beck and call for nothing more than a sore thumb.'

'And I know how much it means to you, poppet. I've always hoped that one day you and Giles might make a match of it, and what better than to have my daughter and her family living close to our country home, which one day will be hers anyway.'

Mary's cheeks flushed prettily. 'Oh, Pa. Don't say such things. There's nothing between Giles and me. It's all in your imagination.'

'Is it, puss?' Sir Hector's deep laugh echoed off the wainscoted walls. 'I'm not blind, my love. Nor have I forgotten what it is to be young and in love.' He turned to Lucetta with a broad smile. 'My little girl thinks I am too old to understand affairs of the heart, but that is far from the truth. I am a man in my prime, am I not, Lucetta?'

Lucetta pushed her plate away, the buttered muffin left uneaten. 'I am sure you are, sir.'

He rose to his feet. 'And I have work to do. When you have finished your breakfast I would like you to join me in my study, if you are not too tired after your long journey, that is.'

'I am not tired.' Lucetta could not face being left alone with Mary. 'I will come now, Sir Hector.'

'But you haven't eaten a thing,' Mary protested. 'You must have something, Lucetta. I'll ring for a fresh pot of coffee, or would you prefer tea?'

'I'll have something later,' Lucetta said, pushing back her chair. 'I'm not hungry and I'd like to make an early start.'

'Capital,' Sir Hector said, holding the door open. 'Your enthusiasm for work does you credit, my dear.'

He glanced over his shoulder. 'And you should rest, Mary. You are still convalescent and must not overexert yourself.'

'Yes, Papa,' Mary said, dimpling. 'But we will have luncheon together, Lucetta, and perhaps afterwards we could walk into the village and I will show you the doctor's house and surgery. I couldn't be more thrilled for Giles.'

Lucetta nodded mutely as she hurried out of the room. It was a relief to know that Mary was in ignorance of what had passed between herself and Giles, but it was just a matter of time before she discovered the truth. Sir Hector strode past her, making his way towards the side of the house where his study was situated well away from the main reception rooms.

'It's good to have you home once again,' he said as he ushered her into the book-lined room. 'I've missed our mornings together, Lucetta. In fact I'd go so far as to say I've never had a secretary who was so compatible to my way of thinking and working. I hope you feel the same, my dear.'

Lucetta perched on the edge of a chair placed strategically in front of the desk. She reached for her notebook and pencil. 'Yes, sir,' she murmured, flicking through the pages to find a clean sheet.

Sir Hector took his seat and began to sift through a pile of correspondence. 'You are happy here with us, aren't you, Lucetta? I mean even if we fail to get a reply from the consulate in Bali, I would hope you might stay on and continue to work for me.'

Lucetta looked up, staring at him with a puzzled frown. She felt drained of all emotion and oddly distant from everything around her. 'I hope that Sir John will confirm my identity, Sir Hector.'

'Yes, of course. That must be so, but supposing the likeness is not true enough or that you have changed considerably since they last saw you. After all, it is over a year since you left Bali and you were little more than a child then.'

'I was seventeen, sir. Hardly a child, and in less than six months I will be nineteen.'

'Yes, that's true. And I am forty-five. That must seem very old to you.'

He was gazing at her with an eager, almost boyish expression in his blue eyes and Lucetta had not the heart to tell him that he was the same age as her father would have been had he lived. She shrugged her shoulders, trying to sound positive. 'Not really, sir. I daresay that age is more to do with how one feels and thinks rather than actual years.'

'Well said. I agree entirely.'

He sounded so relieved that Lucetta was glad she had told a white lie, and she gave him a reassuring smile. 'Perhaps we should start work, sir?'

'Yes, we must begin.' He reached for his spectacles and put them on. He rifled through a pile of correspondence, finally choosing a dog-eared piece of paper covered in ink blots. 'We will begin with a letter to this lady who feels that she has been unfairly dealt with by her landlord.'

Lucetta lost track of time as she took down Sir

Hector's slow dictation, but her thoughts were far away from the study with its well-worn furnishings and faded velvet curtains. While Sir Hector gathered his thoughts, she gazed out of the window at the waving green fronds of a weeping willow leaning at a precarious angle over the stream. The flash of a kingfisher's plumage caught her eye, and the bright colours of its feathers reminded her forcibly of the exotic island of Bali. Had it all been a dream? She chewed the end of her pencil as she waited for Sir Hector to continue. Could the ardent young man she had known then be the same callous philanderer who had abandoned his fiancée and unborn child? Her head was beginning to ache and her heart felt like lead inside her breast. She sighed.

'I think that is enough for today,' Sir Hector said, giving her a worried look. 'You are tired and I mustn't overwork you, Lucetta. Leave the transcription until tomorrow, my dear. There is nothing so urgent than it cannot wait and I have an appointment with the Lord Mayor of Dorchester, which I must keep.' He rose to his feet and came round the desk to stand beside her. 'We will begin again tomorrow, when you are thoroughly rested.' He laid his hand on her shoulder but removed it almost immediately. 'Why don't you go and find Mary?' he said gruffly. 'I'm sure she is dying to show you the house where Giles hopes to start up his practice.'

He left the room without waiting for her response, and Lucetta closed her notebook, setting it back on the desk. She stood up, smoothing down her crumpled skirts. Everything she owned had been bought and paid for by Sir Hector's generosity. He might pretend that she was earning her food and keep, but she knew that she was living off his charity, and despite her feeling of detachment from the real world she was beginning to suspect that there was something underlying his apparent kindness. She had seen a light in his eyes that was neither paternal nor the look of a mere benefactor. She had not given it much thought until now, but she realised that despite his wealth and position, Sir Hector was a lonely man. She hoped that she was mistaken, but his remarks regarding the difference in their ages had left her feeling uncomfortable and a little suspicious. She spent some time tidying his desk, but in the end she knew that she could put it off no longer and she went in search of Mary.

After a light luncheon in the morning parlour, Lucetta and Mary set off for the village, walking through leafy lanes where the trees leaned over to touch branches, forming shady tunnels. The road ran alongside the stream which turned a huge water wheel, sending a fine mist into the air and catching the sunlight to form rainbows as the water tumbled back into the millstream. The mill house resonated with the rhythmic sound of the millstone grinding the corn, and a film of white flour dusted the hedgerows like hoar frost in winter. In contrast the still waters of the millpond were dark and mysterious, but made less sinister by the families of ducks floating on its surface like children's toys. Lining the river banks, half hidden by a curtain of weeping willows, thatched farm workers' cottages were interspersed with a blacksmith's forge, a school house and a village shop selling everything from candles to calico. Behind a grey stone wall lay the graveyard and the Norman church with its square bell tower. Yew trees grew in abundance, shading the moss-covered gravestones, and a funeral was in progress as Lucetta and Mary walked past, the coffin resting temporarily beneath the lychgate as the mourners processed along the street which forked to embrace the village green. On the far side Lucetta saw a three-storey stone house with a tiled roof and mansard windows. Ivy clambered up its walls and roses spilled their scarlet petals in a carpet around the front door.

'There it is,' Mary said proudly, pointing to a brass plaque on the door jamb. 'This is the doctor's house and surgery which Papa wants to help Giles purchase. It is everything I could have hoped for him, and I know he will make a splendid family physician.'

'And you would make him a wonderful wife,' Lucetta said softly.

Mary's cheeks flamed scarlet to match the roses climbing round the porch. 'Wherever did you get that idea, Lucetta?'

'Oh, Mary, I've known all along that you love Giles.'

Mary stared down at her dusty shoes 'I do love him, but not in the way you think. I might have harboured romantic thoughts once, a long time ago, but it was just a silly girl's infatuation.'

'I could say the same for myself, I suppose.'

'I'm so sorry,' Mary cried, throwing her arms around Lucetta and giving her a hug. 'What am I thinking of bringing you here and going on about my family when I know how you must be suffering? You must try to forget Sam. There are plenty of good men who would be proud to love a girl like you, regardless of whether you are rich or poor.'

'And you really do not think of Giles in a romantic way?' Lucetta held her breath, studying Mary's face in an attempt to gauge her true feelings.

'I've told you, Daisy. It was a childish crush. I've outgrown it completely.' Mary turned away to pluck a single rose that trailed over the wall. She inhaled its scent with a smile. 'He should be home tomorrow or the day after, and he will need all our help to make the new house comfortable. I've only been inside once and it was very shabbily furnished. It smelt of dogs and disinfectant and it badly needed a woman's touch. I can't wait to get those dreadful old curtains down and hang something pretty in their place. Of course the whole house needs a thorough clean, but we can get a woman in from the village to scrub the floors and polish the woodwork. Give me a month and I will have the house fit for a king.'

'Or even a country doctor.' Lucetta smiled in spite of her misgivings.

'Especially a country doctor. I want only the best for Giles; he deserves nothing less.' Mary squeezed her arm. 'When Papa returns from Dorchester I'll ask him if we can get the house keys and tomorrow we can go and see what needs to be done, for I'm sure that Giles wouldn't know where to start, and his sisters are not interested in anything other than the current fashions, card parties and balls. I love them dearly, but I'm afraid to say they are all quite shallow.'

'Shallow isn't the word I would use to describe them,' Lucetta said wryly. 'But perhaps they improve on better acquaintance.'

Mary linked her hand through Lucetta's arm. 'Let's stop at the wishing well for tea. I think we both may have something to wish for.'

It was late in the afternoon when they returned home and Lucetta went to her room. She sat on the padded window seat looking down on the gardens basking in the June sunshine. Butterflies flitted about in the flowerbeds below her, looking like tiny pieces of coloured tissue paper blowing in the gentle breeze. She closed her eyes, inhaling the warm scent of roses and honeysuckle as she listened to the country sounds that she had come to love. The babbling of the stream, the buzzing of bees and the twittering of birds in the trees was music to her ears, but the song they sang was one of farewell. She was doing no good by staying here. Despite Mary's protests that she had long grown out of her youthful infatuation, Lucetta remained unconvinced. She was certain that Mary would make an ideal wife for Giles, and that he would come to realise that, but it would not happen unless she removed herself from the picture.

There was only one course open to her now and that was to leave Stockton Lacey and return to London where she truly belonged. She made her mind up to speak to Sir Hector after dinner that evening. If she explained the situation carefully she was certain that he would listen with a sympathetic ear. He had been pleased with her work as his secretary, and if he could be persuaded to give her a good character she might find similar work, maybe for another Member of Parliament like himself. Painful though it might be, the time had come for her to leave before she did irreparable harm to those whom she had grown to love.

'What?' Sir Hector stared at Lucetta with bloodshot eyes. He had imbibed heavily before dinner and during the meal, and he had been in a jovial mood when he returned from his luncheon engagement with the Mayor. Lucetta suspected that they had drunk quite a few glasses of wine with their meal, but his mood had changed suddenly when she had attempted to explain her reasons for wanting to leave. They were alone in the drawing room, Mary having retired early to bed, worn out by the day's excitement and exertion.

'This is utter nonsense,' Sir Hector said, pouring himself a generous measure of brandy. He tossed it back in one gulp. 'I'm sorry, my dear girl. I didn't mean to raise my voice but this is all foolishness and must stop. You cannot run away because you have received an offer of marriage from a besotted young man.'

'It is not any young man, sir. We are talking about Giles, the man your daughter worships and adores. He is the man that Mary was destined to marry, until I came along and almost ruined everything.'

'Giles doesn't know what he wants,' Sir Hector said dismissively. 'He's a good fellow, but he lives in a bubble. His life has been lived in the narrow confines of school, university and then the hospital where the women he meets are either dying of fever or are career-minded blue-stockings.'

'Mary is not like that, sir.'

'Of course not. I wasn't including my daughter with women like Sister Demarest and Matron who would, if she were on the battlefield, have terrified even the Iron Duke.'

'Mary is an angel, sir. I love her like a sister and I would cut off my right arm rather than hurt her. I agree with your assessment of Giles, and that is why I must go away now before it is too late. He thinks he is in love with me, but I have just aroused his chivalrous feelings and he is sorry for me, which he has mistaken for something deeper. Once I am gone he will turn to Mary, of that I am certain.'

Sir Hector placed his glass down on the sofa table. He came towards her, swaying a little as he walked. He was so close that she could smell the alcohol on his breath, with just the hint of a Havana cigar. She dropped her gaze, unable to meet his eyes, but he placed his finger beneath her chin, raising her head so that she was forced to look at him. 'You are a good girl,' he said thickly. 'You are very young, but I think that you are old for your years. You don't have to go, Lucetta my dear. There is an obvious answer to both our problems if you will hear me out.'

She brushed his hand away more in panic than anger. 'Please don't, Sir Hector.'

He caught her round the waist, holding her tightly

so that her body was pressed against his. 'You are not a schoolroom miss. You have known what it is to love and want a man, you told me so yourself. I am not trying to seduce you, my dear. I am offering you marriage, respectability, an old family name. In short, Lucetta, I am asking you to marry me. Disregard the gap in our ages, it doesn't matter. I will do my utmost to make you happy.'

'Please let me go,' Lucetta cried, struggling to break away.

'I won't hurt you, my little dove,' Sir Hector said, smiling tipsily. 'I will treat you like a queen. You will want for nothing.'

She could see that words alone were not going to save her and she went limp in his arms. 'I don't know what to say, sir. May I have time to consider your offer?'

He slackened his grip, staring down into her face with an unfocused gaze, and then he released her, bowing from the waist with a flourish. 'Of course, my pet. Anything you say. But don't keep me waiting too long, Lucetta. I admit that I might have had a little too much to drink tonight, but my blood is hot and I want an answer quickly. I'll give you until tomorrow evening, and when you have made up your mind to accept my offer, we'll be married by special licence and spend our honeymoon in Paris.' He took her hand and raised it to his lips. 'I will buy your trousseau in the top fashion houses. You will be Lady Harcourt, how does that sound to you, my darling?'

Lucetta backed away from him, forcing her cold lips

into a smile. 'Too good to be true, Sir Hector.' She was close to the door now and she made her escape.

She did not stop running until she reached her own room. She locked the door behind her and only just made it to the bed before her knees gave way beneath her. She was trembling violently and for a moment she thought she was going to be sick. Gradually her nerves gave way to anger, but she was furious with herself, not with the hapless lonely man who had offered her a life of luxury and respectability. She must, she thought, have done something terribly wrong in her dealings with men to make both Giles and Sir Hector think that they were in love with her. She had never set out to charm them or to flirt. Perhaps it was her vulnerability and helplessness that had attracted them to her, but whatever it was she could not stay to find out. She must leave now before matters grew too complicated and painful for all parties.

She packed a few necessities in the pigskin valise that Mary had given her, leaving her best silk gown with a feeling of deep regret, but the voluminous skirts would not fit inside the small case, and where she was going she doubted if she would need anything so grand. She waited until the house was quiet and the sound of the servants treading the backstairs to their beds had died away, and then she left her room, creeping downstairs to Sir Hector's study. Taking a sheet of headed writing paper, she dipped a pen in the silver inkwell and wrote a glowing reference for herself, signing it in a fair copy of Sir Hector's hand. Having folded it and put it in an envelope, she took another sheet and wrote a note to Sir Hector. She thanked him and Mary for their unstinting kindness and generosity. She begged their pardon for her manner of leaving, and she urged them not to look for her. She ended by wishing them well, and dashing the tears from her eyes, she blotted the missive and left it in a prominent position on the desk.

She returned to the drawing room and, lifting the sash, she climbed out of the window onto the terrace. It was a fine summer night with a full moon and myriads of diamond-bright stars to light her way. Keeping close to the house, she made her way to the shadow of the trees. She had to struggle with the heavy iron gates but managed to squeeze through without causing the hinges to groan and give her away. Once outside the grounds she set off walking in the direction of Dorchester, where she intended to get the first train to London.

She had no idea how far it was, but she was unused to walking long distances and she soon tired. The valise which had seemed so light at the outset began to feel as though it was packed with bricks, and her arm ached miserably. The thin soles of her boots were not designed for tramping miles on stony roads, and after an hour or so she was forced to sit down by the roadside. She resumed walking after a brief respite, following the Roman road which stretched in a straight line like a silver ribbon between hedgerows and fields where sleeping cows lay like gigantic molehills on the dewy grass. She longed to rest, but it was midsummer and the nights were short As she trudged onwards the end of the road seemed to get further and further away.

She was exhausted and almost at the point of collapse when she heard the clip-clop of a horse's hooves behind her. She stopped and turned to see a farm cart laden with milk churns lumbering towards her. The farmer pushed his billycock hat to the back of his head, staring at her curiously as he drew his animal to a halt. 'D'you want a lift to town, maidy?'

'Oh, yes please.' Lucetta handed him her valise and heaved her tired limbs up onto the seat beside him. 'Thank you, sir. I'm much obliged.'

'Running away, are you?' He clicked his tongue against his teeth and flicked the reins so that his steady old nag lurched forwards. 'Maidservant, are you? Going to meet your lover then?'

'That's right,' Lucetta agreed. She was too tired to argue. She leaned back against the hard wooden rail and closed her eyes.

She was awakened with a jolt as the cart stopped and the farmer leapt from his seat to begin unloading the churns. It was sunrise and to her intense relief they had stopped outside the railway station. She picked up her case and clambered down to the ground. 'How much do I owe you, sir?'

'Nought, maidy. I was coming anyway.'

Before she had had time to thank him he hefted a heavy churn on his back and staggered off towards the platform where a train was waiting.

Lucetta bought a single ticket to Waterloo and was relieved to find an empty compartment. She settled herself in the corner seat and closed her eyes, but a sudden noise made her snap upright as the door to her carriage was opened and three young soldiers climbed in laughing and talking loudly.

'Well, what have we here,' the boldest of the three said, sitting down beside her. 'What's your name, my dear?'

'Leave her be, Joe.' The youngest-looking seemed little more than a boy and he took the seat opposite Lucetta. 'Don't take no notice of Joe, miss. He thinks he's a masher but he ain't.'

'Shut your face, Billy-boy. This young lady knows a gent when she sees one, don't you, dearie?' Joe laid his hand on Lucetta's knee.

The third soldier, who had the raw-boned look of a man country born and bred, slapped Joe on the back. 'I'll have her next, Joe. I'll show her what a real man can do.'

Lucetta leapt to her feet. 'Leave me alone. I'm not that sort of girl.'

'Ho, ho, airs and graces,' Joe said, pulling her down onto his lap. 'I like a bit of spirit. Lady's maid are you, love?'

Lucetta struggled to free herself but he had her tightly around the waist. She took a swipe at his face but she missed and merely knocked his cap sideways over his ear.

'Let her go,' Billy said anxiously. 'There are officers on the train, Joe.'

They had not bothered to close the carriage door and as Lucetta uttered a scream of protest an officer resplendent in a scarlet uniform entered the compartment. 'What's going on here?'

The men stood up to salute their superior and Lucetta slid to the floor in a flurry of petticoats.

'Get out or I'll put you all on a charge,' the officer snapped.

Shamefaced like naughty schoolboys the troopers filed out onto the platform and stood to attention. Lucetta scrambled to her feet listening to the officer giving the men a good dressing down before ordering them to find another carriage. A blast from the guard's whistle was followed by a gust of steam from the engine as it started to pull out of the station. The officer leapt inside the compartment and slammed the door, pulling up the window as columns of steam and smoke blew back along the track.

Lucetta eyed him warily as he took a seat in the far corner. He doffed his plumed hat with a smile and a flourish. 'I apologise profusely for my men, miss. They meant no harm but they are little better than animals with farmyard instincts and have not the slightest idea how to treat a lady.' He rose to his feet, swaying with the movement of the train. 'May I introduce myself, ma'am. Lieutenant Ralph Randall at your service.'

Chapter Seventeen

Lucetta managed a tired smile. Her eyelids were heavy and all she wanted to do was to sleep, but in the presence of a strange man she did not dare close her eyes.

'May I know your name, ma'am?' Ralph settled himself in the opposite corner of the carriage. 'We have not been properly introduced, but I feel in the circumstances that we are no longer complete strangers.'

'I am Lucy . . .' She paused, desperately trying to think of a name other than Cutler. 'Lucy Guthrie, Lieutenant.'

'How do you do, Miss Guthrie? Or may I call you Lucy? My friends call me Ralph, so it would seem a fair swop.'

Lucetta nodded, avoiding his curious gaze by looking out of the window at the green fields flashing past at quite an alarming rate.

'And where are you going, Lucy?' Ralph continued. 'Myself, I am going to London for a week's leave.'

'I see.'

'You are not a great talker, are you?'

'You'll have to excuse me. I'm tired and I don't feel like making conversation.' She could see Ralph's reflection in the window and he was staring at her. She wished he would go to sleep or read a book, anything to stop him asking so many questions.

'Go to sleep then. I promise I won't disturb you, Lucy.'

He was too confident in his own charm and too familiar by half. Lucetta felt suddenly wide awake, but she closed her eyes feigning sleep until the train pulled into the next station. The carriage door opened and she looked up, hoping that he might have decided to change compartments, but to her dismay a burly farmer smelling strongly of the stable yard was about to enter the carriage when Ralph stopped him with a gesture. 'I'm afraid this compartment is taken, my good man.'

'Eh?' The farmer stepped back onto the platform, glowering. 'There's plenty of room. I got a ticket bought and paid for, mister.'

Ralph stood up, squaring his shoulders. 'I am escorting this young lady to London and all the seats are taken. Do you want me to call the guard, sir?'

The farmer backed away. 'No need to take that tone.' He stomped off and Ralph slammed the door, turning to Lucetta with a satisfied grin. 'You will be quite safe with me, Lucy. I will make sure that you have a restful journey to London. You did say that you were going all the way, did you not?'

Lucetta was forced to smile. 'I didn't say, but I am going to London.'

Ralph moved along the seat until he was facing her. 'May I ask what takes you to the metropolis? Are you meeting your sweetheart perhaps?'

'No. Nothing like that.'

'Well, then let me guess. You are returning home after a visit to a maiden aunt in Dorset. Your father is a man of means and you live in Highgate, or maybe in Chelsea.'

Ralph's easy-going manner and undoubted charm, even if he was fully aware of it, was having the desired effect on Lucetta and she began to relax. She had no idea where she was going or how she was going to manage on her own in London. She had enough money to pay for lodgings for a week or even two if she found somewhere cheap, but she would need to find work quickly. 'I am going to London to look for a position,' she said, deciding to trust him. 'I have been working as a secretary. I have references.'

'Well now, that does surprise me.' Ralph angled his head, giving her an appraising look. 'I would have said your clothes cost a lot more than a secretary could afford. I think there is a mystery here, Lucy Guthrie.'

She opened her mouth to protest but he held up his hands. 'All right. I won't ask any awkward questions and I want to help you. Have you anywhere to stay in London?'

Lucetta was about to lie but she was desperate and she shook her head.

'Then I can be of assistance. I am going to visit my aunt who owns a large house in Whitechapel. I know that she would be only too happy to have a young person like you renting one of her many rooms. She is getting on in years and likes nothing better than to have company. She might even be able to put you in touch with a prospective employer. Who knows?'

'Do you really think so?' Lucetta knew she was grasping at straws, but this offer seemed heaven sent.

'I know so,' Ralph said confidently. 'Aunt Matilda will love you.'

The hansom cab drew to a halt in Angel Alley. Lucetta had been under the impression that the aunt's house was similar to those she knew so well in Lonsdale Square, but although this narrow passage running from Whitechapel High Street to Wentworth Street might be the most salubrious address in the area it was not what she had been led to expect. Ralph paid the cabby and alighted, holding out his hand to help her down from the cab. Her expression must have registered the shock and distaste she felt. He shrugged his shoulders and the gold braid on his uniform glinted in the sun's pale rays as they fought their way down through smoke-filled air. Feral cats and dogs foraged in the gutters for scraps of mouldering food, and glistening masses of bluebottles feasted off the horse dung and other waste matter that lay undisturbed on the cobblestones.

'Don't judge the house by the exterior,' Ralph said casually. 'Come inside and you'll see.'

Lucetta glanced nervously up and down the alleyway where barefooted children with scabby faces hung about listlessly in doorways while their slatternly mothers touted for business. The rows of terraced houses were neat enough, with green blinds and brass plates on their doors advertising trades from hosiers and glovers to silk mercers, tailors and bootmakers. It was quite obvious that Aunt Matilda was none of these and as Ralph rapped on the brass lion's head door knocker Lucetta was tempted to run away, but she had nowhere to go. Reluctantly she followed him into the narrow hallway where the surprisingly savoury aroma of roasting meat made her empty stomach rumble with hunger. At least the interior of the house seemed clean and the floorboards had been waxed and polished to a glassy sheen.

'Roast lamb,' Ralph said, sniffing the air. 'Aunt Matty does not stint when it comes to feeding her guests.' He handed his plumed hat and leather gloves to a scrawny maidservant.

'Shall I take your bag, miss?'

Lucetta shook her head. The girl did not look strong enough to carry a sack of feathers, let alone a leather valise. 'I'll keep my things with me for the moment, thank you.'

'Shall you take off your shawl and bonnet then, miss?'

'Not for the moment.' Lucetta clutched her shawl a little tighter around her shoulders.

'You have nothing to fear, Lucy,' Ralph said, eyeing her keenly. 'This is not what you were expecting?'

'Not exactly,' Lucetta murmured.

'You're tired and you must be starving. We'll wait in the parlour for Aunt Matty and the girl can bring us some refreshments.' He slapped the young maid on the bottom. 'Tell your mistress that Ralph is here with a guest, and bring the young lady some tea.'

The girl scuttled off without a word.

'Is that how you treat your aunt's servants?' Lucetta demanded, hanging back as Ralph opened the door to a reception room. 'That was uncalled for.'

He ushered her into the parlour with an unwavering smile. 'Don't trouble your pretty head about matters that don't concern you. I didn't hear her complain, did you?'

Lucetta walked past him, clutching her valise in front of her like a shield. 'It wasn't a gentlemanly thing to do, Lieutenant.'

'It was Ralph just a few moments ago. I thought we were friends, Lucy.'

She hesitated, but his engaging smile reassured her and she sat down on the nearest chair. She was so exhausted that she could not walk another step. 'You have been very kind, Ralph. And I am grateful.'

He produced a silver case from his inside pocket and took out a small black cheroot which he lit with a vesta, inhaling the smoke with a satisfied sigh. 'I'm counting on it, my dear.'

Lucetta was about to challenge his remark when the door opened and a middle-aged woman entered the room. She was tall and slender with her waist so tightly corseted that it was little more than a hand's span. Her grey hair was piled up on her head in a mass of elaborate curls and her cheeks were rouged to an unlikely rosiness, as were her thin lips. Her black bombazine skirts rustled as she moved and she smiled when she saw Ralph. 'The girl said you'd arrived, you scoundrel. I haven't heard from you for six months or more and then you turn up on my doorstep. What am I to do with you, you bad boy?'

Ralph moved swiftly towards her and kissed her on the lips.

Lucetta looked on in amazement. He must be very fond of his aunt, she thought dazedly.

Aunt Matty took the cheroot from Ralph's fingers and sucked on it, exhaling a plume of smoke before handing it back to him. 'And who is your friend, Ralph? You don't normally bring one with you. Are my girls not enough for you?'

Ralph slipped his arm around her shoulders. 'Now, now, Aunt Matty, don't be a naughty girl. You'll shock my new friend who is fresh from the country and unused to city ways.' He turned to Lucetta with a disarming smile. 'May I present Miss Lucy Guthrie, Aunt? She is looking for work in London, and I told her that I was sure you could put her in the way of suitable employment.'

'How do you do, ma'am,' Lucy said, rising to her feet and bobbing a curtsey. 'I hope I'm not putting you out by arriving unannounced?'

Miss Matty nudged Ralph in the ribs. 'What are you doing, boy? This one is a lady.'

'I beg your pardon,' Lucetta said, glancing from one to the other. 'Is there something you haven't told me, Ralph?'

He tossed the cheroot into the empty grate and he pinched his aunt's thin cheek, a little too hard Lucetta thought as Miss Matty winced and her hooded grey eyes watered. 'My dear aunt likes to tease, Lucy. Perhaps you would like to be shown to your room. I'm sure you would like to refresh yourself after our long journey and I need to speak to my aunt in private.' He slapped Miss Matty's cheek with a playful smile.

'Do that again and I'll show you the door,' Miss Matty hissed, and then, recovering her composure, she curled her thin lips into a smile as she moved sinuously to the fireplace and tugged on the bell pull. 'Cora will show you to your room, Miss Guthrie. We dine at nine o'clock.'

'I've told the girl to bring tea here for Lucy,' Ralph said calmly. 'However, I'll be quite happy to take it up to her room.'

'No you won't,' Miss Matty said sharply. She modified her tone, smiling archly. 'I wouldn't expect you to wait on our guest, Ralph. That wouldn't be the done thing, now would it?'

The young maid stuck her head round the door before Ralph had a chance to reply. 'You rang, missis?'

'Show Miss Guthrie to number six,' Miss Matty said sternly. 'And she will take her tea in her room. We will see you later, Miss Guthrie, when you have had a chance to rest.'

Lucetta shot a sideways look at Ralph but his attention was focused on Miss Matty and he seemed to have forgotten her existence. She followed the maid out of the parlour but Lucetta hesitated when they reached the foot of the stairs. She could hear raised voices and bursts of laughter coming from the upper floors, together with scraping and bumping sounds as if furniture were being moved about. She cast a desperate glance over her shoulder, wondering if it would be better to make a swift exit, but the thought of wandering the streets as afternoon wore into evening was even less appealing than accepting Miss Matty's hospitality.

'Shall I take your bag now, miss?' The maid's pinched face was close to hers as the girl stopped on the stairs just ahead of her.

'No, it's all right. You go on, I'll follow.'

As they reached the first landing a door opened and a man lurched out, very red in the face and shrugging on a cord jacket over a coarse calico shirt unbuttoned to the waist. He stopped when he saw them and he pulled a cloth cap onto his tousled head. 'Good day to you, miss.'

Lucetta moved out of his way. 'Who was that?' she whispered in the maid's ear as the man lumbered downstairs, his heavy boots scraping on the bare treads. He left the definite odour of the farmyard in his wake and the stench of an unwashed male.

'He's a farmer's man, miss. They lodge here twice a week when they come up from the country to supply the Whitechapel hay market. They're some of the best behaved ones if you know what I mean.' The girl scuttled up a second and slightly narrower staircase to a narrow landing where she unlocked the door facing them and stood aside to allow Lucetta to enter. 'This is your room, miss.' She slipped the key into the pocket of her apron and was about to leave but Lucetta caught her by the wrist.

'That's my key, I believe.'

The girl's face paled and her eyes opened wide. 'I got me instructions, miss.'

'Why?' Lucetta demanded. 'Why am I not to have the key?'

'I dunno, miss. I just do as I'm told.'

Lucetta thrust her hand into the girl's pocket and took out the key. 'I'm sorry, but you will just have to tell your mistress that if I am paying for my room I expect to have possession of the key.'

'She'll beat me black and blue.' The girl's eyes welled with tears and her lips trembled.

'I'll tell her it was my fault,' Lucetta said, patting her on the shoulder. 'Don't cry, dear. I'm sure we can clear this up. Tell me your name and I'll speak to Miss Matilda.'

'I'm Cora, but if you want to help me, don't say nothing. I'll get twice the walloping if you do.' She turned and ran down the stairs.

Lucetta shut the door and locked it. Only then did she look round the room that she was about to rent and she was not impressed, but it would have to do for one night at least. The floorboards were bare except for a rag rug beside the iron bedstead which was hardly the height of luxury. The bare mattress looked lumpy and a tentative prod with her fingers confirmed her suspicion. Coarse cotton sheets were neatly folded at the foot of the bed with one blanket and a thin cotton coverlet. The pillow ticking was marked with greasy patches where other heads had lain, and the sharp ends of feathers stuck out like the spines on a hedgehog. The walls were whitewashed and unrelieved by any form of adornment, as were the only two pieces of furniture in the room; a pine washstand and dressing table. Lucetta sat down on the edge of the bed and began to unlace her boots. The only good thing that could be said of this spartan bedchamber was that it appeared to be reasonably clean and the bedding had been washed and ironed. It was small comfort but she was too tired to care and she lay down fully dressed and almost instantly fell asleep.

She awakened with a start at the sound of someone thumping on her door. She snapped to a sitting position. 'Who's there?'

'Open the door, Lucy. It's Ralph, I've brought you some tea.'

She swung her legs over the side of the bed. 'Please leave it outside the door.'

'What's all this about, Lucy? You're not afraid of me, surely?'

'I need to rest. Please leave me alone.'

There was a moment's silence and when he spoke his voice was clipped as if he were controlling his temper with difficulty. 'Don't be a silly girl. For God's sake, Lucy, I'm not going to hurt you.' There was a clatter of crockery as if he had placed the tray none too gently on the floor, but he moderated his tone. 'We dine in an hour, my dear. Join us in the parlour for a glass of sherry before dinner. You have nothing to fear.'

She put her ear to the door, waiting until his footsteps died away before unlocking it and opening it just far enough to make certain that there was no one outside. She seized the tray and retreated to her room. She placed it on the washstand, and only when she had locked the door did she feel safe enough to breathe again. She perched on the edge of the bed and drank the rapidly cooling tea in a couple of thirsty gulps. The kitchen staff had been generous with the food and there was a plate of ham sandwiches which she devoured in seconds, followed by a slice of seed cake which was not her favourite but she was too hungry to be fussy. Feeling much stronger, she sat back on the bed listening to the rhythmic creaking of bedsprings from the adjoining room. Naïve she might be, but it was quite obvious what sort of house Miss Matty was running. She knew now that Ralph had tricked her and she realised that she had been foolish in putting her trust in a handsome stranger.

She slipped her feet into her boots and laced them tightly. There was nothing else for it: she would rather brave the city streets than stay in this house of ill repute for a single night. She did not think that Ralph would force her, but she was taking no chances. She packed her bonnet and shawl inside her valise so that if she were seen she would not look as though she intended to make her escape, and she tucked her purse into her stays. Unlocking the door, she paused, listening for sounds other than the ones emanating from the bedrooms, and satisfied that everyone was fully occupied she tiptoed down the two flights of stairs to the ground floor. She reached the front door and was just about to grasp the handle when she heard footsteps behind her. She tugged at the door but it refused to open and she realised too late that it was locked and the key was not in place.

'I thought you might try something like this,' Ralph said with a mirthless chuckle. 'I can't think why you are so eager to throw yourself to the wolves, my dear Lucy.'

She spun round to face him. 'You are the wolf and I was foolish to believe your lies, but you can't keep me here against my will.'

He leaned over her, resting one hand on the lintel and trapping her against the solid wood of the door. 'Can't I? And who is going to save you from my amorous advances, my little innocent? There is no one here who will answer your cries for help, or they might possibly be cries of ecstasy.'

Lucetta pushed her hands against his chest and the braid cut into her fingers. 'You are disgusting and you are no gentleman.'

His smile faded and he took her by the arm, dragging her along the passage towards the parlour. 'I've had enough of your maidenly protestations. You are starting to bore me, Lucy.' Opening the door he thrust her inside and she stumbled, almost losing her balance.

'Ungrateful little bitch,' Miss Matty said, scowling. 'Pour some grog down her throat, Ralph. Maybe that will make her more amenable.'

Lucetta drew herself up to her full height. She was trapped but she was not going to give in so easily. 'Let me go now and I won't report you to the police, but I've got friends in high places. My last employer was a Member of Parliament. I'll see you both behind bars if you don't set me free this instant.'

Miss Matty hooted with laughter. 'What brass! You're a little madam and no mistake. D'you think we're so green as to believe a tale like that?'

'Yes,' Ralph said, seizing a lock of Lucetta's hair and twisting it around his finger. 'If that was true you wouldn't have been running away to London. I think she's a lady's maid who stole from her employer, Aunt Matty. I reckon that the cops are looking for her as we speak.' He tugged at Lucetta's hair making her yelp with pain. 'That's a fraction of what you'll get if you don't do as you're told, my girl.'

Lucetta's heart was thudding so loudly that she was certain they could hear it, but she met his gaze without blinking. 'Let me go. You can do what you like but I won't cry for mercy and I will hate you for the rest of my life.'

'She has spirit, I'll grant her that,' Miss Matty said, taking a lit candle from the mantelshelf and lighting a cigarillo in its flame. 'Shall you dine first, Ralph, or do you want to tame the little shrew before we go to table?'

Ralph released Lucetta so suddenly that she staggered against the wall. He selected a decanter from the table by his side and poured the amber liquid into three glasses. He handed one to Miss Matty. 'I'll savour the moment, Matty. We'll drink to a night of unbridled pleasure.' He thrust one of the glasses into Lucetta's hand. 'Drink this, my pet. It will help you to relax.'

Lucetta dashed the glass to the floor and it shattered into gleaming shards. 'I don't want a drink and I won't eat. You can't make me.'

'You will eat and drink even if I have to tie you to the chair,' Ralph said grimly. 'Ring the bell for the maid, Aunt Matty. We don't want any accidents involving broken glass.' He picked up a sliver and held it close to Lucetta's cheek. 'It would be a pity to spoil that milkmaid skin with an ugly scar.'

Miss Matty reached out to tug at the bell pull and at the same time there was a loud clang from the door-bell. She smiled grimly. 'Ah, good. Another client to keep my girls occupied. I can see that this is going to be a very interesting evening, Ralph, my dear. Refill my glass, there's a good fellow.'

Lucetta could hear voices in the hall, a deep male voice and the higher pitch of Cora's response as she let the newcomer into the house. Lucetta seized her chance while Ralph had his back to her. She leapt from her seat and ran to the door, wrenching it open before either Ralph or Miss Matty had a chance to stop her. She raced along the hall, pushing past Cora and the astonished farmer's man who gaped at her open-mouthed, and she made her escape with Ralph's voice ringing in her ears as he ordered her to stop. She tore across the street and only narrowly missed being run down by a brewer's dray. The stolid carthorse reared and whinnied in fright as she came close to being trampled beneath its hooves. Lucetta tripped over her long skirts, but managed somehow to regain her balance and kept going, dodging between knots of prostitutes standing about chatting as they waited for punters, and drunken men staggering from one public house to another at the start of a long night. She ran until she was out of breath and forced to a halt by a painful stitch in her side.

It had begun to rain. Steady drenching precipitation that trickled down her neck, soaking her to the skin and chilling her to the bone. She had neither bonnet nor shawl and in her headlong flight from Miss Matty's house she had not had a chance to retrieve her valise. She took shelter in a shop doorway only to find that it was already occupied by an old woman who was snoring loudly with an empty gin bottle clasped in her claw-like hand. Lucetta moved on to the butcher's shop next door and huddled against the half-glassed door. The interior was in darkness but the smell of blood and sawdust made her stomach heave. She peered out through the curtain of rain and the oily shimmer of the gas lamps, but the street was deserted. She could hear the faint sound of raucous voices raised in song from a pub on the corner, and she caught the occasional whiff of stale beer and tobacco smoke as revellers went in and out, but to her relief none of them passed her way.

She sank down on her haunches, wrapping her arms around her knees in an attempt to keep warm. She could feel the leather purse lodged between her breasts but it was small comfort. The sum of money it contained was all that she had left in the world and would not sustain her for more than a few days. She had no clear idea where she was, but she knew that this was probably one of the roughest areas in the East End. She had stumbled into a dark underworld where robbery and murder were so commonplace that the news of them rarely hit the headlines. Life was cheap in this part of London and she was totally alone. She dared not fall asleep even though it was almost impossible to keep her eyes open.

Despite her determination to stay awake, Lucetta kept drifting off into an uneasy state between waking and dreaming. Once, in the dead of night, she thought she heard her mother's voice telling her not to be afraid but when she opened her eyes there was nothing but darkness. She drifted back to sleep tormented by nightmares. She felt something soft brush across her face and a weight on her legs. She awakened with a muffled cry to find herself looking into the luminous eyes of a feral cat. It hissed, arched its back and skittered sideways out into the street, leaving Lucetta wide awake and trembling. She raised her eyes to the sky and could have cried with relief to see the pale green streaks of dawn in the east. The rain had ceased but she was so cold that she could not feel her fingers or toes.

Scrambling to her feet she started walking in order to make the blood flow into her cramped limbs. She had no clear idea where she was going, but instinctively she headed south towards the river, as if the great Thames which had almost taken her life might provide her with the solution to all her problems. If she could reach her father's warehouse at least she would be in familiar territory, and maybe just maybe she might find someone there who would recognise her. It was a slim hope but it gave her the strength to put one foot in front of the other despite her physical discomfort and the hunger gnawing at her belly. She was limping now as the blisters on her heels burst, causing her much pain but she kept on doggedly. The sun had risen and the city was slowly coming back to life. Men hurried past her on their way to the docks or the manufactories down by the river. Costermongers pushed their barrows towards the markets and horse-drawn vehicles rumbled past her as she made her way down Leman Street. She could smell roasting coffee beans and the mixed odours emanating from the warehouses that surrounded the docks: cow horn, spices and the burnt sugar smell of molasses all mingled with the stench from the sewers and coal dust from the barges unloading at the wharves.

She had wrinkled her nose at this heady mixture when she had visited her father's warehouse as a child, and the memories of that happier time brought tears to her eyes. She stopped, leaning against a lamp post as a wave of faintness made the pavement and buildings swim in dizzying circles before her eyes.

'Are you all right, my dear?'

Lucetta focused with difficulty on the bewhiskered face of an elderly gentleman dressed in sombre black. 'I think so, sir,' she murmured.

He proffered his arm. 'You look to be in need of sustenance. I can help if you will let me.'

She eyed him suspiciously. 'How so, sir?'

He smiled and she realised that his eyes were infinitely wise and kind. 'Come with me. There is a soup kitchen close by where you will be able to rest and have some food.'

'And what is in it for you, may I ask?' Lucetta was horrified to hear the words spill from her lips, but she was not going to be caught so easily this time.

'I am doing what He would want me to do.' He raised his eyes to heaven and smiled. 'Come. There is nothing to fear.'

She could not doubt his sincerity and Lucetta allowed the gentleman to lead her the short way to a dreary-looking building down a side street. He opened the door and as he ushered her inside she breathed in the welcoming aroma of hot tea and freshly baked bread.

'They will look after you here.' He made to leave but Lucetta caught him by the sleeve.

'You're very kind, sir. Might I know your name?'

'I'm William Booth. God bless you, my dear,' he said, doffing his hat. 'If you feel so inclined you will be more than welcome at any of our meetings. Ask anyone here and they will tell you where to find me should you need help or comfort.'

Lucetta watched him leave with a sigh of regret. She had known him for a few minutes but she felt that she could trust him with her life. She sighed, turning her attention to stare round the large room where ragged men and women sat on benches at trestle tables. They hunched over their food, stuffing bread and jam into their mouths and washing it down with mugs of strong tea which was served from a counter at the back of the room. Lucetta was not too proud to join the queue and her mouth watered at the sight of the food. As she took the plate of bread scraped with margarine and a generous helping of plum jam, she remembered a time when she would have turned her nose up at such food. Now it looked like manna from heaven and she smiled gratefully as she accepted a thick china mug of tea laced with two spoonfuls of sugar. She moved away, searching for a spare seat at one of the tables, and found one next to a shaggy-haired man who sat with his back to her. There was little enough room and she cleared her throat. 'Excuse me, mister. Would you mind moving up a bit?'

Slowly, he turned his head to look at her. Despite his haggard appearance and unkempt beard, his eyes gave him away and they stared at each other in disbelief.

Chapter Eighteen

'Lennie! It is you, isn't it?'

Guthrie blinked and his red-rimmed eyes focused on her with difficulty. 'Lucy?'

She glanced around, realising that many heads had turned their way, and she sat down hastily. 'Yes, it's me, Lennie. But what brings you here and where is Stranks?' She glanced nervously over her shoulder, half expecting to see him queuing for food.

'In jail,' Guthrie muttered, shaking his head. 'Got caught red-handed and sent down for life. Penal servitude he got and was lucky to escape the hangman's noose.'

Lucetta thought it was a sentence well deserved, but she did not want to upset Guthrie by saying so. He looked ill and his ragged clothes hung off him, making him look like a scarecrow whose stuffing had been taken for nesting material by the birds. 'How have you been managing on your own?' she asked, sipping her tea.

Guthrie hunched his shoulders, staring down at his empty plate. 'Why would you care what happens to me? We treated you bad, Lucy. I ain't proud of what we done.'

'You helped me to escape. I'll never forget that. If

you'd followed his instructions I'd have ended up on the streets or worse.'

He shot her a sideways glance. 'You don't look as though you've fared much better, girl. What happened to you?'

Lucetta bit hungrily into the doorstep of bread and jam. She chewed and swallowed, closing her eyes as she savoured the food. In the past she had eaten some of the finest food that the best chefs could produce, but nothing had ever tasted as wonderful as this humble fare. She drank more of the strong sweet tea before answering. 'It's a long story, Lennie. I've had a bit of bad luck, that's all.'

'Looks like you was doing all right until then. Them duds cost more than a bob or two.' He raised his head to glare at the men seated opposite them. 'And you lot can keep your maulers to yourselves, if you takes my meaning.'

The unkempt, unshaven men stared down at their food, muttering into their beards. Lucetta shuddered as she saw a flea clinging to the eyebrow of the man seated directly opposite her. She crammed the last of her meal into her mouth and scrambled to her feet. 'I think I'd best leave now. Are you coming with me, Lennie?'

He reached for his stick, grimacing with apparent pain as he swung his gammy leg over the bench. 'Where are you going?'

She wanted to help him up but she did not wish to embarrass him in front of his peers. 'I don't know,' she whispered, 'but perhaps we should get out of here. I think you may have upset a few people.'

A twisted grin curved Guthrie's mouth and his eyes lit with a flash of amusement. 'They ain't people, ducks. These here are animals fit only to live in the zoo.' He edged towards the street door. 'But you're right, girl. It don't do to get on the wrong side of them as you might meet in a dark alley. They'd slit your gizzard for a ha'p'orth of baccy or a penn'orth of grog, and them duds of yours would fetch a fair amount in a dolly shop and no questions asked. We'd best get out of here.'

Taking her by the elbow, he hustled her out of the soup kitchen. 'You look done in,' he said. 'Where are you dossing down?'

Lucetta smiled tiredly. 'Last night it was in a shop doorway. The truth is that I've nowhere to go, Lennie. I've made a real mess of things.'

He glanced warily over his shoulder as the door to the soup kitchen opened and a man lumbered out into the street. 'I rent the old place, girl. It ain't much but you're welcome to stay as long as you want.'

Lucetta sensed that they were being watched and she slipped her hand through his arm. 'I'd be grateful for a roof over my head, just until I find employment somewhere. I can pay something towards the rent.'

'Who'd have thought it,' Guthrie wheezed. 'It's a far cry from them days in Bali when you was the rich man's daughter and we planned to hold you for ransom.'

'I'm no longer that girl,' Lucetta said, slowing her pace to keep in step with his awkward gait. 'Lucetta Froy is dead and buried. I go by the name you gave me now. I'm Lucy Guthrie.'

Lennie sniffed and wiped his nose on his coat sleeve. 'That touches me to the heart, girl. Here am I, a real villain who did you wrong and you takes me name. I call that a real Christian thing to do, and I'd be proud to have you as me daughter.'

'Then perhaps that is what we should tell anyone who asks,' Lucetta said thoughtfully. 'It would be safer for both of us.'

He nodded wordlessly, and they ambled on through the city streets, passing the Royal Mint and skirting the perimeter of the Tower of London until they came to Trinity Square. In the middle of the street a group of carrion crows were feasting off the carcase of a dead rat, and Guthrie let out a roar, hobbling into the road and waving his arms like a madman.

Lucetta ran to his side, dragging him out of the path of an approaching horse and cart. 'Lennie, what's the matter?' She led him to the safety of the pavement. He was breathing heavily and in obvious distress. 'Are you all right?'

'I hates them bleeding birds. They gives me night-mares.'

'They're just crows, Lennie. They were only doing what was natural to them.'

'I has terrible dreams of them picking me bones.' He shuddered and turned away from the gory sight. 'Let's move on. It ain't far now.'

Brandishing his cane at the crows as they gathered ready to swoop again, he limped off and Lucetta had to run to keep up with him.

'Where are we going, Lennie?'

'You'll remember it when we get there,' he said grimly. 'It's the same drum we took you to in the first place, although a basement room in Black Raven Court ain't what Miss Froy was used to.'

'I'm sure it will suit Lucy Guthrie.'

'You'll be all right, girl. I won't let no harm come to you.' Guthrie paused for a moment, pointing with his cane. 'See that church spire? That's All Hallows and just beyond is Seething Lane. We'll soon be home.'

The entrance to Black Raven Court was almost opposite the police station, the irony of which was not lost on Lucetta as she recognised her grim surroundings. It was here that she had been kept prisoner, but now it was to be her sanctuary. The soot-blackened buildings were a raggle-taggle mixture of warehouses and three-storey dwellings that had known better days. Despite the heat of the day, it was cold in the shadows and the stench of sewage and animal excrement was sickening. Guthrie led the way down the slime-encrusted stone steps and he unlocked the door.

Lucetta followed him into the dank-smelling pit of a basement room, waiting in the doorway until he had lighted the stub of a candle stuck to the table top. Unpleasant memories of the time she had spent in captivity flooded back to her and she had to curb the desire to retreat and run away. The worm-eaten rafters were festooned with cobwebs as thick as lace curtains and the floor was carpeted with dust and rodent droppings. It was quite obvious that Guthrie was no housekeeper; remnants of past meals were scattered across the table and spilling onto the floor where ants and flies feasted on the mouldy scraps.

'This is disgusting, Lennie. How can you live like this?'

He shook his head, sinking down onto a stool at the table. 'There don't seem to be much point in tidying up, and I wouldn't know where to start. I ain't been feeling too good, Lucy. Me leg plays up something chronic and I can't get work.'

She covered her nose and mouth with her hand in an attempt to keep out the noxious smells. 'How have you managed to live?'

'No one will hire a man with a gammy leg. I tried down at the docks but they just sent me away and I was forced to go back on the dip.'

'What is that?'

He looked away, hanging his head. 'Picking pockets. I learned it as a youngster. It's all I knows and me leg ain't healed like it should. I gets eaten up with fever, specially at night.'

'I'm not surprised if you live like this.' Lucetta closed the door behind her. 'I can't live in such a mess. Where is the broom?'

Guthrie stared at her with a blank expression. 'I dunno. I don't think I got one.'

'Then you'll have to go out and buy one,' Lucetta said with a determined twitch of her shoulders. 'And we need coal for the fire, a bucket and a scrubbing brush and some washing soda. I'll write a list.'

'I can't read,' Guthrie said humbly. 'And I got no paper nor a pen. I used to leave all that to Norman.

Like he always said, he had the brains and I had the muscle. Afore I got injured, that is. Now I'm no use to anyone.'

She stared at his bowed head and was suddenly overcome by pity. He was a big man physically but she now saw him for what he was – a child inhabiting a man's body. Without Stranks to guide him he was lost. Disregarding the filth on the floor, she knelt by his side, hooking her arm around his shoulders. 'You mustn't say that, Lennie. I might not be alive now if it weren't for you. Stranks would have killed you too if he had found out that you'd let me go. You did a brave thing and now I'm going to look after you.'

He raised his head and his eyes met hers with an incredulous look bordering on delight that reminded her of a pet dog she had had when she was a child.

'You'd do that for me, Lucy?'

She was already regretting her rash promise but she couldn't go back on it now. She smiled and nodded. 'I won't leave you until I know that you can look after yourself.' She stood up and moved away. The stench of his unwashed body and the sight of lice running through his hair and beard made her stomach churn. She was beginning to itch and the thought of being infested with fleas and lice was enough to galvanise her tired limbs into action. 'I'll go and get the things we must have. You stay here and see if you can get the fire going. We'll need hot water and plenty of it.'

He scrambled to his feet and hobbled over to the grate where ashes spilled all over the cracked tiles in the hearth. 'There might be a bit of coal left at the bottom of the sack. I'll do me best, and perhaps you could get us something for our supper.' He turned to gaze helplessly at the clutter on the table. 'I think the rats must have ate the last of the bread.'

'Just light the fire,' Lucetta said, moving swiftly to the door. 'I'll see what I can do.'

He gave her a gap-toothed grin. 'I got a terrible hankering for cheese. I ain't had none since Stranks got took by the coppers. Bread and cheese would go down a treat.'

Lucetta had to force her aching legs to climb the steep and slippery stone steps to street level, but she was filled with renewed purpose and the determination to survive. At least she had a roof over her head and she was not alone. Lennie might not be the person she would have chosen as a companion, but she could not abandon him now. By some strange quirk of fate they needed each other. She hurried through the narrow passage that led into Seething Lane and she turned her face up to the sun. It was high in the sky, and energised by its warmth she went in search of provisions. In Crutched Friars she discovered a hardware shop crammed in between a public house and a shop selling second-hand books. She stopped outside to take out her purse and count the coins. The train fare to London had depleted her savings considerably but she did a quick calculation in her head and decided that she could afford to purchase the bare essentials. She went inside prepared to haggle.

Less than an hour later Lucetta arrived back in Black Raven Court with the shop boy staggering along behind her toting a bag of coal on his skinny shoulders. He set it down with a sigh of relief and she tipped him a penny for his trouble, which sent him racing back up the steps with a wide grin on his face. At least someone was happy, she thought as she opened the door and stepped inside. The stench almost knocked her backwards and the polluted air outside seemed like a breath of spring compared to the squalor of Guthrie's lodgings. She did not see him at first, and she wondered if he had gone out to look for her, but a loud snore led her to the back of the room, where she found him in Stygian darkness, lying flat on his back with his hands crossed on his chest like the effigy of a Knight Templar on his tomb. She was tempted to rouse him and set him to work, but she relented. He had managed to get a fire going after a fashion, and he looked so peaceful that she had not the heart to wake him. She rolled her sleeves up and set to work.

She banked the fire with coal before going out to fetch water from the pump in Great Tower Street. This, she decided, would be a job for Lennie when his leg was less painful, but she found it oddly comforting to have someone who needed her so desperately. She returned to the basement room ready to begin battle with dirt and disorder. She put the kettle on the hob and began sweeping the floor, shovelling up mounds of dust and filth and tipping them outside into the corner of the area. Clearing that away would be another job for Lennie. She had a mental list of chores that would keep him gainfully occupied while she looked for paid employment. She poured boiling water into one of the buckets and added washing soda and a sliver of carbolic soap. For the first time in her life, Lucetta got down on her hands and knees and scrubbed the floor. Guthrie woke up as she tumbled him off his bed in order to scour the flagstones beneath the two straw-filled palliasses, which she took outside and hung over the railings to air. When she returned she found that he had made a pot of tea and it was brewing on the newly swept hearth.

'You done wonders, Lucy,' he said, gazing around the room. 'I wish I could do something to help.'

'You've made a pot of tea,' she said, wiping the sweat off her forehead with the back of her hand. 'I bought some sugar but I didn't have a jug so I couldn't get any milk.' She saw his gaze flicker towards the newly scrubbed table top where she had left her purchases from the grocer's shop. She smiled. 'And there is bread and cheese for supper, but we will have to make it last, Lennie. I haven't much money left and it will have to do until I can find paid work.'

His mouth drooped at the corners. 'It ain't right that you should have to support me. I never had to rely on a woman afore, let alone a slip of a girl like you.'

'Then you must hurry up and get better,' she said briskly. 'Let me look at that leg. I'm no nurse but maybe I can bathe it or something.'

Reluctantly he rolled up his tattered trouser leg and Lucetta recoiled in horror at the sight of maggots writhing about on an angry-looking wound. She knew nothing about such matters but it was obvious that the bones had not mended as they should and fragments

341

of it had pierced the skin. She frowned, shaking her head. 'You must see a doctor, Lennie. I don't know how to treat something like that.'

'I don't want no doctor. They'll cut me leg off and if that don't kill me I'll be a cripple for life.'

She laid a tentative hand on his shoulder. 'But you'll die of blood poisoning if you don't have that leg seen to. First thing in the morning we'll go to the nearest hospital and get that wound dressed properly. I won't take no for an answer.'

Next morning Lucetta and Guthrie set off a good hour before the outpatients department of St Bartholomew's Hospital was due to open. Guthrie was in a great deal of pain but he insisted that he was quite capable of walking the distance to West Smithfield, and with many stops along the way they arrived soon after the start of the outpatients' clinic. They sat on hard wooden benches set in rows like a theatre audience, although there was nothing to view other than the nurses bustling about in their crisp white aprons and caps as they ferried patients in and out of the consulting rooms. As their turn drew nearer Guthrie became restive and it took all Lucetta's powers of persuasion to prevent him from leaving. His nerve almost failed him when his name was called and he refused to move unless Lucetta accompanied him. Reluctantly, she took him by the hand and they followed the nurse into a curtained cubicle.

The young doctor looked up from writing his notes and he eyed Guthrie warily. 'Good morning. I'm Dr Richards. What can I do for you?'

Guthrie opened and closed his mouth like a fish out of water, and sensing his distress Lucetta laid her hand on his arm. 'It's all right, Lennie. Show the doctor where it hurts.'

Obediently, Guthrie rolled up his trouser leg, pointing mutely to the seeping, maggot-infested wound. The smell of putrefying flesh made Lucetta feel nauseous but the doctor did not flinch. He motioned Guthrie to lie on the examination couch. 'If you would climb up here I can take a better look.'

For a moment Lucetta thought that Guthrie was going to make a bolt for it, but she gave him an encouraging nod and a smile and with the greatest reluctance he did as the doctor asked.

'You ain't going to chop me leg off, are you, sir?' he murmured, wincing as the doctor examined the site of the infection. 'I don't want to end up a cripple begging on the streets.'

'I don't think it will come to that.' Dr Richards turned to Lucetta. 'Are you related to this man?'

'I'm looking after him,' Lucetta said truthfully, but seeing doubt in the doctor's eyes she felt compelled to expand the statement. 'I'm his daughter.'

'I see.' Dr Richards eyed her curiously. 'You must forgive me for staring, but I never forget a face and I feel that I've seen you somewhere before.'

'I don't think we've met, doctor.'

He continued to stare at her, angling his head. 'Have you ever been a patient at this hospital?'

'I was once, but it was some time ago. Now could we get back to Mr Guthrie's condition?'

'Well, Miss Guthrie, the patient will need his wound cleaned and dressed daily. He must keep his weight off that leg as much as possible and have adequate rest and good nourishment.'

'I understand.'

Guthrie moved restlessly on the hard leather couch. 'I can't hear you, mate. What is he saying, Lucy?'

Dr Richards turned back to Guthrie. 'I was just telling your daughter that you must rest and have the wound treated daily, Mr Guthrie. If you will just lie there for a few moments longer I'll get the nurse to attend to you.' He opened the curtains and beckoned to Lucetta. 'May I have a word, Miss Guthrie?'

Lucetta followed him into the busy outpatients department. Having instructed a nurse to attend to Guthrie, Dr Richards drew Lucetta aside. 'If the wound does not respond to treatment there is a possibility that gangrene will set in.'

'And he will lose the leg.'

'It was a nasty fracture and has not been set properly. He might require a below-knee amputation, but that would be a last resort. I would hesitate to recommend such drastic action unless the patient's life was in danger, particularly in the case of a labouring man such as Mr Guthrie.'

Lucetta digested this in silence. She had only thought to stay with Guthrie until he was able to fend for himself. The idea that he might be dependent upon her for life was frankly terrifying. 'I understand,' she whispered. 'What are his chances, doctor?'

'I can't say for certain. He looks to be in a poor state

generally. Were he a younger or fitter man I would give him a fifty-fifty chance of recovery, although he would always be lame. As it is . . .' He shook his head. 'I'm sorry, Miss Guthrie. We will do what we can for him.'

'Thank you, doctor. I'll wait for him outside. I need some air; it's so hot in here. The smell and the maggots . . .' Lucetta turned and was about to walk away, but Dr Richards called her back.

'Miss Guthrie, I've just remembered where I saw you last. It was the night that the two vessels collided on the river. I was on duty and you were one of the survivors of that dreadful accident. You looked like a mermaid with your fair hair fanned out on the pillow.'

Lucetta stared at him, hardly daring to hope that he knew her true identity. 'Yes, I was a passenger on the *Caroline*, and I believe that I was admitted here until I was transferred to the fever hospital, but I don't remember anything about it.'

'I'll never forget that night, but as I recall there was nothing on your person to identify you.'

It had been a slim hope, but even so Lucetta could barely conceal her disappointment. 'No, I don't suppose there was.'

'I arranged your transfer,' Dr Richards said, smiling for the first time. 'I have a good friend who works at the London Fever Hospital, and through him I was able to follow your case. You might remember him, Dr Harcourt? Dark-haired fellow with a devilish sense of humour.'

'I–I'm afraid I can't place him,' Lucetta lied desperately. 'It was some time before my memory returned.'

'You were quite a mystery then, as I think you are now, Miss Guthrie. If you'll forgive my saying so, I don't exactly see you as being related to a man like Guthrie.'

'We are given our relations, Dr Richards,' Lucetta said coldly. 'We choose our friends.' She met his startled gaze without flinching, but inwardly she was quaking.

'I'm sorry,' Dr Richard said stiffly. 'I didn't mean to offend you.' He hurried back into the cubicle, instructing a nurse to fetch the next patient.

Lucetta sighed. She had not meant to speak so sharply and he did not deserve such a put-down, but she dared not admit the truth. If the doctor were to inform Giles of her present situation he would almost certainly come looking for her, and if Giles were to repeat his offer of marriage she was not sure that she would have the strength to refuse him a second time.

'Lucy, I'm ready to go home.'

She turned to see Guthrie limping towards her with the aid of a pair of crutches. A young nurse was at his side and in her hands she held a paper package. She smiled as she passed it to Lucetta. 'There are some dressings for Mr Guthrie. I've written the instructions down for you, miss. Dr Richards suggests that you bring your father back in a week's time so that he can check his progress.'

Guthrie was not a good patient. He made such a fuss when the dressings were changed that Lucetta had to cajole, persuade and eventually threaten him with the dire consequences if he refused to let her carry out the doctor's instructions. Ignoring all her protests, he insisted on going out every morning in search of work on the docks or in one of the manufactories by the river, but the result was always the same. No one wanted to hire a lame man.

Lucetta had also been trying to find suitable employment. She advertised her services as a secretary by putting cards in shop windows, but so far without attracting any prospective employers. She had lost the reference she had written in Sir Hector's name when she fled from Miss Matty's house in Angel Lane, and without a change of clothing she knew that she looked almost as disreputable as Guthrie. No respectable businessman would want such a shabby person working for him. She had wandered the city streets close to Black Raven Court and the Tower, knocking on doors of businesses that she thought might be in need of a secretary, and had applied for more menial positions, but without success.

On this particular day she roamed further afield and found herself in Wapping High Street, close to her father's furniture repository. It was achingly familiar territory, bringing back happy memories of childhood visits to her father's business domain where she was received with kindness and affection from his employees. Jim Jenkins had had a soft spot for her and there was always a tin containing shortbread biscuits baked by his wife tucked away beneath Tommy Hall's desk in the front office. Lucetta stopped on the opposite side of the street, staring at the gilded lettering with her uncle's name sprawled across the frontage of the building. She had received short shrift here on her last visit and a bitter taste in her mouth made her swallow convulsively. Anger roiled in her stomach at the thought of Uncle Bradley and her hateful cousin, Jeremiah, reaping the benefits of her father's lifetime of hard work. Uncle Bradley had stolen her inheritance and he was responsible for her sorry plight. She was about to walk away, but her feet seemed to have other ideas and she found herself crossing the street to stand outside the main entrance. The doorbell clanged as she entered the office.

The clerk she remembered as Perks looked up from writing in a ledger and there was no hint of recognition in his rather startled gaze. 'Er, can I help you, miss?'

She cleared her throat and curved her lips into a smile. 'I would like to see Mr Froy.'

'Which Mr Froy is that, miss?'

'Mr Bradley Froy.'

Perks shook his head. 'Mr Bradley is in the Far East, miss. Mr Jeremiah is in charge while his father is away.'

'Then I would like to see him, please.'

'He's a busy man, but I'll see if he is available. Who shall I say is asking for him?'

'My name is Lucy Guthrie and I am looking for work.'

Perks seemed to shrink before her eyes as he drew his shoulders up to his ears, and his neck seemed to retract as if his head would disappear at any moment, like a tortoise under attack. 'I don't think there are any – I mean – we don't employ young ladies, miss.'

'Nevertheless I would like to see Mr Jeremiah,' Lucetta said boldly. She knew she was taking a chance but she doubted if Jeremiah would recognise her now, especially in her changed state. He was four years her senior and had been sent away to boarding school at a tender age. They had seen little of each other while they were growing up, but she remembered him as a fat, spotty and spiteful youth who had pulled her hair and smashed her favourite doll, denying all culpability when challenged by her father. It was more than three years since they had met at a family Christmas party when Jeremiah had barely noticed her, thinking himself above paying attention to a schoolgirl.

Perks slid off his stool. 'I'll see what I can do, but I can't promise anything.'

'Please tell your employer that I was personal secretary to a very important Member of Parliament,' Lucetta said, hoping that Jeremiah's innate snobbishness would come to the fore when he received this titbit of information. 'I left with the highest of recommendations and it is only a family misfortune that has forced me to come in search of employment.'

Perks disappeared through a door at the back of the room which led directly into the warehouse. Lucetta hardly dared to breathe but she did not have to wait for long. He poked his head round the door. 'Would you come this way, miss?'

She followed him into the warehouse and the smell of the tropics took her instantly back to the heady days in Bali. She felt her throat constrict as she saw the carved teakwood furniture from Indonesia and the bolts of exotic silks from Asia. Umbrella stands spilled over with hand-painted paper parasols from China and the bare brick walls were adorned with tiger-skin rugs from India. Their glass eyes winked at her as she walked past them to meet Jeremiah, who appeared to be idling amongst a collection of smiling, fat-bellied pottery representations of Buddha.

Jeremiah had always been chubby but now his shape was so much like that of the statues surrounding him that she had to stifle a giggle. Somehow she managed to keep a straight face and she raised her chin, meeting his curious look with a slight inclination of her head.

'This is the young person, sir,' Perks said deferentially.

'Yes, thank you, Perks. I can see that,' Jeremiah said irritably. 'Go back to the front office and get on with your work.'

Perks accepted this implied rebuke with sagging shoulders and shuffled away, leaving Lucetta to face her cousin. She would have known Jeremiah anywhere, but thankfully there was no reciprocal spark of recognition in his pale eyes which reminded her of river water on a dull day.

She waited for him to speak.

He looked her up and down from the green-tinged black bonnet, which she had bought for a penny in a dolly shop, to the tip of her dusty boots visible beneath the muddy hem of her once elegant skirt. 'Perks tells me that you are looking for work. Tell me why I should even speak to you, let alone employ a woman who looks as though she would be better suited to scrubbing floors.'

'I will scrub floors if that is what you require of me,' Lucetta replied evenly. 'But it would be a waste of my talent as a letter writer and my experience gained whilst working for a well-respected Member of Parliament.'

Jeremiah curled his lip. 'And who might he be when he's at home?'

'I cannot reveal my former employer's identity. It is an official secret and my work was most confidential.'

'Why should I believe you? And if it is true, then why are you here in Wapping instead of peddling your talents in Whitehall?'

Lucetta thought quickly. 'I have an invalid father to keep and my family have fallen on hard times.'

'What a sad story,' Jeremiah said with a sarcastic snarl. 'Stop wasting my time and go away. Get out before I call one of my porters to throw you out.'

Chapter Nineteen

Lucetta shook her head, refusing to move even though he had taken a threatening step towards her. 'You would find my services indispensable, sir. I am familiar with this type of merchandise and I have some knowledge of import and export laws. I can write in a fair hand, and ...' she paused, trying to think of something that would appeal to Jeremiah's ambitious nature, 'and I very much doubt if any of the other merchants in Wapping can boast of employing a personal secretary.'

A flicker of uncertainty crossed his face and his mouth worked soundlessly for a moment. 'You may have a point there, I suppose.'

Lucetta pushed home her advantage. 'I know the names of the government ministers who deal with matters that concern you, Mr Froy. You might need their assistance at some time in the future.'

'You could be useful at that, but I want to see your references. You can't expect me to hire you without proof that what you have told me is true.'

'I'm afraid they were lost in the fire that destroyed our home,' Lucetta lied glibly. 'But I can write to my former employer and request a copy, although he is away in his constituency at the moment and it might take a little time to receive a reply. Might I suggest you start me on a trial basis? I can begin right away.'

'I should consult my father, but he is out of the country. I suppose a week's trial would be appropriate and I won't hesitate to sack you if you don't come up to expectations.'

Lucetta crossed her fingers behind her back. 'I understand perfectly.'

'And you can't work for me looking like a scarecrow. It won't do.'

'As I mentioned, sir, everything was destroyed in the fire. I will not be able to purchase new clothes until I receive my wages.'

Jeremiah scowled at her and when she did not weaken beneath his fierce gaze he put his hand in his pocket and took out a silver crown. He tossed it to her with a careless flip of his fat fingers. 'There, never let it be said that Jeremiah Froy is a mean man or a bad employer. Get yourself something decent to wear and I want you back here to begin work at seven o'clock tomorrow morning. Leave your address with Perks and if you renege on our agreement I will make you very sorry. Now go away, I'm busy.'

Lucetta walked home in a daze of mixed emotions. She was relieved to have found work but she could hardly believe that she had accepted a job from Jeremiah of all people. It might prove to be the most foolhardy thing she had ever done, and yet there was a small part of her that was comforted at the thought of being back in familiar surroundings. Even in the short space of time she had spent in the warehouse she had felt closer to her father than she had since the night of the shipwreck.

She stopped outside a dilapidated dolly shop with second-hand clothes hanging from nails hammered into the door and window frames. A slatternly woman with yellow snuff stains on her top lip gave her an appraising glance. 'Need some new duds, dearie? You won't get better bargains in the whole of Wapping than you will here.'

Lucetta fingered a navy-blue serge skirt that looked as if it was about her size. 'How much for this?'

The woman put her head on one side, eyeing Lucetta with beady-bright eyes and her thin lips moved as if she were mentally calculating how much her prospective customer could afford. 'A shilling to you, ducks.'

'That's too dear.' Lucetta examined the material closely. 'There's a moth hole and the seam is coming apart.'

'Ninepence then.'

'I've seen another one just the same in Petticoat Lane for sixpence,' Lucetta said, shaking her head. She plucked a grey cotton blouse with white collar and cuffs from its hook. 'A shilling for both items.'

The woman held out a grimy hand. 'Let's see the colour of your money then.'

Lucetta grasped the coin between her thumb and forefinger. She was loth to part with any of it, but she had no choice. 'I'll need four shillings change.'

'Are you suggesting that I ain't got that much?' The

woman produced a handful of coins from her skirt pocket and counted them out one by one.

The shopkeeper obviously considered she had done a good deal and Lucetta walked away feeling that she had obtained a bargain. She spent another tenpence on bread, cheese, milk, tea, and as a special treat for Guthrie, who had a sweet tooth and loved his tea sweet and strong, she added a half-pound of sugar to her purchases.

When she arrived back in Black Raven Court she found him sprawled on his bed with his mouth open and loud snores shaking his whole body. A large black cockroach crawled across his forehead and Lucetta flicked it off with the tip of her finger.

'Wake up, Lennie. I've got some good news at last.'

He opened his eyes, staring at her blearily as he raised himself on one elbow. 'I weren't asleep, honest. I was just resting me eyes.'

She smiled. 'It doesn't matter. You need your rest and I'll soon get the fire going. I've found a job and my new employer gave me an advance. We'll have a cup of tea as soon as the kettle boils, and there is bread and cheese for supper.'

Guthrie sat up, rubbing his eyes. 'I dunno why you're so good to me, Lucy. I ain't forgot that we held you prisoner in this very room.'

'And I haven't forgotten how you helped me to escape from Stranks. We're friends now and we look after each other.' She gave him an encouraging pat on the shoulder before turning her attention to the serious business of relighting the fire. It had not gone out completely and she added the last few lumps of coal, fanning it into flame with a pair of bellows that Guthrie had rescued from a rubbish heap. She placed the kettle on the hob. 'There, we'll have a nice hot cup of tea in no time at all.'

Guthrie sat watching her as she sliced the loaf and cut slivers of Cheddar cheese to make a sandwich.

'I got to find work too,' he said slowly. 'You wasn't brung up to toil like a common person. You should be one of them ladies walking round with a maid at her beck and call. It ain't right that you have to keep me.'

'You have to get that leg better first. Tomorrow is your appointment at the hospital, but I'll be at work so you will have to go on your own. You will go, won't you?' She handed him the sandwich, eyeing him anxiously as he stuffed the food into his mouth.

He nodded his head.

Lucetta was not convinced. 'I want you to promise me that you'll see the doctor, Lennie. He'll give you some more dressings and make certain that you are on the road to recovery. It's very important that you see him.'

'I will,' Guthrie mumbled through a mouthful of bread and cheese. 'Is the kettle boiling yet, Lucy? I'm thirsty.'

She made the tea and gave him a cup of the strong brew laced with sugar. 'You didn't promise. I want to hear it from you or I won't be able to start work and I'll lose my position. We'll be right back where we started.'

Guthrie sipped the tea with a beatific look on his face. 'It's sweet. Ta, Lucy. You're an angel from heaven.'

'Lennie,' she said sternly.

'I promise,' he muttered into his cup. 'I'll go and see the sawbones, but if he says he wants to chop me leg off . . .'

'I'm sure it won't come to that. I expect the doctor will be very pleased with you for being such a good patient.' She perched on the stool at the table and ate her sandwich in silence. She had done all she could to keep Guthrie's wound free from further infection and it seemed to be healing well. If she told the truth she was relieved that she could not attend the hospital with Guthrie. She did not want to risk seeing Dr Richards again in case he started asking questions about her time in the fever hospital. If his curiosity got the better of him and he contacted Giles, the whole story would come out and Giles might try to find her again. That was the last thing she wanted.

'Can I have another cup of tea?' Guthrie asked plaintively. 'Is there enough in the pot?'

Lucetta left for work early next morning having extracted another faithful promise from Guthrie that he would attend the hospital. It was a chilly day for late August and there was a hint of autumn in the air as she walked briskly towards Wapping. She could feel the cold stone pavements through the thin soles of her boots and she was thankful that it was dry underfoot, but at least she was clean and tidy in her new skirt and blouse. She had knotted her hair into a heavy coil at the back of her head and she hoped that she looked like an efficient secretary. Jeremiah would never associate the prim Miss Guthrie with the schoolgirl cousin he had treated with such arrogant contempt.

She arrived early at the warehouse and Perks greeted her with a watery smile. He showed her to a dark, windowless cubby-hole behind the main office, lodged between a mountain of sandalwood chests and a wall comprised of teakwood cabinets and wardrobes. The fragrant aromas of Asia and the Far East mingled with dust and the smell of coal gas from the light above her head and she felt quite at home as she set about tidying the jumble of papers on Jeremiah's desk and sorting them into order. She had spent many hours here as a child and she knew her father's filing system off by heart, although the whole thing seemed to have slipped into a terrible muddle since his demise. She found unpaid bills and accounts long overdue all muddled up together. It did not take her long to realise that there was a small fortune in outstanding debts waiting to be collected and an almost equally large amount due in remittances to the Gaslight and Coke Company as well as suppliers and shippers.

By the time Jeremiah arrived she had made a good start and created a semblance of order out of utter chaos. He eyed her suspiciously. 'I hope you haven't muddled everything up, Miss Guthrie. I will hold you personally to account if anything goes missing.'

She bit back a sharp retort. 'I think you will find everything to your liking, Mr Froy.'

'Yes, well – carry on then. I have to go out this

morning but Perks knows my routine. Ask him if you need any help.'

'Yes, sir.' Lucetta kept her head bowed over her work. She did not think he would recognise her, but it was not a chance she was prepared to take. Melting into the background was the safest option.

'I will probably have a letter or two to write after luncheon.'

'Yes, sir,' Lucetta murmured, flicking him a sideways glance. Jeremiah might be wearing a suit tailored in Savile Row, but the fashionable low-cut black jacket and pin-stripe trousers did little to disguise his corpulent figure. He was not quite twenty-three but his body was that of a man of middle years. Peering over the starched edge of a wing-back collar, he looked like a chubby boy masquerading in his father's clothes.

He swaggered out into the main body of the warehouse, shouting instructions at the men and threatening them with dire consequences if he discovered anyone slacking. He continued this tirade for several minutes, peppering his comments with expletives that made the colour rise to Lucetta's cheek. She was certain that her father had never spoken to his workers in such a blustering, bullying manner, and by the time Jeremiah had finished she felt almost ashamed to bear the name of Froy. He strode into the outer office, shouting to Perks to find him a cab.

He was gone and the warehousemen resumed their work in gloomy silence. Lucetta settled down to work. It took her all morning to sort the documents and the best part of the afternoon to write lists of debtors and creditors. Jeremiah did not put in an appearance until it was almost time to finish for the day and he came in reeking of garlic and brandy. He glanced at the newly tidied desk and shrugged his shoulders.

'The correspondence can wait until morning, but I expect you to stay tonight until all that paperwork is filed away. I can't allow my standards to slip just because you are new at the job.'

'Yes, sir,' Lucetta said, forcing herself to sound meek. 'Of course.'

'I'm off home then. Be on time tomorrow morning, Miss Froy.'

'Yes, sir.' Lucetta bowed her head over her work, sighing with relief when the door closed on her cousin.

At seven o'clock Perks put his head round the door. 'I'm going to lock up now, miss.'

'I haven't quite finished, Mr Perks.'

He pulled his cap on and grinned. 'There's always tomorrow, miss. And Sir won't be in until late. I happen to know he's got a dinner party to go to tonight, so we won't see hide nor hair of him until noon at the earliest. The lads have all gone home and I can't lock up with you still here.'

Lucetta stood up and reached for her shawl. She had been receiving wary glances from the warehousemen and none of them had spoken to her. She had heard them muttering to each other and it was not hard to guess their topic of conversation. She could only think that they suspected her of being hired to spy on them. Perks was the only one who treated her like an ordinary human being. Setting her bonnet on her head, she followed him into the office. 'Goodnight, Mr Perks. I'll see you in the morning.'

He closed the inner door and locked it. 'If that's the case, miss, I'll be richer by threepence.'

She glanced over her shoulder. 'How so, Mr Perks?'

He flushed and looked down at his shoes. 'Er, the men in the warehouse have a bet running that you won't turn up tomorrow.'

She eyed him curiously. 'And what did you bet?'

'I said you'd be back, miss. I seen the look in your eyes when you first come through that door. I know pluck when I sees it.'

Lucetta nodded her head. 'And you're right, Mr Perks. You'll be richer by threepence in the morning.'

She returned to work the next day and the next. At the end of the first week when Jeremiah handed out the wages he was forced to admit that she was doing well. He said, rather grudgingly, that she could stay in the company's employ until his father returned from abroad. Lucetta was relieved to discover that Bradley Froy was not expected to return to London for another six months and maybe longer. He would recognise her for certain, but at least she had employment until that time, and she was beginning to enjoy her work. Sorting out the paperwork was a challenge in itself, and although she had never been particularly good at anything at school she found to her surprise that she had a good head for business.

Within a fortnight she had written to all their debtors and Perks was only too happy to tell her that most of them had actually paid up. By the end of her first month Lucetta had paid off the creditors and a fortnight before Christmas she had balanced the books. Jeremiah was so pleased that he had been moved to give her a bonus, which she used to pay a month's rent in advance on a one up, one down cottage in Samson's Gardens, a narrow road off Great Hermitage Street. Despite its rural name there was nothing green and pleasant about Samson's Gardens. There might once have been a flourishing market garden on the site but the only greenery to be seen now was the slime in the gutters and the occasional sooty dandelion that poked its head up between the cracks in the paving stones.

Lucetta and Guthrie moved their few possessions into the empty house just a few days before Christmas. Guthrie's leg had healed almost completely thanks to the treatment he received at Bart's, and he had found occasional labouring work on the wharves or in the docks. In between jobs he scoured the street markets and second-hand shops while Lucetta was at work, and when she came home she invariably found him scrubbing, sanding or repairing an item of furniture. His first contribution to their new home was a pair of beech-wood kitchen chairs which he had discovered in a second-hand shop in Redmead Lane; his next find was a deal table with one leg missing which he purchased for next to nothing in an auction house, and his most prized acquisition was a rusty iron bedstead that had been abandoned on the foreshore. It was in pieces and looked fit only for the dust heap, but Guthrie spent many hours in the tiny back yard working on his project, which he said mysteriously would be shown to her when he had finished and not before.

It was not until she arrived home late on Christmas Eve that Guthrie revealed his secret. He sent her up the narrow staircase to her bedroom where she had been sleeping on one of the palliasses they had brought from Black Raven Court. On entering the room she held the candle up high and in its flickering light she saw to her amazement that the palliasse had been replaced by an iron bedstead, freshly painted black with gold knobs on the bed ends.

Guthrie had climbed the stairs behind her and he squeezed into the room. 'I couldn't get it done in time for your birthday, but it's a Christmas present as well. So what do you think?

She turned to give him a hug. 'Lennie, it's the best present I've ever had.' She sat down on the edge of the flock-filled mattress. It was hard and a bit lumpy but it was still a million times better than sleeping on the floor. 'I haven't slept in a proper bed since I left the Grange,' she said, smiling. 'Thank you so much.'

'I done it all by myself,' he said, grinning with pride like a small boy. 'I mended it and polished it and painted it, just for you.'

'It's wonderful,' Lucetta said sincerely. 'You are clever, Lennie.'

Guthrie shuffled his feet and his thin cheeks flushed. 'It must be hard for you living like this when you was used to fine things. I wouldn't blame you if you wanted to go back with that doctor fellow.'

'What doctor fellow? What are you talking about, Lennie?'

'I never told him where we was moving to, Lucy. I never said nothing about Samson's Gardens nor about your working at Froy's. I kept me trap shut and he went away.'

Lucetta stood up but her knees were trembling and she sat down again. 'What doctor, Lennie?'

'Said his name was Harcourt and he was a friend of Dr Richards at the hospital. It was that Richards cove what told him about you. I never said a word.'

'When did you see him and where?'

'He came to Black Raven Court the day before we left, but I never said nothing about coming here. I ain't that stupid, Lucy.'

'I was afraid this would happen,' Lucetta said, rising a little unsteadily to her feet. 'But it's not your fault, Lennie,' she added hastily, seeing his crestfallen expression. 'There's no way that Giles could find us here. We'll forget all about him and enjoy our Christmas. I've got the whole day off tomorrow and I've saved enough money to buy us a fine goose with all the trimmings. We'll have our first proper meal in our new house.'

Guthrie raised his head to look at her and a slow grin spread across his face. 'If we go to Smithfield now we can get a bargain. They'll be selling the last of the birds off cheap.'

'We'll take a cab there and back and we'll buy a bottle of wine to drink with our Christmas dinner.'

Guthrie's bottom lip trembled and he wiped his eyes

on his sleeve. 'I never had a proper Christmas afore. It was gruel as usual in the workhouse and prison weren't no better. I've had the best time of me life since you come to look after me. If you was me own daughter you couldn't have done more for me.'

Lucetta swallowed hard. 'Come on, Lennie. We mustn't dawdle or there'll be nothing left in the market and we'll have to have jellied eels or a meat pie for our Christmas dinner.' Putting aside all thoughts of Giles and what might have been, Lucetta led the way downstairs. She had refused both Giles and Sir Hector and she had made her choice. She was earning her own living and even though she would not personally benefit from it, she was doing her best for the business that her father had spent his life building from scratch. She was more content with her lot than she would have thought possible and she was happy to remain single. If she could not have the man she loved, she did not want second best. She might never see Sam again but she would not give up hope. She picked up her bonnet and shawl and turned to Guthrie with a genuine smile on her lips. 'Are you ready, Lennie? Let's go to market.'

She could not match Guthrie's magnificent present, but next morning Lucetta gave him the jacket that she had bought in a pawnshop in Cable Street. It had obviously belonged to a gentleman of means and was made from the best Harris tweed, although it was well worn and slightly frayed at the cuffs. Guthrie was speechless and his eyes filled with tears as he fingered the material.

'I ain't never had nothing so fine,' he murmured. 'I'll feel like the Prince of Wales hisself when I wears this for Sunday best.'

'It will keep you warm and dry in the worst weather, and I'll be very put out if you don't wear it every day,' Lucetta said with mock severity. She handed him a brown paper package. 'And there's a muffler to go with it. I can't have you traipsing round the docks looking for work and going down with a fatal chill.'

Guthrie ripped the package open and pulled out a brightly coloured woollen scarf which he wound round his neck. 'I'll be the smartest bloke in Wapping. Ta ever so, Lucy. I just wish I had something fine to give you. A bed is all right, but it ain't fine clothes like you used to wear in Bali.'

'My clothes are fine enough, and the bed is wonderful. I slept like a princess last night.' Lucetta slid the goose across the kitchen table, which now boasted four good legs thanks to Guthrie's new-found skill as a carpenter. 'You can pluck the bird for me, Lennie. I've never cooked a meal in my life, but I helped Peg Potts in the kitchen at Frog Hall. I'll try to remember what she did.'

Guthrie laid his new muffler carefully over the back of his chair. 'I never plucked a bird neither, but I'll have a go.'

Lucetta stoked the fire in the range, which had an oven just large enough to take a small joint, and between them they managed to pluck the goose. The air was thick with down, which made them sneeze, and the dirt floor was soon carpeted in feathers, but

Lucetta placed the bird in the oven with a feeling of pride. The kitchen might be tiny and ill-equipped, but it was hers and she felt like a little girl playing house. She swept the floor while Guthrie peeled potatoes and for the first time since her flight from Dorset, Lucetta realised that she felt safe and settled. Last night she had been disturbed to think that Giles was trying to find her, but commonsense told her that he would never be able to trace her here. She could only hope that in time he would turn to Mary and realise what a wonderful wife she would make him. She did not think that Sir Hector would pine for long. Perhaps he had already found another lady love. Lucetta hoped so anyway. Sir Hector was a good man and his proposal had probably been born more out of chivalry than from tender feelings. They were all better off without her.

'I'm hungry, Lucy. Will the goose be ready soon?'

Guthrie's voice brought her back to reality with a start. 'I don't know, Lennie. We'll just have to take a peek at it from time to time. I'll know when it's cooked, I think, but we must be patient.'

It was not a bad first attempt, even Lucetta had to admit that, and Guthrie devoured everything on his plate, sucking the bones and licking up the gravy like a hungry dog. Lucetta made allowances for his dreadful table manners on this special day. The goose had been perfectly cooked, but the potatoes had been a bit burnt and the cabbage was not quite done. She had no idea how to make gravy, but all in all she was satisfied with her first culinary effort. She tried not to think about the gargantuan feasts that had been served up by

Cook in Thornhill Crescent. That was then and this was now. She sipped her wine and was content.

But that night she suffered a succession of bad dreams all of which featured Sam in a series of disasters including being attacked by Stranks with a blood-stained machete, and being flogged with a cat-o'-nine-tails by her father. She awakened each time in a cold sweat but the nightmares recurred each time she closed her eyes and then they were on the deck of the *Caroline* as it went down in the Thames. She could hear the shouts and screams of the passengers and crew as people were thrown into the dark, polluted waters near the sewage outfall. Sam held her in his arms as they plunged overboard – she was sinking down and down. The water was ice-cold. She struggled and kicked out with her feet. The current tore her from Sam's arms. She could see his face pale and agonised in a shaft of moonlight striking through the water . . .

Someone was shaking her and she opened her eyes with a muffled scream.

'It's only me, Lucy. You was having a bad dream. It must have been all that good food we ate yesterday.'

Guthrie's face was filled with concern as he peered down at her. She was trembling violently as she pulled the bedcovers up to her throat. He patted her clumsily on the shoulder, but the noise that had awakened her from her nightmare was continuing downstairs. Someone was hammering on the front door although it was dark outside.

'Who could it be at this time of the night?'

'It's seven in the morning,' Guthrie said, peering out of the window. 'Was you going to work today, Lucy?'

She sat up, pulling the coverlet around her shoulders. 'No. I wasn't, but you'd best go and see who wants us so urgently. I'll get dressed and come down directly.'

Guthrie threw up the sash. 'Hold on there, cully. I'm coming.' A gust of icy air flew around the room as he closed the window and Lucetta shivered convulsively as she watched him lumber out through the door. She swung her legs over the side of the bed and reached for her clothes. She could hear the deep rumble of male voices from the living room below but she could not make out the words. She tugged at the laces on her stays and her fingers fumbled with the buttons on her blouse and skirt as she attempted to hurry. She ran downstairs in her stockinged feet with her boots clasped in her hand. She stopped short as she saw that it was Perks who had awakened them so rudely.

'What's wrong, Mr Perks? Has the warehouse burned to the ground in the night?'

He turned to her, with an apologetic smile. 'No, miss. I'm sorry to bother you so early in the morning, and on a bank holiday too, but there's an irate ship's captain demanding to see Mr Jeremiah. There's a question of payment for the cargo and he refuses to let it be unloaded until he's got a promissory note or the money owed.'

'But why come to me? You need to send someone to fetch Mr Jeremiah from Thornhill Crescent.'

'There isn't anyone else, miss. The warehouse is

closed today, but Mr Jeremiah insists that there is always someone on duty in the office.' Perks thrust a bunch of keys into her hand. 'Perhaps you can calm the captain down too. He's hopping mad and I think I would be too if I'd spent six months or more at sea and found there was no money forthcoming.'

Lucetta plucked her bonnet and shawl from the row of pegs behind the door. 'The shipping companies usually handle the payments, Perks. I can't think what has gone wrong.'

'This is different, miss. The captain is the owner of the vessel and Mr Bradley told him he would be paid on his return to London. It was a special consignment of cloth from India ordered by one of them big stores up West. There'll be hell to pay, if you'll excuse the expression, if they don't get it on time.'

'All right, Perks. I'll go to the office right away,' Lucetta said, sitting down on the only chair in the room to put on her boots. 'I'll try to keep the angry captain calm until Mr Jeremiah arrives.'

'D'you want me to come with you, Lucy?' Guthrie said anxiously. 'I'll sort the cove out if he gets above hisself.'

Lucetta flashed him a grateful smile. 'No, thank you, Lennie, I'm sure I can manage on my own.'

'Bless you, miss,' Perks said as he opened the front door. 'I don't know what Mr Jeremiah will say, but he won't be best pleased.' He went outside and was swallowed up in the darkness.

Lucetta followed him, wrapping her shawl around her shoulders as the biting cold gnawed at her bones.

She was out of breath by the time she reached the warehouse and her fingers were so numb that she dropped the bunch of keys on the cobblestones as she attempted to unlock the office door. It was still quite dark although the lamplighter was already on his rounds and had doused the gas light nearest to the warehouse. She crouched down and was feeling around for the keys when someone leaned over her.

'Let me help you.'

She froze as an arm clad in the rough woollen cloth of a pea jacket reached across her to pick up the bunch of keys, and her heart skipped a beat as she recognised his voice. She would have known him anywhere. She turned her head slowly as he helped her to her feet.

Chapter Twenty

Lucetta was trembling violently as she took the keys from him. It was too dark to make out his features. He seemed taller than she remembered and more powerfully built, but she would have known him anywhere.

'Trust Froy to send a woman.' His voice throbbed with suppressed anger. 'Old Henry would be turning in his grave if he knew what had happened to his company.'

She turned the key in the lock and opened the door. 'Step inside out of the cold, Captain. Mr Froy has been sent for and he should be here soon.' Covering her confusion she moved swiftly to the counter where Perks kept a box of vestas. The act of lighting the gas mantles made it easier to avoid the inevitable moment when she must face him. She took off her bonnet and turned slowly to face him, but her worst fears were realised when there was no apparent glimmer of recognition in Sam's hazel eyes. He took off his peaked cap and tucked it under his arm.

'I beg your pardon for being so abrupt, but it is not the first time that this has happened. You must be new here or you would know that getting money out of Froy and Son is more difficult than sailing round the

Horn. I have a crew to pay off and they are eager to get home to their families.'

Lucetta was momentarily lost for words. The soft glow of the gaslight turned his hair to burnished bronze and his clean-cut features were tanned by wind and sun. His features matched the memory she had held close to her heart, but there were subtle changes. The humour had gone from his eyes and there were faint lines etched at the corners of his mouth. Outwardly he was the same Sam Cutler she had known and loved in Bali but he seemed to have forgotten her completely. She thought she had felt pain in the past but it was as nothing to that which she suffered now. Her whole world had been built around the hope that Sam would return to claim her. She had dreamed of their reunion but it had not been like this. She longed to make herself known to him, but something stopped her and it was not simply pride. She shot him a glance beneath her lashes and saw a stranger. Dora Cutler's bitter accusations rang in her ears and Lucetta was too afraid to put her faith in Sam to the test. She moved swiftly to the fireplace and began riddling the ashes.

'I'll get the fire going and make you a cup of tea, Captain.'

'There is no need, miss – I'm afraid I don't know your name.'

She did not look up from her task. 'I'm Lucy Guthrie and I am Mr Froy's secretary.'

'Well, I am very sorry to have called you out so early in the morning, when none of this is your fault.'

'That's quite all right, Captain. I normally start work at half past seven.'

'That doesn't surprise me, Miss Guthrie. Old man Froy is a notorious slave-driver and his son is little better.'

Lucetta let this pass. She finished laying the fire and lit it by striking a vesta on the fireback. She rose to her feet. 'I'll make the tea,' she said, picking up the empty kettle. 'If you'll excuse me, I'll go and fetch some water.'

He held out his hand. 'Allow me. I'm quite familiar with this building and I'm sure I can find my way to the back yard.' His grim expression melted into a warm smile that was so reminiscent of the Sam she knew and loved that Lucetta had to curb the impulse to throw herself into his arms. This time it was her pride that stopped her and she managed a tight little smile in response.

'Thank you, Captain.' She held on to the handle a little longer than was necessary. The brief touch of his fingers still had the power to send thrills through her body. 'You must have been here often then,' she said breathlessly.

'I've had dealings with the family for a good few years, but it's never been the same since Mr Froy's brother Henry was drowned.' His eyes darkened as he took the kettle from her. 'I should have been on that ship. If I had I might have saved ...' He broke off, smiling ruefully. 'But it was not to be. I think we could both do with a cup of tea, Miss Guthrie.' He lifted the hatch in the counter top and let himself into the warehouse.

Lucetta stood as rigid as a stone statue as she listened to his footstep echoing on the bare boards. She picked up the cap that Sam had left on the counter and held it to her breast, closing her eyes and inhaling the achingly familiar scent of him. He might have forgotten her but she clung to the bitter-sweet memories of the past. Was she so very much changed?

She stared into the mirror over the fireplace where she had seen Jeremiah check his appearance a hundred times or more before he went out on business. She ran her finger down the angle of her jaw. Her face was probably thinner than it had been when she first met Sam. Her cheeks were pale and perhaps her hair was a little darker, although scraped back from her face and knotted at the nape of her neck it was not shown off at its best. She looked tired and wan, but that was hardly surprising considering the harshness of her life now. She sighed. She had become plain and uninteresting and perhaps the stories that she had heard about Sam were true. Maybe he had been toying with her affections and had been courting her in the hope of marrying an heiress. She shook her head, frowning at her downcast reflection. If she made herself known to him now he would be embarrassed or even worse, he might wonder what it was that he had ever seen in her. Lucetta Froy was dead and buried. Better to let her remain so.

He returned moments later and having placed the kettle on the hob he took a watch from his pocket and examined it, frowning. 'If your employer has not returned in the next half-hour, I'll have to go about matters in a different way. If I have not received payment by this afternoon, the cargo will be put up for auction.'

Lucetta eyed him curiously. She had grown up in the shadow of her father's business and she knew that he dealt mainly with shipping agents rather than the masters of the vessels. 'Don't you have an agent to do this for you, Captain?'

'I am part owner of the *Sea Eagle* and not yet in a position to pay agents' fees. I handle all our business deals personally, which is why I have not the time or the inclination to await Mr Froy's pleasure.'

He glanced at his watch again and Lucetta was afraid that he would leave before Jeremiah arrived. 'He will be here soon, I am certain. A few more minutes won't make any difference. Won't you sit down and make yourself comfortable? The kettle will be boiling soon and I'll make the tea.'

'Mr Froy is lucky to have such a devoted assistant. I will give him another ten minutes, but I have two days in which to turn my vessel around. I can't afford long delays.'

'You are leaving so soon?'

He met her anxious gaze with a casual shrug of his shoulders. 'An idle ship doesn't make any money, and neither does an empty hold. I was lucky enough to negotiate another cargo bound for France when we docked on Christmas Eve, and when we reach Calais I will look for further business.'

Lucetta busied herself making the tea. 'You can have very little time at home with your family.'

'I am a free man,' Sam said grimly. 'I have no ties in England or abroad. Marriage and seafaring do not sit well together.'

Her hand shook as she selected a cup that had the least amount of cracks and chips from the tray behind the counter. 'I think that if a woman loved a man enough she could put up with almost anything.'

'You have romantic notions, Miss Guthrie. I am afraid that I have no such delusions.'

Lucetta glanced at the clock on the wall, willing Jeremiah to hurry. She knew to the last penny how much the owners of the *Sea Eagle* were owed, and thanks to her efforts in collecting outstanding debts there was enough money to pay them, but it was Boxing Day and all the banks were closed. The street outside was unusually quiet and the only sounds in the room were the ticking of the clock and the crackle of the burning coals. She made the tea and watched Sam drink it in silence. She longed to reach out and smooth away the frown that creased his forehead and she struggled to think of something to say that would ease the situation. The carefree young seafarer she had known and loved had matured into a man weighed down by responsibilities, and worst of all he did not recognise her.

Sam put down his cup and rose to his feet. 'I can't wait any longer. Froy has had his chance and you must tell him that the goods will be sent to auction in the morning unless I receive full payment in cash.'

He was about to leave the office when the sound of an approaching cab made him hesitate. Lucetta could have cried with relief when a hansom cab drew up outside and Perks climbed down, followed more slowly by his master. Jeremiah strode into the office, shaking a powdering of snow from his top hat.

'What the devil d'you think you're doing calling me out on Boxing Day, Captain Cutler? Don't you know that the banks are all closed until tomorrow?'

Sam eyed Jeremiah coldly. 'A promissory note will be sufficient to secure your goods, but they will not be released to you until I have visited the bank first thing in the morning and have the cash in my hands.'

'Are you suggesting that my credit is not good?' Jeremiah's cheeks puffed out and a dull red flush rose up from his throat to suffuse his face.

'I'm not suggesting anything, Froy. I'm merely protecting my own interests. I would be grateful if you would write that note. I have a lot to do today.'

'Fetch me pen and paper, Miss Guthrie,' Jeremiah ordered, waving his hand in her direction. 'And hurry up. I have a house filled with guests waiting for my return.'

'I'll fetch it, miss.' Perks had entered the office in the wake of his master. He gave Lucetta a perfunctory smile. 'Sit down and drink your tea.' He then hurried into the warehouse.

Jeremiah faced Sam angrily. 'You'd better be careful, mister. I'll pay you this time but there are plenty of other shippers who would be only too pleased to carry my cargos.'

'But not as cheaply as I do, and not as quickly either. The *Sea Eagle* is as fast a ship as you'll find, and the mix of steam and sail takes weeks off each trip. Your father knows when he's on to a good thing and he has the final say in business matters, not you.'

Lucetta could see a vein throbbing in Jeremiah's temple and his colour deepened from brick-red to puce. She thought for a moment that he was going to have an apoplectic fit, but Perks reappeared and Jeremiah snatched the pen and paper from him. He scribbled the note and thrust it into Sam's outstretched hand. 'Don't be too sure of yourself, mister. I have some influence amongst the city merchants and I could ruin you if I chose.'

'But that would not be to your best advantage,' Sam said calmly. 'If you put me out of business you would have to pay the going rate to the larger shipping lines, and I'm sure that's not what you want.'

'All right, but I want my cargo unloaded first thing in the morning. See to it, Cutler.' Jeremiah turned to Perks. 'And you deal with anything else that might come up today. I don't want to be disturbed again.' He made for the street door and strode out to the waiting hansom cab.

'Charming fellow,' Sam said, smiling for the first time as he pocketed the promissory note. 'He could at least have offered you a lift home, Miss Guthrie.'

'It's not like it was in the old days,' Perks said gloomily. 'I might not have known him, but I believe that Mr Henry would be turning in his grave if he could see what his brother and nephew have done to the business.'

'I must go now.' Sam put his cap on and he turned

to Lucetta, giving her his full attention for the first time. 'I'm sorry if I ruined your precious day off. Perhaps I could see you home safely?'

He was regarding her so intently that she was taken off guard. Had he remembered her? It was too much to hope for and she could not bear another disappointment. 'No – I mean, thank you, but I don't have far to go. I wouldn't want to put you out.'

'I have business on Spirit Quay. Is that anywhere near your home?'

'Miss Guthrie lives in Samson's Green, Captain,' Perks said before Lucetta had a chance to answer for herself. 'It's on your way.'

'That's settled then,' Sam said, smiling. 'Put on your bonnet and shawl, Miss Guthrie.'

She had been intent on refusing his offer but she was undone by that smile. For a brief moment she saw the Sam she had known and loved, and she knew that she could refuse him nothing. The fact that he did not recognise her hurt more than she would have thought possible, but the light in the office was poor and she was wearing the drabbest of clothes. He was tired after a long sea voyage and his mind was focused on business, not pleasure. Added to all that, he was under the impression that she had died more than two years ago. It was hardly surprising that he did not know her, but she could still hope. She put on her bonnet and slipped her shawl around her shoulders. 'I'm ready, Captain.'

Perks smiled benignly. 'Thank you for helping out, Miss Lucy. I'll see you in the morning.'

'Don't work too hard, Mr Perks.' Lucetta accepted

Sam's arm and was glad of his help as she stepped outside onto the slippery snow-coated cobblestones.

'You'll have to direct me,' Sam said, pulling his cap down further over his eyes as the thick white flakes swirled around their heads. 'I don't know Samson's Green.'

'It's not far,' Lucetta murmured, shivering as the flakes melted on her shawl and the icy water seeped through the thin cotton of her blouse.

Sam glanced down at her and he frowned. 'That is just as well. We must get you home quickly before you freeze to death.' Taking her by the arm, he quickened his pace and Lucetta had to concentrate hard in order to keep up with him. She couldn't help thinking that the old Sam Cutler would have taken off his jacket and wrapped it tenderly around her shoulders, insisting that her need was greater than his. As it was she found herself half carried, half dragged back to the narrow street she called home. She stopped outside her front door, praying that he would not want to come inside. He might not know her but he was almost certain to recognise Guthrie and feel duty-bound to hand him over to the authorities. She stood with her back to the door, peering up at him through the driving snow. 'Thank you for seeing me home, Captain Cutler.'

He nodded his head, thrusting his hands deep in his pockets and turning away as he spoke. 'Good day to you, Miss Guthrie.' He walked off towards Redmead Lane without a backwards glance.

*   *   *

Next day at the office Lucetta could not wait to interrogate Perks. She arrived early just as he was stoking the fire. He glanced over his shoulder as she entered the room bringing with her a gust of cold, snow-laden air. 'You're bright and early, Miss Lucy.'

She took off her sodden bonnet and shawl and hung them over the back of a beech-wood chair to dry. 'I thought we might be busy today, Mr Perks.' She moved closer to the fire, holding her chilled hands out to its warmth.

He struggled to his feet, rubbing his knees as if they caused him pain. 'This weather doesn't help my rheumatics. I'll be glad when winter's over.'

'It must be wonderful to sail off to sunnier climes like Mr Froy senior and Captain Cutler.'

'Yes, miss.' Perks went behind the counter and opened a leather-bound ledger. 'The captain saw you home safely then?'

'Right to the door, for which I was very grateful as the pavements were very slippery. Do you know him well, Mr Perks? He seems quite young to be a sea captain.'

Perks took a pair of spectacles from his jacket pocket and polished them with a cotton handkerchief. 'He was first mate on the ill-fated *Caroline*, but he was left behind in Bali when she sailed for England. He seems to have come into some money and he bought himself a half-share in the *Sea Eagle*. There was talk that Captain Cutler had made his fortune by selling a valuable cargo that Mr Henry had bought and paid for but hadn't been able to bring back on the *Caroline*. I know that

Mr Bradley had his suspicions at the time, but there was no proof. All Mr Henry's papers went down with the ship and there was no one left to say yea or nay to the accusations.' Perks placed his spectacles on the bridge of his nose and his expression changed to one of concern as he stared at Lucetta. 'Are you all right, Miss Lucy? You've gone as white as the proverbial sheet.'

'I'm fine, thank you,' she said hastily. 'Just a bit cold, that's all. I'd best get to work before Mr Jeremiah arrives.' She hurried past him into the warehouse, where the men were just arriving for work. Their initial animosity had lessened gradually over the weeks and now they greeted her with nods and smiles, adding a few grumbles about the weather and the bone-chilling temperature which was little higher inside than out. Lucetta smiled automatically and headed for the relative peace of her tiny office. She sat down, staring into space as she grappled with the notion that Sam had stolen the goods that her father had trusted him to retrieve and send to London on the *Caroline*'s sister ship. She could not believe that he had sold the cargo in order to further his career. Sam would not do such a dishonest thing. She bit her lip as doubts assailed her, but she pushed them to the back of her mind. It was idle gossip, of course, and most likely put about by Bradley himself, who had turned what had been a most profitable business into one that was on the verge of collapse.

While she was growing up, Lucetta had never paid much attention to the dull discourse concerning financial matters that passed between her father and his colleagues, but she realised now that she must have absorbed something from their conversations. She could see why Uncle Bradley was not making money, but she knew that Jeremiah would brush aside any suggestions she might make. He had made it plain that he thought all women were feather-brained creatures put on the earth for one purpose only, and he only tolerated her because she worked for less pay than a man. She sighed and began sorting through the neat stacks of papers on her desk. She must put all thoughts of Sam and what might have been from her mind if she were to keep a clear head. There was rent to be paid and fuel, food and candles to be bought.

Guthrie's injured leg would make it difficult for him to get about on the freezing pavements, and he was fit only for the lightest of manual labours. She had not told him about Sam when she returned home yesterday and she did not intend to, especially in the light of what Perks had just told her. Guthrie was as protective of her as a guard dog, and his lameness would not prevent him from using his fists if he were provoked. Lucetta suspected that he had gone back to his former trade of picking pockets. He had protested his innocence and promised her that he had earned what little money he brought home by honest labour, but doubts still lingered in her mind. She had found a pawnbroker's ticket in the pocket of a shirt she was about to wash, and when faced with it he had admitted one such lapse, but had given her his word that he would not steal again. She could only hope that he would not give in to temptation.

She turned with a start as a sudden gust of cold air blew in from the street. The double doors to the warehouse had been flung open and the men leapt into action, hefting huge crates into the unloading bay. It would seem that Sam had cashed the promissory note and would be preparing to set sail as soon as the next cargo was loaded. Her feelings were so mixed that she did not know what to think or whom to believe. If he had truly loved her wouldn't he have recognised her the moment he saw her?

'Haven't you any work to do, Miss Guthrie?'

Jeremiah's voice behind her made her turn with a start. 'I was just sorting these papers, sir.'

'You were daydreaming, you idle slut,' Jeremiah roared above the noise from the warehouse floor. 'I don't pay you for sitting around and gazing into space. No doubt you were thinking of your lover, or maybe there are several young men sniffing round you like dogs on heat.'

Lucetta rose shakily to her feet. 'There is no call to speak to me like that, Mr Froy. I am up to date with my work, and I came in on a bank holiday to help out in an emergency.'

'Don't answer back, girl.' Jeremiah raised his hand as if to strike her, but he was seized from behind by Sam who appeared suddenly in the doorway.

'Only a coward would strike a defenceless woman,' he said angrily. 'Come outside, Froy, and face me like a man.'

Jeremiah paled and backed further into Lucetta's tiny office, almost knocking her over in the process.

'Wh-what do you want, you madman? Why are you here? You've got your money or you wouldn't have allowed my cargo to be unloaded.'

'Yes, I've got the cash, but I haven't got a vessel. A block of granite fell from a crane and caused serious damage. This is going to cost you dear, Froy. You are going to pay for repairs and compensate me for loss of business.'

'What the hell are you talking about?' Jeremiah demanded, bristling. 'If there's been an accident it has nothing to do with me.'

'You can't lie your way out of this,' Sam said through clenched teeth. 'You bribed that crane operator to make it appear like an accident.'

'That's a lie. You can't prove anything.'

'Oh, can't I? We'll see about that. My men are holding the culprit and he's confessed. Do you dare face him and hear what he has to say? Or shall I send for a constable and have you both arrested?'

'You can't come in here making wild accusations,' Jeremiah blustered. 'I'll not give you a penny piece.'

The warehousemen had gathered behind Sam. They did not appear anxious to stand up for their employer. Lucetta could see that the argument might easily spiral into a fight and she laid her hand on Jeremiah's arm. 'Perhaps you had better go with Captain Cutler, sir. The man might be more willing to tell the truth in your presence.'

Jeremiah turned on her with a savage snarl. 'Mind your own business. When I want the advice of a silly chit of a girl, I'll ask for it.'

The words were barely out of his mouth when Sam grabbed him by the collar and frogmarched him out through the warehouse into the street. The warehousemen abandoned their work and followed them with Lucetta close behind.

'Call a constable,' Jeremiah shouted in a strangled voice as he was forced to cross the street to face a terrified crane driver who was being held by two burly seamen.

Sam glared at the man. 'Repeat what you told me.'

Shaking his head, the man rolled his eyes. 'It's more than me life's worth, guv.' A sharp nudge in the ribs from one of the crewmen made him yelp with pain. 'He give me a sov to drop the block and make it look like an accident. It was Mr Froy what made me do it.'

'Liar,' Jeremiah roared, striking the man a blow across his face that brought blood spurting from his lips. 'Take that back.'

Lucetta glanced at the faces of the men who had surrounded them and she saw amusement wiped away by anger and resentment. They moved towards Jeremiah as one, and she could see the situation turning ugly. She slipped in between Sam and Jeremiah. 'Please, gentlemen, don't you think this matter would be best settled in private? I'm sure neither of you wants a street brawl.'

Sam fisted his hands, squaring up to Jeremiah. 'I'm ready for a fight if he's got the stomach for it.'

Jeremiah seized Lucetta, holding her in front of him like a shield. 'The girl is right for once. We'll settle this in the pub over a jug of rum punch.' He turned to the crowd. 'There's a drink in this for each of you if you get back to your work now.'

A murmur of approval rippled through the small crowd that had gathered and Lucetta felt the mood change in an instant. They drifted off, returning to the warehouses along the street and the ships moored alongside.

'Let me go, guv,' the crane driver whined. 'I got a wife and seven nippers to feed.'

Sam nodded to his crewmen. 'Let him go. I won't press charges as Mr Froy is going to settle the matter.'

'Ta, guv. You're a toff.' The man raced off, stumbling and sliding on the slippery ground in his eagerness to get away.

'The villain should have been handed over to the police,' Jeremiah muttered. 'It's all a pack of lies.'

'We'll continue this in the pub,' Sam said grimly. 'Go back on your word and you'll be sorry, Froy.'

Lucetta glanced anxiously from one to the other. She was shivering violently and her teeth were chattering, but her concern for Sam overrode everything. 'How bad is the damage, Captain? Will it take long to repair your ship?'

He shrugged his shoulders. 'That's for the boat builders to decide, but it won't be cheap.'

'It's none of your business, Guthrie,' Jeremiah snapped. 'Get back to your work or you'll be looking for another position.'

'I'd look for work elsewhere anyway, if I were you,' Sam said, turning to Lucetta with a hint of the charming smile she remembered so well. 'The idiot doesn't deserve loyalty from a person like you.'

Lucetta looked him in the eyes and for a moment she thought she saw a flicker of recognition. She opened her mouth to reply but Sam had turned away as if he had already forgotten her presence.

'Come along then, Froy,' he said, slapping Jeremiah on the shoulder. 'Let's go to the Turk's Head for that jug of rum punch and we'll discuss money in a civilised way.'

Lucetta stood on the wharf, watching them as they strode off towards the pub. Standing amongst the tall cranes with the ships' masts towering above her, she felt small and insignificant. She had once been Miss Lucetta Froy, heiress to a thriving business, and now she was a person of no importance.

'Come back inside, miss.'

She turned to see Perks standing behind her, holding out her shawl. He wrapped it around her shoulders. 'You'll catch your death of cold out here, Miss Lucy. There's a nice hot cup of tea waiting for you in the office, and some of Mrs P's shortbread biscuits what was left over from our Christmas dinner.'

It took several cups of hot sweet tea to warm Lucetta, but the real chill was settled firmly around her heart. She knew now that Sam really had forgotten her. She went about her work that day like an automaton. She did not flinch when Jeremiah shouted at her, taking out his frustration on her instead of on Captain Cutler. It transpired that a witness had come forward, having overhead Jeremiah plotting with the crane driver, and

Jeremiah had been constrained to underwrite the repairs to the *Sea Eagle*. He was not a happy man. Lucetta would have loved to tell him that it was all his own doing and he had brought trouble on himself, but she kept her own counsel. She could not risk losing her job, and if she were to tell the truth her feeling for the business went deeper than that. The warehouse and its contents were her only link with her past. At any given moment of the day she expected to hear her father's voice giving instructions to his men. He was still here in spirit; she could feel him all around her and she would not let him down.

At the end of the day, long after Jeremiah had gone home in a foul mood, Lucetta walked through the warehouse examining the newly unpacked cargo that Sam had brought back from Asia and the Far East. The scent of sandalwood and spices mingled with the smoky sweetness of joss sticks and vetiver. Bales of silk, brocade in jewel colours and cotton threaded with gold and silver were piled high against the walls. Uncle Bradley might be a parsimonious old skinflint but he had an eye for a bargain and the new stock was worth a small fortune if sold to the highest bidders. Lucetta could only hope that Jeremiah had inherited some of the family business acumen. Well placed, this consignment of exotic cloth, furniture and artefacts would bring in enough money to put Froy and Son back in profit.

She was cold and tired and her spirits had never been lower as she trudged homewards. Her bright hopes of a joyful reunion with Sam had burst like a soap bubble soaring towards the sun, only now it was bitterly cold and snow was falling steadily and settling on the ground in a thick white blanket. As she neared the house in Samson's Green she saw footprints and a trail of dark spots leading to her front door. She did not have to examine them too closely to realise that they were drops of fresh blood. She opened the door and stepped inside, hesitating as she found the room in darkness except for a pale glow from the dying embers of the fire. Slumped in a chair she could just make out the shape of a man. 'Lennie, what's wrong?' she cried.

He did not answer, and as she lit the stub of a candle with shaking fingers, she gasped in horror. 'Lennie, what happened to you?'

Chapter Twenty-one

Guthrie's eyes flickered and opened. He stared at her dully. 'It's me leg. Busted in the same place as before.'

Lucetta lit a candle. Guthrie's leg was twisted at an alarming angle and blood was dripping in a steady stream onto the dirt floor. 'How did this happen, Lennie? I told you not to go out in the snow. Did you have a fall?'

'Yes,' he muttered. 'I fell.'

'I'll have to cut the trouser leg so that I can clean the wound and stop the bleeding.' Without giving him time to answer, Lucetta plucked a small cardboard box from the mantelshelf. Opening it she took out a pair of scissors, a needle and a spool of thread. She knelt down in front of him, cutting through the thick material with difficulty. The stench of the blood was making her feel sick but she forced her chilled fingers to work as gently as she could. The smallest movement caused Guthrie great pain, and when she had finally laid the wound bare she had to stifle a cry of horror at the sight of protruding splinters of bone and torn flesh.

'It's bad, ain't it?' Guthrie whispered. 'I'm a goner, Lucy. I'm bleeding to death.'

'You must see a doctor, Lennie. We must get you to the hospital.'

He grasped her by the wrist, forcing her to look him in the eyes. 'No. I can't go there.'

She was startled by the urgency in his voice and the desperation in his eyes. 'You must have proper medical attention. I won't let anyone hurt you.' She spoke softly as she would to a frightened child, but Guthrie shook his head vehemently.

'No hospital. That's the first place they'll look.'

'What have you done, Lennie? Who's looking for you?'

'They'll hang me for sure if they catch me. I was just after the old geezer's half-hunter and he started shouting and calling out for help. I never meant to hurt him, Lucy, all I wanted to do was make him shut up.'

Lucetta had been vainly attempting to staunch the flow of blood with her handkerchief, but this admission made her stop. She raised her eyes to his face and her blood spiked with an icy chill. 'You didn't . . .'

Guthrie closed his eyes and tears seeped from beneath his eyelids. 'I think I killed him, but I never meant to. There was people shouting and I heard a police whistle. I ran and ran and I could hear them close behind. I heard dogs baying and I climbed onto a roof. It was slippery and I fell . . .'

'Don't talk any more,' Lucetta said urgently. 'I can't stop the bleeding, Lennie. I don't know what to do.'

'Yes, you do. Remember what you done in Bali.' He dashed his hand across his eyes, focusing them on her with difficulty. 'Take me belt and tie it tight around the leg above me knee.'

With trembling fingers Lucetta unbuckled his belt.

She slipped it around his injured leg as he directed and fastened it as tightly as she could manage. The tourniquet worked after a fashion and the flow of blood lessened visibly, but she could see that he was very weak. She fetched water from the pump in the back yard and held a cup to his dry lips. 'I have to get help, Lennie. You'll die if you don't see a doctor.'

A grim smile twisted his lips. 'It'll be the noose for me when the law catches up with me.'

She set the cup down on the table well within his reach. She would have to put her personal feelings aside and beg Giles for help, but to walk through the snow to Lonsdale Square would waste precious time and she had no money for the cab fare. There was only one person she could think of who might be persuaded to give her a small loan. 'I'm going out,' she said firmly. 'I'll be as quick as I can and you're not to move.'

'That's a laugh. I couldn't make a run for it if the house was on fire.'

'You'll be all right, Lennie. I'm going to fetch help and you need not worry about the police.' She had not stopped to take off her bonnet when she entered the house and she snatched up her damp shawl. 'I'll be as quick as I can.'

She barely noticed the bitter chill outside as she sped towards Union Stairs and the Turk's Head, where she hoped and prayed she would find Sam. To her intense relief she saw him seated in the taproom surrounded by the warehousemen and dock workers who had taken Jeremiah up on his offer of a free drink. Sam looked up as she threaded her way towards him and he raised his glass to her. 'Well, if it isn't little Miss Prim and Proper from Froy's warehouse. Have you come to taste the landlord's excellent rum punch, my dear?'

Ignoring the leers and suggestive remarks of the men sitting closest to him, Lucetta met his amused gaze without flinching. 'May I have a word with you in private, Captain Cutler?'

'Hey, mate, you're on to a good thing there.' A bearded man nudged Sam in the ribs and winked at Lucetta.

'It won't take a moment,' she insisted.

Sam eyed her curiously and his smile faded. 'All right,' he said, rising to his feet. 'Come outside, young lady, and tell me what I can do for you.'

Howls of laughter greeted this remark and Lucetta felt her cheeks flame with embarrassment. She was hemmed in by curious onlookers but they stepped aside at a word from Sam. The air in the taproom was thick with smoke and alcohol fumes combined with the odour of unwashed bodies and Lucetta took a deep breath as she emerged into the comparatively fresh air outside.

'This is an unexpected pleasure,' Sam said, leaning his shoulders against the pub window. 'What can I do for you, Miss Guthrie?'

'I'll come straight to the point, Captain Cutler. I need to borrow some money. It's an emergency or I would not ask.'

He whistled through his teeth. 'That's to the point, certainly. Can you tell me why I should lend money to a complete stranger?'

Lucetta was desperate. Guthrie's life hung in the balance and whatever his past misdeeds she could not desert him now. She raised her chin to look Sam in the eyes. This was no time for false pride. 'I am not a stranger, Sam. We once knew each other very well.'

He frowned. 'I'm sorry, but I can't place you, although there is something familiar about you and it's been bothering me ever since we first met.'

'I haven't time for guessing games. I wasn't drowned when the *Caroline* went down in the Thames. I was rescued and the man who saved me is badly injured and may be close to death for all I know. I need the cab fare to Islington where there is a doctor who may be able to save his life.'

Sam moved away from the window, taking her by the shoulders and twisting her round to face the light from a gas lamp. He shook his head in disbelief. 'No. It can't be.'

She met his startled gaze with a steady look, willing him to remember those heady days of love and romance in Bali. 'Have I changed so much, Sam?'

'Lucetta? No, it can't be – I visited your grave and I spoke to your grieving relations. I can't believe it is you, and yet . . .' He fingered a strand of hair that had escaped from beneath her bonnet and he held it up to the light where it gleamed like molten gold. 'By God, it is you.' He released the curl, staring at her with wonder dawning in his eyes as he traced the outline of her face with a gentle finger. 'My little Lucetta is alive and has grown up.'

She pushed him away. 'Stop that, Sam. I'm no longer

your little Lucetta and you had quite forgotten me, but that doesn't matter now. I want nothing from you other than a small loan. I get paid on Friday and you will have your money back in full.'

He either did not hear or her words had not registered in his brain. 'I can't believe it. Lucetta, it really is you. But why . . .'

She laid her finger across his lips. 'There isn't time for this. I hold you to nothing, Sam. Five shillings will more than cover the fare. Please, I'm begging you, help me.'

'You must think a lot of this man,' Sam said slowly. 'But I don't understand. Why are you working in the warehouse? You must own it in part at least?'

'It's a long story and this really is a matter of life and death. Are you going to lend me the money or not?'

He took her by the arm. 'I'll do better than that, my dear. I'm coming with you and you can tell me the whole story during the cab ride.'

Reluctantly at first but warming to her story as the hackney carriage trundled on its way to Islington, Lucetta related the events of the past three years, omitting nothing.

Sam sat back against the squabs, listening intently. When she finished he let out a low whistle. 'By God, what a tale. No wonder you look different from the pretty little thing I fell for in Bali.' He hesitated, eyeing her anxiously. 'Not that you aren't attractive now, Lucetta. After all you've been through it's no wonder

397

you look thin and pale as a wax candle, but now I'm here I can put young Jeremiah right. Old Bradley will have to acknowledge you as your father's rightful heiress when I stand up in court and tell them that we are engaged to be married and have been these last three years. You'll be back in Thornhill Crescent in no time at all.'

Lucetta gave him a long look. 'Is that why you accompanied me now, Sam? Are you thinking that you will marry an heiress?'

'I've never stopped loving you, my pet. My heart was buried in the cold earth with the girl I loved and now, by some miracle, she has been returned to me.'

These were the words she had imagined him uttering so many times in the past. She wanted desperately to believe him. 'Are you telling me the truth, Sam?'

He made a show of crossing his heart and his smile embraced her like a kiss. 'I've never lied to you, my love. I am yours heart and soul.'

He reached out to take her hand but the cab slowed down and their fingers barely touched. The spell was broken and Lucetta came abruptly back to reality: this was not the time or the place for a romantic reunion. She peered out of the window as they came to a halt outside the Harcourts' house in Lonsdale Square. Flinging the door open she climbed out of the cab.

'Wait here, please, cabby. I won't be long.' She picked up her skirts and hurried up the path to hammer frantically on the door. Her breath formed clouds around her head as she waited impatiently for someone to answer her urgent summons. There were lights in the windows and in the upstairs drawing room she could see the outline of a Christmas tree hung with glass baubles and tinsel. She crossed her fingers, praying silently that Giles would be at home. She had not considered the fact that he might already be living in Dorset, but it occurred to her now and she became more and more agitated. She could have cried with relief when the maidservant opened the door.

'Is Dr Harcourt at home?' Lucetta stepped over the threshold without waiting for an invitation. 'It's an emergency. I must speak to him right away.'

The maid took a step backwards. 'The family are at dinner, miss. Call back in an hour.'

'No, you don't understand. I must speak to him now.'

'What is all the fuss?' Giles emerged from the dining room, wiping his lips on a spotless white table napkin. It fell from his fingers and fluttered to the floor when he saw Lucetta, and a delighted smile wreathed his face. He came towards her holding out his hands. 'My dear Lucetta, you've come home. Thank God.'

'Giles, I need your help urgently.'

His dark eyes scanned her face and his smile faded into a look of deep concern. 'You are not ill, are you? Come into the morning parlour and let me look at you.'

She shook her head, taking him by the hands and tugging him towards the open door while the maid looked on in astonishment.

'It's not me, Giles,' Lucetta said urgently. 'There is a man bleeding to death who needs your help. You are the only one I could trust.'

He seized his coat and hat from the hallstand, turning his head to address the gawping servant. 'Tell my mother that I've been called out on an emergency.' He snatched up his medical bag. 'I'm ready.'

'Thank you, Giles,' Lucetta breathed. 'I knew I could count on you.' She ran out into the street, giving instructions to the cabby as Sam held out his hand to help her into the waiting cab.

Giles was about to climb in after her but he paused when he saw Sam. 'Is this the patient, Lucetta? He looks hale and hearty to me.'

'This is Sam Cutler, Giles,' Lucetta said, eyeing Sam nervously. She had told him almost everything, but she had omitted to mention that both Giles and Sir Hector had proposed marriage.

Giles eyed Sam with a distinctly hostile glint in his dark eyes. 'So you are Cutler.'

'Get in please, Giles,' Lucetta pleaded. 'It's Lennie who is in desperate need of medical attention. I'll explain everything as we go.'

He leapt in and slammed the door as the cab jolted forwards. 'Why did you leave like that, Lucetta? What made you run away without a word?'

'It doesn't matter now, Giles. The most important thing is to care for Lennie. I'm afraid he will die.'

Giles took her hand and clasped it tightly. 'I've scoured London trying to find you.'

'This is all very pleasant,' Sam drawled. 'But the lady is with me now, cully. We have an understanding, if you get my drift.

Lucetta turned on him angrily. 'You don't own me,

Sam. A great deal has happened since we last met, and I owe Giles and his cousin Mary a great deal.'

'I can see that you're overwrought, my love,' Sam said, making an obvious effort to control his temper. 'When we get back to Samson's Green I'll go on to my lodgings and we'll meet again tomorrow.' He eyed Giles with a belligerent out-thrust of his chin. 'We have the rest of our lives to look forward to.'

Lucetta eyed him doubtfully. This was not the Sam she remembered, but then she was not the same bright-eyed innocent she had been then. She curved her lips into a smile. 'Thank you, Sam. Tomorrow I will give you my full attention.'

Tears trickled down Guthrie's ashen cheeks as Giles finished binding his injured limb. 'There, old chap, it's all done,' Giles said gently. 'Try to get some sleep, Lennie.'

Lucetta picked up the enamel bowl filled with bloodied water and placed it on the table. 'He will be all right now, won't he?' she whispered.

Giles rose to his feet, wiping his hands on a piece of towelling. His expression was grave. 'He's lost a great deal of blood, but providing sepsis does not set in, he should make a good recovery. He looks like a tough individual to me.'

Guthrie grunted and his lips twisted into a parody of a smile. 'I'm that all right, guv.'

'You must rest, Lennie,' Lucetta said gently. 'I'll make you a cup of tea and some toast. You have to keep your strength up.'

Giles glanced round the sparsely furnished room. 'Is this how you live now, Lucetta?'

'We manage very well.' She bent down to pick up the kettle. 'You will stay for a cup of tea, won't you?'

'Let me fetch the water. You look exhausted.' He took the kettle from her. 'Is there a pump outside or do you have to use the one at the end of the street?'

'We have our own pump but we share the privy with twenty other families. This is quite a modern house for this part of Wapping.' She smiled at the shocked expression on his face. 'It's a hundred times better than the basement in Black Raven Court.'

'Maybe so.' Giles opened the door and disappeared into the darkness, returning moments later with a full kettle which he set on the hob. He glanced at Guthrie, who had fallen asleep under the influence of a generous dose of laudanum. 'I hate to see you living like this, Lucetta. Come home with me and allow us to care for you as we did before.'

She sat down on a stool by the fire, warming her chilled feet in the blaze which would consume the last of their coal supply until pay day. 'I can't do that. This is what I was afraid of, Giles, and why I kept away from Lonsdale Square. It was all too complicated, and Sir Hector . . .' She broke off, staring into the flames.

'He told me,' Giles said softly. 'He said he was an old fool who allowed his emotions to cloud his judgement, although I think he was being a bit hard on himself. Was that why you left the Grange in such a hurry?'

Lucetta looked up and smiled for the first time that

evening as she met the irrepressible twinkle in his eyes. 'I couldn't marry a man I didn't love.'

'I know that from bitter experience, my dear.' Giles held up his hand as she opened her mouth to protest. 'I've survived a broken heart. You don't have to worry about me.'

'I must seem an ungrateful wretch to you, after all you've done for me in the past. And Mary too, does she think badly of me?'

'Mary is a saint. She can see no wrong in the people she loves and she does love you, Lucetta. She misses you very much and she would be so happy to see you again.'

'Is she still in Dorset?'

'She is, although they will be returning when the winter recess is over and Sir Hector resumes his seat in Parliament.'

Lucetta eyed him curiously. 'And have you begun working in your country practice? I was afraid that you might not have returned home for Christmas, but I am so glad that you did.'

'I thought about it long and hard and in the end I decided that a comfortable life in Stockton Lacey was not for me. There is so much poverty and want in the East End that I could not turn my back on the people who are in so much need. I'm looking for a practice in an area where I can be of most use, and I think I might have found the ideal one in Hoxton. It's in one of the poorest areas, quite near the fever hospital in fact.'

She felt a lump rise in her throat and she did not

know how to respond, but at that moment the kettle began to bubble. She was touched by his concern for his fellow men and for some unknown reason his words had brought tears to her eyes. She concealed her emotion by making the tea.

'Will you stay for supper, Giles?' She took the toasting fork from a nail by the fireplace and handed it to him. 'I'll slice the bread if you'd like to make yourself useful and toast it by the fire.'

He took the long-handled fork from her, brandishing it in a fair imitation of Britannia holding out her trident on the back of a copper coin. 'I'm a dab hand at making toast. We practically lived on it when I was a medical student.' He was silent for a moment as he watched her slice the loaf that she took from a crock on the dresser. 'Do you love him, Lucetta?'

She looked up, startled by the suddenness of the question and the intensity in his voice. 'That's not a fair question, Giles.'

'I'm sorry. I had no right to ask.'

'Are we still friends, Giles? I couldn't bear it if you hated me for what I did.'

'Of course I don't hate you.' His voice broke with emotion and he turned away from her. 'Why did you run away, Lucetta?'

'You know why. I was the unwitting cause of so much heartache.'

'Your sudden departure made things worse. If only you had waited until I returned from London, we could have straightened matters out. As it was I've spent weeks searching for you.'

'I am so sorry I put you to such a lot of trouble, Giles.' Lucetta handed him a slice of bread. 'I thought I was acting for the best.'

Giles held the toasting fork close to the flames, glancing at her over his shoulder with a wry smile. 'You wouldn't think that if you had seen my desperate efforts to find you. I visited hotels and lodging houses and in desperation did the rounds of the hospitals in case you had met with an accident.'

'Oh, Giles, I am truly sorry.'

'I was frantic, Lucetta. We all were when you disappeared without a trace. Anyway, a couple of weeks ago I happened to meet up with an old friend, James Richards, the casualty officer at Bart's, and he told me that he recalled treating a man who was accompanied by his pretty young daughter. She met your description exactly, and I remembered what you had told me about Guthrie. That seemed to fit too.'

'I'm surprised Dr Richards remembered us when he sees so many cases in a day.'

'You are not the sort of person a man can forget easily, and paired with your friend – it's like the old fairy tale of beauty and the beast.'

Lucetta cast an anxious glance at Guthrie whose mouth was open, and his unshaven chin rested on his chest as loud snores shook his whole body. She smiled in spite of her concern for him. 'That's not fair. Lennie is not a beast. He saved my life and he has stood by me ever since.'

'And he took you to that hovel in Black Raven Court. I wheedled your address from James and I went there in the hope of finding you, but Guthrie said you'd gone out and he didn't know when you'd be back. It was getting late and so I said I'd return next day and I did, only to find the place locked and shuttered. I went back day after day, but none of your neighbours knew where you'd gone.'

'Why did you go to so much trouble when I had treated you so badly?'

'You know the reason why, Lucetta, but in part it was because Sir Hector had received a reply from the British consul in Bali. Sir John Boothby confirmed your identity with a signed affidavit which would stand up in any court of law. You can now prove that you are Lucetta Froy and regain what is rightfully yours.' He handed her the slice of charred bread, which was still smoking from too close a contact with the fire. 'And I am little better than King Alfred who burnt the cakes, but all this will soon be a thing of the past, Lucetta. Burnt toast and dirt floors will become a distant memory. You will be able to return home, my dear, where you truly belong.'

His words lingered in her mind long after Giles had left that evening. He had helped her put Guthrie to bed on the straw palliasse which was kept rolled up in the corner of the kitchen during the day and laid out on the floor by the fire at night. She had banked the glowing embers of coal with cinders saved from previous fires, and on Giles' instructions had given Guthrie a further dose of laudanum before she went upstairs to her room.

She lay in bed staring at the cracks in the ceiling plaster as sleep evaded her. Sam's declaration of love and his assumption that they would be married was not the wonderful happy ending that she had anticipated. Something had changed, but she did not know whether the difference was in her feeling for Sam, or if she doubted the sincerity of his love for her. She had tried to put aside Dora Cutler's vituperative accusations and the animosity that Seth felt towards his cousin, but the poison was insidious and Lucetta had begun to harbour doubts about Sam. There was only one way to solve the conundrum and that was to ask him outright if he had fathered Dora's child and then left her at the altar. Lucetta was no coward, but she was not sure that she wanted to learn the truth.

She tossed and turned but every time she closed her eyes she saw another face and heard a different voice in her head. This time it was Giles who took control of her thoughts. She had left Stockton Lacey hoping that he would turn to Mary who had loved him for years and would make him a good and loyal wife; the ideal partner for a country doctor. But now Lucetta had to face that fact that her sudden departure had done the opposite. Instead of taking up the practice and recognising Mary's silent devotion, he had left behind a comfortable, settled existence and spent months scouring the capital to find the woman who had spurned his advances. It seemed to Lucetta that she had been the cause of much pain and suffering. Eventually, she lapsed into a fitful sleep and awakened next morning with a headache.

A cold white light filtered through the thin cretonne curtains at her window and when she drew them back she discovered that a fresh covering of snow had fallen during the night. The inside of the windowpanes was frosted with ice and when she went downstairs she discovered that the fire had burned away to ashes. She lit a candle and bent over Guthrie, who was mumbling in his sleep. She felt his forehead and realised to her dismay that he was far from cold, in fact he was burning up with fever. She could not move him in order to clear the grate and anyway there was not enough coal to keep the fire going all day. Sam had not actually given her any money, although he had paid the cab fare, and she had just a few pence left until she received her wages in two days' time.

She went into the yard and found that the pump had frozen solid. Icicles hung from its lip and she broke them into the kettle, scooping up a handful of clean snow and adding it to the shards of ice. She hurried back to the relative warmth of the house and mixed a few drops of laudanum with the melting snow, waiting until it had turned back to liquid before she held it to Guthrie's parched lips.

'I have to go to work, Lennie,' she murmured. 'But I'll come back at midday to see how you are.' She was not certain whether he had heard her, but she placed a cup of melting ice at his side. Her bonnet and shawl were still damp but she had nothing else to wear. She must not be late for work; Jeremiah had a nasty habit of docking their wages if his staff failed to turn up on time and she could not afford to lose a penny. She did not want to leave Guthrie in his present state, but it was possible that he might end up crippled for life and she would have to support them both. In any event he would need medicine and good food if he was to make a full recovery.

She arrived at the warehouse on time and set to work immediately. Perks noted her pallor and insisted on making a pot of tea, telling her that if she were any thinner she would slip through the gratings in the street and fall down a sewer. He insisted that she ate the last of Mrs Perks' shortbread and he flapped around her like a mother hen, until Jeremiah's arrival put a stop to all communication between them.

Jeremiah was not in a good mood. He stormed into the office, flinging his top hat onto a peg and cursing as it toppled onto the floor. 'Damnation. As if I have not enough to put up with. Pick it up, girl.'

Lucetta bent down to retrieve the hat and hung it on the peg. 'Good morning, Mr Froy.'

'Good? What's good about it?' Jeremiah waved a piece of paper in front of her face. 'This is the estimate for repairing that bloody boat. Does he think me a fool to part with that amount of money to repair a rotting hulk? I'll challenge it in court if necessary, but I'm damned if I'll pay out that sort of cash for someone else's problem.'

Lucetta glanced over the document. She did not know much about the cost of repairing sailing vessels, but it did not seem inordinately expensive. 'So you will not pay this then, sir?'

'Not a penny.' Jeremiah shrugged off his cashmere

overcoat and allowed it to fall to the floor. 'I doubt if I can pay it anyway. I've just had a letter from my father's agent in Bali. Apparently the old man has had a seizure of some kind and is unable to continue with his tour. He is already on his way home. Hang my coat up, Miss Guthrie, and make me a cup of tea while you're about it.'

Lucetta was about to follow his barked instructions when Sam breezed in with a jaunty swagger. 'Good morning, Froy. I've come to collect the money to pay for the repairs to my vessel.'

Jeremiah puffed out his cheeks and his eyes disappeared into angry slits. 'You won't get a penny out of me, Cutler. This is extortion and I wouldn't be surprised if you had engineered the whole thing yourself.'

Sam's smile did not waver. 'You can argue your case in court if you've a mind to do things the hard way, Froy.'

Lucetta shot him a warning glance. 'I'm just going to make tea for Mr Froy. Would you like a cup, Captain Cutler?'

He put his arm around her shoulders. 'There's no need to keep up the pretence, my love. I think it's time we told your cousin a few home truths.'

She drew away from him. 'No, Sam. Don't do this.'

'What's all this nonsense?' Jeremiah demanded angrily. 'What insane plot have you two hatched together?'

'Nothing,' Lucetta said, shaking her head. 'It's Captain Cutler's idea of a joke.'

Sam smiled benevolently. 'The joke is on you, Froy.

This young lady is your cousin Lucetta Froy. We knew each other in Bali and were engaged to be married. I thought I had lost her when the *Caroline* was sunk, but she was saved, and here she is alive and well as you see. And the bad news from your point of view is that she owns all of this.' Sam encompassed the warehouse with a wave of his arms. 'You work for her now, Froy. And you will be working for me too once Lucetta and I are man and wife. What do you think of that?'

Chapter Twenty-two

'Sam, how could you do that do me?' Lucetta stood outside the warehouse, shivering violently with shock and suppressed anger. Jeremiah had refused to believe Sam and had thrown them out on the street. 'What were you thinking of? I've lost my job because of you.'

Sam hooked his arm around her shoulders. 'My darling, you don't need to slave away for the Froys. You said that your friends have a letter from Sir John Boothby which will establish your true identity. Once we have that, you'll be able to walk into your old home as Miss Lucetta Froy, owner of Froy and Son, importers. You are a wealthy woman, my love, and when we are married we will add exporters and shippers to the name of Cutler above the door.'

Lucetta stared at him in amazement. 'You're mad. It isn't as easy as that. They'll fight me all the way and in the meantime I have no money, and you have no ship. If Jeremiah refuses to pay for the repairs then you stand to lose everything.'

'Don't be such a little pessimist.' Sam's smile wavered but he recovered quickly. 'Come; let's get you back to that hovel you call home before you freeze to death. We'll talk about our strategy over a glass of hot toddy.'

'Haven't you heard a word I've said, Sam Cutler? I can't afford to buy coal for the fire, let alone rum or brandy for a hot toddy. We're down to our last crust of bread and I've only threepence to my name.'

'I'm not a beggar. I've money from my last voyage. We won't starve.'

'You will need every penny to pay for the repairs unless I can persuade Jeremiah that it is all a mistake. I think he will believe it if I tell him you are off your head with some tropical fever. If I grovel, he might just give me back my job.'

She made for the office but Sam barred her way.

'There's no going back now, Lucetta. The first thing we must do is get hold of that document and then I'll organise special licence so that we can be married tomorrow. We'll fight this together, sweetheart. What do you say?'

His eyes were alight with excitement and he grasped both her hands, but she snatched them away. 'Do you want me or my fortune, Sam?'

'What sort of question is that? You wanted to marry me three years ago. Nothing has changed.'

She shook her head slowly. 'Everything has changed, Sam. I am not the same person as I was then, and neither are you. You didn't even recognise me when you first saw me.'

'For God's sake, Lucetta, I thought you were dead. How was I supposed to know it was you?'

'If you'd truly loved me, Sam, I think your heart would have told you.'

He took her by the shoulders, looking deeply into

her eyes. 'It's telling me now.' Ignoring the shouts of the men working on the wharves and the amused glances of the passers-by, he drew her into his arms and kissed her.

Lucetta struggled at first but his mouth was hot and demanding and she closed her eyes, giving herself up momentarily to the thrill of being held in the arms of a man she had loved so passionately. The years seemed to melt away and she was back in the consulate garden, being kissed by her lover beneath the champak tree. She was breathless and trembling when he released her.

'There, now tell me you don't love me.' Sam's smile was triumphant, like that of a child who had just won a race.

'I must go home,' Lucetta murmured, backing away from him. 'We can't do this now, Sam. It's too soon. I don't know what to think.'

He caught her by the wrist. 'Don't be a goose, Lucetta. You want me, you know you do. There's nothing to keep us apart now. Your father is dead and his blind prejudice was the only thing keeping us apart.'

'Don't talk about my pa like that. He might be alive now if it weren't for us. We caused him to have that apoplectic fit. If I hadn't disobeyed him none of this might have happened.' She walked away, quickening her pace as she realised that he was following her.

'That's nonsense and you know it.' Sam caught up and fell into step beside her. 'Your father was a sick man. Anything could have brought about that attack, and, if what Jeremiah says is true, your uncle seems to have suffered a similar fate. We were not to blame for falling in love.' He stepped in front of her, forcing her to stop. 'You do love me, don't you? Say it, Lucetta. Admit it.'

'I did love you with all my heart, but everything is different now.'

'What has changed?'

His angry tone jarred Lucetta's nerves, which were already stretched to breaking point. She met his angry gaze with a steady look. 'You have a child in Salcombe. You left his mother at the altar. She told me so herself.'

He could not have looked more startled if she had slapped him across the face. His cheeks paled beneath his tan and his eyes flashed with anger. 'That's a lie. I suppose she told you that.'

'Dora told me and I believed her.'

'She lied and you were a fool to be so easily decieved. Yes, we were childhood sweethearts and we had an understanding, but while I was away at sea she was carrying on with my cousin, Seth. The child is his, not mine.'

'Why would she lie about a thing like that? I saw the boy. He even looks like you.'

'Well, he would, wouldn't he? He is my blood relation after all, but Tommy is not my son. Dora is a spiteful little bitch who wanted to see me cut out of the family business, and what better way than to make Seth think I had fathered her little bastard.'

'She said you left her at the altar.'

Sam ran his fingers through his hair with an exasperated sigh. 'Yes, I suppose I did, but it was then I found out that she had been untrue to me with my own cousin. She only wanted to marry me because I came home on leave with a pocketful of money, which I can tell you soon went by the time I had bought her all the things she wanted. She was quick enough to turn back to Seth after I left. They deserve each other.'

Lucetta eyed him warily. This angry, bitter man was not the Sam she had known and loved. She believed him, of course, but nagging doubts lingered at the back of her mind. 'I must go home,' she said slowly. 'Lennie needs me.'

'I'll come too. We can talk this over calmly, Lucetta.'

'No. Not now, Sam. I'd rather be alone.'

'Alone with him, you mean. Are you sure that there's nothing between you and that villain Guthrie?'

'That's a dreadful thing to say. There's never been anything like that. Lennie has been like a father to me since he escaped from Stranks. Go back to your ship and sort your own business out. I'm going home.'

'I'll come round this evening then, and take you out to supper. Would that suit you?'

His tone had changed suddenly and his penitent smile made him look like the Sam she remembered so well. She felt herself weakening. 'Yes, all right.' It seemed easier to agree than to stand about in the snow arguing and her nerves were drawn tight as the strings on a fiddle. She felt that any moment something inside her was going to snap. She trudged along the slushy pavement, uncomfortably aware that the icy snow melt was seeping through the cracks in her boots. Even if she begged him on bended knees, Lucetta could not imagine that Jeremiah would take her back in his employ: Sam had seen to that by declaring her true identity and she could not help wondering if he had deliberately manoeuvred her into this position, making it almost impossible for her to refuse his offer of marriage. She paused as she reached her front door. Three years ago she would have fallen willingly into Sam's arms and followed him blindly anywhere he led, but not now. She was no longer that naïve girl with her head stuffed with dreams; she was a woman with a mind of her own and a newly discovered independent spirit. She had suffered but she had overcome the obstacles that fate had thrown in her path. She unlocked the door and went inside.

She found Guthrie lying in the same position as he had been when she left earlier that morning. His skin was grey-tinged and beads of perspiration stood out on his forehead. His eyes were closed but he was muttering unintelligibly.

'Lennie. It's me, Lucetta. I've come home.' She leaned over him, laying her hand on his forehead. The heat from his body burned into her chilled fingers. She knelt down to examine his leg, and as she lifted the thin blanket she covered her nose, stifling an exclamation of disgust at the putrid smell emanating from the wound. The bandages were bloodstained and even more disturbing there was a yellowish tinge to them.

She scrambled to her feet and moved swiftly to the table where Giles had left a small supply of dressings and a bottle containing a solution of carbolic acid. Her stomach heaved at the thought of what she might discover beneath the bandages, but Giles had left her with clear instructions on how to clean the wound and replace the soiled dressings. She took off her bonnet and shawl, and having washed her hands using what was left of the water in the kettle, she set to work peeling the soiled bandages off Guthrie's injured limb. There were livid red and black streaks surrounding the wound and for a moment she thought she was going to be sick, but she steeled herself to follow Giles' instructions. She had watched him carefully the previous evening when he had treated the leg and she did her best to emulate his actions. Guthrie moaned but the fever had him in its grip and he did not seem to be aware of her ministrations.

Lucetta worked as quickly as she could and heaved a sigh of relief when she tied the bandages in place. She diluted the last few drops of laudanum left in the bottle with dregs of water from the kettle and she held Guthrie's head, allowing him small sips of the soothing potion. She stroked his forehead until he lapsed into a deep sleep. The skin on his face was drawn taut across the bones of his skull and his deathly pallor scared her. She stood up, holding the empty medicine bottle in her hand as she gazed at the dying embers of the fire. She had a stark choice to make. She would either spend her last three pennies on food or laudanum. It was not a difficult decision.

She was about to leave the house when a hansom cab drew up outside the door and Giles climbed out carrying a large wicker basket covered with a white cloth. He paid the cabby and turned to her with a question in his dark eyes. 'Have I come at a bad time?'

She stepped back inside the room. 'No. Why do you say that?'

'I hoped that I might catch you before you went back to work, but you were obviously on your way out.'

His twinkling smile cheered her more than she could have thought possible. 'I was on my way to the chemist to buy some laudanum for Lennie.'

'I've bought some with me,' Giles said cheerfully. 'May I come in?'

'Of course. What was I thinking of keeping you standing on the doorstep?'

He followed her into the room and he set the basket down on the table. 'I hazarded a guess that you might need some supplies.'

'That's so thoughtful of you, Giles. We are a bit low on everything.' Lucetta had been saving the last stub of candle for later when it was completely dark, but the room was already deep in shadow and she struck a vesta. 'I was planning to go to the market on my way home.'

Giles hung his hat on the peg behind the door and shrugged off his overcoat. His eyes were serious as he took in his surroundings. 'It would be obvious to a blind man that you are struggling to survive, Lucetta. You must let me help you.'

She avoided his gaze, turning her attention to the basket and lifting off the starched white linen cloth with the feeling that it was Christmas all over again. 'What have you brought us, Giles? It really is too kind of you.'

'You can stop pretending, Lucetta. Things aren't going well for you. Won't you trust me with the truth?'

Guthrie seemed to answer this with a groan and Giles bent down to examine him. He glanced up at Lucetta and his expression confirmed her worst fears.

'He's very sick, isn't he, Giles?'

'It was to be expected, I'm afraid. A chap in his condition has no resistance against infection.' Giles rose to his feet. 'He must go to hospital.'

'No! He's afraid of hospitals and I didn't tell you the whole truth last night, Giles. Lennie was involved in a robbery that went wrong. A man died and the police are looking for Lennie. If they find him he will face the hangman's noose. I can't let him go to hospital and take that risk.'

Giles shook his head. 'I had hoped he was strong enough to avoid it, but I'm afraid he has blood poisoning, Lucetta. His only chance of survival is to go to hospital. You could not be expected to undertake nursing such a sick man.'

'I can look after him if you tell me what to do, Giles.'

'You are not equipped to care for him here and you are out at work all day. Who will care for him then?'

Lucetta began emptying the basket of its contents. 'I have no job now. Jeremiah dismissed me when Sam revealed my real identity.' She held a packet of tea to her nose and sniffed it appreciatively. 'Fresh tea. Thank you, Giles. I'll make some right away.'

Giles reached out to seize her gently by the wrist. 'Stop for a moment, Lucetta. Tell me exactly what happened this morning. If I'm to help you I need to know the truth.'

She sank down on the hardwood chair, resting her forehead on her hands. The fragrant smell of the tea coupled with the baked ham wrapped in butter muslin and a loaf of freshly baked bread, no doubt all coming from the Harcourts' well-stocked larder, were making her faint with hunger. 'I'll tell you when I've had a cup of tea. It's been a difficult morning.'

Giles took the kettle from the trivet. 'I'll make the tea, you sit there. Doctor's orders.'

He went out into the back yard, returning moments later to place the kettle on the hook over the fire. 'There's enough heat left to start warming the water, but you need coal. I'll go out and get some. Tell me what else you need.'

She raised her head, staring at him in wonder. 'How did you get water from a frozen pump?'

He grinned. 'By holding a lighted match to the metal until the ice thawed enough to allow a trickle. It will probably freeze again but we'll worry about that later.' He shrugged on his coat. 'I can see that you need candles and a box of vestas. In fact, leave it to me; I won't be long, and in the meantime I suggest you eat something. Cook put together the basket so I've no idea what is in it, but I told her not to stint and she's a good sort.'

After he had gone the silence closed in on Lucetta and the room looked even smaller, dingier and less welcoming without his presence. She decided that she must be light-headed with hunger. Things would look better if she had some food inside her. She could not remember the last time she had eaten anything other than toast or a sliver of cheese and her mouth watered as she set about making a ham sandwich. The Harcourts' cook had not only sent a large piece of ham, but she had included butter and a chunk of Cheddar cheese, a slab of fruit cake and a bag of sugar. Lucetta settled down to the best meal she had had since she left Stockton Lacey.

When Giles returned with a sack of coal, kindling, a bundle of candles and several boxes of vestas Lucetta was already feeling much better, but he insisted that she rested while he made tea. He had also thought to bring in a jug of fresh milk from the dairy, and when she asked how he had managed to carry so much, he admitted giving the grocer's boy a handsome tip to transport everything on a wooden sled.

'Now,' he said, setting a mug of tea on the table in front of her. 'When you feel able, I want you to tell me everything. I'll do what I can to help you, but I can do nothing until I know all the facts.'

In between sips of hot, sweet tea, Lucetta related the events as they had happened, although she omitted telling him of Sam's repeated proposal and his ideas for a joint venture into business. That was something between her and Sam, and only she could make that decision.

Giles listened intently until she had finished speaking. His expression was unusually serious. 'Do you love this man, Lucetta?'

The question was so unexpected that she was

stunned momentarily into silence. Giles met her startled gaze with a steady look. 'Do you?'

'I don't see that it's any concern of yours.'

'I wouldn't ask if it didn't matter.'

'The honest truth is that I don't know.' Lucetta lowered her gaze, staring at the tea leaves in the bottom of the mug. 'I did love him with all my heart, but things are different now.'

'And you learned things about him in Devon that you had not known before.'

'That's not fair, Giles.'

'Maybe not, but it's true. You were very young when you first met Cutler. You knew nothing of the world of men and it's no wonder your father objected to the match.'

'You sound just like him. Don't say any more. I know you mean well but this is something that only I can decide.'

'You're right, of course, but you really cannot remain in this cold, damp house. For one thing you can't pay the rent, and more important this is not the most sanitary place to care for a patient with septicaemia.'

'I won't let him go to hospital. The police would find him, and he may have committed criminal acts but he doesn't deserve to die for them.'

'I've never supported capital punishment, Lucetta, but without urgent medical attention the poor fellow is likely to die anyway.'

Lucetta shook her head. 'He depends on me, Giles. Lennie is a child in a man's body. He would be terrified if he woke up in hospital.'

Giles was silent for a moment but his gaze never wavered from her face. She was afraid that he would try to persuade her and she felt her resolve weakening, but he seemed to change his mind and he stood up, laying his hand briefly on her shoulder.

'I can see that your mind is made up, so we'll leave the matter there. I'm going now but I'll be back first thing in the morning. Are you sure you will be able to manage on your own?'

'I'm quite sure. Thank you for everything, Giles.'

He moved towards the doorway and then paused, turning his head to give her a searching look. 'You can still change your mind.'

'No, I'm going to care for Lennie myself. This is his home and I won't have him sent away to be cared for by strangers.'

'You are a stubborn woman, Lucetta Froy.'

'If there's one thing that these past few years have taught me, it's how to survive. I was such a silly, thoughtless creature before, and now I've learned to stand on my own two feet and to appreciate the things that really matter, like good friends. And you are the best of friends, Giles.'

His face was in shadow but for a moment she thought she saw his lips tighten as if he were in pain. 'I must go now,' he said abruptly. 'I'll see you in the morning.' He opened the door and vanished into the winter gloom.

Lucetta set about making Guthrie as comfortable as was possible on the thin palliasse. She wished that she could get him upstairs to her bed, but it would take two strong men to carry him up the narrow staircase and any movement caused him excruciating pain, even under the soothing influence of laudanum. She bathed his forehead, and moistened his lips with water when he was too delirious to swallow.

She lost all track of time and she must have dozed off as she awakened suddenly when the front door burst open and a flurry of snowflakes preceded Sam into the living room.

'You ought to lock the door,' he said severely. 'Anyone could walk in off the street and this is a rough area.'

Lucetta stretched and yawned. 'Keep your voice down. You'll disturb Lennie.'

'He looks dead to the world,' Sam said, staring dispassionately at Guthrie's inert body. 'Put on your bonnet and wrap up warm, Lucetta. It's freezing outside.'

She had completely forgotten his invitation to dine with him, but now the memory of their conversation came rushing back to her. 'I'm sorry, Sam. I can't leave Lennie. He's very ill. Giles thinks that—'

'What?' Sam turned to her, frowning. 'Has that fellow been pestering you? Doesn't he know that we are engaged to be married?'

'Giles is a doctor. He came to treat Lennie, not to see me.'

'Well I don't like it, my love. You can't blame a fellow for being a bit jealous when he comes back from a long sea voyage and finds his fiancée being courted by another man.'

425

Lucetta leapt to her feet. 'This is madness. You're talking as though nothing has changed. We aren't engaged, Sam. We never were because my father refused to consider you as a prospective son-in-law. You thought I was dead until a few days ago and you had quite forgotten me.'

'No!' He grasped her hands and clasped them to his chest. 'I'd never forgotten you, my darling. You were always here in my heart. I knew that one day we would be reunited.'

She snatched her hands free. 'Stop talking like that. Too much has happened for us to simply pick up where we left off.'

He tossed his cap onto the table and pulled her into his arms, crushing her against the brass buttons on his pea jacket. His mouth sought hers in a kiss that robbed her of breath and sent her senses spiralling, but a moan from Guthrie brought her back to reality and she pushed Sam away. 'This is madness.'

'You do still love me,' Sam said with a triumphant grin. 'Don't deny it, Lucetta. We were meant for each other and I'm not going to lose you again. We'll go out and celebrate.'

'No, Sam. I've told you that I can't leave Lennie.'

'Then I will bring supper here to you.' Sam snatched up his cap and rammed it on his head. 'We'll dine here and you can keep an eye on the old boy while we share our first meal together.'

He was gone before she could raise any further objections, and when he returned he was carrying a bundle wrapped in newspaper. 'Where are the plates?

I've bought hot pie, pease pudding and baked potatoes. What is more . . .' From his pocket he produced a bottle of rum and a large yellow lemon. 'For hot toddy,' he said proudly. 'Put the kettle on, Lucetta. We'll dine like royalty and drink a toast to our future.'

Sam sat opposite her at the small table and he ate with relish, drinking copious amounts of hot toddy and becoming more and more expansive beneath its influence. He told her stories of his adventures at sea and Lucetta began to relax a little. She had forgotten what an amusing companion he could be and the tension between them eased. She kept an eye on Guthrie but he was heavily sedated and his moans were muffled and less frequent. Lucetta could only hope that the healing process had begun, and that the poisons were leaching from his body.

'He's fine,' Sam said, refilling her glass. 'Stop worrying about him and drink up. This is a night for celebration.' He thrust his hand into his breast pocket, producing a folded document with a flourish. 'And this is the key to our future happiness.'

Despite her misgivings, Lucetta could not help being curious. 'What is that?'

'A special licence, my darling. We can be married when and where you choose.'

Lucetta felt panic rise in her breast. 'I–I can't think about it while Lennie is so ill, Sam. You must give me more time.'

Sam reached across the table to clasp her hand and his eyes shone with an unnatural brilliance. 'Don't take too long, Lucetta. I will have to leave London as soon as my ship is seaworthy. I want to make you mine before I set sail again.'

She could see that he had drunk too much and she was suddenly nervous. 'I think you should leave now, Sam. It's getting late and we're both tired.'

He stood up, swaying slightly as he pulled her to her feet. 'I'm not leaving you alone tonight.'

'You're drunk.' She had not meant to shout but something in the timbre of her voice must have reached Guthrie's drugged brain and he stirred in his sleep.

Sam drew her slowly to him, holding her captive and gazing into her eyes with a triumphant smile. 'I may be drunk but I'm not stupid. You belong to me and tonight I'm going to stake my claim.'

There was no doubting his meaning and Lucetta attempted to break free from his grasp but her struggles only seemed to amuse him and he swept her off her feet, lifting her in his arms as he strode towards the staircase.

'No, Sam, please put me down. I have to stay with Lennie. He might die . . .'

Sam carried her up the stairs to the bedroom and tossed her onto the bed. 'He's had enough laudanum to stun an elephant. My needs are greater than his.' He began unbuttoning his shirt, but a look of uncertainty crossed his features and he sat down heavily on the edge of the bed. 'Hell and damnation.' He collapsed against the pillows, closing his eyes. 'I need to lie down for a moment or two. That bloody rum must have . . .' He drifted off into a drunken stupor.

Lucetta clambered off the bed and ran from the room, closing the door softly in case the sound should awaken him. Her heart was pounding as she crept downstairs and she was trembling with fear and mounting anger. How dare he treat her like a common street girl? That wasn't the Sam she had known and loved. He had been a gentleman. She went to the table and on examining the bottle she realised that he had drunk the best part of its contents. He would have a sore head in the morning but she could not bring herself to pity him. She picked up the empty kettle and went outside into the frozen night, taking a candle with her and holding it to the metal pump until it thawed just enough to allow a trickle of water. Above her the sky was a dome of blackness pierced by tiny pinpricks of twinkling light. A full moon turned the snow-covered yard into a fairyland of sparkling prisms and she took deep breaths of the crisp air. Sam's drunken actions had sullied her home, making her feel uncomfortable and unclean, but out here seemed to have been purified by the freezing temperature and the drifts of virgin snow. It was too cold to linger for long but it was with great reluctance that she went indoors. She hoped and prayed that Sam would sleep until morning when she intended to ask him to leave.

She slept fitfully in a chair by the fire, waking every time Guthrie stirred. She gave him sips of water and when the pain grew too intense she dosed him with more laudanum. She was stiff and sore and it seemed that the night was going on forever, but she must have drifted off to sleep eventually as she awoke with a start to find pale slithers of daylight slanting through the windowpanes. Half awake, she realised that someone was rapping urgently on the doorknocker. She dragged herself to her feet and hurried to open the door to find Giles and Mary standing on the pavement and the Harcourts' carriage and horses waiting at the kerbside.

Mary rushed past Giles to fling her arms around Lucetta's neck. 'Oh, Daisy, I'm so glad to see you.'

Lucetta found herself being hugged until she was breathless, but Mary's enthusiastic greeting was infectious and she returned the embrace. 'Come inside out of the cold.'

'Mary insisted on coming,' Giles said, stamping the snow off his boots before following them indoors.

'Yes, of course I did,' Mary said, smiling happily. 'Giles has told me everything, Daisy, and I've come to help you care for the patient.'

Lucetta stared at her dazedly. 'But I thought you were still in Dorset. Or are you back at the hospital now?'

'I'll tell you everything after Giles has examined Mr Guthrie and given me my instructions. You are not alone now, Daisy dear. I intend to stay as long as you need me.' She took off her bonnet and fur-lined mantle and hung them on the row of pegs. She rolled up her sleeves. 'We will look after him together.'

Lucetta waited hardly daring to breathe as Mary undid the bandages and Giles examined Guthrie's livid wound. The stench of corrupting flesh filled the room and Lucetta clapped her hands over her mouth to stifle a cry of despair. She knew even before Giles confirmed her suspicions that the poison had spread.

Giles rose to his feet and his expression was grave. 'He has to go to hospital, Lucetta. The limb is gangrenous and must be amputated. Even then his chances of survival are slim, but without an operation he has only hours to live.'

Mary put her arms around Lucetta, giving her a sympathetic hug. 'Listen to Giles, my dear. He really does know best.'

'So you're here again are you, quack?'

Lucetta had almost forgotten that Sam was sleeping off the effects of the rum toddy, and he had come downstairs in his stockinged feet. His shirt was unbuttoned to the waist and he leaned against the wall, folding his arms across his chest with a challenge in his eyes as he glared at Giles.

Lucetta could see by the expression on their faces that Giles and Mary had leapt to the wrong conclusion. After all, what would anyone think when they saw a man half-dressed coming from a lady's bedchamber? She raised her hands in a gesture of desperation. 'This isn't what you think, Giles.'

His expression was dark and unreadable as their eyes met. 'It's none of my business, Lucetta. My main concern at this moment is Guthrie. I must get him to hospital right away.'

'That's right, cully,' Sam said, grinning. 'Take the worthless fellow and put him where he belongs. Lucetta and I have a wedding to arrange.'

Chapter Twenty-three

Lucetta sat on a hard bench in the hospital atrium with Mary at her side. They were surrounded by people of all ages, some of them barely conscious and others groaning with pain from multiple injuries. The stench of blood, pus and urine was barely concealed by the strong smell of carbolic acid, and the sound of coughing, sneezing and retching reverberated off the high ceiling, rumbling over their heads like distant thunder.

Every time a nurse walked past, Lucetta was tempted to stop her and beg for news, but somehow she managed to contain her anxiety and maintain an outward appearance of calm. Guthrie had been admitted to a ward immediately on their arrival at Bart's. There had been no waiting in line and Lucetta knew that she had Giles to thank for that. He had sought out Dr Richards, who had examined Guthrie and had had no hesitation in agreeing with Giles' diagnosis and prognosis. The two doctors had accompanied Guthrie to the ward and Giles had returned some time later with the news that the operation was to be carried out with the utmost urgency, and he had been granted permission to be present in theatre. Lucetta had murmured her thanks but she could not look him in the eye. Even now, several hours later, her cheeks reddened as she recalled the embarrassing scene earlier that morning when Sam had appeared at the foot of the stairs, half dressed and tousled from sleep. Despite her attempts to explain that she had spent the night tending to Guthrie, Sam had given her a conspiratorial wink and a smile, as if to confirm the intimate nature of their relationship. To make matters worse, he had produced the special licence, declaring their intention to be married as soon as the necessary arrangements were made. The implication that they had spent the night together was left floating in the air like a putrid waft of marsh gas. If Guthrie had not been quite literally at death's door Lucetta would have refuted this slur on her character, but it had not been the time or the place for heated arguments. She had wished that the dirt floor would open up and swallow her, but Sam had been unrepentant. He had maintained a cheerful flow of conversation while he buttoned his shirt and tied his tie, but Giles had turned his back on him and Mary was too busy attending to Guthrie to pay much attention to Sam's suggestive remarks. Eventually, to Lucetta's intense relief, Sam left the house, promising to return after he had arranged for work to begin on repairing the damage to the *Sea Eagle*.

She would meet that challenge when it happened, but now she sat with her head bowed and her hands clasped tightly in her lap as she waited for news from the operating theatre.

'They'll do everything they can for him,' Mary whispered. 'Try not to worry, Daisy.'

Lucetta nodded and flashed a weak attempt at a

smile in Mary's direction, but she couldn't speak. In the beginning she had hated both Stranks and Guthrie, but Lennie had proved himself to be a true friend. He had stood by her when she most needed help and he had asked nothing in return. In the beginning she had been dependent upon him, but now their roles were reversed and now her feelings for him were verging on the maternal. She could not bear to think of him dying alone amongst strangers.

Mary squeezed her hand. 'I understand. I really do.'

'I know, and thank you for coming with me. I'm sorry I left Dorset without telling you.'

'Don't be. Papa told me everything and he was very ashamed of himself. He said he was an old fool for deluding himself into thinking that a girl like you would want to marry a man old enough to be her father.'

'Sir Hector is a fine man. I was honoured . . .'

'There's no need to explain. I love my papa but you two wouldn't suit.'

'I would make a poor wife for a politician.'

'I didn't mean that, and anyway, you were always in love with Sam. Or has that changed now?'

Lucetta met Mary's steady gaze and she shook her head. 'I don't know, Mary. I honestly don't know. I'm totally confused and all I can think of at the moment is Lennie.'

'I know, dear,' Mary said softly. 'I'm praying for the poor man.'

Lucetta stiffened as she heard approaching footsteps. She knew instinctively that it was Giles and she rose to greet him with outstretched hands. 'Is he . . . ?' the words stuck in her throat.

'The operation was a success. He's back on the ward and you can see him now, but don't overtire him. He's very weak and still has a long way to go.'

'I'll wait here,' Mary said. 'We'll take you home when you're ready, Daisy.'

Lucetta hesitated. 'I don't want him to wake up amongst strangers. Could you get a message to Sam and tell him that I'm here?'

'Of course. You mustn't worry about a thing, must she, Giles?' Mary looked up at him with a trusting smile that was not lost on Lucetta.

Giles nodded his head. 'We will take care of everything, Lucetta. You have no need to worry.'

Lucetta allowed him to escort her to the ward. Their offers of help had lifted a weight from her shoulders, but even though her main concern was for Guthrie, Sam's presence loomed large at the back of her mind. The man she had loved and thought she had lost was now desperate to make her his wife, and yet she was uneasy. Her friends had forgiven her for her ill-considered behaviour and it was obvious that Giles and Mary were as one in their thoughts and actions; she should have been happy for them, but she was not. Lucetta entered the long ward with feelings of deep misgiving and it was not just for Guthrie that she was concerned.

The iron bedsteads stretched in serried ranks down the length of the ward. Nurses bustled about bristling with starched white aprons, caps and cuffs, and there was a cathedral-like hush. The male patients lay on their backs with the sheets tucked up to their necks like well-behaved schoolboys asleep in their dormitories.

Giles led her to the bed nearest the door where the curtains were drawn together. He held them apart. 'You'll be allowed to stay for a short time only. We'll wait for you.'

Lucetta laid her hand on his arm. 'Thank you, Giles, but I'd rather you took Mary home. I'm not leaving Lennie here alone.'

'They won't allow you to stay, my dear.'

She raised her chin. 'We'll see about that.'

He smiled in response and brushed her cheek with a kiss. 'We'll be here when you need us.' He let the curtain fall and she was alone at the bedside.

Guthrie stirred and his eyelids fluttered as if in response to her presence.

'Lennie, it's me,' Lucetta said softly. She pulled up a chair and sat down beside him, taking his hand as it lay on the white counterpane. 'You're going to get better now. You'll soon be home.'

He opened his eyes, focusing them on her face with an obvious effort. 'Lucy?'

'Yes, it's me, Lennie. I'm here.' She squeezed his fingers gently, forcing her lips into a smile, but she was frightened by his gaunt appearance. His skin had a grey tone to it and his eyes appeared sunken in his skull. His lips were dry and cracked and he seemed to find it difficult to speak.

'Thirsty,' he murmured.

Lucetta looked round for water but there was none.

She was about to get up and look for a nurse when the curtains were pulled aside and a nurse appeared as if by magic. She placed a jug and a glass on the locker beside the bed.

'Sips of water only,' she said sternly. 'You can stay for five minutes, miss, but then I must ask you to leave. The patient needs rest.'

She was gone before Lucetta had time to argue. She poured water into the glass and held it to Guthrie's lips. 'Don't go,' he gasped. 'Don't leave me.'

'I'm not going anywhere, Lennie. I'll be here when you wake, I promise.' She settled back on the chair, taking hold of his hand once again and stroking it gently as he drifted back to sleep.

She must have dozed off herself as she awakened suddenly to find the nurse standing beside her. 'You must leave now.'

Lucetta shook her head. 'I would rather stay.'

'It's against the rules, I'm afraid. I must ask you to go now, please.'

'Damn the rules,' Lucetta said stubbornly. 'You will have to carry me bodily from this place. I promised Lennie that I would be here when he woke up.'

'I'll fetch the doctor.'

'Do that, but he won't make me change my mind.'

Minutes later the curtains were pulled apart and Dr Richards faced her with a worried frown. 'I'm sorry, Miss Guthrie, but I must agree with Sister. You should go home and get some rest. Visiting hours are from three o'clock until four on Tuesdays and Fridays, and two o'clock until three on Sundays.'

'Then I'm definitely not leaving,' Lucetta said, settling further down onto the hard wooden chair. 'If I go now it will be two days before I can visit again, and that is just not good enough.'

Guthrie opened his eyes and he gave a start when he saw the doctor. 'Don't let them take me leg, Lucy. Tell him I can wiggle me toes. Look.' He stared down at the hump in the bed where a cage covered the afflicted limb. 'I'm wiggling them, can you see? They itch something terrible. Will you scratch them for me, Lucy?'

Lucetta looked up at the doctor for confirmation, but he shook his head. 'They often feel the amputated limb as if it were still there,' he whispered. 'Don't be alarmed.'

'What's he saying?' Guthrie demanded. 'Tell him to go away, Lucy. I won't have me leg cut off.'

Lucetta leaned forward to stroke Guthrie's brow. 'It's all right, Lennie. I won't let them touch you.'

Dr Richards beckoned to the nurse who was hovering at the far side of the bed. 'Make up a dose of laudanum, nurse. And allow the young lady to stay as she seems to have a quietening influence on the patient. Keep the curtains drawn so that he does not disturb the rest of the ward.'

Lucetta twisted her lips into a semblance of a smile. 'Thank you, doctor. I'm most grateful.'

'Giles told me that you were a very capable young lady. I can see that he was right, but this is strictly against the hospital rules.'

'I understand, and I'll be very quiet.'

He acknowledged this with a nod of his head. The

curtain rings rattled as he drew the curtains behind him and Lucetta was left alone with Guthrie.

She lost all track of time as she kept her vigil at his bedside. The routine of the ward went on outside the curtains but Lucetta concentrated her attention on Guthrie, willing him to pull through. They were left alone except for the occasional visit from one of the nurses as she checked Guthrie's pulse and temperature. The daylight faded and shadows deepened. Lucetta found herself drifting off to the other-world place between sleeping and waking, and although she fought to stay awake she only realised that she had lost that particular battle when she opened her eyes and found the cubicle suffused by the soft glow of gaslight. She was stiff, cold and her stomach rumbled, reminding her that she had eaten nothing since the previous evening. She sat upright, listening to the now familiar sounds of pattering feet and the clank of bedpans, the moans of the other patients and the soft whispering voices of the nurses going about their duties.

She realised suddenly that something was terribly wrong. She could not hear Guthrie breathing. Fingers of panic clutched at her heart as she leaned over the bed. His eyes were closed and his skin was the colour of old parchment, stretched taut over his cheekbones like the skin on a drum. She held her shaking hand close to his mouth. He was cold and still. She grasped him by the shoulders, shaking him like a terrier with a rat. 'Lennie, Lennie, speak to me.' She felt hysteria rising in her throat as his head lolled to one side and his jaw dropped. 'Lennie. Open your eyes. It's me, Lucy.'

Someone was attempting to drag her away from him but she wouldn't let go. She buried her head on his chest, sobbing. 'No, no. I'm sorry, I didn't mean to let you die alone.'

Hands prised her fingers loose and she was lifted bodily. Dimly, she recognised a familiar voice as she was carried from the ward. 'It's all right, Lucetta. I'm here.'

She opened her eyes to find herself lying on a bed in a side ward. Giles was sitting by her side, holding her hand. She snapped into a sitting position. 'Lennie. I must go to him, Giles.'

He shook his head. 'No one can hurt him now. His heart couldn't cope with the toxins already in his system and he succumbed to post-operative shock. It happens all too often in cases such as his, but it was quick and painless. He died peacefully in his sleep.'

She bent her head, hiccuping on a sob. 'Oh, poor man. He was so frightened of dying.'

Giles wrapped his arms around her and held her while she sobbed broken-heartedly against his shoulder. He stroked her hair, speaking to her softly. 'Nothing and no one can harm him now. He was a wanted man, Lucetta. The law would have caught up with him sooner or later and he would have been hanged. This was a far better way out for him and you mustn't feel guilty. You cared for him until the last.' He took a large handkerchief from his pocket and wiped her eyes. 'When you feel strong enough I'll take you home.'

'I have no home now, Giles.'

'Mary has given me the strictest instructions to

take you back to Lonsdale Square. She would never forgive me if I went against her wishes.'

Lucetta took the hankie from him and blew her nose in its pristine white folds. 'I don't know why you are both so kind to me when I've been nothing but trouble.'

'I won't listen to such talk,' he said briskly. 'You'll feel better when you've had a decent meal and a good night's sleep.'

She gave him a watery smile. 'Is that doctor's orders?'

'It most certainly is. Do you feel strong enough to walk or shall I carry you?'

'I'm fine.' She swung her legs over the side of the high bed. 'But what about Lennie? I can't just leave him here.'

'I'll make all the necessary arrangements. Don't worry about a thing.'

'And Sam. I should go back to the house. He'll expect to find me there.'

'A message will be sent to him. He can visit you in Lonsdale Square.'

Obedient as a small child, she placed her hand in his. 'Thank you for everything, Giles. You are a true friend.'

The warmth and luxury of the house in Lonsdale Square was almost overwhelming, as was the welcome that Lucetta received from Mary and Sir Hector. Their unspoken sympathy was more touching than a thousand well-chosen words, and ever-practical Mary had made certain that everything had been done to make Lucetta feel at home. A bath had been run for her and her old bedroom had been made ready with a fire burning in the grate and her nightclothes laid out on the bed.

'Everything is as you left it,' Mary said gently. 'Mrs Bullen has prepared a special supper for you and if you don't feel like coming downstairs, I'll have it brought to you on a tray.'

'I don't know what to say,' Lucetta murmured. 'I don't know why you are being so good to me.'

'We love you, that's why.' Mary slipped her arm around Lucetta's shoulders and gave her a hug. 'Now I suggest you take that bath. The smell of the hospital clings to everything.'

Lucetta gazed longingly at the clean nightgown and wrap laid out on the bed and the starched cotton sheets and pillowcases. 'I've almost forgotten what it's like to feel really clean and to have fresh clothes every day. Having to wash in a basinful of tepid water and using lye soap is the worst torture of all. No wonder the poor find it so hard to keep clean.'

'That's all in the past now, Daisy. I had all your belongings brought back from Stanton Lacey. Everything is here.'

'I won't forget this, Mary,' Lucetta said sincerely. 'But I must return to Samson's Green tomorrow.'

'This is your home for as long as you want it,' Mary said firmly. 'That part of your life is over now. You are Lucetta Froy and we can prove it.'

'Has a message been sent to Sam? He will be wondering why I haven't returned.'

'Everything has been attended to. You'll see him tomorrow but in the meantime you must rest and try not to worry. Things will look better after you've had a good night's sleep.'

Next morning Lucetta was awakened by the now unfamiliar sound of the maid raking the ashes in the grate as she prepared to relight the fire. Lucetta stretched and yawned, luxuriating in the comfort of the feather mattress. The delicious aroma of hot chocolate emanated from a silver pot on the small table close to her bed and curls of steam issued from the hot water jug on the washstand. The maid put a match to the fire and scrambled to her feet, bobbing a curtsey when she realised that Lucetta was awake.

'I hope I didn't disturb you, miss.'

'No, not at all. It's Maisie, isn't it?'

'Yes, miss. It's kind of you to remember. Will there be anything else?'

Lucetta smiled. If only the child knew how she had been living for the last few months she might not be so deferential now. 'No, thank you, Maisie.'

'I'll just pour your chocolate then, shall I?' Maisie seemed reluctant to leave without having performed some small service.

'Yes, thank you.' Lucetta had been going to refuse, but she could see that the girl was eager to please. She accepted a cup brimming with the dark, sweet-smelling chocolate. 'That will be all, thank you, Maisie.'

'Yes, miss.'

Maisie stooped to pick up the bucket and cleaning tools and Lucetta experienced a wave of pity for the skinny little creature as she staggered out of the room.

In the past, Lucetta had never given the plight of their servants much thought and she had accepted their ministrations without question, but now she was seeing things differently. She had learned what it was like to be at the bottom end of the social scale and it had opened her eyes to the hardships and privations suffered by those less fortunate than herself. She thought about the warehouse and the men who slaved away for low wages, receiving little or no thanks from Jeremiah, and she wondered if her father had treated them any better. There was Perks who served the company faithfully and had a position of trust but could not afford to purchase a new shirt when the collar and cuffs wore through on his old one, even though they had been turned and probably turned again. He had been obliged to work on Boxing Day and she had no doubt that Jeremiah would have had all the men in on Christmas Day itself had the necessity arisen.

She finished her chocolate and threw back the coverlet. She might not be able to save the world, but she was Lucetta Froy, the rightful heir to her father's company which was being run into the ground by her uncle and cousin. Perhaps the only way she could lay the ghost of Guthrie's sad past and that of those like him was to stand up and fight the Bradley Froys of this world. She rose from her bed and dressed in one of the elegant gowns that she had thought never to see again. Plain Lucy Guthrie in her second-hand clothes and down-at-heel boots would stand little chance of making a difference, but Miss Lucetta Froy, heiress to a considerable fortune, must be taken seriously. She sat at the rosewood dressing table and put her hair up in coils on the top of her head. A spray of cologne finished her toilette and she was ready to start the day. She was about to rise when she remembered Sam and she paused, staring at her face in the mirror. Was she the same girl who had fallen so madly in love with a young seafarer? Was she still in love with him? She shook her head gravely. 'I don't know,' she whispered. 'I just don't know.'

She stood up with a satisfying swish of silk skirts and starched moreen petticoats and she closed her eyes in a moment of silent remembrance for Guthrie. She could see him now, seated by the fire in their tiny living room with his feet resting on the broken fender that he had liberated from a rubbish tip. He was smiling proudly as she paraded her new-found finery in front of him. She could hear him telling her to 'sort the old bugger out'. She smiled despite the tears that stung the backs of her eyes.

'I will, Lennie,' she murmured out loud. 'When Uncle Bradley returns to London, which must be soon, I'll make him listen to me if it's the last thing I do.' She rummaged in the dressing-table drawer for a handkerchief and dabbed her eyes. Taking a deep breath, she squared her shoulders and left the security of her bedchamber, prepared to fight for what was hers.

Sir Hector looked up from his desk as Lucetta entered the room and half rose from his seat with a tentative smile. 'I'm glad you came to see me, Lucetta. I would hate to think that my ill-judged advances had built an insurmountable barrier between us.'

'Please don't apologise, sir. I should not have run off as I did. It was very wrong of me and I am sorry to have caused you and Mary so much anxiety.'

'Do sit down, my dear. I have something important to tell you.'

Lucetta did as he asked, perching on the edge of the chair where she used to sit and take dictation. 'Mary told me that you had been working on my behalf.'

'I'm not a practising barrister now, but I keep in touch with my old firm and I went to see one of my colleagues who is a notary public. I showed him the letter from Sir John Boothby and he is willing to take up your case. He has applied to the probate registry for a copy of your father's will, and if you make an appointment to see him he will ask you to sign an affidavit declaring that you are Lucetta Froy, as witnessed by Sir John. Mary tells me that your fiancé is forced to remain ashore while his ship is being repaired, and I think that his testimony would add weight to your claim.'

'We are not officially engaged,' Lucetta said hastily. 'I mean, it was a long time ago.'

'I understand, but if the case goes to court, it would help to have someone close to you who is prepared to swear on oath that you are the daughter of the late Henry and Eveline Froy.'

'Do you think it will come to that, Sir Hector? I can't afford to pay a lawyer.'

'Faced with such evidence in your favour, I doubt if Mr Froy will relish the thought of an expensive law suit or the publicity that it would generate.'

'I hope you're right, sir.'

He smiled, shrugging his shoulders and his blue eyes twinkled. 'I am not often wrong when it comes to legal matters. That is one area where I feel quite confident.'

Lucetta did not know what to say. She could not forget his declaration of love for her, and despite his apology, she still felt a little uncomfortable in his presence. 'You're very kind and I do appreciate all your help.'

He cleared his throat and began sorting through the papers on his desk. 'Think nothing of it. After everything you've suffered, you deserve nothing but the best. Now, if you'll excuse me, my dear, I have a lot of work to get through this morning.'

She rose to her feet, relieved to have the excuse to leave the room. 'Yes, of course. Thank you again.'

'I'll arrange an appointment for you to see my colleague as soon as possible.'

Lucetta paused as she was about to open the door. 'Sir Hector, there is another matter – Lennie – I mean, Mr Guthrie – his funeral.'

'I've already spoken to Giles. He's arranging everything. He will speak to you about it.'

Lucetta nodded her head. 'Thank you, sir.' She left him bent over his pile of correspondence and she made her way slowly to the parlour. Her head was buzzing with the unexpected turn of events and she entered the room expecting to find Mary waiting for her, but she was not alone. Giles was standing with his back to the fire and he came towards her with a beaming smile.

'Lucetta, how well you look this morning.' He took

her hand and held it in answer to her mute question. 'It is all arranged. There will be a simple service tomorrow at noon.'

Mary had been arranging chrysanthemums in a tall vase and their spicy scent filled the still air. She hesitated with a bronze-headed bloom in her hands. 'I have a black dress you can borrow, Lucetta.'

'No. Thank you, Mary, but Lennie hated to see women wearing black. He told me once that they reminded him of crows. He had an inexplicable horror of those birds.'

Giles eyed her anxiously. 'You don't have to attend, Lucetta. If it's going to be too upsetting, Mary and I will go in your stead.'

'That's kind of you, Giles, but I will be perfectly fine. I must say goodbye to my old friend.'

Mary dropped the flower on the table and hurried to Lucetta's side. 'Of course you must, and we will be there too. I'm sure Lennie would be happy to know that you are amongst friends.'

Overwhelmed, Lucetta sank down on the sofa. 'He had such a sad life, and he wasn't a bad man at heart.'

'Don't distress yourself, Daisy.' Mary's face puckered with concern.

'He was a good friend to you in the end and you did your best for him,' Giles said gently. 'That's how he would want you to remember your time together.'

Lucetta managed a wobbly smile. 'I know you're right, Giles, but I just wish I could have done more for him.'

'Tell me what Papa had to say just now,' Mary said,

making a valiant effort to change the subject. 'I know that he intends to help you get back what's rightfully yours, but I've no idea how.'

'Don't pester the poor girl,' Giles said, hooking his arm around Mary's shoulders with an affectionate grin. 'Lucetta will tell us when she's ready.'

Lucetta looked up at them and saw them as finely matched as the most expensive pair of thoroughbreds from Tattersall's. Their dark hair and eyes and even their smiles were so similar that they might have been brother and sister. Lucetta could not help feeling a little envious of the ease they found in each other's company. She wished that she felt the same when she was with Sam and instantly felt guilty for even thinking such a thing. She managed a weak smile. 'Hadn't you better put that flower in water, Mary?'

'Yes, of course.' Mary hurried back to the table in the window and she placed the fallen bloom in the vase. 'Aren't these lovely? Giles bought them to cheer a dismal day. He is so thoughtful, sometimes.' She flashed a mischievous smile in Giles' direction, but his reply was drowned by the impatient jangling of the doorbell. Mary leaned over to peer out of the window. 'It's your Sam, Lucetta. Do you feel up to seeing him?'

'Yes, of course,' Lucetta said with as much conviction as she could muster. She was not certain that she was ready to face his demands on her, but there was no point in putting off the inevitable. She could hear his voice in the hallway and the piping tones of the maidservant as she asked him to wait.

Giles made for the door. 'I've business to attend to. I'll say goodbye for now, Lucetta, but I'll be here tomorrow with the carriage to escort you and Mary to the church.'

'Papa might want to take us in the landau,' Mary said, tweaking the last bloom into place. 'You could come with us.'

Giles shook his head. 'I don't think Sir Hector will attend the service. If the news should leak out that a Member of Parliament was at the funeral of a convicted felon, it could damage his career.'

Mary frowned and her pale cheeks were suffused with colour. 'Papa would not let something like that prevent him from doing his duty.'

'It's all right, Mary,' Lucetta said hastily. 'I understand how it is with your papa. Please don't upset yourself.'

Mary looked as though she had a lot more to say but the maid entered without knocking and Sam barged past her before she had a chance to announce him. Ignoring Giles and Mary, he strode over to Lucetta and swept her into a passionate embrace.

Lucetta struggled free and she glanced anxiously at Giles, but he was busy comforting the startled maid. 'Don't worry, Maisie, it wasn't your fault.' He left the room, closing the door behind him with a force that made the windows rattle.

'We are not alone, Sam,' Lucetta said angrily.

He grinned, dragging off his cap and tossing it onto the chair. 'I'm sure Miss Hastings doesn't object to a fellow kissing his fiancée. I've come with good news, my love. I've seen the vicar at the church where your ma and pa are buried and he is free to marry us tomorrow at one o'clock. I wanted to book it earlier but there's a funeral at noon. By this time tomorrow we will be man and wife. What do you say to that?'

Chapter Twenty-four

It was almost as if the huge black birds circling overhead knew of Guthrie's fear and hatred for crows. Their mournful cawing echoed round the graveyard as Lucetta dropped a handful of ice-cold soil onto the coffin lid.

'Goodbye, Lennie,' she whispered. 'I know that you did it for me, but we would have managed somehow. I never told you that I loved you, but I did. You were my special friend and I would have looked after you always.' Her voice broke on a dry sob and she bowed her head, biting back tears.

Giles laid his hand on her shoulder. 'He's safe now, Lucetta. Nothing can harm him ever again.' He allowed the cold dark earth to trickle through his fingers and it fell like rain on the polished oak.

Mary patted her hand. 'It's over, Daisy. Let him rest in peace.'

Lucetta nodded mutely. No words could describe her feelings of guilt and loss. Lennie had turned back to a life of crime in an attempt to provide for her and now he was gone. She was mourning for her father and mother all over again, only this time it was like losing a child that had been given into her care, and she had let him down.

Giles held her a little closer as the biting east wind raked across the graveyard, rattling the bare branches of the trees and whipping dead leaves into eddies around their feet. 'When you're ready, Lucetta.'

She glanced up into his face and she knew that he understood. 'I'm ready to go home.'

With Giles on one side and Mary on the other, Lucetta trod the same path that churchgoers, mourners and bridal parties had taken for many hundreds of years, passing through the lychgate and out into the street where the Harcourts' brougham was waiting to take them home.

During the carriage ride back to Lonsdale Square Lucetta made a conscious effort to face reality. Lennie was dead and gone, hopefully to a better place, and she must face the problems that she had pushed aside until now. Sam had not attended the service. He had been furious when she refused to accept his wedding plans, even though she had tried to explain that the funeral he had talked about so dismissively was that of her friend and protector. Sam had cursed Guthrie, telling her in the strongest terms what he thought of the escaped convict who should have paid for his life of crime at the end of the hangman's noose. He had simply not understood or, Lucetta thought, he had chosen not to understand her feelings, and what began as an argument had erupted into a bitter quarrel. Mary's attempts to mediate had been met with failure on both sides, and Sam had stormed out of the house leaving Lucetta in tears. She had not seen him since.

It had started raining soon after they left the church, and by the time they reached the Hastings' residence what had begun as light drizzle had turned into a steady downpour. Holding up a large black umbrella, the groom opened the carriage door and put down the steps.

'I won't come in,' Giles said apologetically. 'I have an appointment with Dr Glenn, the retiring physician at the practice I hope to purchase. There are just two of us competing now, so I can't afford to be late.'

'I'll keep my fingers crossed for you, Giles.' Mary gave him an encouraging smile as she allowed the groom to help her from the carriage.

Lucetta was about to alight but Giles laid his hand on her arm. 'Are you all right?'

She nodded, resisting the temptation to throw her arms around his neck and sob on his shoulder. 'I'm fine, thank you, Giles.' She shot him a sideways glance, but she couldn't look him fully in the eyes. Something had changed and it felt as though a glass barrier had come between them. She laid her hand on the groom's outstretched arm and stepped down onto the pavement to join Mary who was sheltering beneath the umbrella.

'Oughtn't you to go with him?' Lucetta asked anxiously. 'It's not too late if you call out to stop them.'

'Giles doesn't need me to hold his hand.' Mary hurried up the path and tugged at the bell. 'Don't stand there, Lucetta,' she called over her shoulder. 'You're getting terribly wet.'

Lucetta had barely noticed the raindrops dripping

off the rim of her bonnet as she watched the carriage leave the square, but Mary's comment brought her back to earth with a jolt and she hurried up the path.

'But you will be involved in his work too. Don't you want to see the house where you will spend the rest of your life?'

The door opened and Mary stepped into the hallway, shedding her bonnet and mantle which she thrust into Maisie's outstretched hands. 'What are you talking about, Daisy? I won't be living with Giles. Whatever gave you that idea?'

Maisie moved to Lucetta's side. 'May I take your wet things, miss?'

'Tell Cook we'll have luncheon as soon as possible, please,' Mary said as she entered the morning parlour.

Lucetta realised that she was dripping water all over the tiled floor and she shrugged off her wet garments, handing them to Maisie before hurrying into the parlour. 'But I thought things were settled between you and Giles.'

Mary went to warm her hands in front of the fire. 'What Giles does or doesn't do is his concern, not mine. I'm going back to Stockton Lacey in a week or two and I'm not planning to return to London.' She glanced over her shoulder with a reassuring smile. 'Don't worry, Daisy. We're keeping the house on for the foreseeable future, and you can stay here as long as you like. Papa hasn't decided whether to sell or to let it out to a suitable tenant.'

'But, Mary, I thought that you and Giles had an understanding. I thought that you and he . . .'

Mary threw back her head and laughed. 'Giles and me? Oh, no, we are too much alike. We get on like a house on fire, but there's never been anything romantic in our attachment.'

Lucetta sat down suddenly as her legs gave way beneath her. A multitude of conflicting emotions made her feel light-headed, and the uppermost feeling was one of inexplicable relief. 'I – I thought you were in love with him.'

'I do love him, but I got over my schoolgirl crush a long time ago.' Mary angled her head. 'There's only one person who holds my cousin's heart, and I think you already know her name.'

Lucetta felt the blood rush to her cheeks. The mischievous sparkle in Mary's eyes was so reminiscent of Giles that Lucetta had to look away. 'I turned him down, Mary.'

'I know you did, my dear. Don't worry; he didn't come crying to me. I could see that he was terribly upset about something and I wheedled the truth out of him.'

'What did he say?'

'He asked my advice and I told him to be patient.'

'I love Sam.'

'Are you trying to convince me of that, or yourself?'

'He loves me and he is desperate to marry me. I can't let him down.'

'It's your decision,' Mary said slowly. 'You are the only one who knows what is in your heart.'

'I don't want to talk about it now. I've just said goodbye to poor Lennie, and if I lose Sam it will be

456

like saying farewell to my past and my parents all over again. I do love him, Mary. I do.'

'Then you have made your choice, Daisy.'

'It sounds so simple when you say it like that.'

'If you have any doubts . . .' Mary paused, leaving the end of the sentence hanging in the air. She moved gracefully to a side table and selected a cut crystal decanter. 'You look very pale; I hope you haven't caught a chill.' She poured the amber liquid into two glasses, handing one to Lucetta. 'Drink this; it will do you good.'

Lucetta accepted the glass of sherry and took a sip. The taste on her tongue was pleasantly sweet and nutty and the effect of the alcohol on an empty stomach was instantaneous and warming. She made a valiant attempt to continue the conversation on a less personal level. 'You said you were going to live in Stockton Lacey. Why are you leaving London?'

Mary settled herself in a seat by fire. 'I suppose I'm a country girl at heart. I love nursing, but Papa didn't like me working in the fever hospital. He thought the hours were too long and that in the end I would succumb to some dreadful disease. Besides which, he has decided not to stand at the next election.'

'But he does such good work on behalf of his constituents. Why would he give all that up?'

'I think he's beginning to feel his age. He's no longer a young man.' Mary eyed her over the rim of her glass, but her serious expression dissolved into a smile. 'I'm teasing you, silly. He isn't dying from a broken heart. Papa has been asked to take over from the retiring magistrate in the area. He doesn't think his party will get in at the next election and he says he's had enough of politics. He would rather retire gracefully than be voted out.'

'And what about you? What will you do in the country?'

Mary's dimples played at the corners of her mouth. 'Oh, didn't I tell you? After you left Stockton Lacey, I was introduced to the doctor who had bought the village practice when Giles turned it down. He is a widower with two very young daughters and he needs someone to assist him in his work. I can live at the Grange and have the best of both worlds. I couldn't be happier with the arrangement.'

Lucetta was instantly diverted from her own problems. 'And is this doctor good-looking by any chance?'

'Don't be naughty, Daisy. Dr Goodwin is a very personable man in his early thirties, but that has nothing to do with my accepting the position.'

'No,' Lucetta said, keeping a straight face with difficulty. 'Of course not, Mary.'

'Never mind about me. What about you and Sam? Oughtn't you to make it up with him? If you leave it too long he may think that you really don't care.'

'You're right. I can't leave matters up in the air. I'll go and see him tomorrow.'

'What's wrong with today? I mean, moping about won't bring Lennie back. I think you ought to go this afternoon. I'll come with you if you like. I'll order the carriage and we'll go as soon as we've finished luncheon.'

* * *

Mary's plans came to nothing. Sir Hector arrived while they were in the middle of their meal, announcing that he had made an appointment for Lucetta to see his solicitor friend that afternoon at three o'clock. Lucetta would not have admitted it for the world, but deep down she was relieved. She could not face another emotional battle with Sam, and she knew that he would take her visit as tacit acceptance of his proposal. It would only be a matter of deciding when and where they were to be married. At least she had a valid excuse now for putting off an irrevocable decision.

Mary was waiting for them in the drawing room when Lucetta and Sir Hector returned from the solicitor's office in Lincoln's Inn Fields. She set aside her embroidery hoop and patted the empty space next to her on the sofa.

'Come and sit down. Tell me all about it. Are you an heiress, Lucetta, or shall I still call you Daisy?'

'Leave the poor girl alone,' Sir Hector said, chuckling. 'She must be exhausted after everything that's happened today. Do something useful, Mary. Ring the bell and order some tea and cake. I'll take mine in my study.' He left the room with a nod to Lucetta and a genuine smile on his lips.

Mary reached up to tug at the tasselled bell pull. 'Father's right, of course. You must be worn out. There's no need to tell me now if you're too tired. But I am dying with curiosity.'

Lucetta sat down beside her. 'Well, he was quite

459

amazing. The solicitor, I mean, not your father. Although Sir Hector is very—'

Mary laid her hand on Lucetta's arm. 'I know that my pa is wonderful. Just tell me what the solicitor said.'

'He had sent one of his people out to find my ancient aunt in Surrey, and she had seen the likeness of me and said that I was the absolute image of her mother, my grandmother. She had shown him a faded old daguerreotype of her mother when she was a girl, and apparently it matched. Then he had sent the same person to look up my old headmistress and she had confirmed the likeness too. I had to swear an affidavit, and that, together with the letter from Sir John and confirmation from two respectable old ladies, will, he said, stand up in court. He had a copy of Papa's will and everything was left to me.'

'That's wonderful, but what now?'

'I'm going to see Jeremiah tomorrow. I'll take the affidavit with me and try to persuade him to be reasonable. Perhaps we can come to some amicable arrangement before my Uncle Bradley returns from abroad.'

A thoughtful frown puckered Mary's smooth brow. 'I don't think you ought to face Jeremiah on your own. You should take Sam with you; after all, you do intend to marry him, and the money to repair his ship has to come from the business you are about to inherit.'

Lucetta digested this in silence. The choices she made now would affect her for the rest of her life, and she realised suddenly that she was not the only one involved. There were the men and their families who depended on their wages from the company she now owned. With wealth and position there came responsibility; she could almost wish to be poor again. Life had been much simpler when she was plain Lucy Guthrie. The mantle of Lucetta Froy did not sit quite so easily on her shoulders now.

Next morning Lucetta took a cab to the boatyard in Wapping where the *Sea Eagle* was undergoing repairs. As she had expected, she found Sam on the foreshore supervising the work. Picking up her skirts she made her way carefully across the slippery stones, avoiding the brackish pools filled with rusty bolts.

His expression was not welcoming. 'So you've come looking for me. That's a turn-up for the books. Who are you today, then? Lucy Guthrie or Lucetta Froy?'

'Why are you being like this?' Lucetta demanded breathlessly. 'I know you were angry, but—'

'Angry. That's putting it mildly. You chose that criminal over me and you jilted me on our wedding day.'

'Then you must know how poor Dora felt when you left her at the altar.' Lucetta rarely lost her temper but she had barely slept that night and her nerves were stretched to the point of breaking. She was about to face Jeremiah and she had hoped that Sam might be reasonable, but she could see from the grim look in his eyes and the set of his jaw that he was still furious with her.

He gripped her by the elbow and hurried her out of earshot of the workmen. 'I told you that was a pack of lies.'

She drew away from him. 'And I don't believe you. If you love me as you say you do, why are you behaving like this? If you really cared for me you would think about my feelings and not put yourself first all the time.'

He folded his arms across his chest, glaring at her. 'Did you come here just to fight with me, or is there a purpose to your visit? I think I merit an apology before anything else.'

Lucetta stared up at him. He had changed so much since those heady days in Bali, or perhaps she had never known the real Sam Cutler. His hair was dull and matted to his head and his eyes, which had once danced with golden lights, were now as grey as the skies above them. He was no longer a golden god of love and youth; there was no humour or even a hint of affection in his expression. The intervening years had hardened and toughened him into cold steel and she knew in that single moment that she did not and could not love him.

'I just came to tell you that I can't marry you, Sam. I'm sorry, but you were trying to push me into something that deep down I knew would not work for either of us.'

He gripped her by the wrist, his eyes narrowed and his lips drawn into a thin angry line. 'You've gained proof of your identity, haven't you? You don't need me any more, you cheating, conniving little bitch.'

'Let me go. You're hurting me.'

'Let you go? Never. You agreed to marry me and I'm keeping you to that arrangement. I don't know if a man has ever sued a woman for breach of promise, but if you go back on your word I'm going to have a damned good try. I'll sue your company for every last penny.'

'Let her go.'

The staccato command caused Sam to loosen his grasp just enough for Lucetta to twist free from him. She spun round to see Giles striding across the foreshore towards them. Her breath hitched in her throat as she called his name, and she ran to meet him, tripping and stumbling on the slimy stones. He caught her in his arms and stared anxiously into her face.

'Are you all right, my darling? If he's hurt you I'll break every bone in his body.'

'I'm all right, Giles. But how did you find me? Why are you here?'

'Mary told me where you'd gone. She was worried about you coming here alone, although I don't think she could have imagined that he would actually molest you.'

Sam had caught up with her and he seized Lucetta by the shoulders, dragging her away from Giles. 'Leave my woman alone, Harcourt. This doesn't concern you.'

'I'm not your woman,' Lucetta cried angrily. 'Let me go, Sam. I've told you that I won't marry you and you'll just have to accept it.'

'If you think I'm going to lose my chance to take over your father's business then you are very much mistaken.' Sam let her go so abruptly that she stumbled and would have fallen if Giles had not stepped forward to save her.

'What sort of man are you?' Giles demanded. 'You may be able to bully your crew but you'll leave Lucetta alone or you'll have to deal with me.'

'You!' Sam drew himself up to his full height, fisting his hands. 'Come on then, pill-pedlar; let's see what you're made of.'

Lucetta threw herself between them. 'Stop this, the pair of you. I'll see that you get the repairs to your ship paid for, Sam, but that is all you are ever going to get from me. And you can't sue me because I am still a minor, and will be for another year. I've taken legal advice and although the company belongs to me, it is held in trust until I am twenty-one. Until then my uncle is my legal guardian and whether he likes it or not he has to protect me from fortune-hunters like you.'

Giles slipped his arm around her waist. 'Come along, Lucetta. Let me take you home.'

She smiled up at him. 'There is something I must do first.'

'I'll take you to court over this,' Sam blustered.

Lucetta shook her head, eyeing him sadly. 'It would be a waste of your time and money. I did love you once, but you've changed and I've grown up. Can't we leave it as a happy memory?'

'Bah!' Sam turned his back on them and trudged across the foreshore, kicking at anything that got in his way.

Giles hooked his arm around Lucetta's shoulders. 'What is so urgent that it can't wait?'

They arrived outside the Froy Company's office to find a scene of frantic activity. The double doors were flung open and the goods being unloaded on the wharf were being moved into the warehouse. Lucetta saw Perks standing by a mountain of crates studying a sheaf of papers and marking off each item as it was taken into the storage space. She hurried up to him.

'Is this what I think it is, Mr Perks?'

His eyes lit up behind his steel-rimmed spectacles. 'Miss Lucy, this is a pleasure. Mr Jeremiah told me that you had gone away, but just look at you now.'

'It's good to see you,' Lucetta said hastily. She did not want to go to great lengths to explain why drab Lucy Guthrie had suddenly metamorphosed into a well-dressed young lady. She pointed to the vessel tied up alongside. 'Is that my uncle's ship?'

Perks nodded his head. 'Mr Bradley was taken home first thing, miss. Mr Jeremiah went with him and is not expected back until tomorrow.'

Lucetta knew Perks well enough to realise that all was not well, despite the arrival of new and exciting stock. 'Is something wrong, Mr Perks?'

'Things are bad, miss. You were the lucky one, leaving when you did. Mr Jeremiah has cut our wages and the men have to work twice as hard. He says that it's the current financial situation in the City that makes it so, but I do the books and in my opinion trade has never been better.'

'Why don't you leave and take employment elsewhere?' Giles said, placing a protective arm around Lucetta's shoulders.

Perks shot him a pitying glance. 'You don't know what it's like round here, sir. Mr Jeremiah would make it impossible for any of us to get work. He'd put the word round that we were troublemakers and trade unionists. We've all got families who depend on our wages. We can't afford to be out of work.'

'Don't worry, Mr Perks,' Lucetta said firmly. 'Things are going to change, you'll see.'

Perks managed a weak smile. 'I'll believe that when I see it, Miss Lucy. But if you'll excuse me, I'd better get back to checking the bill of lading. If anything is missing I'll end up hanging in a gibbet like them pirates on Execution Dock.'

Lucetta laughed in spite of herself. 'We won't let that happen to you. I'm going to call on my uncle and set matters right.'

'Your uncle, miss?' Perks looked up from his screed of papers with puzzlement written all over his face.

'I'm surprised that the secret didn't leak out,' Lucetta said, eyeing him curiously. 'Did no one hear the altercation between myself and Mr Jeremiah?'

Perks shook his head. 'No, miss.'

'All will be revealed soon,' Giles said. 'Miss Froy will explain everything once she's settled things with her uncle. Isn't that so, Lucetta?'

'There's a cab now,' Lucetta said, hurrying off to claim a hansom cab that had just deposited a rotund gentleman in a city suit outside a wine merchant's office. Giles caught up with her as she was instructing the cabby to take them to Thornhill Crescent.

'Is this wise, darling?' Giles demanded as he climbed in beside her. 'Wouldn't it be better to wait for a day or two and allow your uncle to settle in at home?'

Lucetta turned to him, clutching his lapels. 'That's the second time you've called me darling.'

'Do you object?'

His smile was tender and she felt her heart sing with joy. She slid her hands under his collar, pulling his head down so that their lips met. 'I love it, Giles.'

'And I love you,' he said softly. 'More than life itself.'

Lucetta sighed as he claimed her lips in a kiss that blotted out the past. Nothing that had gone before mattered. They were the only two people in the world and Lucetta knew that they would be together forever. Giles was her life and her true love. She nestled against him breathing in the scent that was his alone. Her bonnet had fallen off and her hair had come loose from its chignon, but she didn't care.

'I thought I had lost you,' Giles murmured. 'When Mary told me you had gone to find Sam, I thought you had chosen him.'

Lucetta pulled away just enough to look him in the eyes. 'I think I fell in love with you from the start, Giles, but it seemed to me that you and Mary were destined for each other, and I was confused about my feelings for Sam. I realise now that it was puppy-love. My poor father was right, and my wayward behaviour killed him.'

Taking her by the shoulders, he gave her the gentlest of gentle shakes. 'That's absolute nonsense, my love. Your parents were drowned when the *Caroline* went down. As to the stroke, anything could have brought it on. You mustn't blame yourself.'

Lucetta sighed as she rested her head on his shoulder.

'I'm not looking forward to facing Uncle Bradley and Jeremiah.'

Giles held her close. 'I'm with you now and always, Lucetta. We'll face them together.'

Bradley Froy's manservant admitted them to the house with the greatest reluctance. Lucetta was certain that she would have been forced to wait outside in the cold if Giles had not insisted on seeing Mr Froy senior and his son on a matter of extreme urgency.

They were left standing in the hallway while the ageing servant negotiated the stairs to announce their arrival, but it was Jeremiah who descended moments later and the expression on his face was not welcoming.

'What do you want?' he demanded.

Lucetta stepped forward and to her surprise she was not afraid. With Giles at her side she felt invincible, and the affidavit and copy of her father's will tucked away in her reticule gave her further encouragement. 'I must speak to you and my uncle together, Jeremiah.'

'Imposter!' Jeremiah's voice rose to a girlish screech. 'Get out of my house.'

'You're mistaken,' Lucetta said calmly. 'This is my house and I can prove it.'

'What's all the noise, Jeremiah?'

Lucetta glanced over her cousin's shoulder to see her uncle standing at the top of the stairs. He was deathly pale and leaning heavily on a cane, but apart from a slight slurring of his speech he did not appear to have been badly affected by his recent illness.

'Uncle Bradley. It's me, Lucetta. I need to speak to you urgently.'

'I'll have them thrown out, Pa,' Jeremiah spluttered. 'You should be resting, Father. You know what the doctor said.'

'Damn the doctor. They're all a pack of charlatans.'

'I am one of those charlatans,' Giles said with a wry smile. 'If you need medical attention I am on hand.'

'On hand to fleece me,' Bradley muttered, turning away and hobbling along the galleried landing. 'Come upstairs if you must. I suppose I won't get any peace until the girl has had her say.'

Lucetta needed no second bidding. She brushed past Jeremiah and hurried upstairs, following her uncle into the drawing room. She paused in the doorway, gazing round at the unfamiliar furnishings and the heavy embossed wallpaper that made the room seem smaller than she remembered, and depressingly sombre. The only piece of furniture that she recognised was the chaise longue on which her mother had languished during her episodes of ill-health, only now it was reupholstered in crimson and gold damask and Aunt Eliza was perched on it with her thin shoulders hunched and her dark eyes glittering with malice. She reminded Lucetta of the crows that had haunted Guthrie's dreams and circled over his grave. Lucetta shivered and curled her fingers around Giles' hand for comfort.

'What is she doing here, Bradley?' Aunt Eliza demanded, stabbing the Persian carpet with her ebony cane.

Bradley limped over to a wingback armchair close to the fire and lowered himself onto the seat. 'She is after money, no doubt. News of my successful trip must have spread round the city like wildfire.'

Lucetta stood in the middle of the room, taking in every last detail, and to her surprise she felt nothing. This was not the home she had loved and yearned for, it was just a house inhabited by strangers who happened to be related to her. She smiled up at Giles as he held her hand and she knew then that her home would be wherever he was. Bricks and mortar meant nothing. Only people mattered. She braced her shoulders and turned to face her accuser. 'You do recognise me then, Uncle?'

Bradley waved his stick at her. 'Get on with it, girl. What is said between these four walls is between us. You have no proof of your identity.'

'Well there you are wrong,' Lucetta took the papers from her reticule. 'I have a copy of Papa's will and a sworn affidavit from witnesses who are willing to stand up in court and testify as to my identity.'

'We buried Lucetta Froy,' Eliza Bradley cried angrily. 'This house belongs to us.'

Giles moved as if to speak for her, but Lucetta laid her hand on his arm. 'It's all right, Giles. I can deal with this.' She handed the documents to her uncle. 'My solicitor has the originals, Uncle; these are simply copies.'

Bradley cast his eyes over the papers. 'What do you want? I'm a sick man; you must be careful what you say.'

'You are my legal guardian until I'm twenty-one,' Lucetta said calmly. 'I don't want to fight you, Uncle. You are still my father's brother and I believe he was fond of you, goodness knows why. I have a proposition to put to you and Jeremiah.'

'How dare you,' Jeremiah hissed. 'You were a poor girl living with a villain when we last met. How do you think society would view Miss Lucetta Froy if the truth were to come out?'

Lucetta cast him a cursory glance. 'Be quiet, Jeremiah, and listen to what I have to say.'

Later that day, Giles related the scene to a fascinated Sir Hector and an admiring Mary as they sat round the dining table in Lonsdale Square.

'I didn't know you had it in you, Daisy,' Mary said in an awed tone. 'Weren't you terrified that you might faint or burst into tears?'

'She's made of sterner stuff,' Giles said proudly. 'By the end of the meeting Mr Bradley Froy was glad to accept the most generous terms that my dearest Lucetta offered out of the goodness of her heart.'

'Well done, Lucetta,' Sir Hector said, clapping his hands. 'It was a decision that would have done credit to King Solomon himself.'

Lucetta felt a ready blush rising to her cheeks and she shook her head. 'I don't want the house, Sir Hector. I think my papa would have agreed with my decision to let Uncle Bradley stay there rent-free for the rest of his life.'

'But what about you?' Mary asked anxiously. 'Where

will you live? Or should I ask where will you and Giles live? I'm assuming that you plan to marry.'

'We do,' Giles said, reaching out to grasp Lucetta's hand. He raised it to his lips and the gold filigree bracelet on her wrist glinted in the candlelight. 'My dear girl has accepted me and I couldn't be happier.'

'That's absolutely wonderful news,' Mary said, smiling. 'Have you bought her a ring, Giles?'

Lucetta held his hand to her cheek. 'It was too late today, but we are going out first thing tomorrow morning.'

'And the announcement will be in *The Times* on Monday,' Giles added proudly.

Sir Hector raised his glass. 'Congratulations, Giles.' He beamed at Lucetta. 'I hope you will be very happy, my dear.'

Mary drank the toast, but there was a question in her eyes as she replaced her glass on the table. 'What will happen to the business, Daisy? Have you given that away too?'

Lucetta shook her head. 'No, definitely not. It doesn't come to me until I'm twenty-one, but until then I am going to take a keen interest in it. On my solicitor's advice, it's being made into a limited company where I am the major shareholder. Uncle Bradley and Jeremiah have enough shares to give them a modest income, and Jeremiah will be sent abroad to oversee the running of the warehouses in Asia and Indonesia. He will have Papa's trusted managers to guide him and Uncle Bradley will advise him.'

Giles squeezed her fingers. 'I can see who has inherited her father's business head,' he said, smiling.

'And you don't mind your wife having a career of her own?' Mary held her hands up as if she was shocked by the prospect, but the laughter in her eyes belied her words.

'I'm going to promote Perks to the position of manager,' Lucetta explained hastily. 'It's not as if I'm going to work every day, although I will visit the warehouse often to make certain that everything is as it should be.

'And I wouldn't have it any other way,' Giles added. 'I'm not going to make a fortune from practising in one of the poorest areas in London. I'll be glad for our children to have an inheritance to look forward to.'

'My goodness,' Mary said in genuine amazement. 'You've thought of everything, except the most important thing.'

Lucetta raised an eyebrow. She couldn't think of anything that would spoil their future happiness. 'What is that, Mary?'

'Where are you going to live, Daisy? It's all very well giving the family home to your uncle and aunt, but you and Giles can't live in a tent.'

Sir Hector cleared his throat. 'I think I can solve that particular problem. As you know, I'm retiring soon and Mary and I will move permanently to Stockton Lacey. This house will be empty and it is reasonably near your new practice, Giles. I'll be more than happy to give it to you and Lucetta as a wedding present.'

Lucetta gasped at his generosity, but she shook her

head. 'We couldn't accept it, Sir Hector. What about Mary?'

'I can answer for myself,' Mary said, smiling. 'I have more than enough for my needs with a small legacy from my mother.'

'And the Grange will pass to Mary on my demise,' Sir Hector said. 'She is well taken care of and I've always thought of Giles more as a son than a nephew. And don't forget, he has three sisters to marry off.'

'Heavens, what a task,' Mary giggled.

'I don't mind one bit,' Lucetta said sincerely. 'You can't imagine how happy I am to be part of a family once again.'

Giles rose to his feet, moving to stand behind Lucetta's chair and resting his hands on her shoulders. 'We may never be rich in financial terms,' he said, dropping a kiss on the top of her head. 'But if love is counted as an asset, Lucetta and I will be the wealthiest husband and wife in the East End.'

'Amen to that,' Lucetta said, jumping to her feet and flinging her arms around his neck. 'I do love you, Giles.'

Poppy's War

Lily Baxter

August 1939: Thirteen-year-old Poppy Brown is evacuated to a village in Dorset. Tired and frightened, she arrives with nothing but her gas mask and a change of clothes to her name. Billeted at a grand country house, Poppy is received with cold indifference above stairs and gets little better treatment from the servants. Lonely and missing the family she left behind in London, Poppy is devastated when she hears that they have been killed in the Blitz.

Circumstances soon force Poppy to move to the suburbs and into the company of strangers once more. Earning a meagre income as a hospital cleaner, as the war continues to rage, Poppy longs to do her duty. And as soon as she is able to, she starts her training as a nurse. While the man she loves is fighting in the skies above Europe, Poppy battles to survive the day-to-day hardships and dangers of wartime, wondering if she'll ever see him again . . .

Read on for an extract . . .

Chapter One

Barton Lacey, Dorset, August 1939

The wheezy noise made by the steam engine as it chugged out of the station was the saddest sound that Poppy had ever heard. She bit her lip, trying hard not to cry as her last link with the East End of London and home disappeared into the hazy afternoon sunshine.

The woman who had been put in charge of the schoolchildren was not their teacher, and she had warned them before they boarded the train at Waterloo that she was not a person to be trifled with. They were to address her as Mrs Hicks and woe betide anyone who called her miss, although miraculously no one had fallen into that trap during the journey, which had taken three long hours. Poppy could tell by their silence that the other children were also feeling tired, hungry and scared as the formidable Mrs Hicks herded them into a semblance of a crocodile while she performed a roll call on the station platform. She was a big woman, and the buttons on her blouse seemed to be in danger of flying off in all directions when her large bosom

1

heaved with impatient sighs. Her tweed skirt was stretched tight across her bulging stomach, and when Bobby Moss had asked her if she had a baby in her tummy he had received a swift clip round the ear. That had quietened him down a bit, which was a relief to Poppy as he had been a pest throughout the long journey, pulling her hair and calling her silly names, but she had felt a bit sorry for him when she saw him huddled in the corner of the carriage nursing his ear, sniffing and wiping his nose on his sleeve.

'Poppy Brown, stop daydreaming and follow the others outside into the forecourt where the billeting officer will deal with you all as he sees fit.' Mrs Hicks' stentorian voice echoed round the empty station as Poppy fell in step beside Bobby. They were marched through the station ticket hall to stand outside on the forecourt, labelled like parcels and carrying their meagre belongings in brown paper bags, together with that mysterious but compulsory object in a box, a gas mask. Some of the children were snivelling miserably, others hung their heads and stared at their boots, while a few of the bigger boys fought and scrapped like wolf cubs attempting to establish a pecking order in their pack.

Poppy wanted to cry like Colin, the ragged boy standing next to her who had wet his pants and was plainly terrified of being found out. She patted him on the shoulder. 'It's all right,' she whispered. 'I expect they'll take us somewhere nice and give us a slap-up tea.' She did not believe that for one moment, but she was not going to admit to being scared stiff. She held her head high and stuck out her chin. 'Up guards and at 'em' was what Grandad always said, taking his pipe out of his mouth and spitting into the fire as if to underline the importance of his words. 'Don't you let them country folk put one over on you, petal. If they does I'll come down on the next train and give 'em a good seeing to. Chin up, Poppy. You come from a long line of brave soldiers, and don't forget it.'

Poppy did not feel like a brave soldier or a brave anything at that moment. Mrs Hicks had vanished. Maybe she had eaten one too many biscuits and exploded somewhere out of sight, but she had been replaced by a man with a clipboard. He wore a pair of tortoiseshell-rimmed glasses through which he peered at them like a myopic owl.

'I'm Mr Walker,' he announced as if this was something they ought to know. 'I'm the billeting officer and I will find good homes to take care of you for the duration.' He turned to a small group of people who had gathered behind him. None of them looked particularly enthusiastic at the prospect of taking on youngsters from the East End, and the raggle-taggle line of children began to fragment as some collapsed on the ground in tears and several others were sick. Probably from fright, Poppy thought, as she eyed their prospective hosts, recalling Mum's last words to her as they had said a tearful goodbye outside the school gates at five thirty that morning.

'Look at their shoes and their hats, Poppy. Good shoes and a nice hat will mean a clean home and no bed bugs or lice. You be a good girl, wash behind your ears and say your prayers every night before you go to bed. Always remember that your mum and dad love you, ducks. And so does Joe, although he ain't always the best at showing his feelings. That goes for your gran and grandad too. We'll all miss you, love'

Poppy said a small prayer now as she met the eyes of a tight-lipped little woman wearing a felt beret and a mean scowl. Her shoes needed a polish and were down at heel. Poppy looked away and moved her gaze down the line until she came upon a smart pair of high-heeled court shoes, two-tone in brown and cream. Glancing upwards she noted a jaunty brown velour hat spiked with a long feather that reminded her of a film poster she had seen of Errol Flynn playing Robin Hood. The face beneath the hat could have been a female version of the film star's, but the woman's expression was neither charming nor kind. Poppy's heart sank a little as she read boredom and indifference in the hazel eyes that stared unblinkingly into her own. But the shoes were good and the hat was quite new. The woman wore a well-cut tweed costume with a gold brooch on the lapel. Poppy did her best to smile.

The lady in the Robin Hood hat turned to the billeting officer. 'What's the name of that one?' She waved her hand vaguely in Poppy's direction.

Mr Walker scanned the list on his clipboard but he frowned as if confused by the names and ages of the children. He moved a step closer to Poppy. 'What's your name, dear?'

'Poppy Brown, sir.'

'Poppy,' he said with an attempt at a smile. 'Named after the flower, were you, dear?'

'No, mister. I was called Poppy after me mum's favourite perfume from Woollies. Californian Poppy.'

The smart lady cast her eyes up to heaven. 'My God, what an accent.' She looked Poppy up and down. 'But she does look the cleanest of the bunch and she's old enough to be useful. She'll do.'

'You're a lucky girl, Poppy Brown.' Mr Walker took her by the shoulder and gave her a gentle shove towards her benefactress. 'You must be very grateful to Mrs Carroll and I hope you'll behave like a good girl at Squire's Knapp.'

'Follow me, child.' Mrs Carroll strode away towards a large black car, her high heels tip-tapping on the concrete, and as the feather in her hat waved in the breeze it seemed to be beckoning to Poppy. She followed obediently but shied away in fright as a big man dressed entirely in black from his peaked cap to his shiny leather boots leapt forward to open the car door.

'Don't loiter, girl,' Mrs Carroll said impatiently. 'Get in the car.'

Poppy glanced up at the chauffeur but he was staring straight ahead of him. She climbed into the back seat and made herself as small as possible in the far corner. The unfamiliar smell of the leather squabs coupled with the gnawing hunger that caused her stomach to rumble made her close her eyes as a wave of nausea swept over her. The jam sandwiches that Mum had made in the early hours of the morning had all been eaten before the train got to the Elephant and Castle. She had saved the piece of ginger cake until last, but she had shared it with the small girl from the infants class whose nose was permanently dripping with candles of mucus that grew longer each time she opened her mouth to howl.

'We'll go straight home, Jackson,' Mrs Carroll said in a bored tone. 'I've changed my mind about going to the library.'

The car picked up speed as they left the village and a cool breeze coming through the open window revived Poppy to the point where she could open her eyes. She craned her neck to look out of the window.

'You're very small,' Mrs Carroll said, lighting a cigarette that she had just fitted into a green onyx holder. 'How old are you?' She inhaled with obvious pleasure and exhaled slowly as she replaced the gold cigarette case and lighter in her handbag.

Poppy was impressed. Her dad smoked cigarettes but he always rolled them himself and lit them with a match from a box of Swan Vestas. Sometimes when she had earned a bonus at the glue factory, Mum would buy a packet of Woodbines for him as a special treat. Gran said it wasn't ladylike to smoke in the street. Poppy wondered what Gran would say about a lady smoking in her car.

'Well?' Mrs Carroll shot her a sideways glance. 'Have you lost your tongue, girl?'

'No, miss, I'm thirteen. I had me thirteenth birthday in April.'

'You're very undersized for your age, and you say *my* thirteenth birthday, not me thirteenth birthday. You call me Mrs Carroll or ma'am, not miss. Do you understand, Poppy?'

'Yes, mi— ma'am.'

Mrs Carroll smoked her cigarette in silence, occasionally tapping the ash into an ashtray located somewhere by her side. Poppy remembered that Gran also said it was rude to stare and she turned away to gaze out of the window. Through gaps in the hedgerows she could see fields of ripe corn, spiked with scarlet poppies and dark blue cornflowers. She had read about the countryside in books and she had seen the flat fields of Essex from the train window on the annual family August Bank Holiday trip to Southend-on-Sea, but the gently rolling countryside of Dorset was something quite new to her. She moved forward in her seat as they passed a field where a herd of black and white cows grazed on rich green grass, and she was amazed by their size and a bit scared, especially when two of them poked their heads over a five-barred gate and mooed loudly as the car drove past. She began to feel sick again and was relieved when Jackson brought the big limousine to a halt outside a pair of tall wrought iron gates. He climbed sedately out of the car and unlocked the gates, which protested on rusty hinges as they swung open. He drove slowly along an avenue lined with trees that formed a dark tunnel of interwoven branches heavy with wine-red leaves.

'This is like the park at home,' Poppy said appreciatively.

'Really.'

Mrs Carroll's voice sounded remote and mildly bored. Poppy accepted this as a matter of course. Grown-ups never took much notice of what children had to say, and she had just spotted a small lake with an island in the middle and a white marble folly in the shape of a Roman temple. It was like something out of a film and she was about to ask Mrs Carroll if all this belonged to her when she heard the thundering of horse's hooves and the car came to a sudden halt. Seemingly appearing from nowhere, the rider drew his mount to a halt on Poppy's side of the car. The animal whinnied and rolled its great eyes. Its nostrils flared and Poppy thought it was going to put its huge head through the open window to bite her. She screamed and ducked down, covering her eyes with her hands.

'Good God, who have you got there, Mother?'

The voice was young, male and well spoken but Poppy did not dare look up.

'Guy! Do you have to ride as if you're in a Wild West show?' Mrs Carroll said angrily. 'Get that beast away from the Bentley before it does some damage.'

'Have you kidnapped a little girl, Mother? I thought you hated children.'

The humour in the voice was not lost on Poppy. She struggled to sit upright, but as she lifted her head she saw the horse's huge yellow teeth bared as if it was going to snap her head off. Everything went black.

She woke up feeling something cold and wet dripping down her neck. A fat, rosy face hovered above hers and for a moment Poppy thought she was at home in West Ham.

'Gran? Is that you?'

'Gran indeed. What a cheek!'

'Well, you are a grandma, Mrs Toon.'

'That's as maybe, Violet. But I'm not grandma to the likes of this little 'un, come from goodness knows where in the slums of London.'

Poppy was raised to a sitting position and the younger person, who she realised must be Violet, shoved a glass of water into her hands. 'Take a sip of that, for Gawd's sake.'

Poppy gazed in wonder at her surroundings. She was in a kitchen, but it was enormous. The whole ground floor of her home in West Ham would have

9

fitted into it with room to spare.

'We thought you were dead,' Violet said cheerfully. 'But now we can see you're alive and kicking.'

Poppy drank some water and immediately felt a little better. 'I thought for a moment I was back at home.'

Mrs Toon cleared her throat noisily and wiped her hands on her starched white apron. 'There, there! You're a very lucky little girl to have been taken in by Mrs Carroll. I hope you're not going to give us any trouble, Poppy Brown.'

'I never asked to come here, missis.'

Mrs Toon and Violet exchanged meaningful glances, as if to say 'I told you so'.

'None of your lip, young lady,' Mrs Toon said sharply. 'You're a guest in this house, although I'm not sure what we're supposed to do with you. Are you going to be kept below stairs or upstairs? Mrs Carroll never said one way or t'other. But whatever she decides, you must keep a civil tongue in your head, or you'll answer to me.'

'Yes ma'am,' Poppy said, recalling Mrs Carroll's lesson in manners.

'La-di-dah!' Mrs Toon said, chuckling. 'Better give her a bowl of soup and some bread and butter, Violet. And then you can take her upstairs and run a bath for her.'

'It's not Friday.' Poppy looked for the tin tub set in front of the black-lead stove, but there was none. Come to that there was no stove either. There was a large gas cooker and some sort of range with shiny metal lids on the top, but that was all. She breathed a sigh of relief. 'Well, seeing as how you got no hot water, I'll skip the bath, ta.'

'People in proper houses have baths every day,' Mrs Toon said firmly. 'And I don't know what gives you the idea we haven't any hot water. We have the very latest in everything at Squire's Knapp.'

'That's right,' Violet said, nodding. 'We had central heating before even Cook was born, and that's going back some.' She placed a bowl of steaming soup on a stool which she set beside Poppy. 'I daresay you don't have proper bathrooms in the slums. Eat up and I'll show you how posh folks live.'

The soup was as good as anything that Gran could make, Poppy thought appreciatively as she bit into the hunk of freshly baked bread liberally spread with thick yellow butter. She had not tasted butter before as they always ate margarine at home. She stopped chewing as she thought of her family and suddenly it was difficult to swallow. She had lost track of time but a sideways glance at the big white-faced clock on the kitchen wall told her it was teatime. Dad and her elder brother Joe would be home from their jobs on the railways, and Mum would be stoking the coke boiler to heat water for them to wash off the grime of the day, while Gran peeled potatoes ready to boil and serve with a bit of fat bacon or boiled cod. Grandad would be out in the back garden smoking his pipe and keeping an eye out for the neighbour's pigeons. The birds were supposed to fly straight home, but were inclined to stop off in order to sample the tender green shoots of cabbage and a Brussels sprout or two.

'What's up with you?' Violet demanded. 'Don't you like proper food? I bet your family lives on rats and mice up in London.'

Apparently overhearing this remark, Mrs Toon caught Violet a swift clout round the ear. 'Don't tease the kid, Violet Guppy. How would you like it if you were sent away from home and had to live with strangers? You go on upstairs and run the bath water and don't dawdle.'

Uttering a loud howl Violet ran from the kitchen clutching her hand to her ear. Poppy swallowed hard and blinked, determined that whatever happened she was not going to disgrace herself by bursting into tears. Gran said tears were a sign of weakness, like not being able to work a pair of scissors with your left hand in order to cut the fingernails on your right hand. Gran said if you couldn't control your emotions or your left hand, it was just weak will and not to be tolerated.

'Eat up, little 'un,' ordered Mrs Toon. 'I haven't got all day to waste on the likes of you, you know.'

'Mrs Toon. I've got a message from her upstairs.'

Poppy twisted round in her chair to see a maid wearing a black dress with a white cap and apron standing in the doorway.

'Mrs Carroll wants to see you and the evacuee in

the drawing room as soon as she's been fed and bathed.'

Mrs Toon tossed her head causing her white cap to sit askew on top of her silver-grey hair. 'All right, Olive. She's nearly finished her food. You'd better take her up to the bathroom and watch your cousin Violet. That girl's got a spiteful streak in her nature and I don't want her trying to drown young Poppy here. Mrs Carroll wouldn't like it.'

'Mrs Carroll says to burn the evacuee's clothes because they'll probably be – you know.' She winked and nodded her head, lowering her voice. 'She says to find some of Miss Pamela's old clothes and see if they fit.'

'As if I haven't got enough to do.' Mrs Toon clicked her tongue against her teeth. She sighed. 'Dinner to prepare and an evacuee to feed and clothe; I just haven't got the time to go poking about in Miss Pamela's room. You'll have to do that, Olive.'

Poppy leapt to her feet. 'You ain't going to burn my clothes. My mum sent me with my Sunday best and I haven't got fleas. It's only poor folk's kids that have fleas, not people who live in Quebec Road, West Ham.'

Olive reached out a long, thin arm and grabbed Poppy by the scruff of her neck. 'Less of your cheek, young lady. Mind your manners or Mrs Carroll will send you back to London to be bombed by them Germans.'

Poppy felt her heart kick against her ribs. If Olive

had punched her in the stomach it couldn't have hurt more. 'They won't bomb West Ham, will they?'

'Why do you think the government sent all you kids out to pester us in the country? Silly girl!' Olive gave her a shove towards the door. 'Now get up the stairs and we'll make sure you haven't brought any little lodgers with you.'

After an excruciating time half submerged in what felt like boiling water while Violet scrubbed her back with a loofah that felt more like a handful of barbed wire and Olive shampooed her hair, digging her fingers spitefully into Poppy's scalp, she was eventually deemed to be clean enough to be taken down to the drawing room. Dressed in clothes that were expensive but at least two sizes too large for her small frame, Poppy waited nervously outside the door while Olive went inside to announce that she was ready for inspection. Moments later she reappeared. 'Go in. Speak only when you're spoken to.'

Poppy entered the room as nervously as if she were venturing into a cage filled with wild animals. Mrs Carroll was seated in a large blue velvet armchair with her feet raised up on a tapestry-covered footstool. In one elegantly manicured hand she held a glass of sherry and between two fingers on the other hand she balanced her cigarette holder. She was talking to a thin, white-haired man seated in a chair on the opposite side of the huge fireplace.

14

She stopped speaking to stare at Poppy. 'She looks cleaner, Olive. It's fortunate that I hadn't found time to send Miss Pamela's old clothes off to the orphanage. They fit Poppy quite nicely, considering she's so small and thin.'

Olive bobbed a curtsey. 'Mrs Toon would like to know where she's to put her, ma'am.'

Mrs Carroll took a sip of sherry and sighed. 'I don't know. There must be a spare room in the servants' quarters.'

A sharp intake of breath told Poppy that this suggestion was not popular with Olive.

'The ones that aren't used have been shut up for years, ma'am.'

The kindly-looking gentleman had been silent until now but he frowned, shaking his head. 'You can't put the child up there, Marina. What about the old nursery?'

'Don't be silly, Edwin. Pamela will need to put Rupert in there when they come to stay.'

'Well, just for the time being then, my dear. The girl will feel more at home in the children's room.'

Poppy cast him a grateful look. He seemed nice and had kind eyes.

'So you are Poppy Brown,' he said, holding out his hand. 'How do you do, Poppy? My name is Edwin Carroll.'

'Pleased to meet you, mister.' Poppy gave his hand a shake and thought how soft his skin was, not a bit like Dad's which was calloused by years of manual labour.

Marina Carroll groaned audibly. 'The reply to how do you do is simply how do you do, Poppy. Not pleased to meet you.'

The lines on Edwin's forehead knotted together in a frown. 'I think the lessons in etiquette might wait until the child has settled in, Marina.' His eyes, magnified by the thick lenses, smiled kindly at Poppy. 'Now you go with Olive, Poppy, and she'll make you comfortable in the nursery. Tomorrow we'll have a chat and you can tell me all about your family in, where was it? Caterham?'

'West Ham, Edwin,' Marina snapped. 'Take her away, Olive. We'll have dinner at eight o'clock whether Guy gets home on time or not.'

'Yes'm.' Olive seized Poppy by the arm and dragged her out of the room.

Mrs Toon said she was too busy with dinner to think about minor details like Poppy's comfort and she put Olive and Violet in charge of settling Poppy in the old nursery.

Grumbling all the way, Olive trudged up three flights of stairs with the reluctant Violet carrying a pile of clean bed linen and Poppy following wearily carrying nothing but her gas mask and toothbrush, which was all that was left after Mrs Toon had incinerated her few possessions in the thing they called an Aga.

Olive and Violet made up a bed in the night

nursery. After a great deal of bickering and a little half-hearted flapping around with a duster, they agreed that they had done enough for one day, and Olive flounced out of the room followed by Violet, who popped her head back around the door and poked her tongue out at Poppy. 'Sleep tight, Popeye. Don't worry about the ghost. The white lady don't do much more than tug off the bedclothes and throw things about the room.'

The door slammed shut and Poppy remained motionless listening to their footsteps retreating down the staircase, and then silence closed in around her. She was unused to quietness. In the cramped living conditions of number 18 Quebec Road, the house reverberated with the sound of men's deep voices and the clumping of Dad's and Joe's heavy boots on bare linoleum. Mum and Gran chattered noisily as they pounded washing on the ridged glass washboard, riddled the cinders in the boiler or beat the living daylights out of the threadbare carpets as they hung on the line in the tiny back garden. Poppy's eyes filled with tears as she thought of her mum with her tired but still pretty face and her work-worn hands. The smell of Lifebuoy soap hung about her in an aura unless she was going to the pictures with Dad, and then she splashed on a little of the Californian Poppy perfume that Poppy had saved up for and bought from Woolworth's to give her as a birthday present.

The day room was furnished with what looked

like odd bits of furniture that were no longer needed in the reception rooms. A child's desk and chair were placed beneath one of the tall windows and a battered doll's house stood in one corner of the room. A tea table and two chairs occupied the centre of the room and two saggy armchairs sat on either side of the fireplace. It was not the most cheerful of places and Poppy shivered even though the room was hot and stuffy. She could imagine the white lady sitting in one of the chairs or coming to her in the middle of the night. She had read about haunted houses and they were always old and large, just like Squire's Knapp.

She hurried into the night nursery, closing the door behind her. This room was slightly smaller and more homely. A baby's cot stood in one corner, with a large fluffy teddy bear lying face down on the pillow. Twin beds took up the rest of the floor space, separated by a white-painted bedside cabinet that some bored child had scribbled on with wax crayons and pencil. Momentarily diverted, Poppy climbed on the bed beneath the window and dangled her legs over the side as she tried to read the scrawled writing. Apart from matchstick men with six fingers on each spiky hand, the only word legible after many applications of Vim was the name **GUY**, printed in thick block capitals and repeated over and over again. Poppy lay down on the pink satin eiderdown and closed her eyes, too exhausted to go into the nursery bathroom and clean her teeth or to put on the flannelette nightgown that Olive had left under her pillow.

When she awakened next morning Poppy thought for a moment that she was back in the boxroom at home, but the brightly coloured cretonne curtains that floated in the breeze from the open window were not her bedroom curtains. The Beatrix Potter prints on the walls were nothing like the pictures of film stars that she had cut from movie magazines and pinned over her bed at home. She sat up, rubbing her eyes as memories of yesterday flooded back in an overwhelming tide of misery. She strained her ears for sounds of life in the house but there was silence except for the birds singing away in the garden below. She knelt on the bed and rested her elbows on the sill as she looked out of the window. Her room was at the back of the house overlooking a wide sweep of green lawns, just like the cricket pitch in West Ham Park. She caught a glimpse of the mirror-like sheen of the lake between a stand of silver birch trees and a dense shrubbery. A movement down below caught her eye as a disembodied hand shook a yellow duster out of a window and was withdrawn almost immediately.

She slid off the bed and made a brief foray into the white-tiled bathroom with its huge cast iron bath standing on claw feet, a washbasin big enough to bathe in and a willow pattern lavatory. The toilet at number 18 had its own little house situated just outside the back door, which the Brown family considered was quite superior to the back-to-back terraces in the poorer part of town where the lavatory was at the bottom of the yard if you were lucky, and at the end of the block if you were not. She cleaned her teeth and washed her face in what Gran would have called a cat's-lick, deciding that she could not possibly be dirty after the scrubbing she had received at Violet's hands. Reluctantly she dressed in Miss Pamela's cast-offs, and after an unsuccessful attempt to get the comb through the tangles she tied her hair back with a piece of string she found in the day nursery.

She wondered what she was supposed to do now. Her stomach rumbled and she realised that she was extremely hungry, but it seemed that she had been forgotten. She might starve to death up here and her skeleton be found years later amongst the cobwebs in the disused nursery. She opened the door and made her way along the narrow corridor to the landing at the top of the stairs. Leaning over the banisters she strained her ears for sounds of life, and, hearing nothing but the tick of a slender grandmother clock on the floor below, she made her way down three flights of stairs to the kitchen. A wave of sound enveloped her as she opened the door and Violet flew past her carrying a dustpan and brush.

'I'd clean forgotten you, Popeye,' she said, grinning. 'Better keep out of Mrs Toon's way, she's on the warpath.' She slammed the baize door that kept the noise from below from disturbing the genteel calm of the family rooms.

'Oh, it's you!' Kneading bread dough as if she were pummelling her worst enemy, Mrs Toon glared at Poppy. 'I can't be doing with you under my feet today, there's too much to do.'

Poppy stood uncertainly at the foot of the stairs, creating patterns on the floor with the toe of her brown sandal. Mrs Toon's cheeks were bright red, the colour of the geraniums that Gran liked to grow in an old sink in the back yard. Strands of grey hair escaped from her white cap, bouncing about like watch springs as she wielded a floury rolling pin at her. 'I suppose you're hungry. Kids always are in my experience. There's some porridge in the pan on the Aga. Help yourself.'

Poppy approached the monster cautiously and was about to reach up to grab the ladle when Mrs Toon happened to glance over her shoulder. 'Not like that!' she screeched. 'For heaven's sake, girl, you'll scald yourself.' She bustled over and, snatching the ladle, she filled a china bowl with porridge and thrust it into Poppy's hands. 'There's sugar in the bowl on the table. Don't take too much! And there's fresh milk on the marble shelf in the larder. Don't spill it.'

Poppy tucked herself away in the corner of the kitchen and ate her porridge, watching in awe as Mrs Toon barked orders at two women who appeared from the scullery at intervals, carrying huge bowls of peeled vegetables. With a face that Mum would have described as a wet weekend, Olive looked distinctly put out as she clattered down the stairs carrying a tray full of dirty crockery.

'I hate bloody shooting parties,' she said bitterly.

'Language, Olive,' Mrs Toon muttered as Olive disappeared into the scullery.

There was a loud clatter and she flounced back into the kitchen wiping her hands on the tea towel. She stopped and her eyes narrowed as she spotted Poppy, who was trying her best to appear inconspicuous. 'You'd best keep out of my way today. I don't want madam making me look after you as well as doing all my other work.' She snatched an apple from a bowl on a side table and bit into it. 'By the way, Mrs Toon, best keep some breakfast hot for Mr Guy. He went out for his morning ride and hasn't come back yet.'

This piece of information did not seem to go down too well with Mrs Toon, and Poppy finished her food quickly. Taking her empty bowl into the scullery she made her escape through an outside door and found herself in a cobbled yard surrounded by outbuildings. The familiar smell of coarse soap and soda billowed out in clouds of steam from the washhouse, bringing a lump to her throat and a wave of homesickness as she listened to the washerwomen laughing and talking while they worked. She hesitated in the doorway, longing to go inside and find a motherly soul who would give her a cuddle and tell her that everything would be all right, but it seemed as if she was suddenly invisible. They were all too busy to notice her.

She was just wondering what to do when she spotted a gateway in the stone wall, and on closer examination she discovered that it led into the stable yard. The smell of horse dung, damp straw and leather was unfamiliar but not as unpleasant as she might have imagined. A horse stuck its great head out of its stall whinnying at her and stamping its hooves and she backed away. Those teeth looked as if they could bite a girl's head off with one great snap of the mighty jaws. She had been chased once by a carthorse that had seemed intent on trampling her underfoot, and she had been scared of the brutes ever since. She glanced round as a stable lad shouted something unintelligible at her and she panicked, thinking she must have done something wrong. She ran through the yard, past the carriage house and into the safety of a large clump of rhododendrons. The leaves slapped her cheeks and twigs scratched her bare legs as she forced her way through the tangle of branches. A large pigeon flew out of the bush close to her head and she screamed in fright as its wing feathers made a loud flapping noise.

Suddenly, she was out in the sunlight again and her heart was beating a tattoo inside her chest. Her feet crunched on the gravel as she ran headlong down the drive. Close by she could hear a dog barking. Too late she was aware of horse's hooves pounding on the hard-baked grass, and the shouted warning to get out of the way. She turned her head and was paralysed with fright at the sight of flailing hooves. The horse reared on its hind legs as its rider swerved to avoid her. She raised her arm to protect her face and plunged once again into a sea of blackness.

A Mother's Wish

Dilly Court

She was determined to make a home for her son and keep him safe . . .

Since the untimely death of her husband, young mother Effie Grey has been forced to live on a narrowboat owned by her tyrannical father-in-law Jacob. In spite of her own despair, she is determined to protect her brother Tom and her baby son Georgie from Jacob's bullying ways – for she is all they have in the world.

But when Jacob hires villainous Salter and his vile wife Sal to run the barge, Effie's life becomes even more unbearable, and Tom is sent packing without a penny to his name. Living on deck with little to shelter her and Georgie from the elements, and tormented by the Salters, Effie is driven to desperation. And stealing Jacob's hidden cache of money she escapes with her son. As she begins her frantic search for Tom, Effie vows that whatever happens she will make a home for little Georgie and keep him safe from harm.

arrow books

The Cockney Angel

Dilly Court

Only she could save her father from ruin . . .

Eighteen-year-old Irene Angel lives with her parents in a tiny room above the shop where her crippled mother ekes out a living selling pickles and sauces, whilst her charming but feckless father Billy gambles away what little money they do manage to earn. And it is all Irene can do to keep the family together.

Billy's addiction soon leads him into trouble. Despite having been brought up by her father to fear and distrust the police, Irene finds herself forced to collaborate with them to save her father from ruin. But Billy's errant ways finally catch up with him and he is imprisoned in Newgate jail. With her mother away from home, a desperate Irene has little choice but to seek help from Inspector Edward Kent – her sworn enemy. For only she can clear her father's name and unite the family once more . . .

arrow books

A Mother's Promise
Dilly Court

She would keep her family together, whatever it took . . .

When Hetty Huggins made a promise to her dying mother that she would look after her younger sister and brothers, little did she know how difficult this would be. But despite the threat of being turned out on to the streets by the unscrupulous tallyman and the never-ending struggle just to exist, Hetty is determined her family will never starve or want for a roof over their heads.

Longing for something better out of life than the daily grind of making matchboxes for a pittance, she dreams of setting up her own business. With the help of friends she sells hot potatoes on the streets and things begin to look up for them all. But when the tallyman comes calling, they are faced once more with a future full of hardship and despair.

arrow books

The Constant Heart

Dilly Court

Would she risk it all for love?

Despite living by the side of the Thames, with its noise, disease and dirt, eighteen-year-old Rosina May has wanted for little in life.

Until her father's feud with a fellow bargeman threatens to destroy everything. To save them all, Rosina agrees to marry Harry, the son of a wealthy merchant. But a chance encounter with a handsome river pirate has turned her head and she longs to meet him again.

When her father dies a broken man, Harry goes back on his promise and turns Rosina out on to the streets. She is forced to work the river herself, ferrying rubbish out of London and living rough. In spite of her hardships, she cannot forget her pirate and when tragedy threatens to strike once more she is forced to make a choice. But is she really prepared to risk everything for love?

arrow books

A Mother's Courage

Dilly Court

She would do anything to keep them safe . . .

When Eloise Cribb receives the news that her husband's ship has been lost at sea she wonders how she is ever going to manage. With two young children, the rent overdue and left with almost nothing to live on, she has no alternative but to turn to his estranged family for help.

She sets off on the long and arduous journey to Yorkshire, but is met with hostility and soon realises she has little choice but to return to London. Virtually destitute and desperate, Eloise is faced with her worst nightmare: she must either go to the workhouse, or abandon her children at the Foundling Hospital. But she is determined to keep them under her protective wing at all costs . . .

arrow books

The Cockney Sparrow

Dilly Court

She sang with the voice of a nightingale . . .

Gifted with a beautiful soprano voice, young Clemency Skinner is forced to work as a pickpocket in order to support her crippled brother, Jack. Their feckless mother, Edith, has fallen into the clutches of an unscrupulous pimp, whose evil presence threatens their daily existence.

Befriended by Ned Hawkes and his kindly mother, Nell, Clemency struggles to escape from life in the slums of Stew Lane. She finds work with a troupe of buskers and is spotted by the manager of the Strand Theatre. Clemency looks set for operatic stardom, but a chance meeting with the mysterious Jared Stone brings danger and intrigue and threatens to change her life forevermore . . .

arrow books